D1561907

HUNTER
AND HUNTED
Human History of the Holocaust

THE B'NAI B'RITH JEWISH HERITAGE CLASSICS

Series Editors: DAVID PATTERSON · LILY EDELMAN

ALREADY PUBLISHED

THE MISHNAH
Oral Teachings of Judaism
Selected and Translated by Eugene J. Lipman

RASHI
Commentaries on the Pentateuch
Selected and Translated by Chaim Pearl

A PORTION IN PARADISE
And Other Jewish Folktales
Compiled by H. M. Nahmad

THE HOLY CITY
Jews on Jerusalem
Compiled and Edited by Avraham Holtz

REASON AND HOPE
Selections from the Jewish Writings of Hermann Cohen
Translated, Edited, and with an Introduction by Eva Jospe

THE SEPHARDIC TRADITION
Ladino and Spanish-Jewish Literature
Selected and Edited by Moshe Lazar

JUDAISM AND HUMAN RIGHTS
Selected and Edited by Milton Konvitz

*Published in cooperation with the Commission
on Adult Jewish Education of B'nai B'rith*

HUNTER
AND HUNTED

Human History of the Holocaust

Selected and Edited by GERD KORMAN

The Viking Press · New York

Copyright © 1973 by the
B'nai B'rith Commission on Adult Jewish Education
All rights reserved
First published in 1973 by The Viking Press, Inc.
625 Madison Avenue, New York, N.Y. 10022
Published simultaneously in Canada by
The Macmillan Company of Canada Limited
SBN 670-38819-x
Library of Congress catalog card number: 72-139397

Thanks to the Morris Adler Publications Fund of B'nai B'rith's
Commission on Adult Jewish Education for making the
Jewish Heritage Classics Series possible as a memorial to
the late Rabbi Morris Adler, former Chairman of that Commission.

Printed in U.S.A.

Page 313 constitutes an extension of this copyright page.

To Omama and Bobbe

Their kinsfolk fell,
but their children live.

Contents

Preface

If ever there was a time when Jewish life seemed about to end in the Christian West, that time was during World War II. It was as if no one would or could stop the clock of Christian civilization from reaching that moment: "There were thus fourteen generations in all from Abraham to David, fourteen from David to the deportation to Babylon . . . fourteen from the deportation . . . to the Messiah," and seventy generations—to continue Matthew's kind of reckoning, all but twice that number less fourteen—until the Holocaust. Its consuming flames reached out everywhere for every name, scroll, symbol, and ritual linking Jews to one another in time—to Jerusalem, to Babylon, to David, to Sinai, to Abraham, to the Covenant—and thus to God.

Everything about the Holocaust was extraordinary because the systematic destruction of European Jewry eludes the mind and all understanding. Each and every Jew, even if he considered himself a non-Jew or a convert to Christianity, was marked for annihilation. Extraordinary too was the fact that not only did one of the West's most enlightened nations try to exterminate Jews but in addition there was the acquiescence of other nations to the Nazi campaign of mass murder.

How then shall we speak of the Holocaust?

While others have written about the horrors and the death factories, and have sought to interpret their human and their metaphysical and/or theological implications, I have sought, as a historian, to provide a chronological frame of reference by which readers may be better able to relate themselves to those catastrophic events which Western civilization produced one generation ago. To this end, this volume presents several stages in the history of the Holocaust, following an introduction designed to explain the complexities of the subject and to offer a framework in which some of the major features can be understood. These stages may be viewed as floors of a building twelve years high (from 1933 to 1945) standing on a foundation many years deep. The first section deals with the period when the refugee crisis reached its high point—namely, 1938–1939—and seeks to lay bare the kinds of attitudes which had contributed to the isolation of Jewry on the European continent. Section II follows with the beginnings of the war in September 1939 and the diversified responses by Jews, according to the circumstances, in their desperate effort to survive. The third section deals with deportation and the suffering of those in flight under varied circumstances of German occupation. The stress here is on accounts by survivors who reveal in further detail what the struggle for individual survival was all about. Next come descriptions of life within the ghetto. In Section V, *"Akzia* Impossible," the revolt of Jews against their situation is revealed by an examination of the Warsaw Ghetto Uprising, the most famed of the Jewish rebellions, which also serves to disclose rebellion's place in Jewish behavior during the occupation, a phase of the Holocaust which has thus far been little understood. The sixth section, through the words of Elie Wiesel, probes the human and moral aspects of Jewish suffering in the concentration camps. The final section, "Liberation," contains material designed to show the diversity of the reactions of the liberated and their ensuing difficulties.

In preparing this volume, I have incurred several special debts which I gratefully acknowledge. Mrs. Mary Carnell and Miss Ruth Olmstead helped with the typing and other technical chores. Gould Colman, director of the Cornell Oral History Program, facilitated the recording and transcription of interviews. Participants in my Holocaust Seminar, which Rabbi Morris Goldfarb helped arrange at Cornell's B'nai B'rith Hillel Foundation in 1966 and 1967, compelled me to learn how to communicate the subject of this book to the younger generation. Walter Lenz, Dr. Joseph Rothenberg, Professor Sylvester Berki, and Professor Zvi Yavets each shared with me painful memories. Professor David Patterson has been a source of encouragement and, with Lily Edelman, a stimulating editor. Esther Jacobson, a remarkable copy editor, improved the final manuscript.

The subject of the Holocaust does not bring light and joy into a family, but my wife, Ruth, and our children, Malka, Ezra, Joshua, and Arona, accepted my involvement with dignified resignation.

GERD KORMAN

Cornell University
Spring 1972

HUNTER
AND HUNTED

Human History of the Holocaust

Introduction

On Purim in 1941, Jews assembled in the walled-off ghetto of Warsaw to express their hope for a New Purim, surpassing all previous Purims in Jewish history—a day that would celebrate the downfall of Hitler, the modern Haman.[1] Within a few years, except for a handful who outlived the transports and camps, who survived the ghetto's rebellion against the German army, all were dead. Dead, like the six million, destroyed by the madness of German National Socialism.

One generation later, on another Purim day, in 1967, a group of scholars and writers gathered in New York City to try to explain the meaning of the catastrophe.[2] They found this a difficult if not impossible task: the catastrophe had many meanings for each of them. Could the human imagination really understand what had happened? Was there any purpose in trying to define the meaning of the catastrophe? Why bother surviving and escaping to tell the story? "What for?" asked Elie Wiesel. "The world does not deserve your sacrifice or your tale; it won't believe you."

Yet each participant felt he somehow had to make the effort to share his thoughts with others. Convinced that Jews had been singled out for destruction for the sake of evil, not for power or lust or gain, Emil Fackenheim, the philosopher-theologian, was compelled to bear witness by what he called the 614th commandment, a commandment binding upon each "authentic" Jew who

[1] Jacob Sloan, ed., *Notes from the Warsaw Ghetto: The Journal of Emmanuel Ringelblum* (New York: McGraw-Hill, 1958), p. 139.

[2] The symposium gathered under the auspices of the magazine *Judaism;* the proceedings appeared in Vol. XVI (Summer 1967), pp. 266–299, under the title "Jewish Values in the Post-Holocaust Future."

survived or came after the disaster, be he believer, agnostic, or atheist. Like the 613 commandments which traditional Jews strive to obey, this additional mitzvah was bound up with the survival and continuity of the Jewish people and of Judaism itself. According to Fackenheim,

> . . . we are, first, commanded to survive as Jews, lest the Jewish people perish. We are commanded, second, to remember in our very guts and bones the martyrs of the Holocaust, lest their memory perish. We are forbidden, thirdly, to deny or despair of God, however much we may have to contend with Him or with belief in Him, lest Judaism perish. We are forbidden, finally, to despair of the world as the place which is to become the kingdom of God, lest we help make it a meaningless place in which God is dead or irrelevant and everything is permitted. To abandon any of these imperatives, in response to Hitler's victory at Auschwitz, would be to hand him yet other, posthumous victories.

The literary critic George Steiner, impelled by his responsibility as a Jew among men, felt a passionate need to utilize the catastrophe of European Jewry for the benefit of mankind. Less concerned with the Jewish particularity of the disaster than the other discussants, he insisted that we must tell about the Holocaust "to be on our guard, so that our children know when it may happen the next time." Steiner defined the two experiences of horror while in transport:

> One was to be with your child and to know why you were going —because you are a Jew. Worse, was to have to explain to your children, as countless assimilationists did: . . . "Why I? What is all this about?" Thus we owe to our children whatever animal protection it may be to say: Be on your guard! Know the signals! If it be Argentina . . . or Morocco . . . or South Africa, when the hell will break loose . . . it is your and my task to save whom we can. I think it is worth telling the story, so we [Jew and non-Jew] can tell the noise when it comes and be on our toes, and know how to move.

The mystic compulsion of Elie Wiesel was different. On the one hand he did not really pretend to know what had happened. When he once asked an American friend why he had done nothing to save European Jewry, the latter answered, "We did not know what was going on." "Impossible," Wiesel recalled saying to him. "In 1942–43 the whole world knew. After the Warsaw Ghetto Uprising, a clear, full picture was offered to anyone who wanted to see and learn. Unimpeachable documents were available: photographs, figures, facts." "We did not believe they were true," his friend remarked. And suddenly he turned toward Wiesel, looking him straight in the eye, and asked, "You were there [in Auschwitz]. Do you believe it now?" "Well . . . I do not believe it. The event seems unreal, as if it occurred on a different planet."

On the other hand Wiesel insisted that the Holocaust

> can be still experienced—even now. Any Jew born before, during or after the Holocaust must enter it again in order to take it upon himself. We all stood at Sinai; . . . we all heard the *Anochi*—"I am the Lord. . . ." If this is true, then we are also linked to Auschwitz. Those who were not there then can discover it now. How? I don't know. But I do know that it is possible. . . . One does not speak about the beginning of creation and the end-time. . . . Today we know that all roads and all words lead to the Holocaust. What it was we may never know; but we must proclaim, at least, that it was, that it is.

Different though their compulsions were, most agreed with Wiesel, who insisted that the catastrophe must be understood first and foremost as a unique Jewish experience, though not necessarily an exclusive one. And that claim, he insisted, had to be staked out firmly and proudly. "I couldn't care less whether these claims on our part do or do not create bitterness. Listen to such *hutzpa:* first they make us suffer, and now they resent it when we acknowledge the suffering as ours. . . . And why take away from the dead the only thing left to them—their Jewishness and their uniqueness? Don't they deserve at least that?" Some, like Steiner, may have flinched at this insistence on distinctiveness and uniqueness. None, however, could deny that between 1933 and 1945 millions of Jews stared bestiality and absurdity in the face and yet, through what Wiesel called an "absurd faith in their non-existent future," still affirmed Judaism and Jewish peoplehood.

Since the historian has to face as squarely as he can the evidence left in the wake of the catastrophe, he has no choice but to begin at the beginning, and to examine the chronicles of the events in the great disaster. Most general historians in the West have tended to write as if National Socialism and its campaign to destroy Jewry represented an aberration from the past. In their view, a mad genius somehow managed to uncover the weaknesses of the Weimar Republic, and aided by anti-Bolshevik panic and the depression, was able to persuade sufficient numbers of German voters that his party, the National Socialists, offered Germany the way to recapture old glories and build a glorious future. By a double-headed program directed against Jews and the depression, Hitler and his party strangled all political opposition, consolidated their conquest of the state apparatus, and imposed a dictatorship. That in turn unleashed upon the world "horrors and miseries which even so far as they have unfolded," Winston Churchill said in 1948, "are already beyond comparison in human experience." [3]

Secular Jewish historians, too, have tended to treat the years of the Holocaust as a break with the Jewish past. Proclaiming the continuity of Jewish existence, on the one hand, and on the other reaffirming its harmony with the Enlightenment,* they have used the past to show how Jews committed to progress and rationalism could develop Jewish life in the Diaspora and in Palestine. Within that framework the Holocaust made sense only as an aberration, a disaster that had destroyed the continuity of Jewish history. Since the Jews who did not directly face Nazi terror turned out to be as impotent as Hitler's victims, there has been some reason for thinking along such lines. Perhaps this impotence demonstrated that the modern nation and its liberalism had destroyed Jewry's ability to provide mutual aid when danger threatened, and thus had in fact destroyed one of the most characteristic features of Jewish history. In any event the Jewish historian, like his non-Jewish colleagues, has treated the Holocaust as a sudden break with the past.[4]

To be sure, there are historians who see the Holocaust as an integral part of past developments: some regard it as the logical con-

[3] Winston S. Churchill, *The Gathering Storm* (Boston: Houghton Mifflin, 1948), pp. 11, 15, 17, 70, 89, 90.
* Here, the Haskalah Movement (c. 1750–1880) for the enlightenment of the Jews through knowledge of Western languages, culture, and science.
[4] See Leni Yahil, "The Holocaust in Jewish Historiography," *Yad Vashem Studies,* Vol. VII (1968), pp. 57–71.

sequence of Luther's teachings; others insist it was the inevitable fruit of the German character in the twentieth century. For some the Holocaust can be viewed as a part of God's general scheme of things, while others endow the disaster with a purpose by seeing it as the primary cause for the creation of the State of Israel.

Stressing the firestorm's deep-rootedness in the past, certain secular historians, especially in recent years, have seen in German nationalism the traditions of *Volk* faith, and in the prevailing cultural despair, links between the perpetrators and silent onlookers of the Holocaust and earlier generations of Europeans and Americans. Individual scholars have begun systematically to identify and recreate the particular centers in Western civilization where such links were forged; they have also embarked upon an attempt to understand the men who fashioned these centers in the first place and their reasons for so doing. Even the long-neglected subject of Gentile-Jewish relations has started to attract well-trained scholars who can locate a place in the chain of strangulation for anticlerical and often antitheistic radicals as well as for such contemporary heroes of Christianity as Michael Cardinal Faulhaber and Dietrich Bonhoeffer, who represent Christian elements in Germany who fought in defense of Jews. For Faulhaber limited himself to Jews of the Old Testament, while Bonhoeffer insisted in 1933 that Jews "must bear" the curse for their actions "through a long history of suffering." Neither Bonhoeffer nor anyone else has ever repudiated the Christian tradition, or sought, according to Emil Fackenheim, "a bond (even if only in his own mind) with . . . Jews faithful to their own faith because, and not in spite of their faithfulness." [5]

At the end of World War II a number of secular Jewish scholars, too, insisted on moving the Holocaust experience out of its historiographical isolation. Some responded quickly to charges against Jewish leaders for failing to save Jews during the disaster and against rank-and-file Jews for behaving like sheep being led to slaughter. They began to demonstrate how Jews did in fact behave as compared with the surrounding populations; they also began comparing acts of Jewish resistance with patterns of resistance by

[5] "Jewish Faith and the Holocaust: A Fragment," *Commentary*, Vol. XLVI (August 1968), pp. 30–37.

other groups under Nazi domination. Through this very process of comparison, Jewish scholars have begun to give the Holocaust both a past and a future.

This trend was accelerated after the Six-Day War, when the tradition of mutual aid among Jews asserted itself as never before. To the Israeli historian Leni Yahil, the implications were clear: "This very fact will enable us to provide the Holocaust with the place it deserves in Jewish history," she insisted. "We have emancipated ourselves from the distress of helpless slaughter . . . the nation proved by its reaction its desire to live and its ability to survive—not only in Israel, but also in the Diaspora. The people proved its willingness to fight for its life. It did not abandon itself; was not it abandoned? This experience transforms the Holocaust into a part of the past." [6]

Without minimizing the significance of the interpretative frameworks provided by many scholars, one may note that much that transpired can be related to World War I. Recent studies have revealed many continuities between the major policy decisions of the governments in power on the eve of World War I and those existing at the start of World War II. World War I clearly served as a model for the men designing battle strategy against the Great Depression.[7] When we consider the impact of World War I upon victor and vanquished—e.g., the killing of thousands of Armenians, the Belgian atrocities, the Balfour Declaration, and the propaganda campaign by which the Germans tried to gain the support of the Jews as German soldiers made contact with the Jewish populations of Eastern Europe—we come to understand better why, twenty-five years later, Europeans and Americans permitted Germans to destroy European Jewry.

Except for the United States' adoption of restrictive immigration, and the triumph of National Socialism, the major policies of the nations shaping European affairs between 1914 and 1939 were remarkably stable. On the eve of World War I, Germany decided to strike preemptively against Great Britain and her continental

---

[6] "The Holocaust in Jewish Historiography," *loc. cit.*

[7] See especially A. J. P. Taylor, *The Origins of the Second World War* (New York: Atheneum, 1961), and Fritz Fischer, *Germany's Aims in the First World War* (New York: Norton, 1967).

allies in order to acquire Russian Poland and the Ukraine as the equivalent of the imperial market areas owned by her European rivals. That decision called into being a strategy which would ultimately send thousands of German soldiers to the eastern border of the Ukraine, and which projected the obligatory migration of the Slavs living on the land closest to German territory. During the war years, Kaiser Wilhelm's men overran many Jewish communities by virtue of their conquest of Russian territory. In the fall of 1918, Germany and her allies finally stood on the eastern border of the Ukraine; by then they had already dominated, for at least two years, Warsaw and the other centers of Jewish life in Poland. Twenty-three years later a differently governed Germany again saw her troops astride the very same centers of Polish and Russian Jewry.

After World War I, no victorious government considered the establishment of an independent Poland a satisfactory settlement in Central Europe. In terms of the principle of the self-determination of peoples, too many Germans and other national groups had to live in the new Poland despite their preference for Germany, Russia, or the territories of the former Austro-Hungarian empire. Consequently, Germany's recurring grievance that the Treaty of Versailles had placed too many of its subjects under foreign rule usually found support in the foreign offices of Great Britain, France, and the United States. In the 1930's a similar grievance voiced by Germany's Nazi regime received similar support from the former Allies. Regardless of what political circumstances governed European affairs, the possibility of combat aid for Poland in the event of an attack by Germany was remote.

Where all the governments engaged in World War I met in agreement was in the view that Bolshevik Russia had to be contained. Almost from the moment Russia withdrew from the war, the Allies turned against the new regime, and thenceforth they pursued a policy of quiet belligerency. No matter how the military circumstances changed, no matter how necessary the Soviet Union's temporary alliance with capitalist countries against the Fascist threat from the west, Britain and her former allies refused to fashion any arrangement which would move the Soviet armies closer to the German border. Consequently, Poland remained the buffer between Germany and Russia even after that arrangement served the interests of Germany rather than Britain, France, and Poland herself. Hitler's nonagression pact with Russia simply assured him in 1939 that the Soviets would do nothing to destroy Poland except on German terms.

Finally, all of the participants in World War I, as well as the Soviet Union and other states formed between 1917 and the adoption of the Treaty of Versailles, shared the same approach toward their respective Jewish populations. Except in Nazi Germany, where Jewry was made public enemy number one, Jews as a group found themselves treated as a minority standing aloof from the central national passion of the country in which they lived. Though the quality of Jewish life in Britain, France, or the United States differed from that in Poland, Rumania, or Soviet Russia, after World War I a similarity existed in that the Gentile citizen of each nation was usually convinced that the Jew was somehow less patriotic by virtue of his historic and traditional relations with other Jews the world over.

World War I experiences and events thus cast weird shadows over the behavior of men in the interlude years. With the slaughter of large numbers of civilians in different theaters of the war, killing became a matter of indifference, and this attitude remained when similar but far more numerous civilian deaths occurred but a few years later. The Balfour Declaration appeared to make anti-Zionism more urgent. The World War I contact with German soldiers led many Jews of Poland, and other Central and Eastern European countries, in later years to think of Germans as civilized, especially when compared to the barbarians from Russia or Austria-Hungary. And intertwined with these developments was America's decision to restrict drastically immigration to its shores. To European Jewry this act, which closed the door to escape for the Jews of Central Europe, equaled in importance Germany's adoption of National Socialism.

In 1913 President Woodrow Wilson appointed Henry Morgenthau, Sr., ambassador to Turkey, and six years later he used him to further his plans for a peaceful settlement of the war. Out of those experiences Morgenthau was able to report in detail how hundreds of thousands of specially selected civilians had died at the hands of slaughterers authorized or condoned by specific national governments. In 1915, for example, Turkish soldiers participated in the shooting, bayoneting, axing, drowning, burning, and raping of thousands of Armenians. By the end of World War I, a million or more persons had thus been butchered.

Ironically, Baron Hans von Ginheim, Germany's ambassador to her Turkish ally, cabled his government on May 31, 1915, his conviction that under the circumstances the Turks were correct in treating the Armenians as "simply traitors, vermin. I think," he wrote home, "that these [Turks] are entirely justified: the weaker nations must succumb." [8]

Morgenthau later reported on the extermination of other civilians—Jews attacked by Gentiles in Polish cities during November 1918, and April, May, and August 1919.[9] In one town Poles killed sixty-four Jews and destroyed the synagogue with its sacred scrolls. In another town Polish soldiers separated men from their families, stood them against the cathedral wall in the public square, and by the light of military automobiles, shot them dead. In Vilna, during three black days in 1919, Polish soldiers marched eight Jews three kilometers to the outskirts of the town, where they shot them, while civilians joined the soldiers inside Vilna to shoot and beat other Jews, and to plunder over two thousand homes and stores belonging to Jewish inhabitants, 80 percent of whom were already close to starvation. Other Jews were arrested and deported from Vilna, herded into boxcars where they remained without food or water for four days. In Minsk the toll was thirty-one Jewish dead, in addition to beatings and pillage.[10]

In the light of events that were to occur at the time when Henry Morgenthau, Jr., was close to President Roosevelt, these reports by Morgenthau, Sr., to President Wilson were awesome in their implications. Nations could murder huge numbers of their citizens, provide protection for the murderers, and count on the world's silence.

Yet, when the Nazis later launched their campaign against Ger-

[8] Howard M. Sachar, *The Emergence of the Middle East: 1914–1924* (New York: Knopf, 1969), p. 105.
[9] Henry Morganthau, *All in a Life-Time* (Garden City: Doubleday, 1922), pp. 407–423.
[10] *Ibid.*, pp. 409–414.

man Jewry, Franklin Delano Roosevelt and others associated with the Wilson administration, such as Herbert Hoover and Bernard Baruch, reacted as if radically new forms of behavior had suddenly emerged. Roosevelt and Baruch had known of Morgenthau's reports because of their relations with him inside the Democratic party (he returned in 1916 to campaign for Wilson's second election), while Hoover, as a Republican helping to administer relief programs, knew the details of the Armenian situation. Besides, Morgenthau's reports had been made public and in 1919 the Allies wanted the United States to accept Armenia as a mandate.[11] Like Morgenthau's son, who became an important member of Roosevelt's cabinet, many American leaders in the 1930's behaved with respect to Germany as if what they once knew had been obliterated from their minds. Yet these same men specifically called on their war experience to help them in dealing with other matters, such as the problems of depression.

Certain misconceptions about national characteristics may have accounted for this strange phenomenon. Many Americans in public life regarded Turkey, Poland, and Czarist Russia as countries not sharing the Anglo-Saxon or Teutonic tradition: after World War I there was talk about the superiority of the Anglo-Saxon race in comparison to the barbaric Turks, Russians, and other Slavs. The Germans were never associated with the kind of behavior manifested by the Turks, who had been killing Armenians since the end of the nineteenth century, or by the Poles and Russians, who periodically unleashed barbaric pogroms against Jews.

[11] *Ibid.*, p. 235. See also Herbert Hoover, *The Memoirs of Herbert Hoover* (New York: Macmillan, 1952), Vol. I, pp. 385–389; Vol. II, pp. 22–23. In 1916 Morgenthau held conversations about Wilson's campaign with the following: William G. McAdoo, Josephus Daniels, Frank L. Polk, Franklin D. Roosevelt, James O'Gorman, Bernard Baruch, Henry Ford, and others. Although I have no direct evidence that they spoke about the Armenians, it would be astounding if all had ignored the subject, given Morgenthau's activities in Turkey. Years later Hoover wrote that Armenia was probably "known to the American school child in 1919 only a little less than England." Besides the stories of Noah's Ark and of the massacres of "staunch Christians," the "Sunday School collections over fifty years for alleviating" the Armenian misery had helped "to impress the name of Armenia on the front of the American mind" (*ibid.*, Vol. I, p. 385).

After all, after the massacre at Kishinev in 1903 the word "po-grom" came to be used to describe ruthless attacks against any innocent civilians. By contrast, the Germans, whose *Kultur* pro-vided the world with so much sustenance, were thought to belong to the most civilized of populations.

To be sure, during World War I accounts of Hun atrocities toward Belgian soldiers and civilians did unite Americans, Eng-lishmen, and Frenchmen in moral outrage. British propaganda in particular exploited reports about the behavior of German troops executing the Schlieffen plan, a master plan requiring the viola-tion of Belgian neutrality in order to bring about the quick de-feat of France. After the war, however, claims were made that Germany had not really been the primary culprit in causing World War I, and the Belgian atrocities were made to appear exaggerated. By the end of the 1920's, Englishmen and Americans had per-suaded themselves that Germans really did belong to civilized mankind after all. Consequently, few Americans and Europeans, including Jews, associated Germans with the kind of bestial be-havior one might expect from Turks, Poles, Russian peasants, or other Eastern or Central Europeans. In 1941, for example, some Jews in the German *Kulturkreis* in Czernowitz, though fully ex-pecting Rumanians to act like butchers, were convinced that the German soldier himself was too civilized for such behavior.

The fact is that most Jews thought of Germany as enlightened with respect to Jewish-Christian relations. Like most Gentiles, few Jews knew anything of German anti-Semitism prior to World War I; those who did were aware that anti-Semitism had taken a violent turn only occasionally, as in the 1880's. Compared with the Jewish lot in the Russian empire, life in the German-speaking empires was seen to be really far better. The correct behavior of the German army during World War I strengthened this impres-sion. Had not the Kaiser's army provided rabbis and kosher field kitchens for its Jewish soldiers, and allowed them to celebrate their holy days if conditions permitted? In addition, the German govern-ment exploited the traditional Jewish fear of Polish and Russian anti-Semitism by presenting itself as the Jews' liberator: in 1914 the Germans distributed flyers among Warsaw's Jews stating that they had come to liberate them from the yoke of Russian persecution. And, indeed, the Germans seemed to prove their claim by arranging for rabbis in the army of occupation to establish contact with the rabbis of Warsaw and work out specific problems of the occupation.

Wherever their armies went in Europe, the Germans came to be recognized as more civilized in their treatment of Jews than the Russians. By the end of 1918, they had at one time or another exerted control throughout the entire territory in which most Jews lived, and their occupation often spelled, if only for a moment, relief from the oppressor for Jews in Warsaw, Vilna, and Riga; Lublin, Lwow, and Czernowitz; Kiev, Poltava, and Kharkov.

The announcement in 1917 of the Balfour Declaration also became part of a weird shadow play. Itself a product of war-oriented Allied politicians seeking Jewish support in peace-oriented Bolshevik Russia, that declaration aroused strong anti-Zionist feelings, which in turn produced strong disavowals of Jewish nationhood or peoplehood by certain Jews. Henry Morgenthau, Sr., is representative of these. He belonged to a small group of American Jews who had become influential in their country's financial and political circles. He played important roles in national Democratic politics, and like Jacob Schiff, Felix Warburg, Isaac Seligman, Oscar Straus, Louis Marshall, and other such bankers and lawyers, could usually gain the ear of important men in public life on behalf of Jewish communal issues. Men of this sort took their Jewish responsibilities and attitudes seriously: they belonged to Jewish organizations and represented Jewry to the non-Jewish world; they contributed vast sums for Jewish relief in America and abroad. They were active too on behalf of the Jewish working poor in Poland and Russia and when pogroms or other outrageous acts of anti-Semitism occurred, sought the aid of the United States government on behalf of their coreligionists both publicly and in private.

In 1922 Morgenthau recalled with pride a remark President Wilson had made when wishing him Godspeed for his voyage to Turkey in October 1913: "Anything you can do to improve the lot of your coreligionists is an act that will reflect credit upon America and you may count on the full power of the administra-

tion to back you up." [12] Later, in Poland, Morgenthau protested
to the Polish heads of state, in Wilson's name, about anti-Semites
among their countrymen. This concern, in part motivated also by
the Allies' efforts to create a stable and unified Poland as part
of the "clan of progressive people," to serve as a buffer between
defeated Germany and Bolshevik Russia, demonstrated to Morgenthau that American and Jewish interests were in complete harmony.[13]

Within that framework Morgenthau was prepared to do whatever he could to improve the lot of his coreligionists in Turkey and
Poland. But when it came to the place of the Jew in the Gentile
world, he shared with many Jews in Great Britain, Germany,
France, and other countries of the West an optimistic attitude
concerning the impact in this century of concepts arising out of
the Enlightenment, Christianity, and nineteenth-century nationalism. Like Nathan der Weise, the hero created by the eighteenth-
century German philosopher Gotthold Lessing, he was the em-
bodiment of what has come to be known as the ecumenical spirit.
In the spring of 1914, for example, Morgenthau had stood with
some Christian missionaries and a Moslem guide at the alleged
gravesite of Abraham, Sarah, Isaac, and Jacob—the Cave of
Machpelah in Hebron—and he marveled years later: ". . . there
we stood, Moslems, Christians and Jews—all of us conscious of
the fact that we were in the presence of the tombs of our joint
fathers—that no matter in what detail we differed, we traced our
religion back to the same source, and the ten minutes to which the
prayer extended were undoubtedly the most sacred that I have
ever spent in my life." [14]

In that spirit Morgenthau was sure that Jews in each country
would find the true Zion, which he defined "as a region of the soul
. . . inspiring . . . individuals to fight, each for himself, the
battle of life where he meets it; . . . winning through to the
dignity and position to which his native gifts and his self-developed
character entitle him. . . . None of us [Americans] would deny
our race or faith." "Though of various sects, we . . . are Jews

12 *Ibid.*, p. 175.
13 *Ibid.*, p. 358.
14 *Ibid.*, pp. 217–218.

by blood . . . [and] religion," he proclaimed in 1922. He frankly admitted that he had found it "more convenient (as well as quite within the approval of what I regard as my somewhat more enlightened conscience) . . . to pass off the other symbols of the Hebraic faith, such as the Kosher observances, the untouched beard, and the distinctive dress." Of the thousands of Russian Jews in the United States who still retained those ancient symbols, he was certain from "observations and experience . . . that these same orthodox devotees will themselves become enlightened—that they—and certainly their children—will perceive, as I and others have perceived, that the Mosaic admonitions were purely temporal devices, expedient truly for the age in which they were promulgated, useful until modern sanitation and modern education did their work, but now become empty of those first values." [15]

From this vantage point he espoused two related but different positions, both of which he felt to be consistent with his self-image as a Jew. He could view with favor the missionary work of Christians because he saw the missions as fostering "the permanent civilizing work . . . which so gloriously exemplified the American spirit at its best." He recalled telling the Turks in 1914 that America "is constantly receiving hundreds of thousands of immigrants from the Old World and American generosity has placed among these newly arrived citizens the services of expert advisers who use every means to make easy the path of the immigrant, and to induct him as rapidly as possible into the full fellowship of American life." The Christian missions in Turkey, he felt, "carried this work one step further," bringing other lands "some of the benefits which our material prosperity made possible among us." [16]

Simultaneously, Morgenthau was able to feel comfortable living as a Jew among Christians. Addressing himself to Zionists, he insisted that he had "come to see that the worship of the God of Israel, the acceptable obedience to His will, is not contingent upon the clothes one wears, upon the meat one eats. His kingdom is the soul of man. In that boundless temple He receives the priceless sacrifice of the true believer. That time and place and mode are acceptable to Him to which the human spirit brings its richest

[15] *Ibid.*, p. 400.
[16] *Ibid.*, pp. 203–204.

offerings." He was able to say unequivocally that it "follows, then, that the Jew everywhere, in Poland as well as in France and America, can acceptably serve the God of his fathers and still enter fully into the life about him." Proudly he proclaimed that "we in America refuse to set ourselves apart in a voluntary ghetto for the sake of old traditional observances." [17]

As late as 1922, after his stay in Poland and France, Morgenthau was still saying that the Jew should everywhere become part of the society in which he lived. He should "weave himself into the very warp and woof of the main fabric of humanity; and gain the strength which comes from a coordinated and orderly relation to the other strands of human society." His peculiar talents would then take on new value and "a unique splendor and a special luster." Unwilling to "forego this vision of the destiny of the Jews," and speaking against the promise of Balfour, Morgenthau rejected the ways of his coreligionists in Eastern Europe. "They may continue, if they will, the practice of our common faith which invites martyrdom, and which made the continuance of oppression a certainty." But we, "the great body of American Jews," have found a better way, he insisted, and so too had the Jews in France, Great Britain, and wherever else there were men like himself whom he called assimilationists.[18]

The terrible, tragic flaw in this kind of thinking came to light in 1922, when the doors to immigrants from Europe began to close in the United States. It was one thing to fight the Zionists with their Balfour Declaration from the vantage point of the Enlightenment; it was quite another to offer false promises.

Recalling his visit to Palestine, Morgenthau told Jews why Christians in different nations would never allow Jews to reestablish their state in the Holy Land, which had been the historic birthplace of the Hebrew religion and the scene of its one-time temporal grandeur. "Anyone who has observed . . . in Palestine the Christians' suppressed hatred of them all for both the Jew and the Musselman" knows that most Christians regard the Jew "not merely as a member of a rival faith, but [as] the man whose ancestors

[17] *Ibid.*, p. 402.
[18] *Ibid.*, pp. 402–404. He used the word "assimilators" in his discussion of Jews in Poland, *ibid*. p. 364.

rejected their fellow Jew, the Christ, and crucified him." Their fanaticism, Morgenthau insisted, "is a political fact of gigantic proportions." [19] A Zionist state in Palestine "would concentrate, multiply, and give new venom to the hatred which he already endures in Poland and Russia, the very lands in which most of the Jews now dwell, and where their oppressions are the worst." [20]

Most of the American Jews who ran for important political offices, became members of presidential cabinets, or served as advisers to leading political figures shared Morgenthau's sentiment or were even less involved in Jewish affairs. Only occasionally did such men as Louis Brandeis and Stephen Wise, who held far different views about the place of Jews in the Gentile world, gain the ear of a president in complex situations where many interest groups exerted pressures. Usually they had no direct access at all. Thus, whenever Jews as a group became an important subject of foreign relations, the policy maker's conceptions were influenced mainly by views like those of Morgenthau. It was only Brandeis, together with Stephen Wise and Felix Frankfurter, who was able, during World War I, by virtue of his friendship with Wilson, to counteract Morgenthau's position on Zionism and the Balfour Declaration. But Wise was not able to play that role during the 1930's, when Jews as a group once again became an important subject in the United States' foreign relations. In part because this time a basic domestic policy of the United States was at stake, Wise was overwhelmed: "I sometimes felt that not a few of the Jews who had access to the President at this time did us a great disservice. They were so eager not to seem to plead the Jewish cause that they failed to interpret accurately . . . . the tragic plight of their brother Jews in Hitler Europe." [21]

In addition, during the 1930's, when most Americans, caught in the depression, appeared immovable on the subject of permitting more Jews to come to America than were allowed by strictly enforced immigration legislation, the Jews around Roosevelt saw

[19] *Ibid.*, p. 206.
[20] *Ibid.*, pp. 397–398.
[21] Stephen Wise, *Challenging Years* (New York: Putnam, 1949), pp. 224–225.

the world through Morgenthau's eyes. His son, then Secretary of the Treasury and a presidential confidant, knew his place. In 1939, when Nazi terror against Jews had been institutionalized and was already well publicized, when Polish Jews had already been deported from Germany to Poland, and when *Kristallnacht,* the night of the falling glass and burning synagogues, had already occurred, he explained his own position to Undersecretary of State Sumner Welles. He could not, he confided, "stop and think, 'Is this [policy or event] good or bad for Jews?' . . . the minute I find myself doing it, I will resign." [22]

David Lilienthal, Bernard Baruch, Judge Samuel Rosenman, and Felix Frankfurter, other Jews who were also close to Roosevelt, were equally nonvocal. Even Governor Herbert Lehman, the President's political expert on New York's large Jewish vote—independently wealthy, the brother of Judge Irving Lehman (executive officer of the prestigious American Jewish Committee), and head of New York's Democratic party—came nowhere near establishing himself as the standard-bearer for those who advocated changing immigration legislation. To be sure, in 1935, the Governor urged Roosevelt to ease immigration restrictions. But despite his full knowledge of the Jewish disaster in Germany, he chose to accept the oft-heard dictum that it was impossible materially to change existing legislation and practices because the opposition had "raised impossible barriers against such efforts." [23]

There was no doubt about the power of the opposition, but to Jewish leaders such as Wise and others in the American Jewish Congress, for example, that very strength only revealed how much work Jews had to do on behalf of their coreligionists in Europe. The traditional groups supporting strict restrictive immigration legislation had by now been joined by others: the depression had helped fashion political coalitions which could make capital out of the Jewish issue inherent in the immigration legislation. Roosevelt's opponents in the Southern wing of the Democratic party

[22] John Blum, ed., *From the Morgenthau Diaries: Years of Urgency, 1938–1941* (Boston: Houghton Mifflin, 1965), p. 81.

[23] Allan Nevins, *Herbert Lehman and His Era* (New York: Scribner's, 1963), pp. 187, 200. I make this charge in appreciation of the powerful opposition Lehman faced and fully understood.

were eager to unseat him; as soon as the economy began to recover in 1935, there was an upsurge of influential economic interest groups who resented some of the New Deal's anti-depression programs. These joined forces with Republicans trying to recapture political power, and found growing support after 1936 when F.D.R. became embroiled in a fight over the Supreme Court and in the recession of 1937. In combination, these groups presented a formidable obstacle for anyone trying to change legislation and practices which they approved.

Three additional elements worked against the liberalizing of immigration legislation: the Administration was pursuing an economic policy in which one of the aims was to maximize trade with Germany; the Administration was committed to preventing America from becoming embroiled in the controversies raging in Europe in the 1930's; and finally, avoidance of moves which might stimulate anti-Semitism had become a major concern of politicians involved with Jews or Jewish problems. Each time friends of immigration reform tried to act in behalf of their cause, its opponents invoked the danger of arousing anti-Semitism or the risk of damaging German-American relations or of embroiling the United States in European affairs. In short, it was difficult for Democrats to move too close to immigration reformers because of the political advantage such action would provide Republicans and other opponents eager to capture control of Congress in 1938 and the White House two years later.

Under these circumstances advocacy of immigration reform on behalf of Jews required extraordinary zeal and tenacity. But such an effort could hardly be expected from the Jews around Roosevelt, most of whom lacked either the commitment or the courage needed to take the kind of serious political risk necessary in order to save hundreds of thousands of Jews between 1933 and 1941.

A related question also rears its ugly head. Why did the Jewish voters, rooted as they were in Eastern Europe and possessing a more realistic understanding of their Jewish situation, not force the Morgenthaus, who could not or would not understand the crisis, or the Lehmans and other Democratic politicians, to fight for their kinsmen abroad? The answer appears to lie in their low socio-economic position in the United States. Most Jews belonged to the working poor in the larger cities, hit so hard during the depression.

Furthermore, some of them were committed to Socialist and Communist positions, which caused them to minimize the attack on Jews. For the majority of the Jews in America, Roosevelt's New Deal, his policies and laws, represented important measures trying to bring them relief; like all the working poor, the Jews were linked to F.D.R. because his administration was committed to easing their lot.

After 1936, when the Republican opposition—which stood for a program to undermine these efforts—was becoming deeply entrenched in Congress, the Jewish masses were faced with a difficult choice: should they push for immigration reform in order to help Jews abroad, and thus risk Republican victories in 1938 or 1940, or should they rather minimize the campaign for immigration reform so as to deprive Roosevelt's enemies of the Jewish question as a campaign issue?

Most American Jews, who had often resented the German Jew in the traditional antagonism between Jews of Eastern and Western origin, chose the second option, and together with their leaders sought to prevent the growth of anti-Semitism in the United States. Jews in Germany, and later in Poland, demanded appeals on their behalf from American Jews, but these were convinced of the urgent necessity of minimizing their own conspicuousness. The result was the preclusion of substantial campaigns on behalf of European Jewry by any large Jewish group in the United States, and in the end—disaster.

Meanwhile, memories of World War I also continued to work against the development of active concern for Europe's Jews. Following the dramatic negotiations in Munich in 1938, Great Britain was one of the signers of a mutual security treaty which placed itself and France between Nazi Germany and Poland, and thus indirectly between Germany and the Jews of Poland. But there was little chance that this security arrangement would be moved from the conference table to the battlefield by the cautious generation living in the shadow of World War I. For example, how could France help Poland and still remain behind the Maginot Line? In September 1939, Germany's invasion of Poland forced France to provide the answer.

Except for a few advances of several hundred meters, the French standing west of the Maginot took no offensive action, in part because two years earlier the Belgians had returned to a neutral position. No one expected France to violate that neutrality unless Germany did so first. The only major land power free to move against Germany, France had imposed upon herself a defensive posture in the event of war in Poland. Under these circumstances there was no reason to assume that Britain's soldiers would strike offensively against Germany, though her sailors did attack German ships on the high seas and her pilots did bomb targets in western Germany up to a north-south line running from Kiel to Cologne. In short, at the end of September 1939, when the war in Poland was over, the Germans remained free to handle their Jews unmolested. And by winter, after the armies of the Soviets had closed their new borders with Germany, it became all but impossible for Jews in occupied Poland to escape Nazi rule.

So matters stood in the fall and early winter of 1939. Reports coming out of Nazi-occupied Poland made it evident that Jews were dying there as never before. The German regime's starvation policies combined with unchecked deadly diseases in Poland's cities, where more than 78 per cent of the Polish Jews were subject daily to Nazi terror and internment. Unlike the occupation during World War I, this 1939 German occupation encouraged the traditional Polish anti-Semites; they were incited to aid the Nazi drive against Jewry. Within the region established during World War I by the German government, and reestablished by the Nazis between 1939 and 1941, Poles helped destroy the traditional forms of organized Jewish life which just a few years earlier had been protected by German soldiers. This turnabout was swift and dramatic; many Jews themselves did not at once recognize the change. For years they had lived amidst intensely anti-Semitic Poles whom, together with the Ukrainians, they had identified as the crudest of Christian barbarians. Many still regarded the German Christians as civilized gentlemen by comparison although the decade or more of news trickling out of Germany had made large numbers of Jews apprehensive regarding the seriousness of the Nazi threat. But those who remembered the first occupation took a while to rid themselves of the assumption that a civilized army had come to take over.

In France, too, the effect of memories of World War I contributed to the destruction of European Jewry. The French failed to recognize that the war against Polish soldiers and Jewish civilians heralded momentous differences from the days of the Great War. When one of their own military observers sent a detailed report, and later presented a supplementary oral account about the German use of tanks in close cooperation with dive bombers, France's chief military commanders saw no reason for changing their strategy or tactics. The leaders of the great armies of the French Republic persuaded themselves that the amazing success of the Germans could only have occurred on the terrain of Poland and because of the particular characteristics of the Polish soldier. French soldiers, and the terrain of France, were different, not comparable. Even Germany's successes in Denmark and Norway during the early months of 1940 failed to change the minds of French military tacticians.

The military significance of this failure for the fate of Jewry in Poland escaped most people; Jews and other opponents of Germany continued to look to the victors of World War I to rescue them from Germany. Once the combined might of France and Great Britain moved against Germany, they were persuaded, Nazism would be destroyed, and with it, its stranglehold on European Jewry. So long as this French and British might remained unchallenged, and Europeans and Americans were resigned to the existing immigration legislation of their nations, it was generally assumed in the West that only military victory could reverse the fate of Jews and their institutions in Germany and Poland.

The events of May 1940 changed all that. German troops struck through the Netherlands, Luxembourg, and Belgium, and with incredible speed executed the imaginative sweep which drove the French and British armies toward the Channel. In two weeks German columns of tanks and other motorized vehicles had the British Expeditionary Force cornered in and around Dunkerque and had all but crushed French might. To be sure, thousands of British soldiers managed to flee across the Channel before the Germans completed their drive, and France continued to fight. But after Dunkerque, with Russia neutralized by the German-Soviet nonaggression pact, no power remained in Europe that could free Jewry from German rule. Dunkerque symbolized Germany's freedom to do her worst against the Jews of Europe. The death of all Jews under German rule and the death of all forms of Jewish life seemed inevitable.

By the middle of 1939 the fruits of Germany's and Russia's policies toward Jews had already become manifest. Neither country offered a hospitable atmosphere in which traditional forms of organized Jewish religious and secular life could sustain themselves. From the first, the Communist government had declared its unequivocal opposition to any form of organized Jewish existence, other than the use of Yiddish for expressing official Soviet policy. By comparison, and notwithstanding the anti-Semitic character of Polish life, independent Poland remained a place where some three million Jews could still practice their traditional rites. But when Poland fell and its Jews became subjects of Germany or Russia, doom struck. By the end of May 1940, who could not have heard its tolling?

To be sure, the memory of the revelations after World War I that some atrocity tales had been war propaganda made Americans skeptical about the reports now coming out of Central Europe. But accounts in *The New York Times,* and those issued by certain Jewish organizations, did provide detailed descriptions of what was happening, the kind of horror stories Americans had heard about both Armenians and Jews in previous decades. Also, if they could not read the Yiddish press, American Jews had the warnings of Stephen Wise and the American Jewish Congress to help them interpret the situation. And since American Jews had fought publicly if unsuccessfully to force Britain to allow even small numbers of European Jews to go to Palestine, there is every reason to believe that they recognized these accounts of the plight of their kinsmen as true. On October 17, 1939, *The New York Times* reported projected deportations to Galicia, where the Germans planned to develop a Jewish reservation: "The plan in its present stage calls for shipping all Jews from the provinces of Posen and Western Prussia." It was clear that in other areas Jews would also be "ordered out of their homes" and in three hours "with only two suitcases" would be forced to entrain for the reservations. By November 6, a fuller report became available in the *Times:* In German-occupied Poland some

> two million Jews are condemned by the Nazis to starvation. Confiscation of property . . . [begun] in Lodz and other . . . [towns in] Western Poland . . . is now proceeding on a large scale in Warsaw. . . . Funds of Jewish religious groups have been confiscated and hospitals and schools have been requisitioned. . . . Jews . . . are chased from lines in front of food stores. Bread ration cards are not given to Jews. . . . A "specialist" from the Dachau concentration camp has arrived in Warsaw to set up a concentration camp. . . . In the provinces, the situation is worse.

A third account (January 5, 1940) appeared from Lodz, telling how a thousand Jews had surrounded their synagogue in passive resistance "when the police wanted to search." In response, the police opened fire, killing "at least 100," thus adding to the wholesale executions taking place in the city.

The Nazi slaughter of defiant Jews had obviously begun, and between the close of 1939 and early 1940 some observers publicly explained its full implications. On September 12, 1939, the German official news bureau proclaimed that removal to the reservation would "bring a solution of the Jewish question in Europe nearer" because Polish Jewry with its high birth rate had continually fed the growth of Western Jewry, "whose birth rate is small." Commenting on this, the *Times* reporter wondered how Western Jewry could be kept small and weak without the extermination of the removed Jews. Rabbi J. Howard Ralberg, a few months later, recognized that Jewry in Germany and German-occupied Poland was doomed in any eventuality. "If Nazism is victorious, persecution will be intensified," he pointed out. "If Hitlerism should be defeated by an economic blockage . . . Jewry will be the victim of desperate Nazi oppression and ruthless extinction."

Shortly afterward, Nahum Goldmann, president of the World Jewish Congress, appraised the situation. "If the war in Europe goes on for another year," he said months before France was defeated, "one million of the two million Jews in Poland will be dead of starvation or be killed by Nazi persecution." Both British Jews, along with their fellow citizens in the British empire, and American Jews knew what was happening in Central Europe, but they did not mount the kind of campaign which might have changed restrictive immigration legislation in the New World and elsewhere. While it is quite likely that even the best Jewish efforts might not have made much difference in the ultimate number of refugees admitted by America and other countries, the fact remains that, with the United States neutral until December 11, 1941, the world watched as the gravediggers readied themselves for the six million.

During the next few years the slaughter continued unabated, and with increasing efficiency. The rapid conquest of the Ukraine once again put the fate of Russian Jews into German hands. German soldiers moved faster than in World War I, covering more territory during this invasion; between June 21 and mid-December 1941 they traveled from the boundary assigned to Poland at the Treaty of Versailles beyond the Ukraine's western border, moving into an area where the news had been strictly censored and where, since the Hitler-Stalin pact, the Jewish population had been told, often in Yiddish, that Germany was the ally and Great Britain the enemy. *Einsatzgruppen,* consisting of teams of machine gunners in army vehicles, covered this region twice, shooting more than half a million Jews, many just after they had completed the digging of their own graves.[24]

Meanwhile, sectors within the German government began to discover that the ordinary techniques of starvation and disease were not killing Jews off as quickly as had been anticipated. Somehow, the Jews were managing to get enough food to survive, at least in Warsaw, Lodz, Lwow, Vilna, and Kiev. In fact, one thing was becoming clear: the Jews refused to cooperate in their own annihilation. They were following the example of Rabbi Isaac Nissenbaum, the pious and devout leader of Warsaw's Orthodox, who advised his people not to give their lives for the sanctification

[24] My figures here and elsewhere come mainly from the following: Arieh Tartakower, "The Problem of European Jewry (1939–1945)," in Louis Finkelstein, ed., *The Jews: Their History, Culture and Religion* (Philadelphia: Jewish Publication Society, 1949), Vol. I, pp. 287–312; and from studies by Jacob Robinson, Raul Hilberg, and Hannah Arendt.

of God's name, as was traditional, but to defy the enemy of Judaism by saving their own lives, because each Jew saved sanctified God.[25]

Many Jews managed to scrounge enough food to keep alive, and they also refused to turn away from their commitment to Judaism and the Jewish people. In the ghettos, the concentration camps, and the forests where they hid, Jews usually persisted in behaving like the Jews they had been before disaster struck. Depending upon prevailing conditions, they gathered in public or private to worship or to meet as secular Socialists and Zionists. If anything was becoming clear to the Germans, it was the inescapable fact that though some Jews might be prepared to cooperate with them for the sake of power or other forms of personal gain, most refused to die or to cause their religious or secular institutions to die. One diary entry summed up the prevailing spirit: "The Jewish community is on a battlefield, but the battle is not conducted with weapons. It is conducted by means of various schemes, schemes of deception, schemes of smuggling, and so on. We don't want simply to disappear from the earth." [26]

Considering the circumstances, such behavior was nothing short of astonishing. With the exception of the Danes, who helped the bulk of the Jewish population of Denmark to reach Sweden, the Gentile populations in the areas the Germans took over would not generally support or protect Jews. Because the assistance of fugitive Jews placed extraordinary demands on Gentile citizens living under a German occupation which punished "friends of Jews," the hunted could expect little or no aid. So hostile and dangerous an environment made any systematic effort to escape or hide or fight all but impossible. Then too, the Jew was hardly an invisible man, even without the yellow Star of David the Germans forced him to wear. Long before the Nazis had swept over the Continent, only a few Jews in Central and Eastern Europe could easily pass as Gentiles. Thanks to generations of Christian and political anti-Semitism, which contributed to the development of

[25] Shaul Esh, "The Dignity of the Destroyed," *Judaism,* Vol. XI (Spring 1962), pp. 106–107.
[26] *Scroll of Agony: The Warsaw Diary of Chaim A. Kaplan,* trans. by Abraham I. Katsh (New York: Macmillan, 1965), p. 243.

various distinctly Jewish styles of living—especially in the years before World War I, when many Jews lived as cultural minorities in Russia and Austria-Hungary—most Jews were instantly recognizable in Eastern Europe by their distinctive clothing, earlocks, beards, and the like. Under the German occupation, where a mistake could cost a Gentile his freedom if not his life, Jews really had no place to hide.

But, in a striking twist of circumstances, as the Germans emptied ghettos and other centers of concentration, killing Jews with bullets or carbon monoxide, and sending them to Auschwitz and Treblinka and Sobibor, the victims began increasingly to adopt the violent tactics of the occupiers. Many a ghetto and concentration camp witnessed battles with guns as well as nerves, while in the forests guerrilla brigades of Jewish partisans fought the Nazis. This form of response by the Jews was all the more remarkable because they lacked everything that other occupied national groups had: Jewry had few elements in its population with the experience and the legal access to arsenals and training customary for a nation—no armies, no police, no centers of armament production. Nor did Jewry have any government-in-exile to provide support for its fighters. In Europe Jews had always lived in circumstances where others took charge of matters of security and defense.

In most countries Jews had been officially regarded as nationals of the Jewish persuasion, to be treated as Frenchmen, Dutchmen, Poles, or Russians. But they were hunted down by the Germans as if they were a separate organized enemy.

The Allies did not recognize the Jews as a special group and so gave them no aid whatsoever. Up to July 1943, Allied aircraft were prevented from flying beyond western Germany by a combination of the Luftwaffe's defense tactics and the technical limits imposed by aircraft design. Except for Westerbork and Vught in Holland, most of the ghettos and concentration camps were therefore out of range for Allied bombers and fighter planes. After July 1943, the distance of air penetration increased to cover central and southern Germany, which included Bergen-Belsen, Natzweilen, Dachau, and a number of other concentration camps. Only after February 1944, however, did all the battlegrounds on which Germans fought Jews fall within the range of Allied aircraft.

Despite these limitations, Allied aircraft could of course have raided some of those sites, and the highways and railroads leading to them. Such raids would have knocked out the camps' transportation and communication, disrupted their functioning, and revealed to Germany the Allies' genuine interest in the fate of the Jews. The R.A.F. had learned the technique of precision bombing early in the war, and on more than one occasion had used it to destroy inaccessible bridges, factories, prisons. Also the Americans and British at times sent up decoy flights to split and confuse the German air defenses, and since these deceptive runs often brought them near concentration camps in southern Germany, Allied flyers might easily have used these camps as targets without weakening the general war effort.

But even had such raids occurred, most European Jews would have remained out of Allied reach from September 1939 until the end of 1944; during this period the Germans could go on waging their one-sided war of destruction against Jewry. Russian armies did not begin to move westward until after the Battle of Stalingrad in 1943, the year the Americans and the British invaded southern Italy. Allied soldiers did not land on Normandy's beaches until June 6, 1944. Most of the killing of Jews occurred within a 250-kilometer radius of Warsaw, an area the Russian armies did not begin to reach until the spring of 1944. In this sheltered region Germans killed between three and a half and four million Jews, most of whom had formerly lived in that section of Poland, but many of whom had been transported there from Holland, Belgium, and France, and from Italy, Yugoslavia, and Greece. Still others had been brought from Russia.

Here Auschwitz and similar factories of annihilation operated in relative secrecy and safety. In many respects the camps of annihilation defy description. They represent "another sphere of existence," in Elie Wiesel's phrase. Most of them boasted meticulously clean facilities for raising Angora rabbits, ostensibly to determine if Angora wool production might be feasible. The Nazi guardians had the responsibility for providing the best care for the rabbits, coddling them in quiet pastoral surroundings, while at the same time they treated millions of Jews like vermin.[27]

Liberated by Russian soldiers in the early days of 1945, Ausch-

[27] Sigrid Schultz, "Angora: Pictorial Records of an SS Experiment," *Wisconsin Magazine of History,* Vol. I (Summer 1967), pp. 392–413.

witz provided evidence that millions of Jews had been killed. But this did not change the knowledge Americans and Europeans had had all along about the fate of European Jewry. Auschwitz only revealed the new techniques by which large numbers of persons could be killed quickly. Auschwitz also came to serve as the symbol of the six million dead.

All that we can do now is to reconstruct their struggle in that weird place of human habitation and its like.

Spring 1972

PART ONE

Juden Verboten

Jewry was public enemy number one for the German National Socialists. When they captured control of the German government in 1933, they quickly strove to make their policies of modern political and cultural anti-Semitism official. During the next ten years they attacked Jews on many different fronts, succeeding by 1937 in depriving them of their German citizenship and shutting them out from most forms of livelihood. The synagogue, any Jewish secular organization—all were in continuous jeopardy. The streets became battlegrounds where Jews could be attacked without fear of police reprisal. Homes were vulnerable to private and state-inspired marauders.

From the outset of the Nazi campaign, Jews fled Germany. As the turmoil increased, so did Jewish flight. Jewish refugees became a world problem. During the 1930's, over 250,000 left Germany for the United States, Great Britain, Holland, France, and other countries of Europe and the Western Hemisphere. The more intolerable the anti-Jewish pressure within Germany, the graver the Jewish-refugee problem, intensified in part by the official expulsion in October 1938 to Poland of all Jews holding Polish citizenship. The problem reached crisis proportions when it became apparent that refugees were unwelcome in many of the countries which they were trying to enter.

Several facets of the Jewish-refugee problem are discussed in the selections that follow.

On Being a Refugee

MAX O. KORMAN *

This human document, a personal letter, outlines one individual's experience of the travails of refugee life in the twentieth century. After World War I, Max Korman had fled Poland for Germany. On October 28, 1938, he and his family, along with thousands of other Jews, were deported to Zbaszyn, a village in Poland's western border country. The following spring, he was permitted to return to Germany for a month. In April, with his family still in Poland, a friend sent him a Cuban entry permit. With the help of an officer of the Hapag Steamship Company in Hamburg, he booked passage on the ill-fated St. Louis. *The selection that follows is excerpted from a letter he wrote his wife shortly after arriving in Holland.*

On Saturday, May 13, 1939,[1] I and hundreds of other passengers strained the facilities of the Hapag Steamship Company at Hamburg's main railway station. We were about to embark on the *St. Louis,* and were being processed all afternoon. Toward evening

---

* This document, translated from the German, is part of the unpublished *Korman Papers,* Regional Archives, Cornell University, Ithaca, New York.
[1] Twenty years later Max Korman recalled in his personal memoirs his feelings while attending religious services that Saturday morning. He was profoundly aware that he and his fellow passengers were on the "threshold of redemption" while the other members of Rabbi Joseph Carlebach's congregation, who had to remain behind, were doomed to hell.

47

we boarded waiting buses and these took us in about half an hour to our ship.

We boarded the *St. Louis* in a spirit of gaiety, delighted with the sense of relief from the tensions brought on by preparations for the voyage. Most of us explored the ship at once, running up and down staircases, gazing down gangways, and inspecting admiringly the interiors of the halls and dining rooms.

Exactly at eight in the evening, as the ship began to move slowly from its moorings, a grand vision possessed each of us: sixteen days in a luxurious floating hotel; sixteen days of freedom from burdens and sorrow; sixteen days to be climaxed in Havana by the embrace of loved ones, by the chance to send for wives, children, and parents who remained behind. A new chapter was to begin for us all.

In the days following our departure we became absorbed in the routine, the sights, the activities of our ocean journey. Since the *St. Louis* carried more than her usual number of passengers on this voyage, meals were arranged in two shifts to accommodate all one thousand of us. The food was excellent, and ample enough to satisfy the heartiest of appetites; those convinced that they had to eat everything soon discovered the discomfort of overstuffing stomachs unaccustomed to ocean voyages.

Our diversions were many. We could sun ourselves on deck, walk the promenade deck (six times around was the equivalent of one kilometer), or amuse ourselves on the sports deck playing ping-pong, volleyball, ringtoss, or miniature golf. In the evening the program alternated among three activities: movies in one hall, dancing in another, and concerts in still a third. The ladies really came into their own with all these diversions, for they could show off their entire wardrobes, from formal wear to playsuits and swimsuits. Most of them literally transformed themselves, stepping out of their skins, so to speak. They behaved as if they were truly on a pleasure cruise, seemingly forgetting that they were really well-dressed beggars; after all, each of us had only four dollars in his pocket.

The truly beautiful and sublime was nature, yes, only nature. Looking into the ocean we saw the ship splitting the water to create in its wake foam-laden waves that rhythmically chased one another. We saw the watery play of colors: greens, bright greens, blues, dark blues, and the rainbow sparkle as the sun's rays hit the ocean's watery spray. We saw the dolphins trying to overtake the faster swimming *St. Louis* by jumping up out of the water again and again. We saw the smaller flying fish rising suddenly, flying seemingly long stretches only to disappear again. We saw the sun rise and set. And we saw the incredibly beautiful cloud formations. It was a wonder to see all this and at the same time to feel one's aloneness in the ocean's enormous spaciousness.

Daily we tracked our journey west. At twelve noon tiny flags on a large map located the ship's position, helping us to see how each day brought the American continent and our goal closer. One foggy and rainy morning, accompanied by sea gulls, we passed the Azores. Land came into view. We could see steep, boulder-laden slopes and a valley snugly protecting a town and its red-roofed houses. As we continued to travel west the weather became warm enough for us to go swimming in the ship's pool. That day was especially wonderful! Thanks to fine sailing weather we arrived two days early. On Saturday at 4 A.M. we awoke to see Havana, and a few minutes later realized that in fact the ship had dropped anchor in the port. Preparations for disembarking began at once with the screening of all passengers.

The next step was never taken. Everything became quiet. Then we saw a decree from the Cuban police, but at first we did not know what it meant. The most diverse rumors began to circulate. First it was said that the Cubans do not work the Saturday before Pentecost, forcing us to wait until Monday before we could disembark. Then, some told us that because the arrival was two days early the port was not ready for the *St. Louis;* other ships, especially an English one and a French, had to discharge their immigrants first. We were bewildered.

Relatives and friends soon began arriving. They came in small motorboats, circling around the giant ship, calling, screaming, waving, and in other such ways trying to relate themselves to their loved ones aboard the *St. Louis.* Many wept, and no wonder: wife and child above, at the railing of the ocean liner; husband and father down below, in the motor launch. It was a dramatic reunion: months of hope and labor and joyful anticipations consummated as loved ones did in fact see one another, but from a distance. From below they soothed us with *mañana, mañana,* a call we were to hear again and again during the days that followed.

The wildest rumors circulated. The government had issued an injunction against landing. The Cuban President was hopefully being persuaded to change the injunction. Committees were working for us round the clock; five hundred telegrams had been sent to Cuban officialdom. We would in fact land if only we would remain calm.

We tried to influence our fate, but the odds became overwhelming. We formed a committee to represent our interests and negotiate for us; and its members tried everything possible, cabling everywhere, listening for even the feeblest response. But no encouraging sound was to be heard. Each of us became more and more tense and as our nerves began to fray we asked ourselves this question: with legal entry permits in hand, why had we journeyed for fourteen days across the ocean? to sit for three days in the port of Havana and to observe from a ship's railings the customs of the natives? One passenger, whose wife and two children were also on the ship, answered by slashing his wrists and jumping overboard. (A sailor leaped after him and saved his life.) We received news bulletins: the Joint [2] in New York and Havana had entered negotiations with the Cuban Government; in fact, the representative from New York, accompanied by an American senator, had flown to Havana. The Cuban parliament had been called into special session. American Jews had posted a five-hundred-dollar bond for each passenger. The boats with the relatives and friends continued to come, morning, noon, and night. They waved and screamed! "You are sure to embark." "The situation is favorable for us." "The parliament has voted and a majority is with us." "Now it's up to the President only." "Yes, yes." "Sure, sure." "Tomorrow, tomorrow."

Those words, those soothing words, well meant as they were, had the opposite effect on us. Continual disappointment had immunized us. We had learned to believe nothing. So we called back to them, *"Mañana, mañana;* it looks very good for us; keep

[2] The Joint Distribution Committee, an international Jewish agency created by the Jewish community to deal with refugee problems.

calm." Finally, we did not even want to see the boats. The unrest increased. People cursed and wept. Many broke down. We were in a witches' brew, it seemed. On Thursday we heard that the ship would have to leave the harbor early Friday morning, and we feared the worst. The passengers organized young people to stand uninterrupted two-hour watches to prevent the feared effects of frustration—collapses and suicides. Concern about many of the women was especially intense; they now knew that on the morrow they would leave their men behind in Havana, perhaps forever. Thus, we kept watch that whole night, and no doubt prevented many an extreme act of desperation.

Friday morning, around ten-thirty, the gentlemen from the American Joint came aboard, gathered us in the social hall, and declared, "The Cuban Government refuses to continue negotiations so long as the ship remains in Cuban waters. The captain is therefore forced to leave port immediately for the waters outside the three-mile limit. At that point the Government's terms for further negotiations will have been met." The leader of the delegation then asked, "Do you want to trust me?" When all said yes, he declared, "I promise you that you shall not return to Germany. We shall do everything so that you will land outside of Germany." He promised further to inform us every two hours about the developments in the negotiations. In the meantime, he asked us to remain calm. Then his group, and the police guarding us, disembarked.

The ship turned, and slowly, very slowly, left the port, accompanied by the many small boats, and also by autos driving along the harbor front. The harbor front itself was crowded with people, who, as in the preceding days, could not approach the ship. They yelled, and waved, and wept; for in spite of promises that we would return to Havana many had begun to abandon hope of ever seeing their loved ones again. And in that mood we left the port, seeing Havana in all its glorious panorama: the dome of the capitol, the skyscrapers, the attractive landscaping, the palms.

Our frightful pleasure cruise into the blue had begun once again, and with it came an awful feeling of despair. At first, when the ship stopped after a few hours of travel, all sighed with relief: the coast of Havana was still in view. But then, even as the first dispatches came, imploring us to be courageous and patient, the *St. Louis* suddenly resumed its journey at full speed. The next morning, seemingly moving toward Cuba, we found ourselves looking at the coast of Florida: Miami's skyscrapers, beaches, the bridge to Key West. All these wonderful facilities seemed within a swimmer's reach. As the yachts and other luxury boats greeted us, you can well imagine the feeling that dominated me. Here lived our uncle; this was the land to which I was supposed to come. And here I was so near, but oh so far.

I was not alone. The moment of truth had arrived. What rotten merchandise we must be if no one is prepared to accept us. The slaves must have been better: at least people paid for them, but here and now, when many wanted to pay for each of us, we are still rejected. Are we really so bad and so rotten? Are we really humanity's vermin and thus to be treated as lepers? Or has mankind ceased being human? Has it decided to imitate the natural elements and join with them in a war of annihilation against all the weaker and helpless forms of life? If yes, then man stands revealed. You have no capacity for understanding. You have no ideals. You have no noble purposes. Man, you are lower than the beasts; for they fight only when driven by hunger, by nature's survival demands, which leave them no choice. You, man, use your ability to reason, to kill, to destroy. And what a hero you are, man. You battle against the weakest. Among your kind are great scientists: they specialize in studying the most complex, difficult problems. You do everything to help them because you claim that their research will yield the best of all possible results for your kind. But with us Jews, man, you preach one thing and practice the opposite: you destroy what you do not comprehend or do not want to comprehend. Man, you are a lie.

The cruise along the Florida coast lasted until noon, when suddenly the ship turned and with full speed sailed in a northerly direction. The captain explained his new course by telling us that technical reasons required him to leave the Florida coast for a waiting station that offered cooler weather and was about equidistant from Havana, Haiti, and New York. Our tense and fearful mood instantly worsened. The despair became intolerable. In Havana we had not jumped overboard. What should we do now?

The evening brought a reassuring message: everything was not yet lost. Santo Domingo offered haven if American Jews would pay five hundred dollars for each adult and three hundred dollars for each child. A straw, but in the meantime the ship continued to travel in a northerly direction, away from Santo Domingo!

Still another cable arrived that evening: landing permission secured from Cuba's Isle of Pines, south of Havana. Relief! Passengers kissed one another, laughed, danced, and believed: they were free at last from the torture of uncertainty. As if to reinforce the message, the *St. Louis* changed course and drifted; apparently the captain was awaiting orders from Hapag Hamburg for his return trip to Havana. By our calculations we could not arrive there before Wednesday morning.

When we arose the following morning, however, we wondered why the ship was moving so slowly. Our wonder turned to alarm as the *St. Louis* changed course again and steamed with full force in the direction of Europe. Something was wrong. Obviously. Fearfully, we awaited an explanation. It came when the captain told us that efforts were still being made to change the mind of the Cuban Government, that in fact that government now had at its disposal deposits of five hundred dollars for each of the *St. Louis* passengers. He had no choice, however, but to continue sailing northward toward the cooler waiting station. That station would be reached by Saturday afternoon. Any change of course could come only upon orders from Hapag Hamburg. As we clutched our straw of hope, groups of pessimists argued with groups of optimists. On one point all agreed: the news about landing on the Isle of Pines was a delusion or an impossibility, for the island didn't have accommodations for a thousand people.

These were truly the days when our despair reached its lowest ebb, for the weather also turned against us. Rain, fog, and storms unleashed themselves against our already overtaxed nervous systems. Seasickness was accompanied by silence from the world beyond. Instead of coming hourly, or three times a day, the bulletins now came only once each day. They told us nothing new, but still we yearned for them, like dying patients begging for morphine to dull their pain. Many prayed. Many fasted.

Finally, even we insisted upon knowing the full truth. When

we discovered that our passenger committee had protected us from some important information and that one of our New York negotiators had been convinced all along that settlement with Cuba was impossible, the most intense point of our despair arrived. We abandoned faith in our committee and organized a general assembly of all passengers to hear all the latest cable messages. Then, to remind the world again of our fate, we decided to telegraph Roosevelt, the King of England (who was then visiting Washington), the American press and radio, and Jewish agencies in New York and Paris. We begged them to transfer us to another ship, which could be rented and which could await a favorable settlement of our fate.

Into this cauldron of emotions came a cable from a representative of the Joint in New York, trying to instruct the captain to sail into New York Harbor, drop anchor at Bedloe's Island, and wait there while Congress acted on petitions to provide landing arrangements in the United States. As well intentioned as the sender of this telegram had been, his cable worsened our mood because of its futility. We knew that Hapag Hamburg alone could affect the captain's course; we also knew that Hapag Hamburg would not act upon such vague expectations.

Fortunately, the captain now began to play a more direct role in our affairs. We trusted his word, for he had been marvelous in every way, and had worked day and night on our behalf. He now reminded us about the promise that had been made to us: we would not be returned to Germany. He also told us that negotiations were continuing and that the point of no return would not be reached until Sunday noon.

That slight glimmer of hope did not prevent depression. There were some nervous breakdowns. Some wished the ship would sink. But somehow most still hoped for something, although we were all fed up with suffering, the ship, the people, the ocean: this horrible feeling of sailing about on the high seas searching for a harbor that might in fact not exist.

Finally, on Saturday afternoon, as cables came to the *St. Louis* from European capitals and institutions, we realized that the critical stage of the negotiations had moved from the New World back to the Old World, from which we had come. Within thirty-six hours (we heard from Paris) we would have news of our fate. But, having been disappointed so often, we had lost our ability to really believe anything. And we did not believe. The thirty-six hours passed slowly, and with their passage the *St. Louis* came closer and closer to Hamburg, Germany, its home port. The thirty-sixth hour came and went without word from Paris. This we had expected. We were beyond despair.

The cable finally arrived: England, Holland, Belgium, and France had declared themselves ready to accept us *all*. The wording was critical, since much doubt and confusion reigned. Fights broke out as people disagreed over the conditions of acceptance: passengers with affidavits only; men only; no women and children —they had to return to Germany. But it was *all* of us who had really been accepted by these countries. We would land in Antwerp and from there be distributed to the host nations.

And so it came to pass in the glare of worldwide publicity.

One last word. We left Hamburg on May 13. We learned of our fate, our harbor, on June 13.[3]

---

[3] Twenty years later, in his personal memoirs, Max Korman recalled the landing procedures:

"On June 13 we docked in Antwerp. Some people were selected for England, some for France, some for Belgium, and some for Holland. Since my name was not called for the first three countries, I went to the hall where people gathered who were supposed to go to Holland. There I found a group of persons standing on the stage and calling each family or person individually. The person or family called had to go on the stage, where the passports were taken, and then they were welcomed into Holland with a flower and identity card. . . .

"Early next morning we boarded a small boat that navigated through different canals and villages until we arrived in Rotterdam; and from there we were taken to Hy-Pleet, a camp for refugees. There the reception was cold and we were made to understand that we were restricted to the camp area. . . . After a few weeks a group was picked to go to Amsterdam, to the Lloyd Hotel, which had been converted into a refugee center. I stayed there until November, during which time a new camp was opened in Westerbork; I was among the first fifty people recruited for the development and settlement of the camp."

The Refugee Problem

NATHAN C. BELTH *

*The following document surveys what was
actually taking place in the critical months of
1938–1939, when the refugee problem came to
a head. It analyzes the policies and actions of
the various countries toward Jewish refugees.
Of special interest are the sections (pp. 59–60
and 68–70) dealing with deportation to Zbaszyn
and the voyage of the* St. Louis, *episodes experienced by the writer of the preceding document.*

. . . No year since the advent of the Hitler regime was as cruel
or as discouraging for German refugees as the twelve months between the Intergovernmental Refugee Conference at Evian, France
(July 6, 1938), and the meeting of the permanent committee set
up by the Evian conference in London on July 19, 1939.

The Evian conference brought with it high hopes that the democratic nations of the world were at last ready to take the first firm
steps toward a permanent solution of the refugee problem. The
months that followed, however, brought only graver political problems, severer burdens upon the philanthropic organizations engaged in refugee work, unusual and fantastic episodes of human
suffering.

But at the year's close a note of hope was struck again; at the
London conference of July 19, 1939, the British Government expressed the view which had long been held by those engaged in

* "The Refugee Problem," *The American Jewish Year Book, 5700* (Philadelphia: Jewish Publication Society, 1939), pp. 374–391.

refugee work, that the problem was insoluble if the financing of a solution were left to private initiative alone. Britain announced that it stood ready to discuss with other democratic governments a plan for granting governmental financial assistance towards a permanent solution to the refugee problem.

In the twelve months between the two meetings, the plight of the refugees from Germany was accentuated and dramatized by the German annexation of the Sudetenland in September 1938 and the subsequent further dismemberment of Czechoslovakia; the mass expulsion of Jews of Polish origin from Germany to [Zbaszyn] Poland in October; the pogroms throughout Germany in November as a result of the shooting of a German embassy official in Paris, and the accompanying punitive governmental action; the great outpouring of Jews from Austria and other territories that came under German domination; the creation of refugee "no-man's-lands"; the closing of the gates of Palestine to refugee and other immigration; the investigation of mass colonization projects, notably British Guiana; the mass rescue of refugee children; the incident of the S.S. *St. Louis* and similar wandering boatloads of rejected immigrants; and finally, the establishment of a foundation to implement an accelerated and orderly emigration of Jews from the Reich.

These are the incidents which created a spectacular background for the more prosiac efforts of governments and public and private organizations to alleviate the suffering of the refugees. The Intergovernmental Refugee Conference at Evian served to emphasize once more that no nation was ready to throw open its gates willingly and unreservedly to an influx of refugees from Germany. Each nation, in diplomatic language, rationalized its position. But the conference did express the determination of the democratic nations to find some formula for the humane solution of the refugee problem and to establish the necessary machinery to achieve that end. The concrete achievement of the conference was the establishment of a permanent Intergovernmental Refugee Committee with headquarters in London. A less tangible, but equally important achievement, is implicit in the establishment of the permanent committee: the democratic nations had come to the conclusion that the refugee problem was no longer a problem for private philanthropic organizations alone, but that if it was to be solved, liberal governments must take a leading role in that solution.

The first meeting of the Committee was held on August 3, 1938, and its first task was to obtain from the Reich an agreement whereunder emigrants would be permitted to take part of their capital with them, and a guarantee would be given that "normal" treatment would be accorded Jews while still residing in the Reich.

The committee named George Rublee, an American, and a close friend of President Roosevelt, as director of the permanent bureau and set for him the task of obtaining from the Reich the necessary agreement that would lead to an orderly, accelerated emigration program from Germany, and safety for those potential emigrants who would be forced to reside in Germany for some years to come. The difficulties that beset Mr. Rublee were formidable. His efforts to deal with a power that was unwilling even to consider any negotiations on the subject were complicated, on the one hand, by the grave political crisis that preceded the dismemberment of Czechoslovakia and, on the other, by new and violently repressive measures taken by the Nazis against the Jews in Germany.

These measures resulted in such conditions that, for the first time since the World War, the term "no-man's-land" was heard again in Europe—only now it had a different, even more cruel meaning. Not battlefields were these new no-man's-lands, but narrow strips of territory bordering on two or more countries, often nothing more than an open field or a ditch. Not soldiers were their inhabitants, but helpless, miserable refugees, men, women, and children, whom no land would admit—blazing indictments of the brutal lengths to which anti-Semitism could go. The first of these no-man's-lands was an old vermin-infested barge anchored in the Danube near the Hungarian shore. On it were some sixty Austrian refugees, ranging from children to old folk, who had been expelled from Burgenland.

Perhaps, in a truer sense, the first no-man's-lands were on the borders of dismembered Czechoslovakia. With the frontiers undetermined for weeks, groups of Jewish refugees, large and small, were shuttled back and forth in an inhuman game. One group of 300 spent weeks in zero weather in an open field between Mischdorf in Austria and Bratislava. Other no-man's-lands camps were situated at Nitra, Tapolcany, Lilina, Michalovce, Prestany and Zilino. Thousands were marooned in these places. When, in October, 1938, Slovakia was granted autonomy, and a large slice of it was ceded to Hungary, anti-Semitic Hungarians rounded up 10,-000 Jews in the newly-acquired territory within four days and dumped them over the new border. The largest group found itself near the city of Kosice. Slowly these no-man's-lands were liquidated through the efforts of Jewish refugee organizations and the easing of official restrictions.

The largest of the no-man's-lands, however, was created not on the Czech, but on the German-Polish frontier when Jews of Polish origin residing in Germany were rounded up on the night of October 28, taken across the border, and left to their fate. The numbers involved were variously estimated as from 12,000 to 18,000 people. The pretext for the action was a decree issued by the Polish Government requiring Polish citizens resident abroad to obtain renewal of their passports by October 29. The decree would have denationalized thousands of Polish Jews in Germany and would have left Germany with a large group of "stateless" Jews.

Without warning or explanation, on the night of October 28, thousands of Jews throughout Germany were roused from bed, many permitted to take nothing more than the clothes they wore, put aboard special sealed trains and buses and taken to the border, where they were forced out and over the frontier. Many of the deportees, although Polish nationals, had been living in Germany more than twenty years; some of them had even been born in Germany and were Polish nationals *de jure* only.

The greatest concentration of these unfortunates was near the little town of Zbaszyn. Overnight, its population of 5,000 was literally doubled. Refugees slept in the streets, in open fields, in tents, and in abandoned stables. Similar were the conditions near Poznan, Lodz, Lwow, Cracow and other border towns. The situation was unprecedented, the hysteria general. The very barest necessities of life were not available. Within twenty-four hours, however, officials of the American Jewish Joint Distribution Committee in Warsaw organized a relief corps. Physicians and nurses arrived, and truckloads of food, clothing, medical supplies were brought to the scene. Stables were converted into barracks; food kitchens and first aid stations were set up. Slowly the no-man's-lands in all areas except Zbaszyn were liquidated. Those who were not permitted to enter Poland proper were concentrated at Zbaszyn. In the face of this emergency impoverished Polish Jewry itself rose to heroic heights and in special campaigns raised 2,000,000 zlotys (about $400,000) for the aid of the deportees. Approximately 13,500 deportees were registered by the relief committees, and as the year drew to a close nearly 11,000 still required direct relief, although some had been permitted to enter the interior of Poland and some others, as a result of Polish-German negotiations, had been permitted to return to Germany for short periods to liquidate their property.

The shock of the Polish border incidents had hardly subsided when the world was horrified by an event even more outrageous— mass pogroms throughout Germany. The pretext for these excesses was grounded in the events on the Polish border. Among the thousands of Jews at the Zbaszyn camp were a couple named Grynszpan. To their son, seventeen-year-old Herschel Grynszpan, residing with relatives in Paris, they sent a postcard telling of their plight. On November 8, the youth walked into the German Embassy in Paris and shot down Ernst von Rath, the third secretary of the embassy. The death of Von Rath two days later was the signal for nationwide riots, which had all the earmarks of having been arranged in advance, and for a billion-mark fine imposed collectively on the Jews in Germany, and for other punitive measures.

These events, while they further complicated the efforts of George Rublee and the Intergovernmental Committee, shocked the democratic nations into renewed efforts on behalf of the refugees. President Roosevelt on November 15 recalled the American ambassador to Germany in order to get a first-hand view of the situation. President Roosevelt also took steps to alleviate the plight of refugees by issuing an order extending for six months the visitors' permits of 15,000 German and Austrian Jews temporarily in the United States, on the ground that it would be "cruel and inhuman" to send them back to probable imprisonment or internment in concentration camps. He also urged Myron C. Taylor, vice-chairman of the Intergovernmental Refugee Committee, to go at once to London for a meeting of the Committee; and the State

Department, in a public statement, urged the various democratic governments to redouble efforts in finding a solution to the refugee problem.

The following week, Prime Minister Chamberlain, speaking before the House of Commons, offered to open two British colonies to refugee settlement, and to admit an increased number into the United Kingdom. The colonies in question were (1) British Guiana, where the Prime Minister offered 10,000 square miles (later increased to 40,000 square miles) in the interior to be leased "on generous terms under conditions to be settled hereafter" for agricultural development subject to surveys by British representatives and voluntary organizations; and (2) Tanganyika, British-mandated former German colony where 50,000 square miles were offered for settlement. In England, itself, Mr. Chamberlain said, admission of refugees depended upon the ability of private organizations to maintain them; and Home Secretary Sir Samuel Hoare revealed plans to admit several thousand refugee children. France and the Netherlands also came forward with offers to open some of their colonial possessions to settlement.

In the meantime, it became evident that Mr. Rublee was at last making headway in his efforts to negotiate with Germany. In mid-December, Dr. Hjalmar Schacht visited London to confer on economic matters with the Governor of the Bank of England, but at the same time presented a plan to Mr. Rublee and Lord Winterton, Chairman of the Intergovernmental Refugee Committee, whereunder refugee emigration would be fostered through clearing arrangements that would also promote the sale of German goods abroad. Mr. Rublee was invited to continue the conversations in Berlin in advance of the plenary session of the Intergovernmental Committee in January. But as this further meeting lagged, the Committee sessions were set over to the following month. On January 10, Mr. Rublee and two associates met again with Dr. Schacht in Berlin. After two days of conversation, further meetings were postponed to allow the German Government time to study the modifications proposed by Mr. Rublee, which would eliminate the fostering of German exports. On January 21, 1939, Mr. Rublee received a revised plan from Dr. Schacht which differed radically from the original scheme, and a further meeting was scheduled for the following day. The next day, however, the meeting was called off and shortly afterwards it became known that Dr. Schacht had been removed as president of the Reichsbank.

The negotiations had failed at what seemed a most encouraging point. That night, however, the American and British Embassies asked the Foreign Office whether the talks would be continued and on the following day Mr. Rublee was received by General Goering. Mr. Rublee then left for Paris to confer with officials of the Intergovernmental Committee, announcing that the discussions in Berlin would be resumed with Dr. Helmut Wohlthat, of the Economics Ministry, on his return. The discussions were concluded the following week when Mr. Rublee received a memorandum from Dr. Wohlthat which stated Germany's position and the extent to which it was willing to cooperate.

The memorandum was presented to the plenary session of the Intergovernmental Committee in London on February 12. At the close of its sessions, the Intergovernmental Committee issued a communiqué which authorized the director to inform the German Government "that, acting independently, it has been and is using, and will use its best endeavors to develop opportunities for permanent settlement of involuntary emigrants." The communiqué, in effect, also approved a project for "formation of a private international corporation which will serve as the agency for financing emigration from Germany and for maintaining such contacts with the German authorities as might be necessary for this purpose." At the same time, it was revealed that Mr. Rublee, feeling his task completed after five months in office, would resign and that he would be replaced by Sir Herbert Emerson, who, in September 1938, had been named League of Nations High Commissioner for Refugees; thus the work of the Committee and of the League would be under the same direction.

Coincidental with the issuance of the Intergovernmental Committee's statement was the departure of an Anglo-American Commission, sponsored by President Roosevelt's Advisory Committee on Political Refugees, to survey British Guiana, in line with Prime Minister Chamberlain's offer of the previous November. After a two months' survey, the commission reported that ". . . while the territory offered for settlement in British Guiana is not an ideal place for refugees from middle European countries, and while the territory could not be considered suitable for immediate large scale settlement, it undoubtedly possesses potential possibilities that would fully justify the carrying out of a trial settlement project on a substantial enough scale that would make it possible to determine whether and how these potential possibilities could be realized."

It was the especial recommendation of . . . the commission . . . that a two-year project, costing approximately $3,000,000 and involving some 5,000 young settlers, should be initiated. Settlements would be established at certain strategic points which would test the feasibility of large-scale settlement and acquire information which could not be ascertained by a small commission in two months.

The attitude of the British Government toward the report was expressed by Prime Minister Chamberlain in a statement before the House of Commons on May 12. Mr. Chamberlain declared that the British Government stood ready to offer the fullest facilities for any settlement decided upon by refugee organizations. He pledged a large measure of local autonomy and adequate representation in the colony's government, should a large new community be established. The Government, he said, would retain control of general services, such as security, communications, and revenue. Concerning the important factor of communications, he said that if the prospects of development were good and capital was forthcoming adequate for the needs of large-scale settlement, the Government would be prepared to provide needed communications.

During the course of the year, numerous projects and lands for settlement, in addition to those already mentioned, were suggested. While many of them were being investigated by various agencies, none had received as thorough consideration or as favorable a report as British Guiana, though preliminary reports on the island of Mindanao in the Philippines showed favorable colonization conditions. The chief disadvantages faced by most of the projects were complicated political situations.

The general problems of refugee emigration during the period offered far greater difficulties than in previous years. Complicating factors were the territorial changes affecting Czechoslovakia and the anti-Jewish legislation in Italy and Hungary, which created several new classes of refugees. Furthermore, many of the refugees from Germany, during the latter part of 1938, were forced to leave the country hurriedly. Such unfortunates were rarely in possession of legal documents which would regularize their stay in the countries of asylum, a condition which added to the complexities of an already confused situation in the lands neighboring on Germany. In addition, the emigrants of 1938 and 1939 were the poorest of all the refugees, for even those who had been comparatively well off in Germany had lost the bulk of their possessions as a result of the November decrees, and had been forced to leave the remainder in Germany.

According to a report by Sir Herbert Emerson, between 120,000 and 140,000 refugees left Germany during 1938, including one-third of the entire Jewish population of Austria, many of these being helped to do so by philanthropic organizations. In the first four months of 1939, an estimated 30,000 additional emigrants were assisted to leave Germany. To this number must be added a considerable group that did not seek aid. As of February, 1939, the official German Government estimate of Jewish population in Germany, Austria and the Sudetenland was 600,000, of whom 200,000 were considered too old to emigrate.

Domiciled in European lands were upwards of 150,000 refugees, of whom approximately 60,000 were dependent for sustenance upon the various refugee committees. Probably the largest number lived in France. At the beginning of 1938, there were about 10,000 refugees in that country, but, by the end of that year, the number had grown to 25,000 and was further increased during the first half of 1939. French officials estimated that perhaps 10,000 of these were so-called "illegals" subject to deportation, and took steps to check the further entry of such refugees. The Interior Ministry was reported to be willing to legalize the stay of these "illegals," if the refugee organizations would agree not to press for the admission of additional numbers. Permission to work as farm laborers or in the defense industries was also to be granted the refugees. . . .

. . . many of the refugees offered to serve in the French armed forces during the mobilizations in the Fall of 1938 and Spring of 1939. . . . The various refugee committees operating in France took steps during the course of the year to coordinate their work more fully, and a centralized body was organized. The major refugee group expended approximately $170,000 during 1938 in assisting some 11,000 relief cases and in other services.

Very humane treatment was accorded the refugees in the little countries of Belgium and Holland, which permitted large numbers to enter. Following the events of November 10 in Germany, there naturally was an accelerated influx into these countries. To help the refugee organizations cope with the situation, the governments established camps to house the refugees. Similar institutions were established in England and France. In several of these camps rudimentary vocational retraining courses were organized to enable the refuges to fit themselves for new occupations.

More than 1,500 refugees were housed in Dutch camps. In addition 1,200 children were admitted into the country and housed in special lodgings. In the Spring of 1939, it was estimated that there were 22,000 refugees in Holland, of whom 11,000 were permanently settled in the country. The Dutch Jewish communities contributed $1,080,000 during 1938 for local refugee aid.

Belgium was greatly affected by the sudden flight of Jews from Austria and, in the period from May to December 1938, over 13,000 Austrians came to Brussels and Antwerp. The problem raised by this sudden influx was met in part by the establishment of a number of camps by the government and, when relief funds ran short, the government for a time took over the care of about 3,000 refugees. In addition the government permitted 500 children from Germany to enter the country and to be housed in children's camps. During 1938, the Belgium Jewish communities raised $55,-000 for refugee work, and large sums were contributed by foreign Jewish organizations.

Similar conditions were faced during the year by the small Jewish community of Switzerland. During 1938, a total of 9,000 refugees required assistance from the community, and the average relief load was 3,000 cases. Here, too, the government took a liberal attitude and provided public buildings for the use of refugees. The Swiss community of 18,000 Jews raised $340,000 during 1938, and additional subventions came from outside sources. The Scandinavian countries, Yugoslavia, Portugal, Luxembourg and

Albania also had refugee problems, though of much smaller compass. In all countries, the refugee committees maintained vocational training facilities and other services to help prepare the refugees for permanent settlement. The American Jewish Joint Distribution Committee expended a total of $778,000 in 1938 in support of the refugee committees in all European lands.

In the efforts to aid refugees, England played an even larger part than any of the continental countries. Not only did England admit larger numbers of refugees, but through the Council for German Jewry, British Jews raised huge sums which were expended for work within England itself, as well as for the work of committees in Palestine, Germany and Austria, and in other European lands. The German Jewish Aid Committee of England estimated that, in May 1939, 28,000 refugees were residing in Great Britain. This number included some 3,000 children, cared for in special children's camps, as part of the general program to evacuate Jewish children from Germany after the November 10 riots, and perhaps an equal number of adult refugees housed in transit camps. The local refugee committee reported that while it had registered 8,500 in 1938, that number had grown to 18,000 by May 1939.

The British Section of the Council for German Jewry conducted two major fund-raising campaigns during 1938, the Austrian Appeal and its regular campaign for aid to German Jews. The former drive received public contributions of £592,000, of which £145,-000 was appropriated up to the end of the year. In addition a nonsectarian drive known as the Lord Baldwin Fund, headed by the former Prime Minister, raised upwards of £250,000 for general refugee assistance.

The hopes of the refugees for permanent settlement naturally centered about the overseas countries. For the first time since the establishment of its quota system, the United States permitted its German quota to be filled. As a result 27,000 German immigrants entered the country from July 1, 1938, to June 30, 1939. In the same period, Palestine admitted approximately 7,000 refugees from Germany under the immigration schedules and an unknown number of "illegals." . . .

Another of the great hopes were the countries of Latin America. From 1933 to the end of 1938, some 40,000 refugees found homes in these lands, half of them in Argentina. The remainder were scattered throughout the other countries of South and Central America, and the West Indies. As long as the influx was comparatively small, local committees in these lands, with some aid from the Joint Distribution Committee, the Hias-Ica Emigration Association, and the Jewish Colonization Association, were able to cope with the situation. A major problem arose from the fact that, while the Latin American countries chiefly needed agricultural workers, most of the refugees were not trained or suited for farming.

During 1938, a small country such as Cuba, with a Jewish population of only 10,000, accepted 3,000 refugees, and by July, 1939, this number had increased to 6,000. A considerable number of the new arrivals were penniless and forced to seek assistance. Employment possibilities were few since Cuban law required 90 percent of all labor to be native. There was a major relief problem in Cuba, therefore, which had to be met very largely with funds from the United States. In Santo Domingo, there were 125 refugees during the year, and Costa Rica and Honduras had 100 each. The tiny island of Trinidad which, prior to 1932, had a Jewish population of only 10, permitted 450 refugees to enter in the last six months. In Chile, where there were 20,000 Jews, 2,000 refugees gained admission. However, on May 5, 1939, a decree was issued suspending all immigration for a year. In Colombia, 1,200 refugees found havens and the average number of new arrivals was 50 to 60 each month. Paraguay virtually stopped all immigration in September 1938 after it had admitted about 1,000 refugees. In Peru, the Jewish population was more than doubled by the immigration of 2,000 refugees, most of whom were admitted on temporary visas, while Uruguay admitted about 3,000 refugees, 2,000 of whom held transit visas. Bolivia, with an original Jewish population of perhaps 100, admitted 6,000 refugees up to the end of the year.

As in other parts of the world, there was a sudden increase in the number of refugees clamoring to enter these countries after Germany's annexation of Austria and the riots of November 10. The panicky flight caused Latin American countries to bar their doors. They raised the requirements for admission, demanded guarantees and head taxes, and applied all their normal regulations with greater severity. But so great was the pressure that refugees became the easy victims of unscrupulous steamship agents and consuls. Frequently, refugees obtained inadequate or invalid documents from consuls in Europe that were not honored by the central governments represented by these officials. Sometimes regulations were changed while refugees were on the high seas and, as a result, whole boatloads of refugees wandered from land to land and port to port seeking admission.

A shocking example of such a boatload of unfortunates, which focused the attention of the entire world upon this phase of the refugee problem, was the Hamburg-American liner S.S. *St. Louis,** which sailed from Germany for Cuba on May 15, 1939 [actually, May 13], ten days after a decree had been issued by the Cuban Government voiding all landing permits previously issued by the Cuban commissioner of immigration. Nine hundred and seven of the passengers on the *St. Louis* held such permits. The Hamburg-American line, however, announced that it had been assured that the landing permits would be honored because they had been issued before the date of the decree. But when the boat arrived in Havana on May 27, the passengers were not permitted to land. Efforts to obtain a reversal of this order failed, and American relief organizations sent representatives to Cuba to cope with the situation. On June 1, President Laredo Bru of Cuba ordered the ship to leave Havana and threatened to have it towed out by gunboats if it did not go under its own steam. He refused to entertain any further representations in behalf of the refugees until the ship had left.

On June 2, therefore, the ship sailed out of the harbor and wandered for more than a week in Caribbean waters while representatives of the National Coordinating Committee and the Joint Distribution Committee sought to obtain permission for the landing of the refugees. On June 5, President Bru announced that he would grant a temporary haven for the refugees if relief organizations would be willing to provide guarantees, in the form of deposits of $500 each for all refugees admitted. Arrangements to meet these guarantees were then made by the Joint Distribution Committee, but before they could be completed, the offer was rescinded on the ground that the time set for meeting the demands had elapsed. **Fur-**

* See pp. 47–55.

ther efforts to open the question in Cuba failed, and the Joint Distribution Committee turned its attention to finding a haven for the refugees in European lands.

In London and Paris, officials of the Joint Distribution Committee, in conjunction with local refugee committees, petitioned the governments of England, France, Holland and Belgium to admit groups of the *St. Louis* refugees. Financial guarantees that these refugees would not become public charges and that they would eventually re-emigrate were offered by the Joint Distribution Committee and, on the basis of these guarantees, the refugees were admitted by these four countries.

Seeing its entire program of aid to refugees and other distressed Jews endangered by the heavy costs of such incidents, the Joint Distribution Committee, on June 21, four days after the landing of the refugees in Europe, issued a statement of policy declaring that it would not be in a position to offer similar guarantees again, because of the heavy financial and administrative burdens involved, which would disrupt its normal program.

A similar statement was made by a spokesman for the Liaison Committee of the League of Nations High Commission for Refugees who declared: "One thing we must state is that if these [the *St. Louis* passengers] are taken care of by certain governments, it is not to constitute a precedent for other shiploads."

South America was not the only place on the globe where these wandering ships sought to land their human cargoes. Dozens of ships with thousands of refugees wandered in the Mediterranean trying to land their passengers along the Palestine coast, despite the restricted Palestine immigration schedule. The activities of these ships finally prompted the British government in July to shut down all Jewish immigration to Palestine, effective October 1939. The port of embarkation for the refugees on these ships, mostly cattle and cargo boats, ill-fitted for passenger service, was Constanza, a Rumanian harbor on the Black Sea.

When all other doors were shut and when efforts to land their passengers on Palestine soil failed, the ships sometimes made the long trip to Shanghai. Several ships with refugees went directly to that city, so that during the course of the year, Shanghai became a major refugee haven, war-torn symbol of the desperation of these people. Chief reason for this was the fact that Shanghai is a free port where the refugees had no difficulty in entering, though they could not proceed to the interior of China. In this city 10,000 refugees were concentrated by July 1, 1939. Opportunity for employment was small indeed and, as a result, a grave relief problem was created with which the local community alone naturally could not cope. Substantial subventions, however, were made by the British Section of the Council for German Jewry and by the Joint Distribution Committee. Some further relief was afforded the community by the fact that the Philippines accepted several hundred refugees from Shanghai and others were enabled to go to Hong Kong, Singapore, Colombo and Bombay.

American Views on Admitting Refugee Children: 1939

The following texts are excerpted from the transcript of the House of Representatives 76th Congress Hearings Before the Committee on Immigration and Naturalization on the subject of Admission of German Refugee Children, *held on May 24, 25, and 31, and June 1, 1939. They document several different positions taken by Americans who knew of events in Germany and had heard the evidence. The United States Congress still refused to admit twenty thousand Jewish children from Germany at a time when thousands of refugees were seeking havens and when Europe was on the eve of World War II.*

Testimony of
Clarence E. Pickett [1]

MR. PICKETT. We are facing in Germany a catastrophe to 800,-000 people. It is a catastrophe created by religious and racial persecution, which is not duplicated anywhere else so far as I know in

[1] Clarence E. Pickett was an outstanding Quaker who appeared here in his capacity as executive director of the Non-Sectarian Committee for German Refugee Children.

the world, and certainly not duplicated anywhere else in central Europe.

That is the first thing we have to keep in mind. We are not just concerned about the children who are hungry. Our own organization has had a good deal of experience with that. We fed a million and a quarter children a day for a period of three and a half years after the World War was over.

We have been connected with Germans and German life and had a center in Germany and Austria ever since the war, and have had a great deal of contact with the developing of the inner problems of Germany so far as relief is concerned. Those now are not our problems. There was a relief catastrophe after the war. We met that. Now there is a catastrophe created by a religious and racial persecution. We cannot sit by and see that happen. We do not believe Americans want to sit by and see a great catastrophe like that happen not only to 800,000 but at the least at the present time 100,000 of those who are children who come under the category defined in this bill, namely, children from fourteen years and down. . . .

MR. SCHULTE.[2] What organization did you say you represented?

MR. PICKETT. The American Friends Service Committee. You may know them better as Quakers.

MR. SCHULTE. You understand me, that I am very much in sympathy with this bill here, 165. . . . But I cannot understand the all-of-a-sudden interest in refugee or orphan children, and I cannot just understand [George William] Cardinal Mundelein and the other bishop you mentioned there, when this is in 1920, 1921, and 1922, there was real persecution going on to the extent of murdering of Catholics in Mexico, where really orphan children were made orphans because of that religious war, and yet no one voice was raised in the United States to take care of those children, in any manner, shape, or form, but all of a sudden we get an interest in refugees or orphans, and I am sympathetic with this act, you understand, but why were we not sympathetic then?

[2] Representative William Theodore Schulte was a Democrat from Hammond, Indiana.

MR. PICKETT. I think you may have a chance to get that from some one who can answer for Cardinal Mundelein. I cannot answer that. I think it is hardly fair to say we have not been interested for over twenty years as we have been interested.

MR. SCHULTE. You do remember the terrific hardships in the country of Mexico? . . . When thousands of those kids were pushed back into Mexico? . . . And the same holds true during your communistic war they have over there.

MR. PICKETT. I agree with regard to Mexico. We have had no connections in Mexico. I cannot answer your question. I think I remember a great deal of concern on the part of the Catholic Church. I would rather those very much more familiar with it would answer that. . . .

There are certain facts which may not be known to your committee here, which I think may be an outlet for that which does not involve the United States. We certainly want participation of other countries in relieving this situation, where we can get it.

I would like to say a few brief words in the beginning, and then unless you want to consume time in questions, I would like to come back and give data concerning the bill. It is a permissive bill only. It permits, as the bill stands now, in 1939 and 1940, the admission of 10,000 children in each of those two years. I hope you will keep in mind it is permissive.

Nobody knows better than I do that you do not move 10,000 children by snapping your fingers. It is a big job for you to undertake. It involves only voluntary organizations and the most important feature in the whole bill is the consular officers in Germany. So it is permissive legislation. . . .

You will have others testifying who have been in Germany since I have. I was there during the month of September, and conditions then were I thought pretty bad. After the persecution, the pogrom, of November 10, conditions have become a great deal worse.

In the first place, since the 10th of November, German-Jewish children cannot go to the public schools. They cannot play in the public parks. It is possible to have privately set-up schools for these children, but they must be paid for by the Jewish population of Germany, and, of course, they are tremendously reduced in their ability to pay, because of the capital tax and because of various forms of extorting money from them.

I feel tremendously impressed in the way in which the population from this minority group in Germany added the enormous expense to themselves with their reduction in standards of living, and they have done everything they could.

Furthermore, they are not permitted by law to conduct schools for those above the age of fourteen. As I have said, they cannot play in the parks. They are reminded continually and being spat at and being treated in ways damaging to children when they go into the streets to play.

On the nights of the 11th, 12th, and 13th of November, 35,000 of these men were put in concentration camps. Some of them have been let out. So far as the figures go, between seven and eight thousand have been let out. They may stay there for weeks, and sometimes it extends to three months. They make the promise that they will leave the country, but they have no way of fulfilling their promise. Consequently, a variety of things happen. Some of them leave and walk across the border. We are handling that kind of people all of the time in border countries.

The most common thing to happen is, since arrests come at night, they do not sleep two nights at the same place in succession. The influence of that you can see on the family life, which is extremely damaging to a child in the younger years.

Then in mixed marriages forced separation is going on at an increased rate; that is, an Aryan wife is required to divorce her Jewish husband, and it may be the other way around. This is not universal, but it is an increasingly common practice; if they refuse to be divorced then a decree is issued and then they are arrested for living together as unmarried persons. All of this has a direct bearing on the family life in Germany. So far as I know it does not happen in China, even in Poland, and it does not happen in Rumania. I will comment a little later about the Hungarian situation, because I have made a study of what is happening there.

So I think you have here a unique problem of unsettling, breaking down the morale and the nervous energy of these children, which is not an ordinary situation.

Furthermore, we have got to look down the road; . . . 300,000 of these people have already registered there who desire to come to this country. If you have a child five years old and he has to wait until he gets on the quota, I think it is important as to what is going to happen to that child after he goes through five years of that and then comes to us as a citizen. That is a very real thing, because even since the 10th of November the people who are coming through our agency now—men, women, and children—present a more difficult problem because of the nervous strain. Of course it is harder on the children than it is on the adults. That is assuming there is no change in the immigration regulations at all. We take in 27,000 a year. Many of these will come in in the long run. This seems to me from the long-run point of view to be a very practical proposition, because I visualize these children who have been victims of this situation.

Then I want to make one other point, which is extremely important to any minority group. I doubt if most Americans realize that on the night of the 10th of November, all synagogues in the whole of Germany were burned to the ground. Whenever you get a minority group that has a religious conviction tied up with it, the religious element means much more when they cannot associate through their political life, and their church life means much more. . . .

But here is the thing which has happened throughout the Jewish group: there is an intensified increase in religion. They have burned down all the synagogues and they have no religious worship available. That is important in the lives of the children, because they had not only preaching services, but they had religious and educational services which were rendered. So that all of these things have conspired to make anybody at all closely in touch with the situation deeply concerned. You do not see that thing happen before your eyes if there is anything you can do in fairness to the total situation. I certainly want to do something about it.

I might say there were two synagogues that were not burned, because one in Berlin and one in Vienna were bounded by valuable areas of property, and they could not burn them without desecrating the other property. But they did ruin them so that no religious services for the Jewish are being conducted in Germany.

I might add this: About 25 or 30 percent are non-Aryan, that is to say, part Jewish and part Christian in religion, either Catholic or Protestant, but they are now a despised race. They do not find themselves able to go to the Catholic Church or Protestant churches freely and feel at home. I do not say the Catholic Church excludes them.

I had a Catholic priest tell me himself in Vienna the saddest thing he had to handle was to see his own members who were partly Jewish cease coming, not because he did not want them but because the Aryan members would move away when they sat down beside them. The pressure is such that they do not want to have that kind of a thing developing around them.

But, personally, you have on a very large scale a decline in facilities available for the Aryan and non-Aryan and Jewish altogether.

With all of these things in mind I came back in October—the end of October—and I found here that there had been all the time a growing feeling that something in addition ought to be done, particularly for the children, and a few of us got together and talked the matter over, and out of that has come this voluntary committee, which is called the Voluntary Non-Sectarian Committee for German Refugee Children, a step which we have felt was most important that this country could do in terms of their best interests. I feel the people who are closely related to the child-caring agencies in this country feel that this is a step that will not hinder the care of American children.

When you get concerned about children you do not look at their race or color so much, but you want the children taken care of, and if children in Germany are neglected then we are participants in that neglect, and that is a bad example for our children over here.

I am not in the child-caring field myself; I am not an expert there, but I have been interested to see these child-caring agencies take that point of view, rather than saying, "We cannot do anything for them, because we have got all we can do for here."

As a matter of fact, many of them have fewer children than they are set up to take care of. So we set out to foster a move, and it has been partly sponsored by this committee, but there has been a very wide response across the country, and I do not want to claim by any means that this committee is the only one interested, but there has been a very wide interest, as will be shown by these hearings.

We realize, of course, the great financial responsibility involved, but for the most part the people are able to pay for passage in German marks. So our responsibility will probably be the caring for the children, as of course, some will not be able to pay, and some will have to be paid for. . . .

The proposal before you is a very simple one. It is a grant of authority under specified conditions—and nothing more. Under its terms authority is granted to admit into the United States not more than 10,000 German children, in excess of the present quota, during each of the calendar years 1939 and 1940. No child shall be eligible for admission who is over fourteen years of age, and no child may be admitted unless satisfactory assurance shall have been given by responsible private individuals or by responsible private organizations that the child will not become a public charge. This is the whole proposal—a grant of authority, to the extent that satisfactory assurances are given, permitting, as an emergency matter, the rescue from Germany of a limited number of children of tender years.

The need for this measure is overwhelming. A catastrophe has occurred. Unlike such catastrophes as fire or earthquake or tidal wave, which have commanded the help of America to unfortunates abroad so often in the past, this catastrophe threatens not only death, but a living death, to thousands and thousands of children.

During my stay in Germany there was brought home to me, through daily, hourly experiences in working with the Friends' centers, the appalling extent of this catastrophe and the unbelievable consequences to the innocent child victims. I want to portray for you what I myself have seen.

Masses of figures do not bring home the true situation. Although you need the figures to determine the extent of the problem, its intensity and reality can be visualized only if you compare the normal life of a normal child with the life of a rejected child in Germany today. Let us look at that life as it goes on from day to day at this very time. The child cannot go to the State schools. Lacking a school, he also lacks all of the legitimate outlets for play. The parks are closed to him. He walks on the street only at the risk of being taunted or spat on by other children or perhaps beaten by his elders. Even in his home the tension and pressure of the environment are upon him. There is the ever present menace of the concentration camp for his father or his older brother. The child's father, a hunted man, sleeps first in one secret place, and then another, but rarely at home. There is the crashing of glass at any time of the day or night when the neighboring rowdies choose to throw stones through the windows. There is terror at a mere knock on the door. And over and around the child and ever present to him is the shattering anxiety of his parents, upon whom he has been accustomed to rely and whose present insecurity invades his life at every point and threatens to destroy the essential security which must be his. And beyond all this terror and insult, his parents have lost their means of livelihood, his family has been put out of their home and crowded into a small, unheated room, wondering how they will eat when the last bit of furniture is sold. This is the daily life of those children in Germany whom the present regime has elected to disinherit.

I have given here a picture of the general environment. I have not referred to the children whose homes have been broken up. At the time of the November 10 excesses, masses of men were thrown into concentration camps; estimates have run as high as 35,000 during that period alone. Furthermore, the extreme German laws have led to hundreds and hundreds of divorces where Aryans and non-Aryans have been married. In addition, there is the terrible fact of suicide. An undertaker in Vienna told me after the annexation of Austria that while before that time his average rate of burials was five a week, after the annexation the rate increased to 140 per week. The children of families, thus rent asunder by concentration camp, divorce, and suicide, are dependent in many instances upon crumbs from the neighbors' tables, surreptitiously given.

This is the situation as it exists in Germany today. The need is almost beyond description. If you would measure that need, I would request you only to visualize your own children in the situation which I have described and to ask yourself whether you too would not be willing, even eager, to have your children go elsewhere for a haven.

Let me attempt now to give you a few of the data which sum up the situation. . . .

The children in Germany who are now in such dire need are Jews, non-Aryans, and Aryans. We speak of non-Aryans for want of a better term. In this class fall all those who, because they have had at least one grandparent who was Jewish, suffer, under German law, all the disabilities visited upon the Jews; yet the vast majority of these have never considered themselves Jews nor have they been thought of by their neighbors as such, prior to the Nuremberg laws. For these there is not available even such aid as the Jews can give their own. They are outcasts in the most stark sense, and it is they with whom the Friends largely deal. Of the Aryans who are in need, most are the children of families who, because of belief in the principles of democracy, have incurred the wrath of the new State.

Of these three groups, Jews, non-Aryans, and Aryans, our most conservative estimate is that there are today in Germany (outside the territory that was Czechoslovakia) over 100,000 children under the age of fourteen who are in the desperate straits I have already described. My observation in the work of the Friends indicates that about 40 percent of these children are non-Jews. In addition to this 100,000 there appear to be at least 35,000 childern in the same dire need from the territory that was formerly Czechoslovakia, and of these children the percentage who are non-Jews is materially greater.

Other countries have already taken steps similar to that proposed in the pending joint resolution. Five thousand children have been admitted to Britain. Fifteen hundred have been admitted to Holland. Belgium, France, and Switzerland have taken hundreds more, the exact number of which we have been unable to ascertain.

The moving conditions presented to me when I was in Germany at the time of the Munich agreement, and made more graphic after the outbreaks of November 10, led me increasingly to consider what could be done for these children. I returned to this country in the latter part of 1938. When I reached here I found that groups other than the Friends—groups interested in child welfare and child guidance and individuals of generous impulses to whom the spectacle of suffering children presented an incentive to action— had been concerned with the same problem. Out of this common purpose the Non-Sectarian Committee for German Refugee Children was born and I felt impelled to assume the executive directorship of it.

With the announcement of the formation of the committee, these groups drew to themselves like-minded persons throughout the land. I cannot enumerate them here. They include men and women of the most diverse backgrounds and interests who have been impelled to join together in this common purpose. It was these groups which heard with extraordinary satisfaction of the introduction into Congress of the bill which you are now considering.

The purpose underlying the proposal has a fundamental and universal appeal. At a time when age-old standards have been called into question, it is the children who still represent the essential human hope. That hope, a universal expression of the human spirit, transcends national and group lines. In the deepest sense, we affirm and reaffirm our faith in the future so long as we are willing to assume responsibility for, and to give of ourselves for the benefit of, the children of our time. The proposal, however, is something more. It is, I maintain, especially appropriate that the United States should play its part in the work of rescuing these children. It was here that public education was first viewed as a public necessity. It was here that principles of toleration were early adopted as the law of the land. It is, therefore, fitting and proper that the great democracy should evince particular interest in extending hospitality to the children who have been cast out and have been made wanderers on the face of the earth. I say, then, that the purpose of this bill is first to symbolize our hopes by aiding these children and second, to permit us to live out, in kindness and generosity, the principles which we have always regarded as basic to our society.

The Quakers have been known for generations as idealists. They are, however, practical idealists. In supporting this bill they have not been carried away merely by a fine passion to do a kindly act. They have measured the consequences of their support. They have noted carefully the safeguards which have been thrown around the proposal. Is there risk that the children who will be brought here will include any who have been permanently injured by the terror of their recent years? That we find safeguarded by the statutes of the United States—left wholly intact by the pending bill—which prevent the entry here of those who are physically or mentally deficient. Is there risk that these children will aggravate the problem of unemployment? These few children, none of whom is more than fourteen, are not competitors for jobs; it is for this reason that the heads of the great labor organizations of America feel free to support this proposal. Is there risk that these children will become a public charge? That is protected by the requirements of the bill that satisfactory assurances will be given to prevent any possible result of that kind. We say, then, that the plan is practical and we are supporting it because we feel an affirmative need to help these children.

Make no mistake that this bill is the unstudied gesture of a few impractical humanitarians. Plans have been evolved covering every phase of the proposal from the selection in Germany of the children to be admitted, to and including their placement in the homes in the United States.

If this bill is passed, there will be no indiscriminate or wholesale selection of children for admission into this country. The Friends and other American agencies have offered their services to undertake selection of children to be recommended to the American consulates for permission to enter this country. The Non-Sectarian Committee for German Refugee Children will supplement the staffs of these organizations with additional well-trained persons who will investigate the particular children intended to be admitted. In this way none will come here save those who are, in the opinion of trained specialists, good material for American citizenship. I have referred before to the limitations provided by the laws of the United States as to the physically and mentally unfit. It is our intention to apply to these children not merely those minimum tests but others in addition, and persons trained in the field of child guidance and child welfare will investigate every ascertainable phase of the lives of the children to be recommended to the consuls.

I have frequently been asked whether it is our thought, if this bill is passed, to deprive families of their children. Nothing, of course, could be further from our intention. Every effort has been made and will continue to be made to keep families intact. It is only in cases where families have been broken up, or where the parents plead to have the children come, that any attempt will be made to take children out of Germany. Those pleas, uttered in terror and amid tears, I have myself heard in scores of cases.

Questions concerning the placement of children in this country will be handled with equal care. A fundamental of the whole plan is the placement of these children to the fullest extent possible in private homes. This is now considered an essential of sound child nurture, and we propose to follow that policy wherever possible. Homes will be investigated and selected, to the extent possible, before the children are brought over. Then small groups of children who have been selected abroad will be brought here and kept at temporary shelters at ports of entry until they can be properly placed in a simple and orderly way throughout the country. From the time of their arrival in this country they will be under the care of the various social agencies of their own faiths which have signified their willingness to accept this responsibility. And supervision by those agencies will continue even after placement.

That there is every likelihood that most of the children can be placed in excellent free homes is already apparent to us. There will be presented to your committee hundreds of offers to receive these children, constituting a part of the offers which have already been received without solicitation by various organizations. These offers, I understand, have come from more than forty States, and from Jewish, Protestant, and Catholic homes. It thus becomes apparent that a very large proportion of these children can be placed in splendid homes among people sufficiently eager to receive them so that they have not even waited for the passage of the bill to make their desires known. To the extent that free homes are not available, after investigation, it is proposed to place the children who would come here in carefully selected paid foster homes. A few children who would, in the opinion of the agencies responsible, work out their problems better in a group situation, will be handled in that way, either in schools or other institutions.

The financial requirements of this program are difficult to state in definite and specific terms. I have told you before that it is our expectation to place most of these children in free homes which are eager to receive them. It would be part of our plan, so far as possible, to obtain commitments from each home in which a child is placed, agreeing to support that child until it became a self-sustaining member of the community. Thus we would have in most cases an absolute obligation to support on the part of the receiving families. With this as the core of the program, the rest of our needs would be taken care of by funds obtained through the Non-Sectarian Committee for German Refugee Children. That organization would be responsible, first, where necessary, for the transportation costs of the children; second, for whatever costs must be undertaken to expand the staffs of the respective social agencies which will assist in the work; and third, for the cost of maintaining such of the children who are brought over as are ultimately placed in boarding homes. Assuming that we work out the program slowly and ascertain about what percentage of children we can count upon placing in free homes, there would be no great difficulty in sustaining the remaining children in boarding homes.

In this way the requirement of the pending proposal and of other applicable law that there be assurance that the children be adequately cared for would be met. The law sets forth the standard, which must be complied with to the full satisfaction of those executive agencies of our Government who administer it for the protection not only of the immigrant but of our own citizens. To meet this standard, there will of course have to be money. I and the others working with me have consulted with various organizations and foundations, with the religious groups under which these children would be placed, and with philanthropic organizations and individuals who are deeply interested in the plan, and as a result of our discussions with them, we have no doubt whatever that the whole undertaking can be appropriately financed.

Incidentally, our first test has already been met. We have realized that in dealing with so large a group of children, regardless of any general financial provision, emergencies might arise. We, therefore, felt that it would be wise to establish a special fund of $250,000 as a contingency reserve against any unexpected situation. I am glad to advise you that the full amount of this reserve already has been underwritten. . . .

I have described for you the need which has prompted this plan, how we propose to carry it out so far as the children are concerned, and our prospects of financing. Others will go in greater detail into the various aspects of the matters which I have mentioned. I do not believe that the practical aspects of this grant of authority raise any fundamental questions. The essential issues are and remain: Will the United States in a critical emergency in human affairs open its doors to a few thousand children who have been reduced to penury and misery, living in fear and in terror, by no act or fault of their own? Will it in gentleness and kindness suffer little children to find haven here? . . . .

Mr. ALLEN.[3] . . . When you talk about the hard time some of us have had, some of us . . . have had a hard time. I know what it means to be born and reared in a log cabin, and to be hungry and to want, and I needed the things of life, and I want to tell you something . . . that in my district today there are thousands of little children that do not have the things that they need, and there are little children living in cotton patches in a cabin, white people and Negro children, too, that do not have the necessities of life . . . ; we are sympathetic, but our sympathy goes first to the people around our own doors. We will embrace them first in our hearts, and then when our necessities are supplied we will be happy to go out and embrace others.

[3] Representative A. Leonard Allen was a Democrat from Louisiana.

. . . would the gentleman advocate bringing the hordes of Europeans here when the record shows that we have thousands and thousands of poor people in this country who are in want? Right here in my file I have a clipping where the relief director in Washington is praying for more money, asking for more money. . . .

Testimony of
Quentin Reynolds [4]

MR. REYNOLDS. A few months ago, just after the happenings of November 10, in Germany, William Chenery, our editor, dissatisfied with the conflicting stories which had come out of Germany, sent me over to get the story of what had happened, and I spent some time in London, talking to members of the International Committee, the so-called Aryan Committee, and obtained access to their then unpublished minutes and records as to the refugee problem.

While there I heard of three hundred children being down at Dover Court. I met them. I went to Berlin and had several talks with Mr. Geist, who is acting as the greatest diplomat in handling this troublesome matter.

I spent a great deal of time with Jewish, Catholic, and Lutheran people, who were unwanted in Germany. I emphasize the Catholics and Lutherans point, because it might be thought that this was only for Jewish, when naturally there are an increasing number of Lutheran and Catholic children who would come under this bill.

MR. ALLEN. Will the gentleman yield for a question? . . . It is my understanding that Germany is not very kindly disposed toward any religion.

---

[4] A second witness was Quentin Reynolds, the famed journalist, associated at that time with *Collier's*. He described his credentials as follows: "I have worked on newpapers from the time I graduated from college until 1932, when I was with the International News Service, and went to Berlin to cover Germany and Austria for them. I was there until late in 1933, when I returned to be an associate editor of *Collier's Weekly*."

86

Mr. Reynolds. Except their own State-controlled religion. Hitler has appointed State commissars, who have taken the place of the churches. . . .

Mr. Allen. These are new organizations that he has called churches?

Mr. Reynolds. No, he has put sovereign heads over these.

Chairman. He put God on W.P.A.,[5] and he appointed his own God.

Mr. Allen. Let us get that clear. I have some very pronounced views on that. He has put sovereign heads over the churches?

Mr. Reynolds. Yes, what he calls religious commissars.

Mr. Allen. And all the preachers have to listen to this civil head?

Mr. Reynolds. Not the rabbis. They have mostly been liquidated. The priests and ministers have, which has brought out a new type of refugee children, which I do not think has been considered at this hearing, the Lutherans.

Mr. Allen. What is true with the Lutherans is true with the other Protestant denominations, is it not?

Mr. Reynolds. Not to a great extent. The Lutherans have shown much courage.

Mr. Allen. How about the Catholic religion?

Mr. Reynolds. I do not think they have shown much fight. As a Catholic, I say this. They of necessity had to fall in with Hitler's plans to abolish Sunday schools.

Mr. Allen. Has he really abolished all Sunday schools? . . .

Mr. Reynolds. Yes; of course; except in the State-controlled churches. They have a catechism written by Alfred Rosenberg, and not Martin Luther. . . . I would like to talk for just two or three minutes about these children and try to bring them to your attention. There were three hundred of them at Dover Court, and I met all of them, under fourteen years of age.

They were lined up in this dining hall, and a man told them what the rules of the establishment were, and he asked if there

[5] The Works Progress Administration, which operated federally financed work programs for the unemployed. In other words, he put God on relief. The committee chairman was Representative Samuel Dickstein, a Democrat from New York.

were any questions, and one youngster, his name was Joseph Weiner, raised his hand and said, "Could I have a violin?" I talked with him, and it developed that his father had been a violinist with the Berlin Symphony Orchestra. His aim was to be a violinist.

The other question was this: A girl raised her hand and said, "May I walk on the grass?" It is a seashore. There was a stunned silence. Finally, after permission, they ran out like kittens with catnip.

All signs in Germany read at the parks, *Juden Unerwuenscht,* which means that Jewish children are not allowed in the parks. . . .

In Berlin I stood in a bread line, which at the end of November had been going on for two years, what they called *Hilfsverein,* where the Jewish were fed by their own people. Of course, after November 10, all private property was confiscated necessarily, and all of these various *Hilfsverein* immediately stopped functioning.

When I was there for the first time there was a big *Hilfsverein* on the Ludendorf Strasse, and later there was a sign up that it was closed. I asked them where they would eat. They had no idea.

Their children can get no medical attention. The Jewish doctors are not permitted to practice, and Aryan doctors cannot doctor them.

What I am trying to bring out is that these 10,000 children are very normal, healthy youngsters. Of the three hundred I saw at Dover Court, you could not tell them from boys and girls in Washington, or boys and girls in New York.

Of sixty I talked to, I got their case histories. Of the sixty, thirty were Jewish and ten Catholic, and the others did not know what they were. Of these sixty only ten knew where their parents were and knew the parents were alive, which I think answers the Congressman's question about should the parents of these 10,000 have any preference. You will find there will be very few parents of these 10,000. Nearly all of them, I think, will be orphans.

Of this 10,000 I would say possibly 6,000 would be Jewish and the other 4,000 would be Catholics and Protestants, unwanted children, and they of course are increasing in number literally every week, more and more Lutheran and Catholic children.

CHAIRMAN. Could I interrupt you to say something very vital? . . . When you say some of them would be fatherless and motherless. . . . Do you contemplate, if it is not a confidence of your paper, that there will be another pogrom?

MR. REYNOLDS. I not only contemplate it, but I am confident the complete pogrom is not very far away.

CHAIRMAN. In other words, there will be a new slaughter?

MR. REYNOLDS. Yes; there is no doubt about that.

CHAIRMAN. Annihilation?

MR. REYNOLDS. Yes; a complete pogrom. You see Julius Streicher is getting more and more in the Chancellor's confidence. He is the only man in Germany to call Hitler *du*. He gave publicly last November a press meeting, and an off-the-record meeting, in which he said there was only one solution of the Jewish problem, and that was to do as Moses had done, and that the Scriptures said that Moses led the Jewish into the Red Sea and the waters parted, but the fact was that the people arose and drove them into the sea.

CHAIRMAN. In other words, this pogrom will annihilate those they disagree with?

MR. REYNOLDS. Yes. And there will be a lot of Lutherans in that, too.

You see, Martin Lemwright, a Lutheran pastor, is still in a concentration camp, and they are trying to force him to sign papers that he will never preach again. Each week they bring those in.

He was put in prison for a sermon he preached, and the text was, "And Peter and the Apostles said, 'You must obey God rather than men.' " For that statement he was put into a concentration camp.

His followers refused to accept these State commissars. They wanted their own churches. They all left their own services and are now holding services in cellars and attics, listening to the word of God as preached by Martin Luther. They get out circulars, thousands of them, asking why they cannot hear the word of God as preached by Martin Luther. They are not preaching treason. But that is what they call treason. So thousands of them are being sent to concentration camps. There are 148 Lutheran ministers in concentration camps. That is the figure I got from Berlin.

I am emphasizing this to show that this is not predominantly Jewish children which from the hearing yesterday one might think it was there. There are going to be a great many of that 10,000 who will not be Jewish.

CHAIRMAN. Did you see anything unusual about the normalcy of these children?

MR. REYNOLDS. No; except they were more polite than most other children, Congressman.

After two or three days at Dover Court, there were never children who looked any more normal in childhood, and you could see them there playing with toys and playing around on the grass.

CHAIRMAN. What was the youngest?

MR. REYNOLDS. Some, I would say, were four and five. . . . And I think the oldest was fourteen. I think that was the provision under which the British allowed them to come in.

CHAIRMAN. Do you think they would be harmful to this country?

MR. REYNOLDS. Good heavens, no. . . .

MR. ALLEN. Mr. Reynolds, this thing concerns many of us just as much as it does the proponents of this bill. How far are we going? What is going to be the result of this bill? This is a hardship case, there is no question about that. They have got the situation in other countries. Just how far are we going over here with that? How far would you advocate our going? . . . you are asking in this bill to raise the quota from Germany by 20,000. Just how far would you go with Germany to relieve the balance of the oppression over there? Just how far would you go with the other nations also?

MR. REYNOLDS. I certainly would not go so far as to throw any economic wrench into the life of this country. I do not know the figure, but I certainly would not allow more in than we could assimilate. I do not think they would cause any trouble. I think 10,000 could be hidden in New York City. . . .

CHAIRMAN. Between you and I [sic] we can dispose of the 10,000?

MR. REYNOLDS. Yes; in an hour.

CHAIRMAN. Now as to these Lutheran children, they are just about in the same class as the Catholic and the Jewish?

MR. REYNOLDS. Increasingly so; yes. You see, the parents want to get them out before they are lost. These children mostly belong to the Hitler Youth Organization, which corresponds to our Boy Scouts. If you do not belong the kids lose face and are looked down upon. These organizations start every Sunday at 6 A.M. for a trip to the woods, which means the Hitler clever way of keeping them from Sunday school. They leave at 6 o'clock to march in the country. In the country they hear speeches of Rosenberg philosophy, and speeches all about Nazis. So that now there are very few youngsters following the religion of their parents with any degree of seriousness in Germany.

CHAIRMAN. You believe that Ray Geist in Germany is a capable administrator to carry out the intent of Congress if Congress should see fit to . . . provide care of these children?

MR. REYNOLDS. Oh, yes. . . .

MR. ALLEN. Would you think, Mr. Reynolds, we ought to write in this bill that only orphans should come?

MR. REYNOLDS. I would not think so, sir. I think that will almost settle itself. I think most of them will be orphans.

PART TWO

Hunter and Hunted

By invading Poland, in September 1939, the Wehrmacht began World War II. Within a month, Warsaw fell and Poland collapsed. Those Poles who were not subject to the rule of the Germans came under that of the Russians, who meanwhile had occupied eastern Poland and northern Rumania, in accordance with prior arrangements with Germany.

So long as Russian armies were close—no more than seventy-five miles separated Warsaw from the river Bug—escape from German-held Poland was possible for that city's Jews. Many did make their way across the Russian lines, especially in the fall of 1939, when the Soviets and Germans were still placing no serious obstacles in the way of flight. One mother, deported from Germany a year earlier and in Warsaw on September 1, 1939, just a few weeks after sending her son on a children's transport to England, was able to walk out and go to the ghetto of Bialystok, which was then in Russian hands.[1]

Most of the Jews, however, remained in Warsaw. As in World War I, they were trapped by the military disaster, but whereas during the earlier war the German army had treated them as a part of the city's population, this time they soon found themselves living with thousands of other Jews as a special element in the domain of the General Government, newly carved out of conquered Poland. In 1939 this region held about 1.4 million Jews, including the more than 300,000 living in Warsaw at the time of the invasion. In the following months this population increased as the entire area became a point of concentration for all Jews under German rule. The population also rose as more and more came into the city on their own initiative, often in the hope of finding shelter in the largest Polish Jewish community. By the end of 1940, the Germans had enclosed almost half a million Jews in 1.3 of the city's 54.6 square miles.

Until June 21, 1941, the German grip on Poland was threatened by the Russians stationed just on the other side of the Bug, but the invasion of Russia eliminated that danger: some hundred miles east of Warsaw, at Brest Litovsk; twenty-five miles east of Lublin, at Chelm; and all along the river, three million Germans attacked the Soviets. Within ten days the Wehrmacht conquered all of eastern Poland and northern Rumania and then went on to penetrate so deeply into Rus-

[1] Told to the author in an interview with Joseph Kamiel and his mother in London in August 1967.

sia that the Soviets were not to return to the domain of the General Government until the June offensive of 1944.

In this militarily sheltered region of Poland the Germans sought to annihilate most of Europe's Jews in a trilogy of slaughter: by starvation, by killing units, and in annihilation centers. Starvation in the ghettos gradually doomed existence: in Lodz in 1940 the reported monthly average death rate among Jews was 0.09 percent; in 1941 it was 0.63 percent; in 1942, for the first six months it was 1.49 percent; by March of that year it was reported as high as 1.72 percent. "The implication of these figures is quite clear," according to Raul Hilberg. "Assuming a steady monthly death rate of 1.5 percent and an absence of a significant number of births, a community of 150,000 shrinks to 1,000 in just 25½ years." [2] Of Warsaw's Jewish population of some 450,000 in 1941, 44,630 reportedly died that year, and 37,462 in the first nine months of 1942. In March 1942 the Germans reported the death-birth ratio in the ghetto as being 45 to 1. The consequences were predictable: within a two-year period the ghettos killed one-fifth of Poland's Jews.

The mobile units and the annihilation centers of Poland destroyed the others. The killing units traveled in the Wehrmacht's wake and within five months after the June invasion had killed over 500,000 Jews; the annihilation centers did the rest. Bullets, and gas in van or chamber, accounted for the deaths of two million.

The Warsaw Ghetto was in the center of much of this activity designed to eradicate European Jewry. In many ways Warsaw served as the capital city of Eastern European Jewry as well as of Poland's Jews; in 1940 its population of 400,000 Jews made it the largest single Jewish community in all of Europe. (Only New York City contained more Jews.) Geographically, Warsaw was in the midst of the region that German arms protected against the Soviets for so many months: within a range of 50 to 150 miles were Treblinka, Kulmhof, Lublin, Sobibor, Auschwitz, Belzec, Lodz, Bialystok, and about 240 miles, or a little farther, the ghettos of Vilna and Lwow. By virtue of its size and location, combined with its position in the history of Eastern European Jewry, Warsaw continued until the very end to function as a vital nerve center for Jewish activity in the territory of the General Government and as a seedbed for all of Jewry's potential responses to the slaughterers.

Little wonder then that Warsaw's Jewry battled on all fronts dur-

[2] *The Destruction of the European Jews* (Chicago: Quadrangle, 1961), pp. 173–174.

ing the period from 1939 to 1943. Its responses were primarily governed by what the organized sectors of the Jewish community knew of German policy and how they conceived the action to be taken. But one fact about their behavior was clear: they responded as members of a distinctive cultural minority, sensitive to the pressures of their non-Jewish environment but fervently committed to the desirability, viability, and future of the Jewish people, regardless of their differing values and beliefs.

As the pressure of the German occupation mounted, they had little choice but to fall back on their own resources to obtain food and shelter. Organizationally, however, they chose also to respond as a Jewish community, with all its diversity and internal conflicts. Like other Jewish populations under similar pressures, Warsaw's Jews began, in late 1940, to convert the formally established ghetto into a Jewish state, complete with its own civil services. "The residents of the ghetto are beginning to think they are in Tel Aviv," wrote Chaim A. Kaplan in his diary when speaking of the impact of young Jewish policemen upon the ghetto populace. "Strong, bonafide policemen from among our brothers, to whom you can speak in Yiddish! The fear of the Gentile police is gone from their faces." A "Jewish shout," he explained, "is not the same as a Gentile one. The latter is coarse, crude, nasty; the former, while it may be threatening, contains a certain gentility, as if to say: 'Don't you understand?' " [3]

To be sure, Yiddish-speaking policemen were a direct consequence of the German decision to establish a ghetto, and were as necessary as any other group providing the civil services of that ghetto state. But they helped lift the spirit of the Jews, in the same way as did the Yiddish-speaking and Polish-speaking Jewish musicians, playwrights, and actors, especially when they were able to communicate the vitality and purposefulness of Jewish existence.

Participation in the Jewish educational programs, the celebration of Jewish holidays, and membership in the various secular Jewish political associations, riddled though they were with divisiveness, were all acts of defiance by means of which Jews could positively demonstrate their belief in the viability of Jewish communal existence. In February 1941, children studied secretly, in the back rooms ". . . on long benches near a table," following practices first devised by the Marranos (secret Jews) in Spain.[4] In 1941, Zionist soup kitchens served

[3] *Scroll of Agony: The Warsaw Diary of Chaim A. Kaplan,* trans. by Abraham I. Katsh (New York: Macmillan, 1965), p. 234.
[4] *Ibid.,* p. 242.

as the center for all "public" Hebrew-Zionist activity. "On every holiday," noted Kaplan, himself a Zionist and Hebraist, "the guests here arrange themselves at small tables, sip tea, and nibble some sort of baked goods." But that social activity was for show. The important element was the presidium made up of all the leaders of Warsaw's Zionists, speaking and debating usually in Yiddish, but sometimes in Hebrew.[5]

Hanukkah in 1940 was an occasion for parties in nearly every courtyard. "Even in rooms which faced the street; the blinds were drawn, and that was sufficient. How much joy, how much of a feeling of national kinship there was in these Hanukkah parties!" wrote Kaplan on December 26. "After sixteen months of Nazi occupation, we came to life again." [6] By Purim 1941 all forms of public worship and celebration were forbidden in the ghetto, but celebrations took place nevertheless. At the Zionist soup kitchen, Kaplan heard the Book of Esther read in Sephardic Hebrew, ate poppy-seed tarts, sang, and heard "debates and sermons, arguments and quarrels as in the good days." [7] Other sectors of the community responded in their own ways—Socialist, Zionist, or Orthodox, but all together fighters against the death of their community. "The Jewish community is on a battlefield, but the battle is not conducted with weapons," Kaplan observed on February 18, 1941. "It is conducted by means of various schemes, schemes of deception, schemes of smuggling, and so on. We don't want simply to disappear from the earth."

---

[5] *Ibid.*, p. 235.
[6] *Ibid.*, pp. 235, 243.
[7] *Ibid.*, p. 256.

The Beginnings: First
Days of War

CHAIM A. KAPLAN *

*Chaim Kaplan's memories of the early days
of the war provide insights into the changing
loyalties, perceptions, and activities among
Warsaw's Jews before the invader actually
arrived and during the first weeks of the occupation of the city. The dates are those of the
particular diary entries from which these read-
ings are drawn.*

September 1, 1939
A New World War

During the morning hours of the first of September, 1939, war
broke out between Germany and Poland and, indirectly, between
Germany and Poland's allies, England and France. This time the
Allies will stick to their word and not betray Poland as they betrayed Czechoslovakia. For the time being, Poland alone will
suffer all the hardships of the war, because there are no common
frontiers between Poland and her allies. We are witnessing the
dawn of a new era in the history of the world.

This war will indeed bring destruction upon human civilization.
But this is a civilization which merits annihilation and destruction.
There is no doubt that Hitlerian Nazism will ultimately be defeated, for in the end the civilized nations will rise up to defend
the liberty which the German barbarians seek to steal from mankind. However, I doubt that we will live through this carnage.
The bombs filled with lethal gas will poison every living being, or
we will starve because there will be no means of livelihood.

How will I support myself? The schools won't be opened for a

* *Ibid.*, pp. 19–60.

long, long time, and even if they should open, there would be no students in them. Parents will not let their children go outdoors for fear of air raids. I invested all I could in repairing my school (2,000 zloty),[1] and now it is bright, clean, repaired, and redecorated. But it will stand empty.

Poland is the chosen one, and the first arrows of the war between civilization and barbarism are falling upon her. But she will be joined by other nations, and united they will destroy the modern Huns. Since our enemy is the enemy of the whole human race, someone or other will come and avenge our spilled blood. And even the Poles who rejoiced at our misfortune, and not only expressed no word of consolation to us, but threatened to do to us what Hitler has done unless we emigrate from Poland—well, now the Poles themselves will receive our revenge through the hands of our cruel enemy. . . .

As for the Jews, their danger is seven times greater. Wherever Hitler's foot treads there is no hope for the Jewish people. Hitler, may his name be blotted out, threatened in one of his speeches that if war comes the Jews of Europe will be exterminated. The Jews comprehend and sense all that is in store for them wherever Hitler's armies make a temporary conquest. It should therefore not be surprising that the Jews show their devotion to their fatherland in a demonstrative fashion. When the order was issued that all the inhabitants of the city must dig shelter trenches for protection from air raids, the Jews came in numbers. I, too, was among them. I took with me A. W.,[2] whose friend and supporter I have become in this time of tribulation. We signed up with the group of diggers who volunteered on behalf of the Jewish Journalists and Authors Association, and we went to dig at 29 Dluga Street. This was almost the first time in my life that I had done such physical labor, but I did not lag in my work. I returned home tired, but I couldn't eat.

September 2, 1939

The second day of the Polish-German war, which ultimately will turn into a world war and a slaughter of nations. England is in no

[1] The zloty was worth approximately twenty cents at that time.—*Translator*
[2] Anka Welcer. A writer who translated Zalman Shneour's novel, *Noah Pandre*, into Polish.—*Translator*

hurry to declare war on Germany, and France too is delaying. But there is no doubt that the two allies will declare war at the same time. This time they will not betray us. Their representatives have already left Berlin, and their ultimatum to Hitler is that he withdraw his armies from the borders of Poland. In his usual fashion, Hitler has ignored the request. Tomorrow or the next day the cannons will begin to speak. From the moment when England and France join with Poland, the war will cease to be local. Then all of England's allies, such as Turkey and Rumania, will awaken, and the world catastrophe will grow.

Today there were four air raids in Warsaw. The inhabitants have already grown accustomed to them and know what they have to do. We have indeed entered upon a new era. We feared its coming and greeted it with anxious hearts, but since it has come and assumed a definite shape, this era will become second nature. Even abnormal living becomes normal when it becomes constant. But our nerves are working hard. Almost the entire day is filled with air raids whose results are unknown because the communiqués are delivered in a terse, clipped style, and conceal more than they reveal. As is customary, each side proclaims its victories and conceals its defeats, but it is not hard to understand why Poland's defeats are great, for the full force of war with a cruel and barbaric enemy, armed from head to foot, is directed against her. The aid which will eventually come from her allies will be indirect rather than direct.

My brain is full of the chatterings of the radio from both sides. The German broadcast in the Polish language prates propaganda. Each side accuses the other of every abominable act in the world. Each side considers itself to be righteous and the other murderous, destructive, and bent on plunder. This time, as an exception to the general rule, both speak the truth. Verily it is so—both sides are murderers, destroyers, and plunderers, ready to commit any abomination in the world. If you want to know the character of any nation, ask the Jews. They know the character of every nation.

The hour is fateful. If a new world arises, the sacrifices and troubles and hardships will be worthwhile. Let us hope that Nazism will be destroyed completely, that it will fall and never rise again. But our hearts tremble at the future . . . what will be our destiny? . . .

September 3, 1939

Historic events! One cannot guess at the results of them. If a German bomb doesn't cut our lives short, and we are privileged to reach the end, it will yet be worthwhile living. England and France stood by their word, their promise to their ally, and the world conflagration has been ignited. There is no counting the number of victims which this slaughter will bring as sacrifices on the altar of Hitlerian barbarism. But there was no alternative. It was impossible to sit in silence and abandon Europe, carved up into small states, to the savage domination of the German terror. The end of this war is not in doubt. The tyrant will receive his punishment, his payment in kind. At that time Providence will also avenge the spilled blood of the German Jews. . . .

Today (from 2:30 to 7:00 P.M.) we again went to dig at 29 Dluga Street and worked for four hours. By immersing myself completely in the physical labor, I freed myself from the sad thoughts which darken my world. There is no happier moment now than the one which is free of thoughts!

From the communiqués it appears that there are no victories. If there were any they would be proclaimed in the loudest of voices. But one cannot describe how great the rejoicing in the capital city is upon hearing that England and France have declared war on Hitler. In an instant the entire city was bedecked with flags.

The joy of the Poles is unbounded. They are fighting for freedom, for the progress of humanity, for international ethics, and for all the lofty ideals for which the chosen few of the human race have sacrificed their lives. A true metamorphosis! The time is not long past when Hitler was their prophet. When they mentioned his name they were greatly pleased, and he served as an example to them, particularly in regard to the Jews. Now everything has changed completely.

How would my mother-in-law have said it? We have a father in heaven!

That Czestochowa was taken by the Germans was just verified a moment ago by the Polish radio as well. "The enemy concen-

trated immense forces and forced us to leave the city of Czestochowa."

> Woe unto the Jews of Czestochowa.
> There is no calamity like unto theirs!

September 4, 1939

Bit by bit we are beginning to feel wartime living conditions.
Normal life has ceased and our world has turned into chaos. There
is no mail; there is no train travel unless one has a permit; the
banks are paying their depositors just a part of their deposits; and
there is no way to earn a living. All trade has stopped except in
food stores and medical supply houses, which are being besieged
by customers. . . .

. . . In the course of four days, the enemy attacked on the
northern front, where he reached Przasnysz, and on the south-
western front, where he reached Ostrow, and he is approaching
Cracow. I am a novice in matters of military tactics and therefore
it is difficult for me to determine whether this retreat is a stratagem
or weakness. In any case, it is not a good sign. Where is Poland's
strength, its might? If this is not a stratagem but rather a weakness,
the enemy will reach Warsaw in another couple of days. And what
will become of us? In the meantime Poland is being devastated.
This is not the Germany of 1914—bad as it was, it had some con-
ception of moral principles and international law. . . .

September 5, 1939

. . . We are left abandoned and the shadow of death encircles
us. When you see all that is taking place, evil thoughts awaken
within you and disturb your rest. The Germans destroyed the
Catholic church in Czestochowa, the most important Catholic
shrine in Poland. The Poles call the Germans all sorts of derisive
names and threaten them with revenge. Good! They are bitter.
And when a nation is bitter, it cries out to avenge its blood and the
desecration of its holy things.

But why did not the Poles join in our sorrow when Hitler ordered
the burning of our synagogues, which were consumed in smoke
together with scrolls of the Torah? We didn't hear a word of consolation. On the contrary, they enjoyed it; they were happy at our

misfortune. We, however, share their sorrow and pray to the God of Israel to avenge their blood and ours. . . .

September 6, 1939

. . . In Warsaw an evacuation has begun of government departments and of the government itself in all its glory, this pompous government which pursues praises and accolades. According to the Breslau radio, this government fled for its life to Lublin while there was still time. The government is fleeing and at the same time tries to soothe and placate the panicked masses.

All day long thousands of wagons come into the city laden with personal possessions—the "property" of the refugees, inhabitants of the cities where the enemy is wreaking destruction. The unfortunate Jews are running for dear life from the wrath of the oppressor. O God! Who can reveal to me what is yet to come?

September 7, 1939

The enemy is at the gates of Warsaw, and we are a beleaguered city. The masses have an eye that sees and an ear that hears. I too perceived it in the darkness of the night. The window of my bedroom faces toward Karmelicka Street, and even though I was sunk in slumber, voices and the noise of passersby reached my ears. I got up and looked out the window, and I knew at once that the government was fleeing. . . .

September 10, 1939

The streets are sown with trenches and barricades. Machine guns have been placed on the roofs of houses, and there is a barricade in the doorway of my apartment house, just under my balcony. If fighting breaks out in the street no stone will remain upon another in the wall within which I live. We have therefore fled to my wife's sister's at 27 Nowolipki Street, which is nearby. Her apartment is supposed to be safer, since it faces a courtyard.

The enemy of the Jews attested long ago that if war broke out, Jews would be eliminated from Europe. Now half the Jewish people are under his domination. Why has God embittered our lives so cruelly? Have we indeed sinned more than any nation? We are more disgraced than any people!

September 12, 1939

It is beyond my pen to describe the destruction and ruin that the enemy's planes have wrought on our lovely capital. Entire blocks have been turned into ashes and magnificent palaces into rubble. Every incendiary bomb dropped in the stillness of the night brings havoc and death to hundreds of people. Dante's description of the Inferno is mild compared to the inferno raging in the streets of Warsaw. Today the Jewish Polish-language newspaper, *Nasz Przeglad,* published a description of last night's raid and I couldn't read it through. . . .

I myself still have something to eat as well as some money. But how long will it last? I am now out of work. Despite all this, however, I still live with hope. This too shall pass. We will yet come out of this alive!

September 14, 1939
Eight in the morning, the first day of Rosh Hashanah, 5700

I have returned to my own apartment. The danger is great everywhere. There is no hiding from fate.

It is difficult to write, but I consider it an obligation and am determined to fulfill it with my last ounce of energy. I will write a scroll of agony in order to remember the past in the future. For despite all the dangers I still have hopes of coming out of this alive.

Yesterday was a day of horror and destruction. Between five o'clock and seven o'clock on the eve of Rosh Hashanah [3] there was an air raid on the North Quarter, which is predominantly Jewish. From where I was, I could see with my own eyes all the horror that such a murderous attack can bring upon quiet residents, who in their innocence were busy preparing themselves for the approaching holiday. A rumor had spread that Hitler had ordered the cessation of air attacks. He was forced to do this by Stalin "the merciful," who threatened to "void" their pact unless attacks against the peaceful civilian populace ceased. Despite my bitterness, I could not help smiling at this bit of "consolation." And immediately we were all shown the veracity of this rumor.

[3] Most air attacks and evil decrees later on in the ghetto were launched on Jewish holidays and Sabbaths.—*Translator*

The enemy mercilessly poured his wrath on the Jewish quarter with incendiary bombs. We too experienced such a bomb at 22 Nowolipki Street, opposite where we are. The effect is like an earthquake. But worst of all is the chaos which follows among the victims. No one knows where he is running. Each one runs to a place that has already been abandoned by another as unsafe. Carrying babies and bundles, distracted and terrified people desperately look for a haven. Tens of thousands of broken refugees find themselves lost in a strange city. These people fill every courtyard and every stairway, and during the turmoil of the fires there are none more miserable. Afterward you hear details that curdle the blood. Hundreds of families are left with nothing—their wealth has been burned, their apartments destroyed, their possessions lost.

How has Warsaw, the royal, beautiful, and beloved city become desolate!

September 15, 1939
Second day of Rosh Hashanah, 5700

Everything and everyone bears the stamp of war. Instead of Jews wearing prayer shawls and carrying prayer books rushing to the synagogue, one sees stretcher bearers carrying the dead and wounded dug out from the ruins of bombed buildings. Yesterday passed uneventfully, and already the populace of the besieged city seems hungry for amusements, promenades, work. That is—outwardly. Inwardly, everyone is busy preparing himself for death. Everyone senses that what we have already experienced is nothing compared to what we will yet experience. . . .

September 20, 1939

. . . Human beings spend all their energies and talents in the pursuit of bread. Man has become an animal, concerned only with brute existence and fear of starvation. Holidays and festivals no longer exist. During Rosh Hashanah, haphazard public prayers were held in some synagogues, but will we be able to recite the Kol Nidre? [4] I doubt it! Israel's prayers in a city surrounded by German soldiers—what dissonance!

[4] A prayer that is part of the service on the eve of Yom Kippur, the Day of Atonement.—*Translator*

September 23, 1939
End of Yom Kippur, 5700

Our holy day is over. Mourning is on every face. As our prophet said, "The whole head is sick and the whole heart faint." There is not one family who has not endured a sacrifice of some sort, human or material. Many of my friends have turned gray. It is hard to recognize them.

On the Day of Atonement the enemy displayed even greater might than usual. He did not give us an hour's respite. The heavy artillery rained fire and iron upon our heads, destroying one apartment house after another and killing dozens of people with every burst. Perhaps it is good to die. Anticipating death is worse than death itself, since death brings release from consciousness, and an end to one's suffering. Everyone feels that his staying alive is merely a matter of chance. Last Thursday the Free Burial Society buried eighty people who had been killed by bombs and grenades. This is an everyday occurrence.

September 25, 1939

Our minutes are numbered. For forty-eight hours the enemy has unleashed the furies of death upon us. It is impossible to describe them.

September 29, 1939

. . . And we are waiting for Hitler's army. Once again, woe to us!

After all the horrors that we have endured, we wait for Hitler's army as for the spring rains. We are without bread and without water. Our nerves are shattered from everything that has happened during the last awful days. In such a condition, our only desire is to rest awhile, even if it is under Hitler's rule. And so, today at 8:00 P.M., Hitler's soldiers will enter the gates of Warsaw like victorious heroes.

Poland has fallen. Will she yet arise?

October 1, 1939

Now I will try to put the whole thing down in an orderly fashion. I was surrounded by disorder, and therein lay the difficulty—how was it possible to describe a disorderly thing in an orderly fashion?

I find it hard even to hold a pen. My hands tremble; I have lived through a catastrophe that has left me crushed and physically broken. And what is worse, even as I sit writing these lines, I am still not certain that the catastrophe is over; I only comfort myself with the hope that I will come out of this alive.

The Germans entered the capital in a disciplined way. They immediately announced that they are distributing free bread to the needy. Before the entry—bombs; after the entry—loaves of bread to the starving. They appear to be a charitable army, but in the midst of their charitableness, their planes did not forget to circle over Warsaw and take pictures of the long lines waiting for free bread from the "charitable" enemy. Thus two birds were killed with one stone: material for propaganda and for films to prove it.

I also stood in line, but not to receive bread—only impressions. I wanted to see the Nazis when they are engaged in charitable work. Also, at that time the entry into the city was being completed, and this too was a good opportunity for impressions. I studied Hitler's army into which he had sunk, according to his own words, ninety million marks within six years—and I was amazed to see how well fed, sleek, and fat it was. The Germans who entered the city amazed you with their healthy appearance and marvelous uniforms. You almost began to believe that this was indeed a people fit to rule the world by virtue of power and strength. But perhaps this too was merely a propaganda display, since everything the Nazis do is motivated by a plan to impress the masses. But even if it was only propaganda, it must still be reckoned with. A doubt stole into my heart: perhaps it was I who had been deceived? Until now I had been certain that they were starving and we were well fed; now I see the exact opposite. We are hungry and they give us free bread. They are well fed and wealthy, and we are starving and impoverished.

October 2, 1939

. . . I was suddenly informed that the newly arrived Germans had already managed to requisition five houses on Nowolipki Street —numbers 12, 14, 16, 18, 20—and to expel all their Jewish inhabitants. They did not permit them to take even a shoelace out of their apartments; they did not permit them to don even an over-coat. In a matter of minutes, all the Jews were expelled and all the houses cleared. The Jews went out afraid and shocked, in a state of confusion and wearing house clothes. Two or three soldiers arro-gantly and noisily stormed into every apartment and shouted: "Jews, *heraus!*"

They were not permitted to utter a syllable. Within minutes, hundreds of families were left without a roof, without clothes, without food, without an apartment, without money—and I among them. And to add to my misery, I had left all my savings in my apartment. My last straw to cling to in an hour of need had been taken from me. Up to now, during the dangerous days, I had left my money in safekeeping with my wife; after things quieted down a bit, we put it in a box which we locked in a chest in the closet. Now I am stripped of all my possessions. I don't even have a roof over my head.

They comfort us with the promise that the apartments were taken for only a few days; that the Germans will not ransack them; that everything will be returned to us in perfect condition. This does not appease me. I am caught between the jaws of the lion; will I emerge unscathed?

October 3, 1939

According to rumor, the German Supreme Commander has let it be known that he wants no difficulties set in the way of the Jews; but this is merely a political move. In the reality of everyday, the Jews are discriminated against. Perhaps the soldiers do this on their own accord, since they are rabidly anti-Semitic, but it matters little to us from whence the evil stems. We are always candidates for double troubles.

We run around like madmen trying to obtain help in entering our apartments and taking out some clothes and other necessities from them, but all our efforts are in vain. It is impossible to return to the apartment without permission, and permission can only be granted by the Commandant, and his office is surrounded with long lines of thousands of waiting people. My sick wife got up at four o'clock this morning and (at 3:00 P.M.) has not yet returned. And I am certain that after waiting ten hours she will return empty-handed. Broken, depressed, and weak, running a fever, hungry and thirsty, she will return home in despair and disappointment.

I am like the man who watches his ox being slaughtered: sad to lose a companion and hungry for meat. From time to time I walk along the left side of Karmelicka Street and gaze at the windows of my lovely apartment, now in the hands of strangers; the sons of Ham took over my property as though it belonged to them. My heart is broken: I sank a whole lifetime's work into that apartment: I lived in it for twenty-four years; I decorated it and beautified it and adorned it; and in one confused hour I lost it.

October 4, 1939

We are at the mercy of shameless murderers. The "charitable" army distributes bread and pottage to the hungry, and the poor unfortunates must wait in line long hours to get their meager portions; but when it comes to a Jew's turn, he is roughly pushed aside and compelled to return home shamed and mauled as well as hungry and thirsty. Incidents of daylight robbery are on the rise. My friend Szlofsztejn told me today that his son was robbed in broad daylight yesterday of 1,000 zloty. A Nazi invited him to the gate, pointed his pistol at him, searched him, and took 1,000 zloty out of his pocket. And this is typical. They rob in secret; the Commandant claims to know nothing about what is going on. But the troops know which way the wind is blowing. People are so overcome with fear that they are afraid to shout. The pillage and plunder are committed only against Jews. The Christians are spared these troubles. They are treated "charitably": they are given food and drink and offered sympathy, because their government deceived them and brought this great misfortune upon them.

We are in a state of double darkness. Physical darkness, because the electricity has been shut off; and mental darkness because the news from the outside world has been shut off. The same day that the electricity stopped, the radio and newspapers also stopped. Undoubtedly, great events have taken place outside our dark world.

Since we have no reliable means of receiving news, rumors abound about the political situation in the world and the military situation on the Western front. Some say that the Soviets are eying

Warsaw and a war is bound to break out between them and the Germans. A peculiar rumor, but one that does not cease. The interminable voice of the people. Others say the Germans are being beaten and battered on the Western front; in fact, the French have already captured twelve cities! In view of the deteriorating and dangerous situation on the Western front, the German Command has decided to transfer several divisions from here to there. In spite of all these peculiar rumors whispered from mouth to ear, no one really knows what is going on.

But politics is far removed from our world. We simply do not have the time to engage in it. We are too busy fighting for a piece of stale bread, a sip of water, the primary necessities of life which even money can no longer buy.

We have turned into animals: some of us into domestic animals; and some of us into carnivorous animals.

. . . The Nazis promised that at 8:00 A.M. the senior officer of the division would appear and permit all the displaced people to enter their apartments, and take out their possessions. But as usual, they lied. A few were permitted to enter their apartments; most of us stood by passively and lost hope of ever entering at all. One of our women friends succeeded in getting into her apartment and nearly fainted. Chaos and disorder reigned everywhere. Everything had been thrown together and the apartment looked as though a pogrom had taken place in it. I took a daring step and decided to get our things out through the window facing Karmelicka Street. Since our apartment is on the first floor, it was easy for our things to be lowered outside. Our maid Irka and our friend Aniuta went into the apartment and handed out everything they could lift. We stood outside—in sight of hundreds of passersby with nothing better to do than watch us for diversion—and caught the things as they came out. It was a scene worthy of being filmed. We worked under these circumstances for about two hours, until we had managed to retrieve all our possessions. With the aid of the women we made packages and bundles which we placed at the gate near 24 Karmelicka Street. Afterward, we brought them to our relative's house.

October 5, 1939
Eve of Simhat Torah,[5] *5700*

Our holiday is no longer celebrated. Fear has displaced gladness, and the windows of the synagogues are dark. Never before have we missed expressing our joy in the eternal Torah—even during the Middle Ages. After 7:00 P.M. there is a curfew in the city, and even in the hours before the curfew we live in dread of the Nazi conqueror's cruelty. The Nazi policy toward Jews is now in full swing.

Every day brings its share of grievous incidents. Here are some typical occurrences: Bearded Jews are stopped on the streets and abused. During the morning prayers on Shemini Atzeret,[6] a hundred and fifty men were pulled out of the Mlawa Street synagogue, herded into a truck, and taken to enforced labor. A Jew was stripped of his coat in the street and the coat was given to a Christian, so that he could benefit from the theft. A broken Jew, standing in a food line for long hours, was picked up for a twenty-four-hour work detail, hungry and thirsty as he was.

Midian and Moab have joined forces in order to oppress Israel. The last lesson has not yet been learned by our wise Polish neighbors, for even though they have suffered a national catastrophe as horrible as hell, they have not forgotten their animosity toward the Jews. Even though they are dull-witted and uncultured and do not know German, they have nevertheless learned to say: *"Ein Jude!"* in order to get him thrown out of line.

Dark and heavy clouds darken our sky. There is no gleam of hope, no ray of light.

The masses comfort themselves with groundless rumors, offspring of their own imaginings. Man believes what he wants to believe. In the thick darkness surrounding us, we have ample opportunity for imaginings. This time, they are not Messianic dreams but political fantasies: in a little while the Nazis will leave and the Soviets will take over; war will break out between Germany and

[5] The holiday of "Rejoicing in the Torah," at the end of Sukkot, when the weekly Sabbath reading of the Pentateuch is completed and begun anew for the coming year.—*Translator*

[6] The Eighth Day of Assembly, celebrated after the seventh day of Sukkot, as the concluding festival of the harvest season.—*Translator*

America; war will break out between Turkey and Germany; there are Nazi defeats on the Western front; Berlin has been destroyed like Warsaw, etc.

Where are we to look for salvation? It seems as though even our Father in Heaven—the mainstay of our fathers—has deserted us. Are we indeed to sing with the poet: [7] "Heavenly spheres, beg mercy for me. Behold, the path to God no longer exists! God of Israel, where art Thou?"

October 6, 1939

. . . At this point I must record the double miracle that happened to me.

I had placed all my money, along with some important documents, in an expensive copper box decorated with Bezalel art work. I had 600 zloty in the form of twelve notes, each worth 50 zloty. The notes were in a sealed envelope. The envelope and some other papers were in a small linen bag inside the box. The soldiers of the "ruling race" broke the lock of the box, took out the bag, and cast it aside as valueless. When the open and broken box was handed out the window to me I thought I would faint, so certain was I that my money had been stolen. But when we returned to our new apartment and began arranging our things—what joy when among our other possessions—which are practically valueless—we found the bag containing the money and documents.

From all the excitement my wife came close to fainting. The money found in the bag was our last bit of security in these turbulent times.

I, to whom this miracle happened, do most certainly appreciate my good fortune. Sinful and murderous men searched for my money in order to rob me of it, and they were smitten with blindness. A double miracle!

October 7, 1939

The conquerors and the conquered find common cause in their hatred of Israel. Jewish morality demands: If a man suffers misfortune, let him examine his deeds. Not so Christian morality. Mis-

[7] Ch. N. Bialik, 1873–1934, then considered the national Hebrew poet.—
Translator

fortune does not trouble the hearts of these practitioners of the "religion of love." When they suffer misfortune, they merely cause others to suffer in turn—especially if they are strangers and not friends. During these confused times, when everyone grieves and worries about the most basic problems, when a common enemy has overrun the country and threatens to swallow both peoples, when their misfortune is even greater than ours since theirs involves a nation and ours involves individuals—and since we are used to suffering and punishment from time immemorial and for them it is a new experience—despite all this, animosity toward Jews continues to grow even during these times of poverty and distress. . . .

October 10, 1939

Only Jews are taken for forced labor. Young, energetic, muscular Poles stand and mock from afar the Jews who kneel under the burden of their toil. The enemy picks Jews particularly for the most distasteful work—cleaning toilets, scrubbing floors, and other jobs of this sort. And there was an occurrence that I heard of from a youth—"It happened to me, myself!" he said. They caught him for work and ordered him to clean out filthy places and gave him no tools. When he asked for tools, they advised him to do it with his hands and to use his coat in place of a vessel. When he objected to this they beat him. Some soldiers were present at the time who couldn't stand to see an innocent man tortured, and explained to the strongarm that one should not behave in that manner toward a human being. The officer replied to this that the Jews wanted the war so it was just that such great misfortune befall them; that more than ten thousand German soldiers have already fallen victim, and that the Jews are making a business out of this war. Afterward they beat him some more, and after seven hours of degrading and despicable work, without tasting bread or water, he returned home.

October 13, 1939

The electricity has been only partially restored. I am still immersed in darkness. And because of the curfew in the city, it seems as though we are under house arrest. But worse than that is the mental darkness. We are cut off from the democratic world and all that is taking place there. All the newspapers, even the Polish ones, are suspended. This week, in their place, a Polish-language paper—a rag, the conquerors' brainchild—has begun appearing. The news from the world at large filters out through this paper, given, to be sure, a particular slant and coloration. Germany is praised above all; conversely, England has no equal for ugliness. In spite of that, they praise and laud Soviet Russia, a Communist state, the nest of world filth with whom, only a few months ago, the Führer refused even to negotiate. The local wits want to find a contradiction in the Führer's approach. Bolsheviks and Jews are one and the same thing, and therefore whoever likes the Bolsheviks likes Jews.

But you can't ask a Führer hard questions, and the mystique of his world is unknown to us. Furthermore, the first victims of Russian Bolshevism were the Jews, and the Jewry of Russia, too, has been driven from the earth. There are no signs of Jewishness at all in Russia. Yet nevertheless, when the news reached us that the Bolsheviks were coming closer to Warsaw, our joy was limitless. We dreamed about it; we thought ourselves lucky. Thousands of young people went to Bolshevik Russia on foot, that is to say, to the areas conquered by Russia. They looked upon the Bolsheviks as redeeming Messiahs. Even the wealthy, who would become poor under Bolshevism, preferred the Russians to the Germans. There is plunder on the one hand and plunder on the other, but the Russians plunder one as a citizen and as a man, while the Nazis plunder one as a Jew. The former Polish government never spoiled us, but at the same time never overtly singled us out for torture. The Nazi is a sadist, however. His hatred of the Jews is a psychosis. He flogs and derives pleasure from it. The torment of the victim is a balm to his soul, especially if the victim is a Jew.

Thus there is little wonder that the Bolsheviks became, in our eyes, the saviors of mankind. Everyone rejoiced as they neared Warsaw. Ceaseless rumors passed from person to person: the Messiah is coming! It was said, as if it were an actual fact, that war had broken out between the Russians and the Nazis. But to the sorrow and misfortune of tens of thousands of young people, it was only a pleasant dream. The Bolsheviks, it is true, marched forward, paying no attention to the line of demarcation established at the outset between them and Germany; but later a change took place. The Russians turned on their heels; they began to retreat to the

east, and the Germans marched after them—and our fate was
sealed.

October 14, 1939

. . . Warsaw has become full of all good things, but they are
not being sold in the normal way. The stores are still closed and
the markets have been burned and destroyed, therefore all the
trade has been brought out to the street. Whatever used to be done
indoors is now being carried on outside, and the streets have begun
to resemble a fair. They are full to capacity. There is no room to
pass; everywhere selling and bargaining, trade and barter are going
on under the sky.

This is the order of trade: the street vendors buy secretly from
the owners of the closed stores at high prices, then sell the produce
out of doors to the passersby at still higher prices. Never have there
been so many vendors among the Jews as in our own days.

Tens of thousands of people are left without a source of livelihood. There is no possibility under current conditions for them to
return to their previous occupations, so they turn to new ones.
And there is no better source of livelihood than trade in produce—
in necessities. Now—everything is saleable. Rotten, stinking goods
that used to be considered unfit to eat or use are now brought outside, and at once long lines are formed to grab up the bargain.

All trade, except the trade in produce, has stopped. And just as
everyone is selling, everyone is buying. Men who until now were
totally ignorant in matters of food, who always found their table
laid with all kinds of delicacies without their having lifted a finger
to prepare it, now get up at the crack of dawn to fetch water, to
look for bread, to search for potatoes, or to find a butcher shop
open to sell them a kilo of kosher meat for the price of 10 zloty.
Every important man now carries a bag full of potatoes on his
back, and a live chicken or a duck in his hand, and he wears a
look of triumph for having managed to supply himself with food.
No one is interested in anything but matters of eating.

The conquerors have left this whole business alone. They
haven't even attempted to make any sort of order in regard to
profiteering, so each man can charge as much as he wants. It is
quite possible that free trade is the better arrangement. The prices

go up sometimes and down sometimes. Everything finds a level without pressure from any direction. There is one constant: Warsaw is Warsaw. You can find all manner of delicacies and luxuries, provided you have the money.

October 15, 1939

The offices of the Joint [8] are like a madhouse. There are tens of thousands of needy. All the rooms are full of people. The noise and tumult never cease throughout the working day. At the door there is a guard who sticks to his orders but not to his place—the people who wish to enter ignore him, and push their way in by force. All manner of entrepreneurs have attached themselves to the Joint and everyone wants to enjoy pleasure and profit. The whole thing is marvelous—this whole "country fair" going on without the conqueror's knowledge or interest. In general, the Nazis have no dealings with the wielders of power among the Jews simply because there really is no such power. Our leaders abandoned us in time of danger. They scattered in all directions like mice, and so we are left neither a nation nor a community, but rather a herd.

October 16, 1939

. . . Here are a few pearls in the course of one day: First, Mayor Starzynski, in the name of the local commissar appointed by the German military command, announced with special pleasure that the German-appointed courtyard commandants are required to furnish a list of the residents of each courtyard who require public assistance, and on the basis of this, everyone will receive a legal document entitling him to receive, free of charge, bread, meals, clothing, and linen which the city will furnish at its own expense—except for the Jews.

Second, in a conversation which lasted two minutes, and which assumed the character of an order through the addition of a threat that "otherwise, they alone are responsible for their lives," the Jewish Council [9] was ordered to furnish a list of the Jewish resi-

8 The Joint Distribution Committee.
9 The Jewish Community Council (Hebrew: *Kehillah*) had been replaced, at German orders, by the Jewish Council (German: *Judenrat*) on October

dents of Warsaw from sixteen to sixty years of age. For what purpose? Nobody knows. But it is certain that it's not for the benefit of the Jews. Our hearts tell us that a catastrophe for the Jewry of Poland is hidden in this demand.

. . . there is a widespread rumor that Vladimir Jabotinsky has founded a Jewish Legion of 200,000 men; that England has proclaimed a Jewish State in Palestine and an Arab State in Syria; that Chaim Weizmann has been made President, and so on. I don't believe any of these rumors. I record them only for remembrance.

October 18, 1939

Our lives grow gloomier from day to day. Racial laws have not yet been formally decreed, but actually our defeat is inevitable. The conqueror says bluntly that there is no hope for Jewish survival. There is room for the assumption that a beginning is being made now.

So far there has been free trade in the streets. This is a trade of pennies, whose practitioners are boys and girls, young men and women driven to this sort of business by poverty. It is destined to be forbidden. It too will be taken out of the hands of the Jews. Every public place shows hatred and loathing toward the Jews. Isolated incidents by blows and violence against Jews have grown too numerous to count. Eyewitnesses tell horrifying stories, and they are not exaggerations.

The future of the schools for Jewish children is not yet known. In general the conquerors have no dealings with Jewish representatives. We are like grains of sand. There is no prior consultation regarding our own lives. They make decrees by themselves and there is no changing them. Reasons are not required. There is only one reason—to destroy, to kill, to eradicate.

Let anyone who wishes to consider the depths of the tragedy of Polish Jewry come to the Joint building (13 Leszno Street) and

---

4, 1939. The last head of the *Kehillah,* Mauryc Majzel, was not elected but was appointed by the Polish Government. He fled Warsaw immediately after the outbreak of the war, and Adam Czerniakow was the appointed head of the *Judenrat.—Translator* see the vale of tears. But even the Joint has no legal authority, and the conqueror knows nothing of its existence. It is our good fortune that the Joint's funds are in the hands of the American consulate and the enemy has no access to them. Otherwise he would confiscate them to the last cent. But the Joint's relief money is like a drop in the ocean. Great God! Are you making an end to Polish Jewry? "Your people" cannot understand: Why is the world silent?

October 20, 1939

Besides the economic disaster, we suffer from particular misfortunes—Jewish misfortunes. Eyewitnesses tell that even officers and high military officials are not ashamed to chase after an old Jew with scissors in their hands to cut off his beard. When they start chasing a bearded Jew, an uproar starts in the street and all the passersby and tradesmen flee. It strikes fear into all the Jews, and they are afraid to go outside. Their fear is far from groundless. First of all, they are seized for forced labor; second, they are seized for beard cutting; and third, they are afraid in general of Esau and Amalek. In the light of all this, our lives are no life at all; we are not secure either outside or at home. In the house they are afraid, "Lest they come . . . ," outside, lest they be seized for forced labor. Everyone goes outside wearing old, torn clothes, and I know one clever Jew who doesn't permit his house to be cleaned, so that it will have the look of a poor man's dwelling—thus he will fool the conquerors.

The *Judenrat,* which was orphaned when its money was stolen and its appointed president (commissar) fled, attempted to organize the matter of seizing people for labor. Czerniakow offered to supply a certain number of workers if only they would stop seizing for forced labor whoever comes to hand in the streets. They scarcely listened to this proposal, merely explained in passing that it was not detailed enough. Finally they agreed that the *Judenrat* will supply five hundred laborers a day, and that the street captures will stop. Tomorrow will be the first day for this new arrangement. The *Judenrat* will pay each worker 4 zloty a day out of its treasury. Let us see if they find people willing to work, if the *Judenrat* can meet its obligation, and if the conqueror will be satisfied with the new arrangement. If, heaven forbid, the contract with the enemy doesn't succeed, the evil will be worse than it has been up to now. We have all become orphans. Out of the depths I called Thee.

October 21, 1939

Some time ago I stated that our future is beclouded. I was wrong. Our future is becoming increasingly clear. Today the legal destruction began, with an order barring Jews from the two branches of the economy in which 50 percent of the Jewish community supported itself. It makes one's blood freeze, and a man is ready to commit suicide out of desperation. This isn't just a small economic deprivation that makes things difficult but will not endanger our survival. It is a savage slash that has no equal in the history of the oppression of the Jewish people. The cruel decree is short and decisive, comprising only seven paragraphs, but it suffices to topple our entire economic structure. The decree says: It is strictly forbidden for Jews to trade in textile goods (manufactures) and processed hides (leather) and any sort of manufacturing that involves these materials. With terrible savagery the ax has struck at the most active artery of the Jewish economy. All violators of this order will be severely punished, even by capital punishment.

After this it will be proper to say "blessed be the righteous judge" [10] for Jewish business in Poland. . . .

October 22, 1939

. . . Radios are being confiscated. Through the long chilly evenings we sit desolate and mournful, and there is no end to our tears. In every family there is misfortune and in every house, destruction. The "legal" destruction has darkened our world, but even this has become a subject for Jewish jokes. But this is gallows humor. I am afraid of a despair psychosis which is permeating our whole lives. We have stopped reacting. Even if they forbid us to breathe, we will make peace with that too. This too will furnish a subject for a new joke.

[10] The prayer said at funerals and upon hearing of a death.—*Translator*

October 25, 1939

There aren't enough words to describe the confusion in our minds. Blatant signs prove that some terrible catastrophe, unequaled in Jewish history, is in store for Polish Jewry.

There is no end to the rumors, and one must admit that there is some basis to them, for the Führer in his speech before the Reichstag on June 10 listed, among the aims of the war, the uprooting of various national groups in the areas under his domination. In all this strange business there is one central objective: to Germanize the conquered areas and to settle German populations in them which will become rooted there and turn the occupied areas into German regions joined to the Reich as one German-national unit.

The migration of communities, meaning the uprooting of communities from their native soil and the resettling of them in a strange land, is an economic catastrophe for the communities themselves. But wherever there is politics, no attention is paid to economics. And here the Jews will be the victims. The Tyrolians, the Letts, and the Estonians are under the administration of a government which seems to take care of them with friendship. For them the government is a solution; it is concerned with them and fulfills all their wants. But for us Jews the government is an enemy out to annihilate us.

Yesterday we heard over the London radio that the Jews of Vienna have received an order to be ready to leave their native city and migrate to the Lublin district of Poland. This means: Prepare yourselves for total destruction.

Another sign that bodes ill: Today, notices informed the Jewish population of Warsaw that next Saturday (October 29) there will be a census of the Jewish inhabitants. The *Judenrat* under the leadership of Engineer Czerniakow is required to carry it out. Our hearts tell us of evil—some catastrophe for the Jews of Warsaw lies in this census.[11] Otherwise there would be no need for it.

The day before yesterday, like true Vandals, the conquerors entered the Tlomackie Library, where rare spiritual treasures were stored. They removed all the valuable books and manuscripts, put them on trucks, and took them to some unknown place. This

[11] This census showed about 360,000 Jews in Warsaw.—*Translator*

is a burning of the soul of Polish Jewry, for this library was our spiritual sanctuary where we found respite when troubles came to us. Now the fountain which slaked our thirst for Torah and knowledge is dried up. The hands of Nahum Sokolow and other men of stature established it. They invested great spiritual powers in it and lately had even built a beautiful building.

October 26, 1939

In our scroll of agony, not one small detail can be omitted. Even though we are now undergoing terrible tribulations and the sun has grown dark for us at noon, we have not lost our hope that the era of light will surely come. Our existence as a people will not be destroyed. Individuals will be destroyed, but the Jewish community will live on. Therefore, every entry is more precious than gold, so long as it is written down as it happens, without exaggerations and distortions. . . .

October 28, 1939

We move along the earth like men condemned to death. It is clear to us that we will die by expulsion, but we don't know when the sentence will be carried out. Such a beginning was made in Berlin before the expulsion there. The order for a census stated that it is being held to gather data for administrative purposes. That's a neat phrase, but it contains catastrophe.

In the eyes of the conquerors we are outside the category of human beings. This is the Nazi ideology, and its followers, both common soldiers and officers, are turning it into a living reality. Their wickedness reaches the heights of human cruelty. These people must be considered psychopaths and sadists, because normal people are incapable of such abominable acts. There are army officers whose greatest pleasure is to lie in wait for bearded Jews on Nalewki Street, to attack them, and to cut off half their beards. The unfortunate Jew is afraid to oppose this, lest his opposition be considered a crime for which he will be punished. Jews are pulled out of lines and beaten for no reason. Nevertheless, one must admit that there are also some soldiers who possess human feelings. P. K. told me that a certain German officer ran into his wife on the corner of Chlodna and Zelazna streets. He asked her if she was a *Jüdin* and gave her half a loaf of bread.

Our tragedy is not in the humane or cruel actions of individuals, but in the plan in general, which shows no pity toward the Jews. We are certain that this census is being taken for the purpose of expelling "nonproductive elements." And there are a great many of us now. No one knows whose lot will be drawn and therefore sorrow is on every face. We are caught in a net, doomed to destruction.

Now the sad news has reached us that the border has been closed; some people say temporarily, others say it is for good.

Warsaw *Judenrat*

One View of
Adam Cherniakow

SHMARYAHU ELLENBERG *

*Within the general circumstances described by
Kaplan, the Germans established Warsaw's*
Judenrat, *or Jewish Council, which like those
of other ghettos and camps, was designed to
mediate between Jews and Germans. At the
time, and afterward, these councils and their
members evoked much discussion, controversy,
and bitterness. Adam Cherniakow became the
head of the* Judenrat *in Warsaw and consequently his name has become especially associated with the entire question. Shmaryahu
Ellenberg, knowledgeable in the affairs of
Warsaw's Jewry, was a contemporary of Cherniakow.*

. . . I encountered the late Adam Cherniakow from time to time.
. . . Early in September, 1939, I escaped from my home town
of Lodz, together with tens of thousands of other Jews, but having
been injured on the way, not by a bullet but by the wheel of a
Polish gun carriage which ran over me during my flight in the dark,
I was forced to remain in Warsaw, which was still open to traffic,
but closed by the Germans several days later. The siege of Warsaw, and the incessant bombardment of the city by German planes
day and night, continued . . . till the end of September, 1939. . . .

* "My Meeting with Adam Cherniakow," *Yad Vashem Bulletin* (February
1965), pp. 50–54.

124

The Zionist Parties in Warsaw, together with the Jewish Merchants and Artisans Organizations in the capital, had joined forces in . . . the "Jewish Public Committee" for extending assistance to Jews through guidance, representation with the Polish authorities, monetary aid and so on. On my arrival at Warsaw, Dr. Chaim Shoshkes immediately suggested I take over the administration of the office of this "Public Committee." I willingly accepted his offer, which enabled me to continue my public activities, even in besieged Warsaw.

The office was in the Community Building at No. 26 Grzybowska Street. The Committee meetings were generally held in the offices of the Chairman of the Committee, Mr. Abraham Gepner, Chairman of the Merchants Association, and a well known personality among Polish Jewry. . . .

My position as Secretary of this Public Committee was very difficult. It's true I was given every technical assistance in the Community offices, but no official was prepared to endanger himself by going out into the streets on the frequent and urgent missions that had to be undertaken. The town was under incessant bombardment at all hours of the day. Warnings sounded and there was a serious shortage of public air raid shelters. I had, therefore, myself to visit public offices, hospitals and various institutions for the purpose of receiving and giving information, and investigating the situation of people applying for aid. The members of the Committee, and in particular the Chairman, Mr. Gepner, and his deputy, Mr. Moshe Kerner . . . , encouraged me in this work and closely collaborated with me. I often visited them at their homes to report on my work and consult them.

I shall never forget the horrifying scenes in the hospitals: they were crammed with the wounded, lying on the floors and in the corridors, in indescribable circumstances, particularly after night bombing, which started enormous fires. Physicians and nurses scurried backwards and forwards, at their wits' end. There was a shortage of personnel and the supply of medicines and bandages was running out.

The calls on the offices of the "Public Committee" increased in number, but we lacked necessary financial means. Nor did we receive sufficient assistance from the Polish authorities to be able speedily and effectively to help all applicants. The Mayor and his staff were always very polite, but the effective aid that they offered us was very slim indeed. The Jewish public workers fully appreciated our work and promised to come to the aid of the "Public Committee," but in actual fact they were unable to assist because their personal troubles and cares sapped them of all energy. We remained, therefore, almost alone and unaided in the committee work.

Adam Cherniakow was among the less active members of the Committee and was generally absent at meetings. It was also very difficult to get hold of him elsewhere for advice; or to induce him to make representations with one or other of the authorities.

It is difficult to describe the confusion in the city streets after the lifting of the siege. The inhabitants went out into the streets in the thousands, to visit relatives, to call at places of work, but first and foremost to draw water in buckets from the river Vistula, because the water supply was not repaired for a long time. Regiments of German soldiers marched backwards and forwards along the principal streets and German placards covered signboards and walls of houses.

To the surprise of the inhabitants, ambulatory kitchens cropped up at central points in the city during the morning and noon hours. These had been sent by the German army authorities to distribute loaves of bread and plates of warm soup among the population, without any discrimination. After some misgivings, people began approaching these kitchens in order to receive the rations offered them; there was famine in the city, all food stocks had been depleted.

Jews also were to be seen among those queueing up; the German soldiers did not discriminate between Polish Gentiles and Jews. Reports of this spread with lightning speed, and the following day these ambulatory German kitchens drew tremendous crowds of Jews and Christians, which increased hour by hour. The Germans had a hard time controlling the crowds. They tried issuing orders, Prussian fashion. Thousands lined up near the kitchens and many others who observed this strange spectacle of an invading army evincing such generosity towards vanquished citizens also took advantage of their kindness. There were many spectators, but it was a painful scene, and they quickly made their departure.

That day towards evening I made my usual visit to Mr. Gepner's home. I was surprised to find him packing a small suitcase. He sensed my surprise, returned my greeting and informed me that, on orders from the German authorities, he had to leave home that same evening and, together with the representative of the "Bund," [1] to present themselves as hostages in order to ensure that the Polish and Jewish inhabitants of the city conduct themselves properly. The news stunned me, and I couldn't even utter a word of consolation to this fine man and proud Jew, who had obviously fallen a victim for his people. Gepner did not give me an opportunity of speaking to him, and of consulting him on Committee affairs. He took his leave of me, saying he had now to give me his last instructions in the name of the Committee, in conformity with the order of the Mayor.

First of all, he asked me whether I had seen the large crowds around the German kitchens in the city. When I answered in the affirmative he said that the Germans had complained to the Mayor that the Jews . . . whose welfare the German army had at heart —and he was prepared to prove it—were undisciplined, refused to obey orders and were the cause of disturbances in central thoroughfares in front of the kitchens where food rations were being distributed to all applicants. The Mayor, who had maintained contacts with the "Jewish Public Committee" throughout the period of the siege, had turned this matter over to Mr. Abraham Gepner, its Chairman, and asked him to appeal immediately to the Jewish citizens, demanding that they behave themselves when applying to the Germans for their food rations.

I wanted to say something, but Gepner said that he understood my feelings very well, and that he had no intentions to comply

[1] The Bund was a Jewish Socialist organization with mass membership among workers in Poland and Russia. Its origins went back into the nineteenth century. The representative mentioned here was the late Szmul Zygelbojm, who later fled to London, where he committed suicide. Several other Polish public figures, headed by the Polish Socialist leader Niedzalkovski, also received these orders.

with the Mayor's request but rather to submit the matter to the Committee in order that it may decide in his absence. Since the implementation of the Mayor's instructions could not be deferred he asked me immediately to contact Adam Cherniakow and to pass on the information to him. He was head of the Jewish community and the task of directing all activities concerning the Jewish population now fell to him.

I agreed, and so we parted in silence. I never saw him again. . . . That autumn evening I made my way to the home of Cherniakow, to inform him of the order issued by the Mayor. Before we parted, Mr. Gepner had advised me to take a coach to Cherniakow's home and not to go on foot because he lived in a non-Jewish district and he did not know what might happen if I walked around there at night. I followed his advice. I found a coach with great difficulty, and paid an exorbitant price to the coachman to take me to Cherniakow's house. We made our way slowly and I had a chance to observe what was happening in the non-Jewish districts. There was complete silence. Darkness reigned in the city, and I was full of painful thoughts. We approached the district where Cherniakow was living. Since I knew neither the name of the street nor the number of the house, I was forced to get down from the coach and enter the houses, in order to read the name-plates. In doing so, I was shocked to see Polish servant girls and German soldiers making love in almost every corridor I entered. Since I disturbed them I feared I might invite attack by a German soldier disturbed by my intrusion. The danger side-tracked my thoughts about this unholy friendship struck up so rapidly between Polish girls and German soldiers. Despite my fear, I decided to carry out Gepner's orders.

At long last I found the house. I climbed the stairs and rang at the door of Cherniakow's apartment. No one came to the door. After ringing incessantly for some time I heard rustling at the door of the flat opposite. A man appeared and asked what I wanted. While I tried to explain, Cherniakow came out. He did not let me in to his house nor to the house he had come out from. Both of us stood on the stairs by the window. He asked why I had come at that late hour. I conveyed to him the message handed over by Gepner on orders from the Mayor. I did not mention that Gepner had been taken as hostage. Cherniakow's features conveyed a sense of dissatisfaction, but he tried to overcome his mood and replied that on the following day he would issue a proclamation to the Jews of Warsaw . . . in keeping with the Mayor's instructions.

. . . I left the house and returned on foot to my own home. That very same night I told Doctor Shoshkes of my meetings with Gepner and with Cherniakow. We continued our conversation long into the night . . . about human nature, public figures and the fate that awaited them.

A few days later the activities of the "Jewish Public Committee" came to an end, and the offices of the Committee at No. 26 Grzybowska Street were taken over by the Community, which only then began to function under the direction of Adam Cherniakow.

I returned to Lodz in the middle of October, 1939. On arrival, my wife told me that the Germans were looking for me as one of the active figures in Jewish public life in the city. I had hardly managed to rest at home and to return to my work in the Jewish Gymnasium in Lodz when I was handed a letter signed by the Chairman of the *Judenrat* in Lodz, informing me that the German Commandant of the city had appointed me a member of the *Judenrat,* and that I was to attend the forthcoming meeting in the Community Building. After consulting friends and colleagues, I decided not to accept the invitation, but by every means possible to implement my plan of immigration to Eretz-Israel. . . .

In the middle of February, 1940, while in Warsaw to complete my preparations for the journey, I called at the offices of the Community, at No. 26 Gazidovska Street. A large crowd had gathered there and it was only with the greatest difficulty that I was able to make my way to the room occupied by Cherniakow, the Chairman, in order to take leave of him. When he heard of my arrival, he asked me in at once. The door opened, and Dr. Alfred Nossig and his secretary emerged. . . .

My talk with Cherniakow was very short. He complained of the great burden of work that weighed upon him and of his daily troubles. Every word of his indicated depression. At last we took leave and he wished me a happy journey.

A Second View of
Cherniakow

A. H. HARTGLASS *

*One of the leaders of the Jews of Poland was
A. H. Hartglass. Here he portrays in some
detail the context in which the* Judenrat *and its
head began to function.*

. . . The last Jewish Community Council before the outbreak of
the war had not been elected, but rather appointed by the Government. The appointed head of the Community was Mauryc Majzel,
a very clever man who knew how to deal with the authorities, but
who had no political views of his own. Majzel fled from Warsaw
immediately after the outbreak of the war. Since there was no
council enjoying public confidence, and since the body nominated
by the Government was no longer functioning, the political parties
suggested the establishment of a Citizens Committee composed of,
among others, representatives of those parties. I was among them.

The question also arose if members of the former Council,
who had agreed to their being appointed by the Government,
should be accepted on the new Committee. But since only a few
had remained in Warsaw, among them people of some importance,
it was decided to co-opt them to the Committee. Among them
was Cherniakow, an engineer, with whom I had been well ac-
quainted from my university days. He was an able and also quite
a decent man. He had no clearly defined political ideas. While
he was a university student he avoided all political activity. After-

* "How Did Cherniakow Become Head of the Warsaw *Judenrat?*" *Yad
Vashem Bulletin* (August 1964), p. 47.

wards he declared himself an assimilationist, and became a high official of the Polish Government. When the Provisional National Jewish Council began to win public recognition and the American Joint Distribution Committee began its activities in the country, Cherniakow, while still retaining his Government post, drew somewhat closer to the Jewish nationalists.

Afterwards, he served for a time as chairman of the Craftsmen Association. He did a great deal of work, concentrating mainly on public displays: flags, parades, participation in Government demonstrations, etc. When the Cooperative Bank was established with the assistance of the "Joint," Cherniakow was appointed head of its Rehabilitation Department, after which he resigned from his Government post. He afterwards hoped that the Joint Distribution Committee would send him as its representative to the Jewish Agency, and there was some chance of this being done. In any case, that is what he said when he told me, as he frequently did, of his plans. When the Cooperative Bank was dissolved, Cherniakow received a considerable sum in severance pay, which he invested in a joint venture and lost almost completely very soon thereafter. Then he received a post in a semi-governmental institution. . . . At the same time he was named as a member of the Council of the Jewish Community.

While the shelling was still infrequent, we met every day. Cherniakow was among those participating in the meeting of the Public Committee, but he always came late.

Once, during the hours when the Public Committee was meeting, I had to go to the Municipality to take care of a certain matter. To my great surprise I saw Cherniakow in the waiting room of the Mayor, who at the time was also commander of the city. When I asked Cherniakow what he was doing there, he told me frankly that he was trying to gain appointment as head of the Jewish Community. The next day Cherniakow showed me an official letter of appointment signed by the Mayor. A few days later the meetings of the Public Committee ended, since people were afraid to leave their homes because of the increased shelling.

Generally meetings would take place on Krolewska Street, in the offices of a well-known leader of the merchants, Abraham Gepner, who was a good and honest man. At that time we were trying to provide assistance to those Jews who had lost their apartments during the shelling or had been expelled from other towns by the Germans. There was also the urgent question of burying the dead, who were scattered in the streets and among the ruins, as well as the question of feeding the wounded people in the hospitals and finding means to cure them.

We had only a few meetings. At one of them Cherniakow showed me his new calling card, on which was inscribed (in German) Senator Engineer Adam Cherniakow, Chairman of the Warsaw Jewish Community.

I was rather taken aback by these cards. When I asked him why he called himself a senator, though he wasn't one, he explained that since his name on the list of candidates to the Senate followed that of Prof. Schorr (who was elected), and since Prof. Schorr had fled to the Russian-occupied territory, he, Cherniakow, automatically occupied Schorr's seat. If the Polish Government had not fled he would now have been a real senator. Aside from that, he added, he needed the title in order to obtain greater respect from the Germans.

Around October 14, perhaps on October 17, though I am not certain of the exact date, the janitor entered during our meeting in the Jewish Community hall and announced that the Germans had come. Cherniakow was, by chance, not there. Several other members of the Committee were also absent. We took note of the announcement about the arrival of the Germans—and we continued the meeting. Suddenly several Gestapo officers burst noisily into the room. They acted like wild animals and without offering any explanations they shouted at us: *"Raus"* (get out). We all rose and went out to the corridor. After a time the janitor told us that the Germans had demanded that we give them all the keys to the locked doors, as well as the key to the safe. The janitor explained to them that the key to the safe was in the hands of the chairman of the Community. When asked who was the chairman of the Community and where he could be found, the janitor announced that the chairman was Cherniakow, the engineer, and that he would certainly arrive shortly. We also wanted to await his arrival, but the Gestapo men present threatened us, crying out: *"Raus aus dem Gebäude, sofort nach Hause* (get out, leave the building, go home immediately)!" We went out just as Cherniakow arrived in the Community's carriage. He was return-ing from the hospital. We told him everything that had happened and we agreed that he would go to the Gestapo, and that the next day at 9 A.M. we would again gather at the Community's build-ing. If something should happen to Cherniakow, we would be informed by the janitor and would then decide what to do.

The next day we all met at the building, but not in the assembly room, since the Gestapo men had taken the key to it. Cherniakow told us that the Germans had taken the 9,000 zloty from the safe, and had ordered him to establish a Council of Elders (*Rada Starszych*) composed of twenty-four members and twenty-four alternates, and said that he would be the head of the Council. We began to prepare the list, which was supposed to be ready by twelve noon. In contrast to the situation during the formation of the Citizens Committee, when everyone tried to become a member and every faction argued that it was not being given sufficient representation on the Committee, everyone now asked to be freed of the responsibility of being a member of the Council of Elders. Yitzhak Meir Levin also asked to be freed of the responsibility of being a member; he was really in danger of being harmed by the Germans because of his beard and kapota.* But we did not agree, though we said that he could avoid coming to meetings as much as possible. I also wanted to escape appoint-ment, for it would not have been worthwhile becoming too prom-inent in German eyes in view of my anti-Hitler articles, but Cher-niakow and others did not agree. Finally we decided that I would be included in the list under . . . *Maximillian.* My second given name, *Apolinary,* with which I had signed my articles, would not be mentioned. I proposed that my alternate be a man who had once done his apprenticeship in my law office. . . . I also pro-posed, among other things, that our friend Yaacov Gamarnikow, the lawyer, be an alternate delegate. He had never participated in political or public life. I only suggested his candidacy at his wife's request, because she believed that if he had some sort of official position the Germans would not harm him.

At twelve noon the list was ready. The Gestapo men arrived

* Long black coat, worn by Orthodox Jews.

and their leader gave us letters of appointment signed by him. They said that the person named had been appointed a member of the Council of Elders and that his task was to carry out their leader's orders. This ended the matter and each of us returned home.

The next day, while I was in the Community building, Cherniakow showed me and others that he had placed in the drawer of his table a small bottle with twenty-four cyanide tablets, one for each of us, and he showed us where the key to the drawer could be found, should the need arise. . . .

Youth Movements in Czernowitz

ZVI YAVETZ *

Elsewhere in Europe, Jews struggled to live. The Jews in Czernowitz found themselves in a special set of circumstances. In 1940 they had come under Soviet rule and faced conditions entirely different from those they had known under the Rumanians. In 1941, when the Germans attacked Russia, the Jews had to decide whether to run with the Russians or to risk living under German rule; later, the Jews still in Czernowitz struggled against German terror. This selection from historian Zvi Yavetz's memoir is based on his recollection of these events many years later. Since Professor Yavetz was a teen-ager at the time which he describes, his remarks offer insights into the views of Czernowitz's ideologically committed Jewish youth.

. . . We had all sorts of youth movements in Czernowitz. The strongest was, of course, Hashomer Hazair, the left-wing movement, which had the best brains. But this was a movement into which my mother would never let me go: "It's Communist, it's Red. . . . They never wear a tie, and they . . . they discuss Karl Marx . . . oh, bad things. Gordania and Dror"—that means Poalei Zion and Dror, which is a little bit like Ahdut Avoda—"these two movements, well, they're nice, but people there are too common, because they really come from the working classes."

* The original transcript is on deposit with Cornell University's Oral History Program, Ithaca, New York.

That was not good enough for Jewish petty bourgeois. The youth movement of Chaim Weizmann, Nahum Goldmann, Nahum Sokolow [Hanoar Hazioni]—not bad. They were not Socialists—good democrats, *"ganz fein, anständig* [respectable citizens]."

Well, those four movements, even though our parents did not favor them, had to stick together because we had our own national enemy, Betar, the Zionist Revisionists. Vladimir Jabotinsky was their leader. We, of course, fought each other, and I must admit that sometimes we had more in common with the Communist youth than we had with the Betar because we were all brought up to believe that they were Fascists. When we saw them in their brown shirts, and you know what a brown shirt meant in those days, and when they were shouting, *"Hedat Betar"* [1] and worshiped the personality of the great Jabotinsky, they made us furious. So we had our big fights with them, through '39 and '40.

Of course, we didn't like the Communists because they always said that Zionism was a bourgeois movement, reactionary, and although we were bourgeois, none of us wanted to look the part; and we said it's not true, we were poor people, working people, and so on, because to be a bourgeois in those days was quite offensive. Nor did we like the Communists' saying that only capitalists can go to Israel—because at that time certificates were given only to persons who had a certain affidavit, which cost a thousand pounds. I remember how in school a friend of mine, who was a member of the illegal Communist party, said, "Well, that might be a solution for you because your parents are going to pay the thousand pounds; but is this a solution for me? If the Red Army is not going to save my life, what am I going to do?"

My grandfather, who was very religious, thought these youth movements were troublemakers. The Germans? They're not so bad. Rumors! And he also tried to convince my mother of this.

When Premier Octavian Goga [leader of the National Christians] took over the government in December 1937, my grandfather immediately went to Palestine and bought a few plots of land. He had plenty of money. But after Kusa and Goga fell the following February, and a so-called democratic government took over, he said, "Oh, we'll stay here. It's all right."

[1] "Hurray Betar." Vladimir Jabotinsky (1880–1940) was the hero of the Revisionist Movement, which advocated militant Zionism.

Only the youth movements were fully aware of what was going to happen, and we really envied the Betar people who started the illegal emigration at that time from Rumania to Israel, even though our own groups had been forbidden to support it. I can still remember Jabotinsky's words when he came to Czernowitz in 1938. "If you're not going to Palestine," he said, *"Yiddishe kinderlech, lernt eich schiessen,"* "Learn how to shoot!" But Weizmann and Nahum Goldmann tried to calm us by saying: "Oh, it's not so bad. You know Jabotinsky." When they sang the Betar song, we booed and started to sing the *Tehezaknu,* the song of the Histadrut,[2] in order to prove we were Socialists an.] workers.

But still, we shared the view that the Nazi danger was imminent, it would come, and it was going to be bad. We never thought in terms of a huge extermination, but we did think that many people would be put to death. Everyone was sure there would be pogroms. Our fear was that the Ukrainians and Rumanians would be let loose to unleash terrible "Kishinevs." [3] The Rumanian government had so far restrained them. It was very democratic from one point of view—every minister had his price. The minister of justice could be bought for so much money, the minister of commerce and industry for so and so much, and so on. And the Jews had the money. My grandfather never paid a penny of income tax because the king was a silent partner in our factory, though he had never seen it.

We believed the Germans would never dirty their hands with Jewish blood, the Germans would not do it themselves. We never thought in terms of a scientific extermination of Jews.

When the Soviets came in 1939 many things changed. Betar disappeared, disintegrated. They had always been brought up with the slogan: "It's good to die for our country." [4] They had always been prepared to do a big job, and even sacrifice their lives. But to do a tough job day after day—this they never had considered; and as long as they could run about in their brown shirts shouting,

[2] The organization of trade unions belonging to the Labor Zionist Movement in Palestine.

[3] Kishinev, then part of Russia, was the scene of a major pogrom against the Jews in 1903.

[4] These were the dying words attributed to Joseph Trumpledor, a fighting pioneer in the early days of modern Jewish settlement in Palestine.

"Hedat Jabotinsky"—that was fine. But when the Soviets came, and we had to go underground and act illegally, and really do things—well, it was very, very dangerous. To be caught by the Soviets in a Hebrew class meant Siberia the next day. The four left-wing groups, including Hanoar Hazioni, which was to the right of them, the center, all worked closely together in small groups in those days. Everybody learned Hebrew. Our first decision was to go to Yiddish schools because the assimilationists had all sent their children to the Russian schools, saying: "The Russians are here. Tomorrow we've got to find jobs in the government, Communist or not Communist." Therefore, the Yiddish schools were packed with people from the Zionist youth movements and the Bundists. The Revisionists had completely disappeared.

It was a great relief, I must say, for all of us when the Russians came; I would be lying if I denied that people were really happy because that was the first time in our lives that we could come home safely at night. We could walk in the streets. Nobody would bother us. We could go to school and not be ashamed of being Jews; and we went to a Yiddish school. The Soviets appeared very attractive even though our parents were upset. I must say that none of my friends was sorry when the Russians nationalized all our properties. On June 28, 1940, I was the son of a millionaire. On the twenty-ninth, I was the son of a pauper because there was nothing left.

My most interesting experience came a few months later, when the Russian officer from the NKVD—the secret police—came to our house and said, "Comrade Stalin says people who don't work should not eat. Why don't you work?" My mother had remarried, and my stepfather had a large store, a sort of supermarket. That was nationalized. But if we had sold a diamond once a year or used a few dollars we had hidden, we could have made a good living even under the Soviets for many years to come. But the Soviets wanted everyone to work. "If you don't work, we must assume that you live on the black market, because otherwise, how *can* you make your living?" the officer asked. So my mother was compelled to accept a job for 280 rubles a month.

The only thing we could not stand was that in school we had

to say that Hitler was fighting a progressive war; in those days of
the Stalin-Hitler pact, Hitler was fighting British imperialism and
British capitalism, and he was from that point of view progressive.
And to hear all that nonsense in Yiddish in a Yiddish school
repeated by my history teacher, Yonit Abramovitch Gettels, a
Jew from Cracow, was revolting.

There were other problems with the Soviets. Everyone was
afraid of everyone. One of our family friends was sent to Siberia
for twenty years because someone reported to the police that he
had told a dirty joke: *"Wos geht, singt, und stinkt?"* he had asked.
"What walks, sings, and stinks?" And the reply was, "The Red
Army." And that brought him twenty years in prison.

But there were always jokes. They were the only things that
kept us alive, our only outlet. The pro-German attitude which we
were forced to take was demoralizing. I myself was expelled
three times from school. I was also thrown out of the Komsomol,
the Communist youth movement, because I used to crack jokes.

In those days the members of the Zionist youth groups were
really in danger. We were reported, and our leaders, who were at
that time university students in their first, second, or third
university years, were all taken to Siberia. Some were later shot
by the Soviets. It was a dangerous game, and our parents were
scared.

The Soviet occupation was temporary, we all hoped. No one
believed, as far as I knew, that the Germans would attack us. We
all thought they would eventually lose the war. Although this
was hardly an ideal way to survive the war, it was better here
than under the Germans.

Not for a single moment did we have the slightest doubt concerning the British victory, even in 1940. Nobody spoke in those
days of America's joining the war, but everyone knew that
America would not let England fall. We heard all sorts of rumors
when we went to synagogue. Under the Russians, we went to
synagogue out of protest. I didn't go to school on Rosh Hashanah
and Yom Kippur; I refused to write on Shabbat in school. Though
we were non-religious, this was the only way we could protest.

Notwithstanding these difficulties, life under the Soviets had
certain advantages. The workers really supported the regime.

For the first time, Jews could send their children into schools free—high schools, universities, teachers' colleges. Theaters cost pennies, cinemas cost pennies.

In June 1941 everything changed and Czernowitz Jews found themselves faced with a terrible dilemma. On the twelfth, the headmaster called a girl from our class into his office and warned her that she and her parents should not stay in their house that night or the next day, nor for the next two or three weeks. Nobody knew exactly what was going on, but I ran and brought the news home. Once this information was confirmed there were conferences in many Jewish houses. News got around that Jews should disappear. We all had Soviet passports, and it was said that all who had Number 39 were in danger.

That number passport was held by all listed as donors to the Keren Kayemet (Jewish National Fund), and also by those with confiscated property—that is, factories, shops which employed other people. Those suspected of political subversion also had a "39."

The rumors said that the Russians had gotten lists and addresses; and we received news from Poland that the Lwow Jews had suddenly disappeared. . . . My grandfather, all my uncles and aunts —that is, my father's brothers and sisters, who had always been good citizens, *die guten Deutschen Stadtsbürger,* claimed it was a rumor started by panic-makers, and they stayed home. The next day, at about one o'clock, hundreds of NKVD lorries surrounded all the houses, and some three thousand leading Jews from our community were transported to Siberia in cattle trucks—the same trucks later to be used by the Nazis. In one of these trucks, my grandfather was suffocated. My grandmother somehow got to Siberia, but died a few weeks afterward.

To have taken Zionist leaders was one thing; after all Zionism was illegal and Zionists took full responsibility for their actions. But so many distinguished members of the community were deported to Soviet Russia! Nobody knew why. Nobody gave us any explanation. There was nothing in the newspapers about it. All of us were terribly upset, especially those who were not living at home. Between June 13 and June 22, I felt myself to be in terrible danger because I was on the list. But they never found me.

My parents and myself, like many other Jews, were hiding in various places—former employees, friends, all sorts of people offered shelter.

Three thousand Jews disappeared in one night—and nobody knew why. In one wagon they had rounded up all the former prostitutes of Czernowitz; under the Rumanian regime prostitution was legal, while under the Soviets it was not. Nobody could figure out what was going on here—Zionists, capitalists, anti-Communists, prostitutes. It was one huge puzzle. And on June 21, my entire class went to see a Jewish play, Abraham Goldfaden's *Machashefe* [*The Witch*]. When I came home late in the evening, my mother shouted, "Why are you out so late? Don't you know how dangerous it is now?" At three or four in the morning, we heard shooting and saw planes bombing the city. We found out the next morning that war had broken out. Complete confusion. And all those Soviet officials, running like mad, frightened. The Germans had attacked. We all came out from hiding because no NKVD officer was trying to find poor Jews who had hidden themselves. Immediately our congregations and organizations came to life again.

And now the dilemma. The Soviets offered to enable all who would like to flee to Russia to depart on trains, though they had few left for the transportation of civilians. And many Jews were prepared to do so, even though they knew it was a bad regime. But wouldn't the Germans be worse? Many of our youth leaders left, but not too many of the elder generation. The Communists —let them go!

We in our youth movement had a meeting to discuss orders received from our leaders in Poland. Since they were already at the university and we were still in high school, we considered them wiser and more intelligent.

And they said: from Czernowitz to Russia—never! Try to push through to the Black Sea. That was the decision, and so we stayed.

On July 5, Czernowitz was occupied by Germans and Rumanians. And that was the beginning of the Holocaust.

The first troops to come in were Rumanian troops who had joined the German war effort. They caught Jews at random. The Germans were saluted by the Ukrainians and by the Rumanians, who hated the Russians, and who could easily point us out to the occupying troops: this one is a Jew, that one is a Jew. They lived in our neighborhood and knew us.

I was on the street with friends and we were caught. My watch was taken away immediately, I was beaten up by two Rumanian soldiers. And we were taken to a former Soviet barracks and ordered to clean it up.

One of my friends was recognized by the Rumanian corporal in charge, who warned us: "You must get away from here because as soon as you finish the job, you'll all be shot." We both suggested that it would be a good idea to let us go and bring some water to clean the floors, since the Russians had blown up the water tower and we knew about a well where we could get water. The officer agreed, and detailed two rifled soldiers to accompany us. We misled them and spoke Yiddish to one another. When we came to a small wood, I ran left, he ran right. They shot, but both of us managed to survive.

After I returned home we learned that about three thousand Jews had been taken down to a place we used to call the *Schiesstelle*—where the soldiers used to have target practice—and were killed. Included were the Chief Rabbi of Czernowitz, some of the Jewish leaders, along with other Jews caught at random. They were all buried in a mass grave in the small woods near the Prut River. That was our first taste of the German regime.

But Jews refused to understand. In the synagogues they continued to say: that was only a Rumanan piece of work. Were the more civilized Germans around, this could never have happened.

Very soon we discovered that practically all the Jews who lived in isolated communities outside of Czernowitz had been slaughtered with axes and knives—by peasants living in the vicinity. And everything was looted. Some forty members of my family died in that pogrom during the first days of July.

News came in practically every half hour. This man had been taken away, that man had disappeared, another had been shot. The panic really started growing, especially because the Nazi-supporting population was so enthusiastic about the German victories achieved during those days.

It was a dreadful period. Many, many times I was caught and beaten by Rumanians. The main job of the Jews was to do forced labor, reconstructing bridges and roads that the Russians had blown up before their retreat.

On Rosh Hashanah, 1941, rumors spread that we were going to be ordered to leave our homes and probably be deported. Our youth movements had just finished licking their wounds—we had lost part of our membership who had gone with the Russians, and another group had been shot during the pogroms. Somehow we had managed to reestablish our links with the movement in Lwow.

On Hoshanah Rabbah, 1941, at six in the morning, posters all over the town announced that about fifty thousand Jews were to leave their homes and assemble on four small streets. By ten, all Jews were in the ghetto. We were allowed to take along only one suitcase. Some forty or fifty of us were crowded into a small room. The Rumanians sent word into the ghetto that this was only temporary, and that we would soon get new housing, but not in Czernowitz. We would be sent to Mogilev or maybe to some other place. And immediately the Jewish community sent out its leaders to negotiate with the Rumanians. How should this be organized? It was Simhat Torah. The Horedenke Rebbe, with a Torah in his hand, and his followers were the first to go to Mogilev because they would get better housing. In those days, members of our movement, youngsters of sixteen and seventeen, ran from house to house telling people to hide because nobody would return from the transports. But who listened to us?

They had some reasons for not believing the kids. Everyone lost faith in us after the *Struma* affair, when we had said that instead of paying so and so much money to stay in Czernowitz, why not pay double in order to get away from here—get to Bucharest somehow and get on a boat? Some rich Jews, eight hundred of them, did go on the *Struma,* among them many of our friends and classmates. They reached Istanbul safely, and then the British said they were German enemy citizens, aliens, and were therefore not to be given visas for Palestine. The Turks sent them back, the ship was torpedoed, and eight hundred Jews were drowned. When this news reached Czernowitz, everyone said: what about your

Palestine, what difference does it make? Out of the frying pan, into the fire—or into the deep sea! What difference does it make? So the *Struma* was really a very bad thing for us. But the youth movement continued to believe in escape by boats.

All those who did listen and stayed were saved. It was not easy. We had to run from one cellar to the other, from one house to the other, to find an officer and bribe him, so as not to go on the transports. But many Jews went. One of my aunts considered it stupid to stay and wait for her turn. She voluntarily went into the street whose residents were being deported on that day. . . . She never came back. Neither she, nor her child, nor her husband —none of them, thousands.

There were four huge transports; and about fifteen thousand Jews, most of them rich, remained behind. Then suddenly the ghetto was abolished, and all fifteen thousand who had remained behind were allowed to return to their houses. They all had special permits to stay in town, one because he was a doctor and was needed, another because he was an engineer and was needed, another because he had the right connections with some Rumanian officer and happened to bribe him well. This was all done by Rumanians. We had no Germans there. Our community leaders did not seem to know what was happening.

For the people who had remained behind, the best move now seemed to be to run away from Czernowitz and other places in Bukovina and Bessarabia. In Rumania proper Jews were not as badly treated as in those places. In Bukovina and Bessarabia, Jews had a double stigma: we were not only Jews but we were also considered to be Communists—who had lived happily under the Soviet regime. In 1941, as Jews in Czernowitz we were in a dilemma whether we faced Russians, Germans, or Rumanians.

There was another option. In the ghetto, the major ideological struggle between the Zionist youth and the Communists was whether to flee to the Black Sea or join the Partisans. The Communists had a point. They always advocated joining the Partisans, which was the right thing to do. But our question was: point them out to us—where are they? And they were nowhere. In those days there were no Partisans in Bukovina or Bessarabia. All of them supported the Nazis wholeheartedly. There was nobody to join. It was just talk.

There was a possibility, of course, of organizing guerrilla-fighting, but with whom? A few Jewish kids? No weapons. Hostile Ukrainians. Who could do it? It was an idea, but it was as utopian as our dream about Palestine. But we believed. Were it not for that faith, no one of us would have survived at all. But we believed, and I shall never forget the great enthusiasm in our cellars when we heard over BBC that the Germans had had to evacuate Rostov. That was the first German setback, the beginning of the end. Then came Pearl Harbor. Well, we were sure the Germans were going to lose the war, but then we were really asking: are we going to survive it? Are the Jews going to see the peace?

PART THREE

In Flight

The selections * that follow tell of individual cases of tribulation and survival outside the camps of annihilation. Each has its own nuances, and differs from the others. Each reveals the critical role played by non-Jews as the hunted Jews succeeded in outwitting their pursuers. The very imperfection of their English adds to the poignancy of their narrative.

* These accounts were printed for the United States House of Representatives 79th Congress (1945) Hearings Before the Committee on Immigration and Naturalization, *Problems Presented by Refugees at Fort Ontario,* pp. 151–154, 155–162, 165–167, 169–173.

On the *Pentcho*

HANS GOLDBERGER

*This is a report, by one of the passengers, of
an "illegal" trip to Palestine on the Bulgarian
vessel* Pentcho, *made by 511 Jews fleeing from
Slovakia, Germany, and other areas under the
Hitler terror.*

. . . Hitler occupies the "protectorate" [March 15, 1939]; at the
same time hell breaks loose for the Jews in now "independent"
Slovakia. The Germans of Slovakia and the "national" Slovaks
wish to prove that they can do even better in cleaning out the
Jews than the SA and SS did in Germany and Austria, and they
work hard to catch up as fast as possible. Demolition of Jewish
stores, expropriation of Jewish property, imprisonment in concentration and so-called labor camps, burning of synagogues, for-
bidding Jews to visit any parks, restaurants, and other public places,
police raids, deportations to the borders where for weeks women,
children, and old people live in no-man's-land, in forests and on
the barges on the "international" Danube River.

We have to get out of this hell at any price, even if it means
death. Only away from it. . . .

Special transportation bureaus, founded by private persons,
speculative entrepreneurs, or Jewish organizations, are mushroom-
ing. Showing a registration card given by one of these bureaus
often protects you from arrest and deportation, but you can be
sure that the police officials don't close their eyes for nothing.
These "transportation agents" are mostly Rumanian or Greek
traders on the white-slave market. They call themselves "ship-

owners" and charge fares for which, in the good old days, one could travel first class around the world. . . .

For a year now our group was supposed to start its trip almost every week. But again and again there were not enough "victims" collected. An indescribable, terrible year; to be ready to leave from day to day, most of us now without any position or means of subsistence, without living quarters, under constant terrific pressure. Nobody knows where to turn. On the streets Jews are assaulted and mistreated, even trampled to death. Buying a little piece of bread becomes a problem because you have to cross the streets. Sometimes, there is still an Aryan who, because he disapproves of all this silently, helps us, although this is not without danger for him. . . .

Today is the day of our departure [May 16, 1940]. Mr. Anatra from Rumania, the "shipowner," apparently has received enough money at last. It was good that we had not seen the ship before, otherwise most of us would rather have committed suicide than put our feet on this ship, the *Pentcho*. A ship of 270 gross tons, to hold approximately four hundred persons at first. Most of them were young people, since the transport was organized by a Jewish agency which intended to bring young people, above all, to Palestine. It was a remodeled, eighty-five-year-old, paddle-wheel steamer. "Remodeling" meant that the ship had received a second structure designed to harbor more people, but endangering the ship's stability. It sounds incredible, but it is a fact that whenever you knocked with a hammer against the walls of the machine room, the ship sprang a leak and the water rushed in. During our trip, such leaks had to be filled frequently. Above the paddle-wheel case there was a small cabin whose floor was simply torn away by the waves in the course of the trip. Under your feet you could see the water moving. . . .

Down the Danube we went. We had been assured that for the trip on the open sea we would have another ship at our disposal; otherwise, there would have been a revolution on board. After three days, we were completely out of food supplies. After another five days, we were held up at the Hungarian-Yugoslav entrance into the Yugoslav part of the Danube. This would not have constituted the biggest problem for Mr. Anatra, but he had discovered a group of about a hundred German Jews who had been released from concentration camps on the one condition that they would leave Germany within eight days. These unfortunate people had no other choice but the *Pentcho*. Anatra sent them after us in a small river boat, and now something began, compared with which Dante's *Inferno* must have been child's play. They were mostly elderly and sick people. There was not enough sleeping place, the bunks were triple-decked and hardly thirty centimeters [about one foot] wide for each person. Sleeping was done in shifts. Thank heaven we all had very little baggage, since the police had not permitted more than a bag of fifteen kilograms for every person.

We were poorer and more miserable than the poorest beggars, although most of us had lived in comfortable circumstances and had held good social positions before. The kitchen for those five hundred people was one room, 1½ by 2 meters in size. The main meal was a soup prepared in two kettles under great difficulties; on account of the ship's rocking the kettles constantly overturned and burned the feet of the cook. Not only the meals but also the air was rationed, since no more than thirty persons were permitted on deck at a time; otherwise there was danger that the ship might keel over. The air below deck was indescribable, so thick you could have cut it with a knife. There were only two toilets for all the people aboard and we had bedbugs in uncountable millions; we found no remedy against them. Yet to keep things sanitary, we introduced a draconic routine and, although there was only one improvised shower on board, we didn't have a single case of infection or typhoid fever. God was with us on the whole trip.

One country passed us on to the other, and whenever the Danube States could not agree about us, because none of them wanted to have us, we lay in the middle of the river, once for several weeks between the Rumanian city of Guirgiu and the Bulgarian city of Rusczuk. We were able to see the restaurants on the river banks, we heard concerts from the cafés, and starved. In three languages we wrote on the outer planks of our ship the word "Hunger," but it didn't help. Many of our young people jumped into the Danube to swim ashore, but they were all brought back except one. He succeeded in escaping and, with the help of the Jews of Bulgaria, reached Palestine. Whoever left the ship was shot at. After two weeks a Bulgarian priest came to our ship in a little steamboat and brought us food, in spite of the protests of the police. Our ship had no fuel for its engine, and so Rumanian soldiers permitted us to steal wood in the forest at the river bank in return for some "baksheesh." It took us four and a half months to travel down the Danube to its mouth at Sulina. The few Rumanian sailors on board refused to participate in the sea trip and left the ship. Only the captain and his wife, both heavy morphine addicts, had to stay on board since they, too, were emigrants like us and were not permitted to go ashore. The captain's wife later died from morphine.

Warships forced the *Pentcho* to proceed into the wide-open Black Sea. Our equipment consisted of only one anchor, and we had no lifeboats, no life preservers, no radio—in fact, nothing at all. Those were terrible moments when our river boat first came into contact with the waves of the open sea. Rumanian warships escorted us until we reached Bulgarian territorial waters. We arrived in Constantinople, where they refused to give us water and bread, and we were driven on into the Aegean Sea. Now we began a wild, aimless journey among the Greek islands which lasted for weeks. The Greeks were the first who admitted us to their harbors and permitted us to buy food and to take on water. In Piraeus, the local Jews provided us generously with food and fuel. And then came the climax of our tragedy: war had broken out between England and Italy. We saw no more ships and, as we learned later, we actually sailed right through some mine fields.

Our *Pentcho* survived, as if by a miracle. Once we saw two points on the horizon, which advanced in our direction at terrific speed. At first we thought they were amphibious planes; but they turned out to be Italian PT boats which sped toward us with their torpedoes ready. At the last moment, the commander must have seen the women and children on board and concluded that we could not have been a British warship. With the threat of being torpedoed, we were forced to follow the speedboats into the harbor of the Dodecanese island of Stampalia, where our ship was thoroughly searched. The Italians were very touched when they saw our miserable condition on board the ship, and one officer told me: "Until now, I always thought we who are stationed on this island and fighting the British constantly are heroes; but now I declare the fight that you Jews are putting up is far more heroic and noble, and that is why you shall win."

Early in the morning we were escorted through the mine fields by an Italian minesweeper who directed us toward Greek territorial waters. On account of bad weather we were held up offshore from a Greek island, the penal colony Anafi, and then we proceeded in the direction of Crete. Suddenly, at one o'clock in the afternoon, came the big catastrophe. The boiler, which had been filled frequently with salt water, exploded. The engine room became flooded and the engine stopped. It was a godsend that most of the passengers did not realize the seriousness of the situation, otherwise there would have been a panic. In order that the ship might go on, all of us contributed our linen sheets, and our wives speedily sewed up some sails.

The wind was increasing slowly, and even without sails the ship began to pick up speed. Seeing the outlines of an island in the far distance, we took our course toward it, although our captain did not know, as usual, where we were. I was on the bridge until approximately 11 P.M., but then I became so deadly tired that I went below deck where I fell asleep on my cot instantly. The people aboard were quiet. We had told them that we would anchor near the island and repair the damage there. However, I must have anticipated that something would happen, for I told my wife to lie down but to keep her air cushion inflated and ready. Around 1 A.M. I was awakened by a terrific noise. It was as if the ship was jumping from one rock to another. The sleeping quarters were empty and outside a heavy storm was blowing. The captain had tried to lower the anchor, with the effect that the only chain had broken like a piece of thread. The ship was thrown against the rocks with terrible force. Our only salvation was the ship's paddle wheels which were jammed between the rocks. A few yards more, and our running aground would have meant death to many of us.

While the ship continued to bump against the rocky coast, we were able to bring women and children ashore, or rather, on the gigantic rocks. All this took place in utter darkness, with a few flashlights providing the only illumination. Everybody remained lying just where he stumbled. Then we brought some food supplies ashore, as much as we could still lay hands on, because most of the ship was already filled with water. The drinking water tanks of the ship were also flooded with sea water so that we could not bring any drinking water ashore.

Thus we waited for morning to come. It was a small, uninhabited rock island, no animals, no birds, no plants, and no water. We spent eleven days on this island; the *Pentcho* itself had broken into several parts after two days and disappeared in the sea. We had almost a feeling of relief, remembering the bedbugs and the lack of air from which we had suffered for so long. On the first day we all really believed that the island was tottering. We hadn't touched land for five and a half months.

The name of the island was Camilloni; it belonged to the Italian Dodecanese. There, too, we organized our life. In one of the rocky grottoes we found some water which fortunately was not so salty. We painted large SOS signs on linen. We dropped bottles with messages into the sea, and we burned large fires at night. We had saved some heavy fuel from the *Pentcho* wreck. Four men went out on a mad adventure, trying to reach Crete, approximately sixty miles away, in our only rowboat. They did not succeed, of course, and after two weeks a British warship fished them out of the sea, more dead than alive, and brought them to Alexandria, where they spent six months in a hospital. . . .

After eleven days had passed, Italian warships rescued us from the island in two successive nights and brought us to Rhodes, where we spent the next year and a half in a concentration camp. We spent the Day of Atonement on this island, and all five hundred of us fasted that day with full hearts.

Rhodes—a year and a half of hunger, hunger, hunger. The island was under blockade, and for a solid year not a single ship arrived from Italy or from nearby Turkey. Forty grams of macaroni or beans were rationed to each person per day, 150 grams of bread, and many undefinable green leaves. The small Jewish community gave us one lire per day per person, [which was] one cent in American money. The first two months we spent in tents. November and December are the rainy season on Rhodes, and we were literally lying in water. Now, we got our first epidemic—dysentery —and many of our good friends died within a few days. Whatever we still had in gold or watches was spent for the little food which we were able to buy from our Fascist guards secretly for fantastic prices. In the concentration camps Greeks were imprisoned together with us. In January 1941 we were transferred to a military barracks which was dry at least.

During our stay we lived through approximately a hundred British air raids. The planes came with such punctuality, frequently several times a night, that we would set our watches by their arrival. The Italian soldiers went into the air raid shelters, but we had to stay in the barracks. Once we were thrown off our cots by the air pressure caused by an exploding bomb. It is strange we never felt panic or fear. Even more, we actually missed the attacks when the planes did not come. We almost enjoyed watching the fires and explosions from our barracks, which were located on a hill; each air attack was a symbol to us, as if the hour of our liberation had arrived and we now could say to our guards, "See, these are our friends. Soon they will be here to rescue us."

Four men intended to flee from Rhodes, this time to nearby Turkey. Leaving the camp at night, they succeeded in getting away in spite of the coastal guards. They tried to man a boat and row out onto the sea, but their attempt ended in tragedy. The boat had been ashore for months and completely dried out, so that after a few hundred yards it was flooded by water. Two young men drowned; the other two were able to rescue themselves by swimming. They were sentenced to one year imprisonment, charged with "stealing" a boat and leaving the island without permission. They spent this year in a prison camp, not caring much whether they were there or in our concentration camp. Neither of the bodies of the two who were drowned, nor the boat, was ever found.

Finally, the Italians no longer knew what to do with us on Rhodes, and so they sent us in two groups of 250 persons each to Italy, where we were again put into a concentration camp—this time, Ferramonti. The "masters of mare nostrum" needed no less than four weeks to bring the ship from Rhodes to Bari. It was our third war voyage, and we thanked heaven that the British did not send our ship to the bottom of the sea. On our voyage we saw in many ports how the British had wrecked Italian ships, to say nothing of those ships which we could not see, because they had disappeared in the bottom of the sea.

From Mannheim

JACOB KAHN

When, in the autumn of 1940, the first series of the fiendish deportations of Jews and the poor Jews of Mannheim without any exception, even people ninety years of age and mothers who but a few hours before had given birth to children, were assembled like cattle at the station to be deported to the south of France, I felt sure that a similar fate would befall all German Jews sooner or later. I set to work to get away from the fatherland at the earliest moment, no matter where. I had had my name registered at the American consulate at Stuttgart, but my waiting number was so high that my prospects of being called at an early date were next to nil. I therefore decided to try to get to Shanghai and from there to America in due course. But just in those days no more permits were issued by the Shanghai authorities, and following the advice of the Jewish committee set up to facilitate emigration, I got a visa for a Central American republic (Honduras) against payment of a considerable sum. This should enable me to travel "via Shanghai," my intention being, of course, to stay there until I could continue my journey to the United States of America. Before getting the above-mentioned visa, I had naturally to obtain my German passport. My application was at once communicated to the Gestapo and shortly afterward there came a post card from the chief of the Gestapo asking me to present myself that very day at three o'clock at their offices. I must confess that this invitation was received by me with mixed feelings, because in most cases to be cited before the Gestapo meant at least to be detained for some time. Having no other choice, however, I went and presented the invitation card at the entrance to an official who took it, looked at it, yet again asked my name. When I had given it, he wished to know my Christian name, though both appeared quite clearly on the post card I had handed him.

Thinking that he only wanted to make quite sure that I was the man required to present himself, I repeated them, omitting, however, the most important part of my name, that is, the additional name, Israel, which by law every male Jew has to bear. The consequences of this heinous offense I had thus committed were at once made clear to me. The enraged official went for me, abused me as I have never been in my life, and moreover telephoned at once to his superior, informing him of this awful omission. When I came to this official things looked consequently very black for me. I should almost certainly have been sent to a concentration camp had not, very, very fortunately for me, just at this very moment, the Chief Rabbi of our city entered. He was, strange to say, very much respected by the Gestapo and, rightly so, everywhere else by the way. He at once grasped the situation and owing to his pleading I got off with a severe warning after having been given an opportunity—owing to the rabbi's intervention only —of explaining how the misunderstanding had arisen. I was then questioned [concerning] at what date I would leave Germany, since I had applied for a passport. On my stating, "As soon as possible," they gave me one month to do so. In the days that followed I wrote, telephoned, telegraphed incessantly to all sorts of committees, authorities, and agencies in order to get the documents, etc., which were necessary and I was promised every assistance, particularly by the Jewish committee for emigration. It would take up too much space if I were to enumerate all the obstacles I had to encounter. Manchukuo and Japan suddenly stopped giving transit visas, whereas the Russians who—as I was told—had agreed to a special train to Vladivostok "within a few days" did not stick to their promise. So the month elapsed without my having been able to get away. I had, however, got together the great number of documents from the customs department, the exchange authorities, the police, etc., etc., all of which were to be handed over before the definite permission to leave Germany was given by the passport department.

Punctually, I was cited again before the Gestapo on the expiration of that month and after a rather lengthy interrogation and pleading they extended the limit they had given me by yet another month. I had proved satisfactorily that I had done all I could do to get away by showing them originals of telegrams and letters I had received and submitting the above documents and letters to them. I was told, however, that the inevitable consequence of my not leaving within the time would be the concentration camp. They warned me, moreover, not to tell abroad any fairy tales about their "alleged" cruelties (*Greuelmärchen*), as they had their agents in every country and their arms were long enough to reach me anywhere in the world. Emigration to Shanghai seeming, and as a matter of fact being, impossible, there remained only one country to go to, Yugoslavia. The permission to go there I obtained as far as the Germans were concerned, but it was impossible for a German Jew to get a "visum" from the Yugoslav consulate. But "unofficial" immigration to Yugoslavia on a large scale and organized by a man, S., in Graz was then taking place, who, against payment of a considerable sum, had brought many thousands of Jews across the frontier. To him I was sent by one of the committees set up to help the Jews in acute danger. I dare say the story of the trafficker in "human bodies," who did a lot of good though he did it for the mere sake of earning a fortune, will be written some day after this war. It will be an interesting story forsooth. He was on the best of terms with the local Gestapo, who quite evidently were his "partners" in his lucrative business. I was, by the way, one of the last he had helped to cross the frontier, because shortly afterward he was arrested for quite a lot of violations of all sorts of laws. For some of these offenses he could have been condemned to death, but he got off with about six months' imprisonment and a fine—if I remember rightly—of about seven million marks. All this shows that he must have had helpers in very influential quarters. But to return to my narrative: When I got to Graz I found a large number of people of all sorts huddled up in a small back room, some of them clad in furs. They had just arrived from Berlin, Hamburg, or Vienna by airplane.

We were in that room two days; as it was suggested to us that going out might endanger us, very few of us went out into the town.

Still more fellow sufferers, among them two ladies of over eighty years, arrived, and we were transferred one night to a so-called farm, in reality an unused cowshed, on the outskirts of Graz. After a week's stay there, packed like sardines, we set out on our journey one morning at four o'clock, accompanied by several friendly Gestapo so that people should think that we were placed under arrest. After a journey, first by rail, carefully distributed in many wagons, and then in motor lorries, we eventually arrived three hours later in a village near the frontier where we were received by yet another set of Gestapo officials, who, after some hand-shaking with our guide, i.e., the man, S., did not take any further notice of us, except that they took us to the customhouse, where a close examination of our persons and our luggage should have taken place. Everything had been so arranged that we arrived there after office hours and the inspection, if this is the right word to use, was performed by two male and two female officials, all most certainly in league with our guide and the Gestapo. In reality we were not examined at all. They merely asked me, e.g., whether I had any gold, foreign exchange, or other valuables with me, which I truthfully denied. But they were satisfied in every case. Some people were careless enough, to use a mild expression, to endanger all of us by taking these forbidden things with them. Toward evening our march began. After three hours' walk we arrived at a large farm, half frozen, where the greater number of us stayed. But there was not room for all of us. So we had to walk on for yet another hour, higher up in the Alps to another farm. In the meantime a blizzard set in which lasted several days and which caused much suffering among us. The ordeal was all the greater, as the place we stayed in was indescribably dirty. I had never seen such a filthy place before, which lacked even the most elementary or primitive requirements. I felt such a disgust that I was absolutely unable to touch any food except boiled potatoes, or a little milk—but only when it was taken from the cow in my presence and when it was put into an aluminum pot which, luckily, I had in my handbag.

What a relief for me when we started eight days later on our first attempt to cross the frontier. At twelve o'clock on an icy February night we left at last, shivering yet glad to get out of our den. Our guide and his delegate or lieutenant arrived on the scene with four or five Gestapo men, bribed to protect us against any eventual interference from other official or officious sources. They accompanied us right up in the mountains to the actual frontier, one of them even carrying my handbag for me, which was much too heavy. Before they departed they gave us some instructions in case we should not succeed in getting to our destination. They told us to ask for Mr. this or that in case we should have the ill luck to have to return to the German side. We subsequently had to climb up again shortly afterward. The ways were so slippery that we fell down continually on the ice-covered ground. Now and then we had to cross a stream, which caused us to get wet feet, which subsequently were frostbitten. No one was allowed to speak, of course. Thus we marched on for almost thirteen hours, resting sometimes for five or ten minutes. I was more dead than alive; in any case I was, and most of us were, completely exhausted when at last we reached a river. If I remember right, it was the Sava. Upon a signal a ferryman came noiselessly across to ferry us in batches of about ten persons at a time. Though we were unspeakably tired we had to walk on, until suddenly we were stopped by what proved to be Yugoslav soldiers, who had completely surrounded us. We had been given away by some rival or enemy of our guide, who was put in fetters, whereas all others were marched off to some building, fortunately but one-half hour distant, which eventually proved to be a sort of prison. I then was indifferent to everything. The only thing I wanted was to sleep, sleep, sleep. I never before or after slept so deeply. We were treated very well. The Yugoslavs fed us well, gave the men cigarettes and wine, and candies and chocolates to the women. After a brief interrogation we had to march back to the German side of the frontier accompanied of course by a detachment of soldiers who, just like their superiors, evinced great sympathy for us but who had to obey orders. This time it took us but five or six hours to reach the frontier, as we could use the highway. Much depressed, yet not entirely downhearted, we returned to our den which we had hoped never to see again.

I went to sleep again immediately, though not quite so deeply as before. About a week afterwards we started afresh by another route, which proved to be more treacherous and fatiguing still than its predecessor. This time we marched on for about six hours until on the slippery ice several people fell, spraining their ankles or, in one case, breaking several fingers, or hurting themselves in some other fashion [so] that it was impossible to walk on, especially as so many of us declined to go on climbing on the ice- and snow-covered brink of a precipice. The third attempt took place—minus some of the injured persons—five days afterwards by yet another way. After great sufferings, most of us being frostbitten and completely exhausted, we reached—after about ten hours' Alpine climbing and descending—a point where motor lorries were waiting for us. In order to hide us, blankets were put on top of us, and all went well until we reached the city of Maribor, where, owing to some congestion of traffic, we were compelled to pull up. There, unfortunately, our vehicles somehow roused the suspicions of a policeman, with the inevitable result that we were discovered, brought before the chief of the police, and finally escorted back once more to the German frontier. It was quite evident that this time, too, the police felt sorry for us. For a little while it seemed to me and even to others that we should . . . be allowed to continue our journey. In any case I think that the chief of the police would have done so if it had not been for the fear lest some of his subordinates might talk. He offered us food, wine, and cigarettes and caused some motor vehicles to take us back to a spot near the frontier. There we were received just as before—I had forgotten to tell that—by some people who in some mysterious way had been informed of our mishap and who conducted us once more to our old dirty lodgings. When we had been on our way for about five weeks in all, yet another expedition ended similarly; after long and wearisome climbing up and down, we were caught once more, exhausted, and escorted back this time with fixed bayonets under the command of an officer who seemed not so well disposed toward us.

The next attempt was made a few days later, although many of us had declared [we would not] . . . try it again. This time we had a guide who proved to be most experienced and resourceful. He had got in touch with some Yugoslav soldiers, who kept military vehicles at our disposal, two lorries and two large private cars.

These we succeeded in reaching after a terrible march through sleet and a snowstorm. I was trembling all over, so exhausted was I, and most others too could not have walked on any more. Those like myself who had to get into the lorries were entirely covered up with oilcloth; some light cases and chairs and I don't know what else were put on top of us. We were nearly suffocated. The ladies began to weep, thinking it impossible to hold out. But they did and when we arrived after a few hours in a suburb of Zagreb, our destination, most of them were in a state of collapse, from which they recovered, however, in a remarkably short period. . . . We were helped to find lodgings, in many cases of the most inferior type, it is true, and expensive into the bargain, especially for us who had been allowed to take with us ten marks (about four dollars in all according to the official quotation at the German exchanges, but in reality probably worth about two dollars). I may mention, by the way, that the occupants of the private military cars which I spoke of never arrived and were never heard of again. How we had envied them and how deeply we pitied them now. I was rather fortunate as I found a letter waiting for me . . . upon my arrival. My brother who had emigrated to Yugoslavia some time before me and who got across the frontier right away had left a letter for me saying that he had retained for me good lodgings. I had written to him previous to my emigration that I, too, was starting after all for Yugoslavia and he had expected me and waited for me all those weeks, but as I did not show up, had left Zagreb with its perils for illegal immigrants for some camp (which with the open or veiled consent of the Government had been set up for some cases) just two days before my arrival.

Another rather agreeable surprise for me was the fact that my luggage had arrived, untampered besides, whereas many of my associates had found their trunks broken open and empty or at least partially robbed of their contents. A lady, a relative of mine, had, e.g., been robbed of almost all her clothing, her shoes, etc. Being illegal immigrants we could, of course, make no claims for compensation. We had to be most cautious and careful, all the more because none of us was able to speak the Yugoslav language. I hardly dared to go out and I most carefully avoided restaurants because I had been told [to do so] by my landlady. . . . As I found out later, she did this in order to keep me in a constant state of fear and to show why she was entitled to ask so high a rent. She always spoke of the risk she was incurring by harboring me and she kept on increasing the price. But I had to make the best of a bad job and as the sword of Damocles hung over me, the illegal immigrant, I had to grin and bear it. Yet it was a good thing I stayed there, because most of the cheaper lodgings were raided one day, their occupants arrested and probably sent back to Germany. I was in Zagreb about a fortnight, when one Sunday morning some acquaintances of mine rushed into my room, telling me that Germany had declared war on Yugoslavia and that Belgrade had been heavily bombarded. What a shock to me from a personal point of view as well as from a general standpoint! What would happen next? Zagreb was soon occupied and from one day to another all foodstuffs disappeared as though locusts had eaten up everything. The German soldiery crowded all the shops and bought up everything almost indiscriminately. Gestapo men and all the other various Nazi formations cropped up everywhere and it was not long before the first anti-Jewish measures were taken. Space forbids to enumerate all of them.

I will mention only one which was typical: all Jews were ordered to wear both in front and at the back a yellow piece of cloth (about the size of this page) with the Star of David and a Z (abbreviation for *Zidov*—Jew) on it. Now a strange thing happened. Many Jews put this distinctive sign proudly on, which was meant to shame and to disgrace them, whereas the population either evinced their horror or their sympathy with the Jews. No Jew was, as far as I could see, derided or molested by their non-Jewish co-citizens. But I saw on two occasions men rushing up to a Jew, who was decorated, and kissing them on both cheeks. These sympathizers were Serbs, I was told. Even babies in their cradles had to have the yellow rag pinned on. The whole thing proved such a failure from a propagandistic point of view that soon afterwards the yellow rag was replaced by a kind of yellow medal of the size of a dollar to be worn on the chest. When I read the proclamation about the yellow badge I found that exceptions were made in the case of Hungarian and some other categories of Jews and, having a kind of presentiment that, at some future date, there might be some peril for those wearing the badge, I took the bull by both horns and went to the German consulate thinking it immaterial whether I would be devoured by the German Scylla or the Croatian Charybdis. But a great surprise waited for me. I was admitted to the German consul, who was very nice toward me and said to me that he saw no reason why the German Jews should wear the badge, after I had drawn his attention to the fact that Jewish subjects of some other nationalities were exempt. He, moreover, told me that as German subjects we were under the protection of his consulate and it was quite evident that he was well disposed towards the Jews, an attitude which eventually led to his dismissal. Later on, acting under instructions from superior quarters, he had to advise other inquirers to wear "that thing" (so he called it), but I and some friends of mine never wore it. Fortunately, because on a Saturday, when many people, among them a lot of Jews, were out of doors, the latter who were wearing the badge were surrounded by hundreds of agents in plain clothes, put into cars, lorries, etc., etc., and subsequently sent to a concentration camp.

There were thousands of them. Husbands were thus torn away from their wives, wives from their husbands, children from both of them, in most cases never to see each other again. Many committed suicide, others died from shock or starvation soon afterwards, others on their journey to the concentration camp. I remember the case of one dear old lady whose husband had been arrested on his way to the doctor. After waiting for his return in vain for many hours and on hearing of the numerous arrests she sent her only son with some blankets and food to the jail where his father was reported to be. But there they retained the son as well and she never saw either of them again. On another occasion a bomb was thrown (in the university, I think). On the next morning a proclamation was issued that a great number of Jews whose names were given—mostly intellectuals, professors, doctors, lawyers, judges, consulting engineers, scientists, etc., who had been arrested long before the attempt—had been executed as a deterrent. Most of them were well known and highly respected persons who had never had anything to do with politics. Their only crime was their Jewish descent. The police now began to come to the houses to arrest the Jews. Life began to be a hell on earth. I got notice by my landlady to leave and only after many exciting and anxious days I succeeded in finding another room. Fortunately I had obtained the address of a lawyer, well connected with the police, who procured for myself and some friends of mine permits to stay for a month, with the possibility of monthly renewals. As a matter of fact those permits were always renewed, in my case at least. Though probably the costs, i.e., the lawyer's bills, were not too high I had to sell some of my belongings to defray them. For a little while I breathed more freely, yet I began to think of leaving that inferno. But where could I find a place of comparative safety? The only country not yet under the Teuton heel was—in spite of its anti-Jewish laws—Fascist Italy. But how to get there?

By some chance (or, as it turned out to be, later on, mischance) I had made the acquaintance of a man who was well connected with the police. He seemed to be a kind of secret agent or something like it and he had some connection with the Germans, too. I had been introduced to him by a refugee whom I had done some favor and who had been helped by the above-mentioned man, too. The latter I consulted now and then about the advisability of our staying in Zagreb or not, and for some time he said that we were quite safe. One day, however, he changed his mind and he advised us to leave for the Dalmatian town of Sebenico, then under the Italian rule. He offered his services for obtaining permits for myself and my friends against payment of considerable sums. I obtained the amount required by selling lots of things on his promising to have everything ready within a week. I thereupon gave notice to my landlady for the end of the month (i.e., about three weeks later). But when that date came I had neither the permit nor did I have a room. I was put off by the man L. from day to day, from week to week. I considered myself very fortunate when after prolonged searching I found at last a room at a Jewish lady's, paying a month's rent in advance. It turned out to be a blessing that she had insisted on it. For I had hardly come to her house, when the lady became very nervous because some Jews had been arrested and their belongings taken away in neighboring houses. She therefore hurriedly sublet her apartment to a man who turned out to be one of the Poglavnik's (Croatia's dictator's) chauffeurs, who, being glad to find decent lodgings, paid her quite well for it, instead of sequestrating it or taking it away from her as he probably might have done with impunity and as actually had been done in a number of cases. At first he wanted me to leave on account of my being Jewish. But on my explaining to him that I had paid my rent beforehand and on my former landlady's paying him the amount I had handed over to her, he agreed to my remaining until the expiration of the month.

After a few days when I had had a few talks with him, he took a liking to me. He confessed never having met a Jew to speak to and that he began to see that they were being wronged. So friendly did he finally become that he brought me every day wine, butter—a rare object there—grapes, chocolate, and many other things worth much more than the rent I had paid. And when, one day I informed him of my intention of going to Italy, he tried to dissuade me from it, asserting that I was quite safe with him, where nobody suspected a Jew to live. The reprisals against the Jews increasing, I felt that it was high time to get away. As my plans regarding Sebenico did not seem to materialize, I went to the Italian consulate to try to get a regular visa for Italy, though I was almost convinced beforehand that I would not succeed. They told me, however, there that there was some prospect, provided I brought a recommendation from the German consulate. What seemed to me incredible and impossible happened. I got it. I still hold a photo-copy of this document in which the German consulate asks the Italian authorities to grant us the permission to go to Italy. Yet the Italian consulate refused to accept my application form when they saw that the item "race" was filled out with "non-Aryan." Being determined to go away, I saw only one possibility, i.e., to get across the Italian frontier without a visa and leave everything to chance. As many were in the same predicament as myself, several organizations of persons had set up who undertook against considerable payment to conduct persons to Italy, especially to Lubiana. Selling some more of my belongings, I succeeded in raising the amount I needed. I took with me, I am glad to say, two others who had nothing and paid for them as well. In vain I tried to have my money refunded by the man L., who had so definitely promised to get me through to Sebenico. So one day we started first by train and then walking through some woods until we were held up by a Croatian frontier patrol, who asked us to hand over our hand luggage to them. This we refused to do, and they then asked us for ten thousand krunas (dinars). Again we refused point blank. As a matter of fact we did not own such a sum. Thereupon, we were brought to some frontier police station.

Things looked rather black for us, though we had regular permits of the Croatian Government to emigrate. Fortunately I had a document with me, issued by the friendly German consul, in which all Croatian authorities were requested to respect my property. And so we were finally, after lengthy discussions, and a tip of about a hundred krunas, allowed to go. As it had become dark in the meanwhile, we had to stay overnight with some peasants, who received us quite hospitably. On the next morning we left at dawn, were ferried across a little river, and then handed over by the man who had hitherto conducted us, to some young people who were to act as guides up to the next railroad station, which was situated on Italian soil. When we had walked on for about an hour through some woods our guides suddenly stopped and demanded from each of us an additional payment, which was about twice as much as we had already paid to the man who had undertaken to get us across to Lubiana, the sum we paid to include everything. We did not have that much money, as a matter of fact, but had we possessed it, we should not have paid it either. Upon our refusal our guides became impudent, abused us, and finally threatened to give us away to the Italian frontier police. We, thereupon, decided to return rather than go along under such circumstances. When the fellows saw that we were in earnest they changed tactics. They began to ask what we were willing to pay. I may add that we were five persons in all. We declared that we had made full payment, from which they had received their full share. After some lengthy discussion and haggling [we] agreed to pay about one-tenth of what they had demanded: one-half to be handed over at once, the other half upon our arrival at the station. Just in that moment a couple arrived on the scene who spoke broken German. We told them what had happened to us. They told us they had some business to do in a nearby village on Croatian soil. We should wait for them an hour or two; they would come with us then, since they lived in Lubiana.

We were suspicious, however, about their intentions and told them we should rather walk on to the station in order to be sure to catch the next train; we should meet them at the station upon their return. We went along with our guides, were ferried over what appeared to be a large pond, but what was really some river, when in the middle suddenly our boat was filled with water so that we got soaked but we managed to come across. I may add that in another party on the very next day one of two brothers was drowned on the very same spot in consequence of the boat's going down midstream. (The tragic story of those brothers would fill a book if it were told.) We duly arrived near the station and paid the guides the money they had extorted from us. They had, however, the good sense to recommend us not to wait at the station itself, but rather go to an adjoining house where a Slovenian schoolmaster lived. We found there a friendly reception. They brought us something to eat and to drink and we remained until about the time the train was due. They even accompanied us, ready to affirm if it should have proved necessary that we were their relations. The couple we had met had turned up in the meantime. They were Slovenes, too, and eventually proved to be very good and generous people who, though they were poor, did all they could to assist us. Our suspicions had been absolutely unfounded. They took our tickets and our party of five divided itself in three groups so as not to rouse the suspicion of the carabinieri (military police) who were walking up and down this station so near the frontier. All went well this time. When one of the carabinieri came near me, one moment the Slovenian man, who was known to that particular official, talked to me in his own language (which the carabinieri understood as little as I did), as though I were a relation or friend of his. And so we finally arrived in a suburb of Lubiana. We thought it safer to get out there than at the central station.

The Slovenian couple being fully aware of our plight invited us so cordially to their little cottage that we could not resist. They had quite a tiny cottage, put their own bedroom and that of their sons at our disposal with fresh linen, etc., and made it as comfortable as they could. We afterward found out, to our regret, that they slept in the attic on some straw. The man was but a humble railroadman, but he and his family had hearts of gold. I shall always include them in my prayers. They refused any payment and all I could do was to leave a parcel with some undergarments secretly with the old grandmother, who promised to hand it over when we were gone. Not intending to abuse these good people's hospitality or to sponge upon them, we went after a day to town, presented ourselves at the Red Cross, which in those days had established a special shelter for refugees. We were given some cards for meals after being registered and told to go to an old sugar factory, where beds had been put up. There were already some hundreds of refugees there, the rooms were so crowded, the air so stifling, that I and my companions decided to look for some private lodgings. I was fortunate enough to find a room after a prolonged search in the house of a policeman. The price was rather high and I had only forty lire (40 cents) in my pocket, after having paid the rent. I paid it in advance, though not asked to do so, in order to be sure to be able to retain this room for a month. With a sigh of relief I brought my hand luggage then from the railwayman's house, where I had left it. My larger trunks had in the meantime arrived as well, to my great surprise, and I got them handed over at the customhouse without any formalities. The firm of carriers in Zagreb that had undertaken the forwarding had not held out much hope that they would arrive safely or even arrive at all in Lubiana, so that I had reckoned half and half with the loss of my belongings.

In no case had I expected to get my things so soon. The sugar factory being the emigrants' center, I called there every day to learn what was going on. When I came there a few days afterward I was told that police agents had been there asking about twenty people who had arrived in the last few days to present themselves at the *questura* (police station). The Red Cross always transmitted the names of the recent arrivals to the police authorities. My name was included in the list, which, by the way, had to be signed by every individual asked to present himself. Since I had not done so I expressed the opinion that for the time being there was no cause to go. The man in charge of the emigrants who lived in the factory thought I had better go, saying that all was but a formality and that he "guaranteed" that nothing disagreeable would happen. And he succeeded in persuading me and two of my companions to come with him the next morning. I shall never forget our walk to the police station on that bleak morning. It was October 31 and it snowed ever so hard. From nine to ten we waited and then one after the other went in to the *questor* (chief of police) and I began to be fidgety when by eleven o'clock none had come out again. Finally at eleven-thirty one of them came out saying, "We shall all be detained." Upon hearing this we three walked or rather ran out as fast as we could, though the man who had guaranteed that nothing would happen to us called out to us to stay. It was probably no bad intention on his part, only stupidity, when he said to the policeman in charge that there were three more, though I had given signs to "shut up." We were rather upset, of course, and the next day or two always went out very early in the morning and came home late at night so as not to be at home should the police call. The cold days we spent in the streets or in libraries or in churches.

The meals (two cents cash) we took in a large restaurant, run, I think, by the Red Cross. Only once did we go into a cafe where I spent one lire (one cent) each on a cup of coffee to get a bit warm and to read the papers. When I got home the third evening, my landlord knocked at my door, saying that police agents had called requesting me to appear next morning at the station. What I had feared all along had come through. I besought my landlord to come with me and to put a good word in for me, to which he agreed. When I reported next morning the *questor* was not there and I was told to come back in the afternoon. A little respite I thought. I may add that I had taken a handbag with the most necessary things and some edibles with me in case I should have to go to prison. When I returned in the afternoon the *questor* had not yet come, but his representative wrote out a warrant for my arrest. I pleaded to be allowed to go home, stressing the fact that I was staying with a member of the police force who (as they remembered at the station) had testified as to my respectability and I succeeded in the end in persuading them to let me go, promising to put in an appearance next morning at ten o'clock. This I did, once more taking my things with me in readiness for the prison. I was brought before the *questor,* who asked me by which way and which means I had come to Italy. I told him frankly the circumstances and appealed to him to take a humane "attitude" in accordance with the noble Italian tradition. I particularly begged him not to send me back to Croatia as was usually done in such like cases and as was done with the others who had been detained. I visibly made an impression on him, especially since I was able to express myself in Italian. " I won't send you back to Croatia," he replied finally, "I shall send you to Germany, where you were born." I knew he did not mean it in earnest and I said, "I should prefer to be shot there and then." . . .

From Belgrade

ALEXANDER GRIN

I left Belgrade before the war started in Yugoslavia. It was March 31, 1941. The war started April 6. The revolution had taken place March 27 in Belgrade. Prince Paul, the regent, was fired and King Peter came into his majority. As a minor, King Peter had a regency of three members; the president of the regency was Prince Paul. Paul worked with the Germans; it was he who signed the pact with the Axis. Peter broke the agreement when he came into his majority. With the revolution of March 27, the Government of Prince Paul and the old regency fell.

It was clear that there would be war against us. Our people were more than 90 percent against the Germans. The Germans had a tourist office which was an out and out propaganda office. All the documents were there on file against the personalities who were friendly with the Allies.

Two big things happened in Yugoslavia on March 27 and 28. On March 27 a crowd broke into the tourist office, took all the papers and pictures of Hitler, and made a bonfire in the middle of the street and burned everything.

The next day, March 28, Peter was crowned King in the church. All the ambassadors were present, the German Ambassador, Von Herren, too. As he went out of the church after the coronation, the people broke into the auto and spat in the Ambassador's face.

By March 30, it was certain that war would come with the Germans. On March 31 I left Belgrade for Dubrovnik on the Adriatic coast. It is a beautiful city—many Americans had been there as guests. I [remained] . . . in Dubrovnik until May 19, the day when the Government of Italy made a pact with Poglavnik (Duce) Pavelich, the Yugoslav Fascist, in the name of the independent state of Croatia.

Dubrovnik was the capital of the new Croatian state. I was with my family at that moment in a restaurant. I heard this news by radio. I immediately took a car—put my luggage in it and fled. I was just as afraid of the Croatians as of the Germans. I was afraid of the Ustashi, the Yugoslav Fascists. I fled to Hertzeg Novi in the Gulf—one of the biggest gulfs in the Adriatic, south of Dubrovnik. It was a big military harbor. We fled there because we knew it would remain under Italian occupation, not Croatian. In the past, Hertzeg Novi and the whole region south of it were given to Italy. The people were mostly Serbians.

We remained there from May 19 to July 22, 1941. The night of July 22 the Italian carabinieri encircled the hotel where we were. They arrested all the Yugoslav Jews in the hotel. My boy was three years old then. It was nighttime. We had to awaken him. They brought us in trucks to a school where we remained until the afternoon of July 23. There were about 190 people from many hotels, and so forth. They took all our money—we could keep only five hundred lire, five dollars, at the official rate of exchange. It was the Italians who did it.

Then they took us to the vicinity of Cataro in a Yugoslav ship called *King Alexander*. It was a luxury ship, but it was dismantled and nothing worked. The toilets and the plumbing had all been stopped. We had to sleep on the floor of the cabins. It was no longer luxury.

The next day we were transferred to another ship, *Kora* or *Kumanovo,* named after a city in Yugoslavia. All of us had our cabins on this ship. We remained four days; something was wrong with the ship. They repaired the machines. July 26 we left for Durazzo, the biggest harbor in Albania.

We were all prisoners, suspected as Jews, as Yugoslavs, suspected of having financed the revolution. It had broken out in Montenegro two or three days before; it was the first revolution in Yugoslavia. The twenty-seventh of July they took us in cars to the concentration camp of Cavaia in Albania. It was the most terrible camp I have ever heard of. We were in one room, men, women, children, sick people, all together. We slept on wooden slats—no mattresses. It was full of insects. Thousands of fleas and bedbugs. In the morning when we awakened we were full of red sores. No windows. It was open where there should have been doors and windows.

We remained there for three months. After that, we left from Durazzo for Bari in a transport ship with Italian soldiers. Our wives and children had cabins first and second class. We men had a salon in the first and second class. The soldiers had third class decks. It was a short trip; it took only one day.

In Bari they disinfected us, bathed us, disinfected our clothes. That was October 24 and 25, 1941. We remained in Bari one or two days. The Italians brought us to the concentration camp at Ferramonti. Italy had entered the war on June 10, 1940, against France. That was the stab in the back.

We stayed in Ferramonti until June 15, 1942. The circumstances in Ferramonti were different for the people who had money and for those who had none. I was among the unfortunate people who had no money. We had nothing with which to get clothes and food. We got some food from the Government, especially for the children, so they would not suffer. My boy had no milk for months and months, and very little bread. The people who had money could buy anything on the black market. Italian agents sold everything. There was big corruption. The Italian director of the camp got jewels from our people to give them liberation. He wanted gold coin all the time. We called him a numismatist—an old-coin collector. But of course he wanted new coins.

Then, because of my rheumatism (I have arthritis, with a stiffness of the hand) and because the climate in Ferramonti is very damp, with much rain, I couldn't stay there. After eight months, I got into free confinement, *libero confino,* in the province of Pezaro. It is a city on the sea. We were in Pran di Milito, a village of five hundred inhabitants. Then we transferred to Urbino. We were there until September 1943. I got eight lire a day, eight cents per man. My wife got five lire, my boy got three lire, sixteen cents daily for the family. We got 150 lire a month for rent. The Italian government of the village gave it to us. Every day we had to go to the police station of the caribinieri to present ourselves. I and my wife—we had numbers—we just gave those numbers to the police.

We had a great deal of trouble with the police secretary of the Fascist Party. He was very hostile. He wanted to do everything to make our condition worse. We bought our food from the Italian people and they were good to us. On the sixth of September I was transferred to Pezaro. September 10 I left Urbino for Pezaro. In Pezaro we had to go to the police station too every day. We remained there until the end of November 1943. We were still in *libero confino*. Then I heard that they were gathering together the Jews to put them into a concentration camp and deport them to Poland. Because my father was an Ashkenazi Jewish rabbi in Yugoslavia, the Fascists deported my father and sister to Poland. The Ustashi killed my brother-in-law.

The most famous concentration camp in Croatia was Jussenowac. In three years, out of 50,000 men, there remained 1,500. They had killed all the others.

When we heard this thing, I tried to escape. I got a false Italian identification card for my wife and myself, saying I was an Italian Aryan. In a truck which brought chickens to Rome, I escaped on November 27, 1943, without my wife and boy. I didn't know if they could find me. . . .

From Brussels

SAMUEL SILVERMAN

I came from Tarnow, Poland. In 1928 I left Poland and went to Belgium where I worked as a furrier. In 1940, when the Germans came to Belgium, all the Jews—there were about eighty thousand —began to flee. Part of them went to France, part to the Belgian coast. For two days there was a panic. Many Jews left their baggage and everything else they owned and escaped to France by way of Dunkerque. They heard that the Germans were marching quickly through Belgium.

We had two small children, a two-year-old girl and a four-year-old boy. When we came to Boulogne on the French coast, we met thousands of Jews who had fled there. We went on by foot from Boulogne for fifteen kilometers. There the people told us that the road was already closed by the Germans.

We were cut off. Ninety percent of us were from Belgium; the rest were French people from Dunkerque, Calais, and Boulogne. When the Germans came to Boulogne, my wife, my two children, and I ran into a cellar. We were three days without food and water. The children drank wine brought us by Belgian soldiers who were also trying to escape to southern France. After three days the soldiers told us, "You can come out—the Germans are here." I looked out. There were the German soldiers and the German tanks. German officers stood up in the tanks and looked around into all the corners with binoculars. Other soldiers stood in the cars holding machine guns.

The Germans told the Belgian soldiers to go home, "Belgium

is free." The Germans believed that when Germany had conquered it, that meant it was free. They even said, "Jews, go home.
Belgium is free."

We had left Belgium with my brother and sister and their
children. In the flight we lost them. Now we began to go back
to Brussels alone on foot. The Germans had told us to go, but
now they put up placards. "It is *verboten* to go to Belgium." They
advised the refugees to go to the villages and stay there for a few
days, until they would be allowed to go home. I was in one of the
villages with my children for fourteen days. At first we had enough
to eat, but we slept badly on straw. The English and French were
not coming back, and we could not get through France.

We didn't know where to go. The only thing to do was to go
back. We thought, the Germans have achieved such victories,
maybe they'll forget the Jews. On the way, the Germans helped
the refugees, even the Jews, to go home. They brought them to
Brussels in cars. It made no difference to the Germans whether
they were Jews or not.

When we came to Brussels, we met many Jews who had come
back before us. They said the Germans have gone, we should
never have left Belgium. We had lost our belongings. I lost my
baggage in a railway station. All the refugees from northern
France began coming home. Some began to do business with the
Germans, mostly with the German and Austrian Jews. But the
Polish Jews in France were afraid. There were many Jews from
Belgium who had gone directly from Brussels to Paris to southern
France to escape the Nazis. But now all foreign Jews who had
come to France since 1936 were interned. In order to escape
being interned many fled back to Belgium, where they heard that
everything was good, even though the Nazis were there.

The first Jewish law the Germans instituted in Belgium was that
"No Jews may return." But the Jews kept coming back. The
Germans knew it and did nothing. The law was only on paper. In
time, 80 percent of all Jews who had been in Belgium before the
war came back. We heard terrible things about what was happening to Jews in France. The French were putting Jews into concentration camps and were collaborating with the Germans. In
Holland they were making Jewish laws like Germany. Holland had

a civil administration under a gauleiter, an Austrian who had betrayed Schuschnigg.

In Belgium, there was a military commandant, a military administration under General von Falkenhausen. In the beginning of 1941, there was a fight between the Belgian Fascists and the anti-Fascists in Antwerp. The Germans blamed the riots on the Jews and gave orders that as punishment the Jews must not go out on the streets after seven o'clock in the evening and before seven in the morning. It was forbidden for two Jews to stand in the street; they were not allowed to stand on the streetcar safety zones. They had to keep walking up and down. They couldn't sit in the streetcars; they had to stand on the front platform. Those orders were only in Antwerp.

Then the German order came that Jews could live only in four towns—Brussels, Antwerp, Liège, and Charleroi. Every other place was forbidden. After these orders many Jews left Antwerp and came to Brussels. The people in Brussels treated the Jews better than they were treated in Antwerp. Antwerp is Flemish, Brussels is more French and more sympathetic.

The Germans now said that every Jewish store had to print the word "Jewish" in three languages—French, Dutch, and Flemish. In the big stores, they put in Aryan managers and threw out the Jewish owners. They didn't do it in the small stores because those stores didn't make enough to pay for the salary of an Aryan manager.

In the middle of 1941 the order was put out that Jews must give up their radios. The Germans declared that the Jews were the ones who spread the propaganda from the enemy radio stations. The Nazis were clever propagandists. When they gave out a Jewish order they always motivated it.

They promulgated an order for the four cities. A curfew was set after eight and before seven in the morning. They explained that the Jews were black marketeers, that they carried on their best business in the dark. They would be prevented from doing it now, and this curfew would be in the interests of all. Belgium laughed at the explanations.

In the spring of 1942 they sent out, under the signature of the commandant of northern France and Belgium, an order that all

Jews must liquidate their businesses immediately; the deadline was April 30, 1942. The Jews were told to send their material to a certain address.

They created a Jewish council of Belgian Jewish citizens, Association Juif Belgique. It was a group who had to collaborate with the Nazis. The first job of the council was to count all the Jews. They did it exactly. After that they reported that 42,000 had come and registered. How many didn't come, we don't know. They said that over 40,000 were foreigners. At that time Belgium made it very hard to become naturalized. I was there fifteen years and couldn't be naturalized.

After the Jewish census, the Nazis called the Belgian Jews, saying, "We have nothing against the Belgian Jews, but the foreign Jews must return to their homelands. There they will work. We will do them no harm. They are doing nothing here. This is war and everyone must work."

The order of June 6, 1942, came next; all the Jews had to carry the Jewish Star of David on their hearts. It had to be sewed on well; if not, they would be punished in concentration camps. The Nazis called the mayors of the four cities where the Jews lived, telling them to distribute the stars for the Jews. The stars were yellow, about four inches square.

You must know that in Belgium every city is divided into communes, and each commune has its own mayor. Brussels had nineteen communes and a million people. The four cities had ninety-six mayors. Vandenmulenbrouc was the chief mayor of Brussels. He called a conference of the ninety-six mayors to discuss this question. They decided they would not do this work for the Nazis. They refused to collaborate. The Germans saw that the ninety-six mayors would be hard to work with, that they were from the old regime. They decided to change them and to find ninety-six collaborationists. But they couldn't. So they decided to make a Great Brussels with only one mayor. When the Germans began to dismiss the mayors, Vandenmulenbrouc issued a proclamation. The Germans had no right to dismiss him. He was elected by the Brussels people. The election was certified. Only the people could depose him. He hoped shortly to take his office back. The Germans arrested him, and arrested the chief of police for permitting the proclamation to be issued. He was shipped to Germany; no word has been heard from him since. All of this political upheaval had been caused by the Nazi orders forcing the Jews to wear the Star of David.

Through the Belgian committee, made up of the collaborationists who had gotten all the addresses by means of the census, the Germans now sent invitations to all boys and girls between the ages of fifteen and twenty, to come to Malines to work. The invitation was signed by the order of the Jewish citizens of Belgium. It would be advisable, they wrote, to take work clothes along, food for ten days, dishes, etc. They were warned that if they didn't come, the family would have to pay reparations. "We guarantee it is absolutely for work. Not for deportation. We beg you to come—if you don't, all Jews will have to pay reparations."

Then we saw the most terrible picture in Brussels. Thousands of young men and women walked on the street, carrying rucksacks. Parents accompanied them, weeping.

Every day in the station, a thousand children came. Every day five thousand people came, weeping at the departure of their children. Many didn't come; they had a feeling they would never see their children again. So the Germans began to snatch people. They closed certain streets and pulled off every Jew caught in those streets. The Jews began to hide, so the Germans worked at night. They closed off the streets, and then entered every house. The first night they took over three thousand Jews. Now the Jewish council had no more work. The Germans were doing everything.

The Jews, mostly Polish Jews, now broke into the office of the Association Juif Belgique and burned all the documents and killed Gottesmann, a Belgian Jewish collaborationist.

Many Jewish young people joined the Brigade Blanche to do underground work. They were very active. They burned trains taking raw materials out of Belgium to Germany. They murdered active Belgian collaborationists. They began to make raids on the bureaus which printed meal tickets, the *Timbres de Ravitaillement* (food wasn't free, but you had to have cards anyway). Each month they got about 200,000 to 300,000 food stamps. One time they got all the 275,000 meal tickets from a train going from Brussels to Ghent. Half the cards were distributed to the members of the underground, to the resistance movement, and the Jews; the other half they sold to other Belgians in order to get money for their activity.

The Jews began to move out of their houses and hide. Ninety-five percent of the Belgian population was very good to the Jews. Jews found places to hide yet it was very difficult to stay in them.

L'Ami du Peuple (*The Friend of the People*), an anti-Semitic paper, appeared. Each week, the opening remarks of the paper were, "Don't tell me where a Jew lives—just tell me his phone number; we'll get him and you'll be rewarded."

It became terrible. Unfortunately, many Belgians began to [do this] work to obtain money. In October 1942 I found a place to hide. I was hidden there three and a half months in a room with my wife and children. We didn't go out for air all the time. I thought I was the only one there and I thought I was hidden safely. But one day the owner came and said that the newspapers had printed, "Whoever hides Jews will be killed."

I went away. My wife wept. We all had two apartments then. We always thought we could go home. The owner of my apartment came to me and said, "Twenty-one families in my village were taken by [the] Gestapo. They came two days after you left and they broke into my villa looking for you."

The Association Juif Belgique now began to do something for the Jews; they no longer collaborated. They began to send food to the Jews in the prison at Malines.

Every two or three days the Gestapo brought dead people to the Jewish council in Brussels. They had died of hunger. Food was terribly hard to get in Belgium; the Jews were all starving.

Malines was the assembly point for Poland. The Jewish young people who worked for the underground began to help save men and women from being deported, as well as those in hiding.

The Gestapo deported people first in passenger trains. Some of the men jumped out of the trains. The Gestapo deported them then in baggage cars. They jumped out of the baggage cars by breaking open the top of the trains; fifteen or twenty men would escape each time. Each train carried from 1,500 to 1,800 Jews to Poland.

Once, in the beginning of 1943 the underground organization

stopped the train in the middle of the night. There was shooting between the Germans and the organization. The organization stood at the door and gave each Jew a hundred francs and told them to disappear immediately. From this train, over six hundred Jews came back to Brussels. The next train carried many German soldiers. The organization again stopped the train. There was much shooting again. Unfortunately only three or four escaped; but over twenty women and children were brought dead to Brussels, shot with machine guns.

Until September 5, 1943, when I left, the Germans had deported twenty-one trains with Jews, each carrying over 1,500 Jews. Over 40,000 had been deported; we had no more knowledge how many more Jews were left. I was one of the last.

The underground organization gave my family and me French documents. My wife didn't want to leave. She said that tens of thousands of Jews in Paris had fallen into the hands of the Gestapo. It was true. In fact the demarcation line between Vichy France and Free France was one of the most terrible places of deportation. That's where the Gestapo really caught them.

I said no. I want to save myself, not wait for the Gestapo. We Jews had given our children to Belgian families and to monasteries. They all had false papers. From the beginning it was the most terrible experience for the children. My son of six years had to wear the Star of David and yet live among the Christian children. He wouldn't go in the streets any more. "I won't go. I won't go."

My wife and I went to France to a residence. We waited to see how we could get our children. September 5 I left. On the sixth I came to Grenoble. Fortunately, there was no passport control. I had only an identification card. Those were terrible moments for Jews in Grenoble. The Jews saw the Italians leaving and knew the Germans were coming. It was impossible to sleep in a hotel. I would have fallen immediately into the hands of the French Gendarmes and they would have turned me over to the Gestapo. Some Jews told me to go six kilometers to friends who were Jews and sleep there. Fortunately I saw some trucks with Jews. They told me the Italians from San Gervais and other places were going to Nice and taking Jews along. I said I would go along with the Italians. I asked one of the chauffeurs. I told him I was from

Belgium. He allowed me to go along. On the seventh, I came to Nice with my wife.

In Nice the mood was better. There I went to the Jewish Committee, mostly Polish Jews. They were very sympathetic. They hardly believed that the day before yesterday I was in Belgium; they couldn't believe I could make such a fast trip. They told us every fifty or sixty kilometers there was a control. They gave us meal tickets, rest, and told us not to worry. "We'll get your children." The next morning the Jewish Committee gave us new papers permitting us to walk on the street.

In the evening the news came of the capitulation of Badoglio. That was terrible news for the Jews in Nice. There were over 30,000 Jews in Nice alone. In Grenoble, there were twice as many. They all began to worry, our protectors are going away (the Fascists were our protectors). Early on September 9 (I was still in the fever of the trip) I saw an Italian officer. He parked a truck with telephone wires. I said, "Take me to Italy."

He said, "No, I can't."

I said, "Take me to Italy."

"Why?"

"Because I'm followed by Germans."

He said, "Come along. When are you ready?"

I said, "In half an hour." . . .

PART FOUR

In the Ghetto

The period between the time Jews organized themselves inside the Warsaw Ghetto and that of the Uprising in the spring of 1943 was one of ultimate despair. All options for survival disappeared. To the toll wrought by hunger and disease in the summer of 1942 was added that of the systematic mass deportations, which destroyed whatever was left of the Jews and their possessions. Illusion after illusion, hope after hope, ended in despair as German soldiers and Jewish police forced Jews to board trains leaving the city.

Systematic Starvation

RAUL HILBERG *

The policies of systematic starvation and massive expulsions devastated ghetto populations everywhere. This brief excerpt depicts vividly the terrible toll Germans exacted by starving Jews to death.

In the "free" economy of the Warsaw Ghetto [in 1941] the amount of food a man ate depended on the amount of money he could spend. The poorest sections of the population depended on soup kitchens and begging. Employed groups could buy inadequate quantities of rationed products. (Ration cards were distributed by the *Judenrat* upon payment of monthly fees.) Only "capitalists" could afford to sustain themselves on a steady diet of smuggled foods at the black market prices. . . .

The situation in the Warsaw Ghetto . . . deteriorated. The Warsaw epidemics started in the synagogues and other institutional buildings which housed thousands of homeless people. During the winter of 1941–42 the sewage pipes froze. The toilets could no longer be used, and human excrement was dumped with garbage into the streets. To combat the typhus epidemic the Warsaw *Judenrat* organized disinfection brigades, subjected people to "steaming action" . . . set up quarantine stations, hospitalized serious cases, and as a last resort instituted "house blockades" imprisoning in their homes the sick and the healthy alike. The one useful article, serum, was almost unavailable. A single tube of anti-typhus medicine cost several thousand zloty.

* *Op. cit.,* pp. 171–173.

All over the incorporated territories and the *Generalgouvernement* the ghetto hunger raged unchecked. A primitive struggle for survival began. On March 21, 1942, the [German] Propaganda Division of the Warsaw district reported laconically:

> The death figure in the ghetto still hovers around 5000 per month. A few days ago, the first case of hunger-cannibalism was recorded. In a Jewish family the man and his three children died within a few days. From the flesh of the child who died last— a twelve-year-old boy—the mother ate a piece. To be sure, this could not save her either, and she herself died two days later.

The ghetto Jews were fighting for life with their last ounce of strength. People collapsed at work and in the streets. Hungry beggars snatched food from the hands of the shoppers. Corpses were lying on the sidewalk, covered with newspapers, pending the arrival of cemetery carts.

Expulsion

CHAIM A. KAPLAN *

*This selection from Kaplan's diary reveals the
despair resulting from the massive expulsions
in the summer of 1942 and sets the stage for
the Uprising in the Warsaw Ghetto later in
1942 and in 1943.*

The terrible events have engulfed me; the horrible deeds committed
in the ghetto have so frightened and stunned me that I have not the
power, either physical or spiritual, to review these events and
perpetuate them with the pen of a scribe. I have no words to
express what has happened to us since the day the expulsion was
ordered. Those people who have gotten some notion of historical
expulsions from books know nothing. We, the inhabitants of the
Warsaw Ghetto, are now experiencing the reality. Our only good
fortune is that our days are numbered—that we shall not have
long to live under conditions like these, and that after our terrible
sufferings and wanderings we shall come to eternal rest, which was
denied us in life. Among ourselves we fully admit that this death
which lurks behind our walls will be our salvation; but there is
one thorn. We shall not be privileged to witness the downfall of the
Nazis, which in the end will surely come to pass.

Some of my friends and acquaintances who know the secret of
my diary urge me, in their despair, to stop writing. "Why? For
what purpose? Will you live to see it published? Will these words
of yours reach the ears of future generations? How? If you are
deported you won't be able to take it with you because the Nazis

* *Op. cit.,* pp. 323–340.

will watch your every move, and even if you succeed in hiding it when you leave Warsaw, you will undoubtedly die on the way, for your strength is ebbing. And if you don't die from lack of strength, you will die by the Nazi sword. For not a single deportee will be able to hold out to the end of the war."

And yet in spite of it all I refuse to listen to them. I feel that continuing this diary to the very end of my physical and spiritual strength is a historical mission which must not be abandoned. My mind is still clear, my need to record unstilled, though it is now five days since any real food has passed my lips. Therefore I will not silence my diary!

We have a Jewish tradition that an evil law is foredoomed to defeat. This historical experience has caused us much trouble since the day we fell into the mouth of the Nazi whose dearest wish is to swallow us. It came to us from habit, this minimizing of all edicts with the common maxim, "It won't succeed." In this lay our undoing, and we made a bitter mistake. An evil decree made by the Nazis does not weaken in effect, it grows stronger. The mitigating paragraphs are increasingly overlooked and the more severe paragraphs intensified. At the beginning, the time of the "negotiations," a directive was issued to the *Judenrat* to deport 6,000 a day; in point of fact they are now deporting close to 10,000. The Jewish police, whose cruelty is no less than that of the Nazis, deliver to the "transfer point" on Stawki Street more than the quota to which the *Judenrat* obligated itself. Sometimes there are several thousand people waiting a day or two to be transported because of a shortage of railroad cars. Word has gotten around that the Nazis are satisfied that the extermination of the Jews is being carried out with all requisite efficiency. This deed is being done by the Jewish slaughterers.

The first victim of the deportation decree was the President, Adam Czerniakow, who committed suicide by poison in the *Judenrat* building. He perpetuated his name by his death more than by his life. His end proves conclusively that he worked and strove for the good of his people; that he wanted its welfare and continuity even though not everything done in his name was praiseworthy. The expulsion proclamation posted in the city streets on the afternoon of July 22 was not signed in the usual manner of

Judenrat notices, "Head of the *Judenrat,* Certified Engineer Adam Czerniakow," but merely *"Judenrat."* This innovation astonished those circles who examine bureaucratic changes in notices. After the President's death, the reason became clear. Czerniakow had refused to sign the expulsion order. He followed the Talmudic law: If someone comes to kill me, using might and power, and turns a deaf ear to all my pleas, he can do to me whatever his heart desires, since he has the power, and strength always prevails. But to give my consent, to sign my own death warrant—this no power on earth can force me to do, not even the brutal force of the foul-souled Nazi.

A whole community with an ancient tradition, one that with all its faults was the very backbone of world Jewry, is going to destruction. First they took away its means of livelihood, then they stole its wares, then its houses and factories, and above all, its human rights. It was left fair prey to every evildoer and sinner. It was locked into a ghetto. Food and drink was withheld from it; its fallen multiplied on every hand; and even after all this they were not content to let it dwell forever within its narrow, rotten ghetto, surrounded with its wall through which even bread could be brought in only by dangerous smuggling. Nor was this a ghetto of people who consume without producing, of speculators and profiteers. Most of its members were devoted to labor, so that it became a productive legion. All that it produced, it produced for the benefit of those same soldiers who multiplied its fallen.

Yet all this was to no avail. There was only one decree—death. They came and divided the Warsaw Ghetto into two halves; one half was for sword, pestilence, and destruction; the other half for famine and slavery. The vigorous youth, the healthy and productive ones, were taken to work in the factories. The old people, the women, the children all were sent into exile.

The president, who had a spark of purity in his heart, found the only way out worthy of himself. Suicide! In the end the Nazis would have killed him anyhow, as is their custom in the areas from which they expel the Jewish population; nor would the president have been the last to be shot. From the moment of his refusal to sign the expulsion order he was a saboteur in the eyes of the Nazis and thus doomed to death. With a president one must be very exacting. In any event, he did well to anticipate the Nazis.

He did not have a good life, but he had a beautiful death. May his death atone for his wrongs against his people before becoming president. There are those who earn immortality in a single hour. The President, Adam Czerniakow, earned his immortality in a single instant.

July 27, 1942

Anyone who could see the expulsion from Warsaw with his own eyes would have his heart broken. The ghetto has turned into an inferno. Men have become beasts. Everyone is but a step away from deportation; people are being hunted down in the streets like animals in the forest. It is the Jewish police who are cruelest toward the condemned. Sometimes a blockade is made of a particular house, sometimes of a whole block of houses. In every building earmarked for destruction they begin to make the rounds of the apartments and to demand documents. Whoever has neither documents that entitle him to remain in the ghetto nor money for bribes is told to make a bundle weighing 15 kilos— and on to the transport which stands near the gate. Whenever a house is blockaded a panic arises that is beyond the imagination. Residents who have neither documents nor money hide in nooks and crannies, in the cellars and in attics. When there is a means of passage between one courtyard and another the fugitives begin jumping over the roofs and fences at the risk of their lives; in time of panic, when the danger is imminent, people are not fussy about methods. But all these methods only delay the inevitable, and in the end the police take men, women, and children. The destitute and impoverished are the first to be deported. In an instant the truck becomes crowded. They are all alike: poverty makes them equal. Their cries and wails tear the heart out.

The children, in particular, rend the heavens with their cries. The old people and the middle-aged deportees accept the judgment in silent submission and stand with their small parcels under their arms. But there is no limit to the sorrow and tears of the young women; sometimes one of them makes an attempt to slip out of the grasp of her captors, and then a terrible battle begins. At such times the horrible scene reaches its peak. The two sides fight, wrestle. On one side a woman with wild hair and a torn blouse rages with the last of her strength at the Jewish thieves, trying to escape from their hands. Anger flows from her mouth and she is like a lioness ready for the kill. And on the other side are the two policemen, her "brothers in misfortune," who pull her back to her death. It is obvious that the police win. But during the fight the wailing of the captives increases sevenfold, and the whole street cries with them.

But isolated incidents don't hold up the operation. The police do what is incumbent upon them. After the completion of the arrests in one house, they move on to another. The *Judenrat* prepares a daily list of houses in which blockades will be made that day. And here a new source of income is opened up for the graft-chasing police. The wealthy and the middle class have yet to be brought to the transports. For those who have no documents, banknotes turn into documents. There is almost a fixed price for ransom, but for some it is cheaper, all according to the class of the ransomed one and the number of people in his household.

Two actual cases are known to me. One of the members of our family ransomed himself off with a substitute for money. In place of the ready cash which he didn't have at the time of the hunt, he gave a silk umbrella as a "gift" not to be returned. An acquaintance of mine, a Hebrew teacher, a downtrodden pauper with a crippled son, was forced to give 300 zloty—his last nest egg, since he has no expectation of new earnings from teaching Hebrew. In this instance the price was high, for expulsion of a cripple means expulsion to the gates of death. Sick people and cripples are killed by the Nazis while still en route.

But from the time they began to hunt down passersby on the street, the sorrow of the expulsion became even greater. For this barbarism the beloved *Judenrat* will find no atonement. One who is seized in his apartment supplies himself with some clothing and food for the journey. His loved ones take their leave of him, fall on his neck. Not so one who is seized on the street. He is taken to the transport as he is, without extra clothing, without food and sustenance, and usually without a penny. No entreaties avail him. He is led out to the transfer point like a lamb to the slaughter.

Life in the ghetto has been turned upside down. Panic is in

its streets, fear on every face, wails and cries everywhere you turn. Trade has ceased; bargaining has been silenced; and most important, smuggling has stopped. When there is no smuggling, costs go up, so that the price of bread has reached 60 zloty. Prices have increased tenfold, all businesses have ceased to exist. Everyone's staff of bread has been broken. From whence cometh our help? We are lost! We are lost!

July 28, 1942

The situation grows graver by the hour. Through the window of my apartment near the scene of the "hunting" I beheld those trapped by the hunt and was so stricken that I was close to madness. For the detainee, the thread of his life is cut in an instant, and the work of an entire lifetime in which his best efforts were invested becomes abandoned property.

Before my very eyes they capture an old woman who walks with a cane. Her steps are measured, and she makes her way with great exertions. She is unable to straighten up. On her face there are marks of nobility and signs of a family status now past. She too was arrested by a lawless Jewish scoundrel. He needs clients, and even this old lady counts, "as is," without clothes or linens, without even food. She will be sent "to the East." She will be fortunate if she doesn't live long.

A young mother of two little children from 19 Nowolipki Street was caught and sent off. The dear children were left orphans. There is no comfort for her husband and their father. And there are similar victims by the hundreds. Today about 10,000 people were taken. They are shoved into freight cars which have no places to sit and no sanitary facilities. If anyone survives that journey, it is nothing less than a miracle.

In truth we have reached extremity. Death is precious when it is quick and swift, when it takes your soul and you pass on into your eternity. But a death which comes by the agonies of starvation and the tortures of the oppressor, who prolongs the death agony and turns his victims into living skeletons—this is the cruelest of punishments. Have we truly sinned more than any nation; have we transgressed more than any generation?

Never in my life had I known the pangs of hunger. Even after I was pushed into the ghetto I ate. But now I too know hunger. I sustain myself for a whole day on a quarter-kilo of bread and un-sweetened tea. My strength is diminishing from such meager fare. At times I can't even stand up. I fall on my bed, but rest eludes me. I am in a state of sleep and am not asleep, of wakefulness and yet am not awake. I am plagued by nightmares. Fear and worry preoccupy me—fear lest I be seized and deported; worry about where to find my bread. My income has stopped. The sums owed to me by others are lost. Besides what he needs for food, no one has a penny to his name, and payment of debts isn't taken into consideration at all.

But the main thing is fear of expulsion. The only ones partially insured against expulsion are workers in the factories that German firms have taken under their protection. Many factories accept workers skilled in their trades, and even those who are unskilled but have money. Thus a new economy has begun in the lives of the ghetto Jews who have not yet been expelled.

I am tired. The sequel will come tomorrow, if I'm not caught.

July 29, 1942

The expulsion is reaching its peak. It increases from day to day. The Nazis are satisfied with the work of the Jewish police, the plague of the Jewish organism, and the police too are satisfied: the Nazis, because through industry and cruelty the police have succeeded in supplying exiles above and beyond the daily quota originally specified, and close to 70,000 people have already gone into exile; the police, because they are lining their pockets. This income is fortuitous and apparently not dangerous. The Nazis don't bother about details. Give who you will, as long as there is no shortage of human material for expulsion. In any event, the respite that the bribe creates is only temporary. A house which is blockaded today can be blockaded tomorrow too, and the next day, and so on ad infinitum. A man who was released once can be caught again—even by the same policeman who let him go the first time—especially since the police have nearly 2,400 dogs. The wiles of the policemen know no bounds. Besides taking bribes, they also steal and rob. How? They order the inhabitants of the house to go down, while they themselves remain in the unguarded apartment. Thus they profit from all that is abandoned.

This criminal police force is the child of the criminal *Judenrat*.

Like mother, like daughter. With their misdeeds they besmirch the name of Polish Jewry which was stained even without this. At the transfer point where the exiles are collected, the policemen traffic in bread. These loaves of bread, which the police force gets in abundance free of charge, are sold to the hungry and oppressed captives at 80 zloty a loaf. For delivering a letter, ten zloty. They are growing rich on these profits, and for the time being they are experiencing the eternal reward in this life—until the Nazis take pity on them as well. Their day will come, and they too will be destroyed, but they will be the last.

Nazism is not original. They took everything from Bolshevism, only that they expanded its rottenness. This is the same Bolshevism in black paint. There is no difference but that of color. Bolshevism came and said: "Everyone must work!" Nazism came after it and said likewise: "You are idle! Go ye unto your burdens!" But Bolshevism spoke out of its desire to improve the world; Nazism spoke out of hatred for the Jewish people.

With one stroke of the pen the face of Warsaw was changed. They made an end of its peddlers; its beggars and paupers and down-and-outers were collected; its stores were closed; its streets were emptied. Everywhere there is the silence of the graveyard. Everything has passed away—disappeared in one day. It is as if the earth had opened and swallowed up all its crowds and noises, its secrets and vices, and the entire tribe of ants that scurried through its streets from dawn until curfew.

When the Nazis decreed expulsion for the "unproductive population," people went into hiding as though they had been erased from the face of the earth. Now there is hunting for the sake of expulsion, where once they traded and bartered.

The unproductive population included most of the ghetto dwellers. In the eyes of the Nazis, anyone who doesn't take a needle or a shovel in hand is in no way productive. Based on this, the entire population of the ghetto was scheduled for expulsion. They therefore tried to save themselves by a change in approach: You want us to work? By all means—only allow us to live. One is not overscrupulous about the means in time of danger. Immediately a great movement arose to set up factories to work for the good of the German army, and the German commandant invited German firms to establish branches in the General Government. The Jewish shop-factories received raw materials from these firms and began to manufacture for each one what was required to meet their obligations to the commandant. In this way factories for various trades were opened which employed tens of thousands of people. Thus the expulsion decree caused people who had been store-keepers, tradesmen, peddlers, servants, teachers, lawyers, engineers, and all kinds of other middle-class people to stream toward the factories. Henceforward, only one who is enrolled as a worker in one of the factories under the protection of some German firm has the right to remain in the ghetto. A certificate (*Ausweis*) granted by a firm of the Reich has the power to save its bearer from expulsion and from all the other troubles that have attached themselves to us. Within a week, tens of thousands of tradesmen, peddlers, unemployed men, idlers, spreaders of false rumors, and bums have been turned into creative workers, into a productive element; they sit hunched over a needle, sewing buttons on a pair of army pants.

The entire ghetto is a mammoth factory producing for the good of the German army. We have become a laughingstock!

July 30, 1942

The seventh day of the expulsion. Living funerals pass before the windows of my apartment—cattle trucks or coal wagons full of candidates for expulsion and exile, carrying small bundles under their arms. Their cries and shrieks and wails, which rent the very heavens and filled the whole area with noise, have already stopped. Most of the deportees seem to be resigned to their fate. Only an occasional sound, the tear-drenched echo of a protest, is heard from some unfortunate seized while she was engaged in the activities of everyday life. Misfortune descended upon her unforeseen. She knew that there was an expulsion, but she was almost positive that it would never come to her. And behold, it is come! Woe to her! Alas for her soul! But her shrieks and plaints are sown upon the wind. It is finished, decided. She is going toward a new "life."

Amid all the tragedy of sudden expulsion, one minor detail is perhaps the most tragic of all: People come to the transfer point voluntarily, saying: "Take me! Save me from the quagmire of the ghetto! I will die anyhow; there is famine in the ghetto. Comfort the dying!" But these are the words of a small minority of people with no roots in the soil of the ghetto.

Besides the blockading of houses and hunting in the street, there is still a third method of expulsion—premiums. Large posters have been put up in many courtyards to say that all those who voluntarily come to the transfer point for expulsion will receive three kilos of bread and a kilo of marmalade to take with them in their wanderings. They are given until the thirty-first of July.

Today I haven't gone outside the house, because the sword of expulsion strikes in all the streets of the ghetto. They take everyone who comes to hand, those dressed in finery and those dressed in cast-offs—all of them, all of them swallowed up by the wagon. They are not even paying attention to the certificates of those who work for the German factories, which should be a protection for them.

The soothing rumors that the expulsion will cease, that only a certain percentage will be exiled, that the many factories abetting the victory of the German army will enable the rest of the Jews to remain in the ghetto, have not materialized. Nothing of the sort. The tempo of the expulsion increases from hour to hour. On every hand there are catchers. Besides the uniformed Jewish police and the nonuniformed auxiliary police, pure Germans have also come to this task. They dress in civilian clothes so that people won't spot them.

All day long the ghetto has been deathly silent. During the working hours in the factories the number of passersby decreased to a minimum. Those who have not yet managed to be accepted in some factory are afraid to stick their noses out for fear of being caught. They hide until the wrath shall pass. Perhaps salvation will come! Perhaps there will be a change for the better! But for the time being, the oppressor does not stay his hand.

There is one category among those "insured" against expulsion whose eyes reflect fear, who despite the documents in their pockets never go out of the doors of their houses and, within their houses, hide in inner rooms. These are the "officials" of the Jewish Self-Aid Society, who numbered over two thousand at the outbreak of the catastrophe. It is the strength of the Jewish people that in time of disaster they invent something out of nothing, build bridges out of paper. If it works, it will work; and if not, what have you lost? Before the expulsion, the Self-Aid employed about four hundred people who were registered with the labor office, and there were also full-time officers who held work cards in accordance with the laws of officialdom. Suddenly, the calamity! Thousands of people were left without legal protection and doomed to exile. Accordingly the directors of the society, with the consent of the *Judenrat,* decided to provide their friends with a legal haven in the form of "legitimizations," documents stating that so-and-so was an official of the society. They based their plan on the fact that the expulsion decree had a paragraph which stated specifically that officials of the Jewish Self-Aid Society would have privileges comparable to those of officials of the *Judenrat.* A veritable factory for legitimizations was set up. Anyone who had had any connection whatever with the activities of the society from the time of its establishment to the present day, whether as a salaried employee or a volunteer, received certification as one of its officials.

Within three days, over two thousand certificates were prepared and distributed—a tremendous job even for a well-equipped and refined technical apparatus, let alone an organization as inefficient as the Self-Aid. Here no one stood in long queues, but rather on top of one another. The pushing and crowding of hundreds of people with the fear of death in their eyes reached horrible proportions. Mobs pushed their way into the officials' offices and urged them to speed up their work. The result was exactly the opposite. Order was disrupted, work was interrupted and delayed: anger and hysterics from both sides. No one had any assurance that such a certificate would be legally accepted, but it is good to have something in writing to lean on. People seek comfort in the fact that for the time being the Jewish people are handling everything, and the police are under the orders of the *Judenrat,* which considers these certificates legal. Everyone said, "It carries no real guarantee. In the end it will come under censure and be nullified. But for the time it has validity in the eyes of the Jewish police, and that's enough for me. I'll at least be able to go and look for a more secure hiding place." In point of fact it did save many people. They were seized and later released. I too find refuge in the shadow of a certificate. Blessings upon the Self-Aid!

I have just been informed that 57,000 people have already been deported. The teacher and writer Aron Luboszycki, a refugee from Lodz, was among them.

July 31, 1942

The hunting goes on full force. The living funerals never cease. The Jewish police are fulfilling their humane duty in the best possible manner, and the Nazis are so pleased with their work that some of them are being sent to Radom and Kielce, where expulsions have now been ordered as well. These cities are both smaller than Warsaw, and local elements are not particularly desirable for this sort of operation, so the strangers from Warsaw come where no one knows them to carry out the Nazis' wishes.

Yesterday and today were "days of awe"; no *Ausweis* was honored. Workers were taken out of factories protected by the German firms of Többens, Schultz, Mangesten, and the like. Thousands of people were seized whose documents were questionable, having been given only as protection from the destroyers, and whose bearers were not expert in the trades ascribed to them in their certificates. These are documents given out of kindness, like those of the Self-Aid Society, and are of no value. Sometimes they help if by a miracle you chance to meet a policeman who shares the distress of his people—but the Nazis are insatiable.

The sum total is that there is no Jew who has not insured himself with some piece of paper, and there is no Jew who doesn't hide in the inner recesses of his house, certificate and all. It's just that with a certificate in your pocket, hiding is more comfortable.

More factories are established every day. This is the only source of salvation now, even though every one of them is built on sand. Many people scurry to register for the factories. Merchants and tradesmen, intellectuals and Menachem-Mendels,[1] are turning to handicraft in order to be saved from deportation. Everyone is pushing his way into a "shop" and is prepared to sell all his pos-

[1] From a character created by Sholem Aleichem—an impractical dreamer. —*Translator*

sessions and give away his last cent, if only to be considered productive.

How great the panic of the factories has become! Everyone fights to be enrolled in them, and everyone gives thousands of zloty for this privilege. For a genuine laborer it is enough if he brings a sewing machine with him, but a business or professional man contributes ready cash in place of a machine. None of the newly erected factories has any validity or future unless they are incorporated into the network of factories of some German firm; and this privilege too must be bought with cash from the Germans, who demand immense sums in return for the right to work for the German army. But no one has scruples about the size of the sum. A man will give everything he has in exchange for his life. The whole matter is clouded in doubt and no one knows what the day will bring, but the people of the ghetto, who see death face to face, are seeking security not for a day, but for an hour.

Be that as it may, we are like rams and sheep bound for sacrifice, except that it is hard to determine the exact instant at which one will be put upon the altar. The sword has already been removed from its sheath, but we haven't yet stretched out our necks for the slaughter.

My powers are insufficient to record all that is worthy of being written. Most of all, I am worried that I may be consuming my strength for naught. Should I too be taken all my efforts will be wasted. My utmost concern is for hiding my diary so that it will be preserved for future generations. As long as my pulse beats I shall continue my sacred task.

August 1, 1942

The enormity of the danger increases our strength and our will to save our lives, like a fever which gives strength and power to one who is dangerously ill. But all this is merely a momentary relief; afterward the weakness returns sevenfold.

Yesterday the murderers from the SS came to assist the Jewish police, and within two hours, i.e., from seven to nine in the evening, the entire Jewish population of Nowolipie Street—from the corner of Karmelicka to Smocza—was forced to leave its homes and go into exile.

Blessed is the eye which has not beheld all of this!

The expulsion decree is a twofold one: expulsion for the non-productive, and after this the terrible edict of evictions. A command is suddenly given to evacuate an entire block of apartment houses within a single hour. This starts an uproar, a turmoil that Dante could not have envisioned. It is the Nazis' intention that every decree come as a complete surprise. Hundreds of families hurt by this decree become frantic from the enormity of the misfortune. Where will you go? What can you save? What first? What last? They begin to pack bundles in haste and fear, with trembling hands and feet which refuse to do their bidding, and to take their belongings outside, for they no longer have a home. Hundreds of women and swollen infants rend the heavens with their cries. The sick are taken outside in their beds, babies in their cradles, old men and women half-naked and barefoot.

At seven in the evening the SS arrived and ordered the Jewish police to blockade an entire block. They made an announcement in each courtyard: "Prepare bundles weighing 15 kilos and go down into the courtyard. No one is exempt!" Terrible fear gripped the whole area. Everyone sensed that his fate had been given over into the hands of insatiable murderers. With the Jewish police the inhabitants could come to a compromise in one way or another, but this time the decree was inexorable. Submit yourselves to your bitter fate!

About 10,000 people were deported and disappeared.

August 2, 1942

Jewish Warsaw is in its death throes. A whole community is going to its death! The appalling events follow one another so abundantly that it is beyond the power of a writer of impressions to collect, arrange, and classify them; particularly when he himself is caught in their vise—fearful of his own fate for the next hour, scheduled for deportation, tormented by hunger, his whole being filled with the fear and dread which accompanies the expulsion. And let this be known: From the beginning of the world, since the time when man first had dominion over another man to do him harm, there has never been so cruel and barbaric an expulsion as this one. From hour to hour, even from minute to minute,

Jewish Warsaw is being demolished and destroyed, reduced and decreased. Since the day the exile was decreed, ruin and destruction, exile and wandering, bereavement and widowhood have befallen us in all their fury.

For five days now the Nazis have been "helping" the Jewish police. Since then the expulsion has begun to leave a trail of innocent blood behind it. A man who is ordered to leave his apartment must go as he is, for if he tarries a single moment he is put to death at once.

After Nowolipie, henceforward to be known as Schultz Street, came the turn of Leszno Street from the corner of Zelazna to Solna. The population of Leszno was not struck by the evacuation order, but rather by the decree of expulsion. A blockade was made on Leszno Street, and within two hours about 2,000 people were brought to the transfer point. . . . All their possessions were left in the hands of the enemy.

Jewish Warsaw is turning into a city of slave laborers who have nothing of their own. The German companies that own the factories concentrate their employees in one section. To achieve this, they confiscate all the houses near a factory and settle the workers and their families in them. Without them there would be no Jewish community. Every activity in the ghetto, and all its establishments, are being brought to an end. Jews who are not employed in one of the factories will be expelled from Warsaw. For the time being they are busy with schemes and plans for hiding until the wrath passes, but the wrath of the Nazis never passes. On the contrary, it increases. Concessions granted on paper never materialize in practice. All of the various *Ausweisen* are voided and nullified. In the end, everyone will be expelled.

Today I heard from Dr. Lajpuner, who in turn heard it from rumor, that the houses from 12 to 21 Nowolipki Street will be confiscated and turned over to the workers of a brush factory. This news will affect us both, for he is a resident at Number 14 and I at Number 20. If the rumor proves true I shall have no place to lay my head. And his fate is like mine. We shall both sleep out of doors—until we are caught and deported. Meanwhile we are without food—not even enough for a single meal.

We have no information about the fate of those who have been expelled. When one falls into the hands of the Nazis he falls into the abyss. The very fact that the deportees make no contact with their families by letters bodes evil. Nothing that is related—and many things are related—is based on exact information. One person says that a certain family has received news of one of its members who was deported, that he arrived in the place intended for him alive and well—but he doesn't name the place nor give his address, and he doesn't ask them to write to him. Certain other unconfirmed reports are widespread, but no one knows their source nor lends much credence to them. Nevertheless, there is some local information about one segment of the deportees—the sick, the aged, the cripples and the other invalids, the weak ones who need the care and help of other people. They have returned to the city, not to the living but rather to the dead—to the cemetery. There they have found rest for their oppressed souls, and there they attain eternal peace. I have not yet verified this information myself. I record it as I heard it from the rumor.

August 4, 1942
During the morning hours

I spent yesterday in hard and tiring work, packing boxes and making bundles of pillows and blankets, and particularly in hiding my library, the joy of my life and the delight of my soul. My block is insecure. We are on the verge of expulsion and the confiscation of our houses. It is a time of danger. Our living in Warsaw has become illegal; we await calamity at any moment. The houses are being confiscated for the factory workers, to whom the idlers must give up their apartments. And I, and all those like me, are idlers, for we haven't a place in a factory. Therefore it behooves one to be ready for the coming catastrophe.

I packed my possessions to send them to a relative of mine who has succeeded in getting a "worker-status" (*Placowka*) outside the ghetto for 2,000 zloty. He is more secure in life and property than I. An apartment was even set aside for him at 15 Leszno Street, a building whose inhabitants had already been expelled. He thus becomes my savior and refuge in my time of need. The furniture, glassware, and other household goods will remain where they are and strangers will inherit them for themselves. It is obvious that my privileged relative can protect only part of my property; there is no one to protect my life and my liberty. My life is forfeit and suspended over nothingness.

Yesterday, the third of August, they slaughtered Zamenhof and Pawia streets. They did not confiscate houses, but blockaded the entire block for expulsion. The SS killers stood guard while the Jewish police worked inside the courtyards. This was a slaughter in proper style—they had no pity even on infants and nurslings. All of them, all, without exception, were taken to the gates of death. The fabricated papers of the Self-Aid Society were as useless as though they did not exist.

In the Zamenhof-Pawia blockade, unlike the Nowolipki disaster where hundreds perished, innocent blood was not spilled on the spot, because the SS did not go through the apartments.

The rabbi of Radomsko and his entire family—six people in all—who lived in Nowolipki Street were murdered.

In the evening hours

I have not yet been caught: I have not yet been evicted from my apartment; my building has not yet been confiscated. But only a step separates me from all these misfortunes. All day my wife and I take turns standing watch, looking through the kitchen window which overlooks the courtyard, to see if the blockade has begun. People run from place to place like madmen.

On the very day that I packed my possessions to turn them over to the relative who is my protector, my friend M. from Nowolipki Street brought me some of his belongings because he had heard that his block was in danger of blockade. My friend M. is "kosher" by virtue of the fact that he has an administrative position at the *Judenrat*. His documents are valid and carry full privileges. But the size of the ghetto is being steadily decreased, and there is therefore a danger that the function of an administrator will cease to exist. What did he do? He looked for some kind of factory, and found one, but only upon payment of ransom. Because he had no cash, he gave its equivalent, a precious stone worth several thousand zloty. This was the last of his savings for the bad times to come. When he handed over the stone he was destitute.

My lot is even worse because I have neither money nor a factory job, and therefore am a candidate for expulsion if I am caught. My only salvation is in hiding. This is an outlaw's life, and a man cannot last very long living illegally. My heart trembles at every isolated word. I am unable to leave my house, for at every step the devil lies in wait for me.

There is the silence of death in the streets of the ghetto all through the day. The fear of death is in the eyes of the few people who pass by on the sidewalk opposite our window. Everyone presses himself against the wall and draws into himself so that they will not detect his existence or his presence.

Today my block was scheduled for a blockade with Nazi participation. Seventy Jewish policemen had already entered the courtyard. I thought, "The end has come." But a miracle happened, and the blockade was postponed. The destroyers passed on to the Nalewki-Zamenhof block.

When the danger was already past I hurried to escape. Panic can drive a man out of his mind and magnify the danger even when it no longer exists. But already there is a fear that my block will be blockaded tomorrow. I am therefore trying to lay plans to escape with the dawn. But where will I flee? No block is secure.

Thousands of people in the Nalewki-Zamenhof block were driven from their homes and taken to the transfer point. More than thirty people were slaughtered. In the afternoon, the furies subsided a bit. The number of passersby increased, for the danger of blockade was over. By four in the afternoon, the quota was filled: 13,000 people had been seized and sent off, among them 5,000 who came to the transfer of their own free will. They had had their fill of the ghetto life, which is a life of hunger and fear of death. They escaped from the trap. Would that I could allow myself to do as they did!

If my life ends—what will become of my diary? [2]

---

[2] The volumes were smuggled out of Warsaw, and were found, some time after the war, buried in kerosene cans on a farm outside the city.

PART FIVE

Akzia Impossible:
Warsaw Uprising

Many facts about the Warsaw Uprising are known, but considerable confusion remains, and will probably always remain, in part because of ideological rivalries on the part of witnesses and analysts and in part also because of the scantiness of the source material. The excerpts by J. Kermish reveal the difficulties inherent in studying wartime underground activity. Raul Hilberg provides an overview of the Uprising based primarily on German sources, especially accounts by the German military commanders who destroyed the ghetto. The very last days in the Warsaw Ghetto are poignantly recalled by survivors.

First Stirrings

J. KERMISH *

Kermish, former director of the Polish Central Jewish Historical Commission, discusses sources and events so as to reveal the complexities and passions inherent in the subject; he also shows a strong interest in determining when the first stirrings of military insurrection began among Jews.

. . . The discovery of the second part of the Ringelblum Archives [1] has given us a number of important documents testifying to the shock of the ghetto experience after the deportations in the summer of 1942, and to the far-reaching changes in the attitude of the surviving Jews of Warsaw, in the concluding months of that year.

It is noteworthy that when the Poles living in the "Aryan" sector of the city heard of the transports leaving for Treblinka they criticized the Jews and made the familiar charges: Why did you not defend yourselves? Why did you go like sheep to the slaughter? Why did you not attack the Germans, when you learned that you were being led to your deaths? And so forth and so forth.

In these acrimonious debates the leaders of the Jewish Resistance Movement had preferred to make it clear that against the murderous terror practised by the Nazis in the ghetto, no group, however disciplined and battle-trained, could hope to stage a

---

* "First Stirrings," *Yad Vashem Bulletin* (October 1963), pp. 12–19, and (August 1964) pp. 22–33.
[1] Emmanuel Ringelblum, an historian, maintained an archive during the period of the Warsaw Ghetto. Most of the material accumulated was published as *Notes from the Warsaw Ghetto* (New York: McGraw-Hill, 1958).

mass organized resistance. This terror, combined with the ruses, adopted by the Hitlerite deportation headquarters, was capable of effectively breaking the back of any community, and particularly one which for years had lived under the conditions of a prison or a concentration camp. In the course of these discussions the Jewish leaders informed the Poles of the preparations being made by the Jewish Resistance to strike when the time came.

But in fact much of the responsibility for the conditions prevailing in the ghetto prior to the large-scale deportations in the summer months of July–September 1942 rests upon the "Aryan" sector. For many, many months the Jews had appealed to Polish governmental circles for arms for the ghetto, but what was received after prolonged effort was so insignificant in quantity and so poor in quality that any defensive action was out of the question. Moreover, "in the course of the forty-four days of the *akzia*," [2] according to Dr. Ringelblum, "nothing was heard from the 'Aryan' sector. There was complete silence there as the drama unfolded before the eyes of hundreds of thousands of Poles. . . ."

Underground Government circles, there is no question, knew of the fate of the Jews of Lublin and they were aware of the true function of the Treblinka Camp. But they did not find it necessary to warn the Jews that what was called "the eastward transfer of population" was a euphemism for mass murder, wholesale slaughter. These circles did not issue a call for self-defense, they did not utter a word of encouragement, they gave no promise of help, even of moral assistance.

"We can say with certainty," Dr. Ringelblum wrote, "that if responsible Polish circles had extended moral aid and help in arms, the Germans would have been compelled to pay a high price for the Jewish blood that flowed in August and September of 1942."

We must point out at this juncture that it was only the Polish Socialist Party (PSS) that published a circular addressed to the Jews (it reached only that one section of the ghetto known as the "Little Ghetto"), indicating the true nature of the "population transfer." This circular stated that seventy thousand of the Jews of War-

[2] *Akzia* ("action") can be taken to mean the entire campaign by the Jewish resistance in Warsaw, or an engagement between one or more of the ghetto fighters and one or more of the soldiers under German command.

saw had already been gassed in Treblinka and that resistance was therefore necessary.

It was only after a number of inmates of Treblinka had fled from the camp that the eyes of the Jews were opened and they began to appreciate what the "population transfers" really meant.

The Jewish Fighting Organization (established, as Ringelblum puts it, "at a time of extreme spiritual collapse among the Warsaw Jews") published already a number of placards in August 1942 explaining what Treblinka signified, and called for resistance. But the Jewish masses refused to believe this unverified evidence.

The leaflets distributed by the Jewish Fighting Organization were regarded as German acts of provocation, to induce acts of resistance which could serve as a pretext for the destruction of the last survivors of Warsaw Jewry. The Jewish Fighting Organization, which at this time had no arms in its possession, was compelled to look on helplessly and in despair while hundreds of thousands of Jews—workers, intellectuals, women, and children—were sent to their deaths.

It was only in the second half of the month of August that the first signs of reaction to the slaughter manifested themselves. The Jewish Fighting Organization set fire to a number of buildings which had been cleared of their residents. These acts reached their culmination August 20; the first shot was fired by the Jewish Fighting Organization. Israel Kanal, a leader of the Akiva Youth Organization, severely wounded Joseph Sherinski, commander of the *Judische Ordnungs-Dienst* (Jewish Order Service) in the ghetto. An assassination attempt aimed at Schmerlings, an officer in the Jewish Service, was unsuccessful.

Tales of individual acts of resistance, such as the throwing of a heavy ashtray by Severin Majda, a former theatre director, at the Hitlerites who came to arrest him (one of the Hitlerites was wounded in the head and Majda was shot dead on the spot), were related with satisfaction. There were also other acts of individual resistance during the siege.

Pain, grief and regret were voiced on the day after the first *akzia* had been completed. All the surviving inhabitants deeply regretted their submission, and the fact that they had not demonstrated any resistance even to the Jewish Police. "Why was everything so easy for the cruel enemy? Why did the Nazi hangmen not suffer even a single casualty?" The general opinion was that submission had not only not reduced the dimensions of the catastrophe, but had magnified it. "We must go out into the streets. We must set everything alight!" In these words Ringelblum transmits the mood of the street. "We should have broken down the walls and crossed into the 'Aryan' sector. The Germans would have taken their revenge. It would have cost us tens of thousands of lives, but not three hundred thousand."

Grief at the loss of relatives and anxiety for what lay ahead were now mingled with a powerful urge for vengeance.

Most of the population was now ready for resistance. On November 5, 1942, Ringelblum wrote: "The people want the enemy to pay heavily. They will attack with knives, staves, bullets. They will no longer permit mass arrests. They will not allow themselves to be kidnapped in the streets. Now they know that every work-camp means death. . . . Now everybody, old and young, must defend himself against the enemy." In such a climate, with such a mood, the Jewish Underground could launch large-scale operations. In this period collaboration between the parties and the youth organizations became closer.

There are few sources for information on this preliminary period of organization and training of the various fighting units. This was particularly the case with the younger unit of Hashomer Hazair, Dror, Gordonia, Poalei Zion, the Bund and others. The older members of the fighting units had been trained in physical training courses held before the War. These courses had actually been devoted to self-defense against Polish anti-Semitic hooligans. (In the winter of 1938–1939 Hechalutz had organized a six weeks course at Zhclonka near Warsaw. Forty members took part in the course, the instructors of which came from Eretz Israel.)

Among the documents preserved in the second part of the Ringelblum Archives are a number of leaflets of the Jewish Underground, dated December 1942 and January 1943, indicating the true character of the murderers "who wish to exploit our labor to the last drop of blood and sweat, till our last breath." They also revealed the falsity of the reports disseminated by the enemy agents, e.g., "letters coming from Jews deported from Warsaw and now in labor camps in Minsk or Bobruisk." The bloody murderers," states one leaflet of the Jewish Fighting Organization, of January 1943, "have a clearly defined purpose: to keep the Jewish population calm, and thereby to ensure that the deportation is carried out without a hitch, with the use of minimum force, and without casualties on the part of the Germans." The Jews were called upon to resist actively: "Not a single Jew must enter the truck. Those who cannot resist actively must adopt passive resistance; in other words they must hide."

The leaflet entitled, "Get Ready for Action! Be Prepared"—undated but apparently issued in December 1942, by the "Jewish Military Union"—explicitly states: "There is no salvation in going to die apathetically, like sheep to the slaughter." Only "those who resist have any hope of being saved. Let the enemy pay with his own blood for every Jew. Let every house become our fortress. Jews, rouse yourselves and fight for your lives!"

In another leaflet the Jewish Fighting Organization issued a warning. "Let no man lift up his hand to help, actively or passively, the hangmen, in handing over his brethren, his comrades, his neighbors, or workmates. The despicable traitors who help the enemy will be cast out of the community."

Even before the establishment of the Coordination Committee in October 30, 1942, the Jewish Fighting Organization decided to clean the ghetto of the internal enemy, by the liquidation of the lowest criminal types who had sold themselves to the Germans. Thereby they sought to intimidate the *Judenrat* and the Ghetto Police. The killing of Yaacov Leykin, Deputy Commander of the Ghetto Police, on October 29 by Eliyahu Rozhansky (assisted by M. Growas and Margalit Landau), served as a warning to his comrades in the Police. This was also the case with the death sentence imposed on Israel First, executed by David Shulman (assisted by Berl Braude and Sarah Granatstein).

In the public warning given by the Jewish Fighting Organization, on October 30, on the day following the assassination of Leykin, we read: "The public is hereby informed that following the arraignment of the officers and constables of the Jewish Police of Warsaw—as indicated in the notice of August 17—sentence was carried out on Yaacov Leykin, Deputy Commander of the Jewish

Police, in Warsaw, at 6:10 P.M., October 29. Further acts of reprisal will be taken with the full force of the law. The public is also hereby informed that the following have been arraigned: (1) the Warsaw *Judenrat* and its Presidium for collaboration with the occupant, and assistance in acts of deportation; (2) the managers and officials of the shops oppressing and exploiting the workers; (3) group leaders and officials of the *Werkschutz* [factory guard] for their brutal attitude towards workers and the 'illegal' Jewish population. Rigorous reprisals will be taken."

It is, of course, well-known that in January 1943 (that is, before the *akzia* was renewed) the Jewish Fighting Organization launched a number of acts of terror against persons guilty of various crimes against the Jewish people. The punishment took the form of pouring vitriol on them. The Fighting Organization planned a big reprisal operation against the Jewish Police on January 22, 1943—six months after the great *akzia* set in motion in the summer of 1942.

Thanks to the Diary of Shmuel Winter and other authentic documents from Jewish and Polish sources we know that a network of secret agents of the Gestapo was thrown over the shops. It was only in regard to some of them that the Jewish Fighting Organization had precise knowledge. Most of them were successful in covering up their tracks and it was only by chance that their true function became known.

At this time the German agent and spy Ganzweich made an appearance in the ghetto. In his lectures, Ganzweich called for the establishment of a Jewish Anti-Soviet League. He collaborated with the "Torch" (*Zagiew*) group which was in the service of the Gestapo. Kalmanowich, an agent of the group, sought to obtain from Winter—who supplied food to the Jewish Fighting Organization—rations for a "fighting" group named *Traugut* [the undercover name for the "Torch" group]. At the same time Ganzweich and his gang spread optimistic rumors about the prospects of the ghetto.

Illegal newspapers and underground leaflets continued to be published in the Ghetto. (In November and December 1942 *Der Sturm,* organ of the Underground, was published. The last issue was published in April 1943.) The group in the service of the Gestapo also issued organs: *P.O.B.* (Ganzweich's paper) and *Żagiew* (published by Kalmonowich, the Gestapo agent).

The brushmakers issued a secret radio bulletin, which was circulated among the Jews of the "shop." The reports from the fronts, printed in this bulletin, emanated from abroad. But the light in which events within the ghetto were reported was astonishing. The "editor" assured his readers in his bulletin that his group had succeeded in introducing a number of Jews into the Gestapo, who were playing a double role. Thus the "shop" would always have information on every *akzia* that the Germans were about to launch.

Thanks to the vigilance of the Jewish Organization a secret investigation was undertaken. It was proved that the "editor" of the bulletins in the brushmakers' "shop" was the leader of a group of Gestapo agents, who left the ghetto on frequent occasions. He was executed by two *halutzim*. On his body a document issued by the Gestapo and a large sum of money were found. A note bearing the legend "For treachery" was stuck onto the corpse.

The Fighting Organization declared war to the death on the traitors collaborating with the Germans, and responsible by their despicable behavior for moral corruption in the ghetto. They were sentenced to death and saved themselves from the hands of the fighters by flight to the "Aryan" side of the city. The most important operation against Jewish agents of the enemy, in which fifteen persons took part, was carried out on February 21 . . . on 38 Swietojerska Street. . . . The attempts were made against the lives of Leon (Lolek) Skosovsky, Pawel Vlodarsky, Adek Weintraub, Mangel, Lidia Radziejewska (Ania). Skosovsky was seriously wounded, while the rest were killed. No casualties were sustained by the assailants. The latter captured a M.N. 7657 revolver and seven rounds of ammunition, the property of Skosovsky.

Operations against the traitors and spies also included the members of the *Werkschutz* who had oppressed the workers. For example "Pat," one of the most hated members of the German *Werkschutz,* was shot. A notice was published regarding every death sentence carried out by the Fighting Organization. As a result of these operations, the organization began to be called "The People's Avengers."

"The Jewish Military Union," established by the Revisionists, also carried out a number of death sentences on traitors, who had collaborated with the Gestapo. Among others the policeman Kosowsky was shot dead.

In the course of a short time, the Jewish fighting organizations had succeeded in gaining the confidence of the Jews in the ghetto. Their renown grew during the January *akzia* and subsequently, proving the far-reaching changes that had occurred among the Jewish survivors in the ghetto. The fighting in January between the Jewish Fighting Organization and the German gendarmerie and the SS was a source of encouragement, indicating a new spirit among the Jewish combat units. It caused shamed surprise among the Germans. The legend of the "invincible Germans" who could seal the fate of hundreds of thousands of Jews if they so willed was destroyed.

The reports of the first act of Jewish resistance spread like wildfire through the whole city of Warsaw. The first account of the fighting in the ghetto was rendered in the "Aryan" sector by "Jurek" (Aryeh Wilner), representative of the Fighting Organization accredited to the Polish Underground, who engaged in smuggling arms in the ghetto. Wilner had taken part personally in the ghetto fighting.

The Gestapo headquarters reacted characteristically. It resolved to confuse and demoralize the two fighting organizations. It established its "own" Jewish organization called "The Free Jews Organization," headed by Captain Lontzki. This organization issued an "illegal" newspaper which by the use of "revolutionary" phraseology sought to lead the Jews astray. The Jews were called upon to take up arms forthwith against the Germans, and not to wait for the destruction of the ghetto. The true purposes of this organization, however, were transparently clear. They wished to sow confusion in the ranks of the fighting organizations and upset the preparations for the Rising. Immediate action, accordingly, was necessary to forestall this satanic plan. The headquarters of the Fighting Organization and the Military Union published a circular warning the inhabitants of the ghetto against the provocations of Gestapo agents and informing them that these were the only two bodies heading the resistance movement. Only instructions issued by them were to be heeded.

In view of these circumstances the Jewish Fighting Organization accepted into its ranks only those whose past was well-known, preferring members of the Zionist youth organizations, known for their loyalty and devotion, who had had an ideological training. After the January *akzia* twenty-two combat units were organized on a movement basis. The military discipline of these units was essentially a function of this movement character. The members knew each other well and there was a strong spirit of mutual confidence and esprit-de-corps among them.

After the events of January all fighters had to live collectively, principally in *kibbutzim,* which were the bases of the Fighting Organization. Half of the twenty-two combat units belonged to the youth movements, which, as stated, constituted the backbone of the Fighting Organization. Collective living . . . welded these units closely together in the dangerous conditions under which they lived and in view of the struggle that lay ahead. They were inspired by the defenders of Tel Hai. More than others they stressed that the struggle of the ghetto was the fight for Jewish dignity and honor.

The exemplary esprit-de-corps within these units was demonstrated in a terrorist action against the "shop" of Halmann in Nowolipki Street, before the January *akzia.* On January 17, a number of fighters threw vitriol at a Jewish policeman. The fighters were successful in making their get-away. One of them, however, Zandmann, a member of Hashomer Hazair, was apprehended by a watchman of the *Werkschutz,* who informed the managers of his capture. When Mordecai Anielewicz, commander of the ghetto fighters, heard of this, he made his way to the "shop" to get Zandmann out of the clutches of his captors. On the night of January 17–18 a number of fighters attacked the office in which he was being held and liberated him. Dr. Ringelblum, who was employed in the Halmann "shop" and took part in the consultations regarding the freeing of Zandmann, emphasizes Anielewicz's readiness to undertake any risk for his comrades, just as the latter were willing to lay down their lives for their commander.

We have less information about the internal organization of the Military Union, established after the January *akzia* by the Revisionists. The Union also included members of various other youth organizations—including Communists—as well as non-party members. After prolonged negotiations and much effort the Fighting Organization succeeded in establishing contact with the Military Union and common forms of organization were introduced (especially in the acquisition of arms). The basic principle in both was that only three or at most five members knew each other. The ghetto was swarming with provocateurs and informers, and exceptional precautions were necessary to protect the organization, which could have been destroyed in a single swoop of the Gestapo. . . .

Eventually closer contact was discontinued and relations between the two organizations were restricted to joint meetings on a command level and cooperation in the acquisition of arms. There was also an agreement dividing the defence sectors in the ghetto between the two bodies.

When the preparations for the Rising were in progress, however, and when the fighting had started the differences between the two dwindled. Zionist *halutzim,* Bundists and Communists fought shoulder to shoulder. Many of the fighters could smuggle themselves out of the ghetto and escape the fighting, but they refused to do so. They were inspired by a profound sense of duty, by a burning desire to avenge themselves and their people and to fight for their people's honor. Revenge and honor inspired all of them.

When, for example, a suggestion was put to the renowned fighter Aryeh Wilner that he remain in the "Aryan" sector, he declared that he had no wish to remain alive while most of his comrades were being killed. He preferred death with honor.

It was this aspiration to die honorably, to defend human and Jewish dignity, that generated the Rising.

We have no authentic information about the "activities" of the Free Jews Organization prior to the outbreak of the Rising, but it is known that on the first day of the Rising, leaflets bearing the signature of "Captain Lontzki" appeared on the walls of the ghetto, declaring that "the time for action and vengeance has come." He called all men capable of bearing arms for active service. The aged and the women were required to contribute money. In the concluding passage of the leaflet "Captain Lontzki stated that "from this day the system of quintets has been abolished. All must come to headquarters in their masses." The aim of the leaflet was abundantly clear, to sow confusion at the crucial moment in the ranks of the fighters. The attempt, however, failed.

After the armed Rising of January 1943, in the comparatively short interval until April of that year, the Jewish Resistance Movement registered notable achievements in the organization and arming of the ghetto. The Fighting Organization, which was mainly responsible for the resistance, won the confidence of the Jewish masses and established its authority. The construction of underground bunkers and tunnels was taken in hand energetically, arms were acquired to equip the largest possible number of Jewish fighters and to establish lines of communication between the combat units.

The present is not the place to enter into any account of the magnitude and the tempo of these preparations for the Rising, and of the organizational capacity of the leaders, thanks to whom the ghetto was converted into a stronghold, able to resist for many weeks the criminal and murderous designs of Himmler. It is, however, rewarding to review, albeit in brief, the unceasing guerrilla warfare which the Fighting Organization conducted after January 18, 1943.

On February 11, three fighters took part in an operation in which an SS man was killed. The booty, a Mauser revolver and a sum of money, was handed over to the regional commander.

Nine fighters were involved in an action on February 19 within the precincts of the ghetto. Two German gendarmes were killed. The booty: uniforms, two revolvers of the Parabellum and Wis types—and a sum of money.

A major act of sabotage was carried out on March 6. The storehouses of the SS and the police of 31 Nalewki Street were set on fire. These stores with workshops attached supplied equipment to army hospitals: mattresses, beds and blankets. Five men, reinforced by a local group of nine, took part in this operation. Incendiary bottles, thermite bombs, petrol and kerosene were used in setting the stores on fire. Immense damage was caused. The withdrawal was carried out according to plan and without any casualties, before the gendarmes were called into action.

In the February–March months the Fighting Organization operated resolutely against the German plans for "the transfer of the ghetto to work camps in Poniatowa and Trawniki." The first enterprises to be transferred included the shop of Halmann and the brushmakers. But on the night before the planned removal of the Halmann factory, at the end of February, a Fighting Organization group (comprising thirteen fighters under the command of Shelomo Winogron) penetrated via the factory walls and set the buildings aflame. The factory premises included a row of buildings from the corner of Samoce Street to the corner of Wolnosc Street. The fire destroyed all the raw materials and the machinery which had been put together ready for dispatch. The Germans on the factory premises fled in panic. The combat group withdrew without loss.

Similar operations were undertaken by the Fighting Organization against the brushmakers' shop and the shop of Schultz and Schilling.

A large-scale combat action was carried out by the organization on March 13 in the vicinity of Mila and Zamenhof Streets. A combat unit attacked the German factory guards of the Steyer works, who for weeks had been responsible for acts of shooting and robbery in the ghetto. In this action one German was shot and his arms confiscated, while another German was shot dead in flight. The guards were reinforced by SS men and police. In the affray which ensued another SS man was severely wounded and arms taken from six Ukrainians. No casualties were suffered by the Jewish unit. The civilian population actively assisted the Jewish fighters. In a reprisal action, however, several truckloads of gendarmes surrounded Mila Street, to Muranow Square, and shot all passersby in addition to people who were taken out of their homes and hiding places. (One hundred and seventy Jews, including fourteen children, were killed in this operation.)

On March 15, 1943 the Fighting Organization issued leaflets

calling upon the Jews to resist the transfer order to Poniatowa and Trawniki. The leaflets stressed that compliance meant the destruction of the ghetto, as Poniatowa and Trawniki were no more than transit stations on the road to Treblinka. This time the German efforts to put an end to the ghetto "quietly"—failed. The enemy's attempt to rob the Jewish fighters of their natural battle-ground, the ghetto, was foiled by the Jewish Resistance.

The dramatic appeal made by the commander of the Jewish Fighting Organization to the armed forces of the Polish Under-ground to supply the ghetto immediately with one hundred grenades, fifty revolvers and ten rifles, and thousands of rounds of ammunition of various calibres was explained by the "low state of our arms after the repeated operations of recent weeks, in which a large amount of ammunition was used up. . . ." "We shall not try to convince any one of our determination or ability to fight," wrote Mordecai Anielewicz bitterly. "From January 18 the Jews of Warsaw have been fighting ceaselessly against the occupant and the collaborators. Those who doubt or deny this are deliberate anti-Semites." The commander of the Jewish Fight-ing Organization indicated his "willingness to furnish precise plans of our situation, together with maps, to establish beyond a shadow of doubt the need for arms."

Unfortunately Anielewicz's dramatic appeal did not meet with the response it deserved. . . .

. . . Significant Jewish documents which have reached us re-cently are the Statutes of the Jewish Fighting Organization (*Yid-dische Kanuf Organizatzie*—YKO), dated December 2, 1942, the reminiscences of Hirsch Berlinski, accounts of the Ghetto Rising, and a profile of the commander of the Jewish defenders, Mordecai Anielewicz, written by Dr. Emmanuel Ringelblum.

The memoirs and other writings of Hirsch Berlinski, the heroic commander of the Left Poalei Zion unit, and a member of the Headquarters of the Jewish Fighting Organization, constitute a major discovery. As one of the leaders of the Left Poalei Zion (after the deportation of Schachna Sagan to Treblinka in the *akzia* of summer 1942, Berlinski, together with Paula Elster, headed the Central Committee of the party), he took part in all the secret conferences preceding the establishment of the Fighting Organization and the Jewish National Committee. Berlinski was also active in a number of expropriation operations for the Arms Fund of the YKO.

As commander of the Left Poalei Zion unit Berlinski fought at the beginning of the Rising in the area of the brush factory, and later in other sectors. Berlinski was also a member of the group which organized the rescue of sixty ghetto fighters, who after the crushing of the Rising sought to reach the "Aryan" sector of the city through the sewers. Only part of this group, including Berlinski himself, succeeded eventually in reaching the partisan units in the Wyszkow forests. Later the Jewish underground smuggled him into the "Aryan" sector of Warsaw, where he was active in the work of the Underground and had time to write his reminiscences and other accounts of the Rising. . . .

Berlinski's writings were found in the ruins of the building at Suwalska No. 25, between Zoliborz and Powaski on January 2, 1943, by Joseph Ziemian,[3] and were transmitted to Dr. A. Berman, a leader of the underground Jewish National Committee on the "Aryan" side of the city. The original mss. is today in the possession of the Warsaw Jewish Historical Institute (a photostat is in the Yad Vashem Archives).

Berlinski, together with his comrades Paula Elster and Eliahu Erlich fell on September 27, 1944, in hand-to-hand fighting with Nazis during the Polish Rising in the Zoliborz Quarter, in which a unit of the Jewish Fighting Organization took part. He was thirty-five years old at the time of his death.

Hirsch Berlinski took part in the first conference of the workers movements (Hechalutz, Right Poalei Zion, Left Poalei Zion and the Bund), held at the end of March 1942, in the People's Kitchen at No. 2 Orla Street, and remembered all the details of the discussion that took place at the time. The first item on the agenda was the defence of the Warsaw Ghetto. At the end of his speech on this subject the Hechalutz representative, Yitzchak Zuckerman, proposed that a leadership be established to undertake organiza-

[3] His book *The Cigarette Sellers of Three Crosses Square* (London: Valentine, Mitchell and Co.) appeared in 1970.

tion of the defence of the ghetto. Maurycy Orzech, representative
of the Bund, however, expressed his strong opposition to the
creation of a single Fighting Organization: "the fighting unit of the
Bund will not reveal to any general Fighting Organization the lines
upon which it is organized or its aims, as these are military secrets,
which must be carefully safeguarded." What he meant to say was
that the Bund (like the Polish Socialist Party) had close connections with the Polish Underground under the authority of the latter,
and that for this reason he could not disclose the secrets of the Bund
to other underground groups. Thus a united defence committee was
not set up, notwithstanding the fact that the representatives of all
the other parties were in favor of the establishment of such a body.

In deliberating on the problems of the Rising, Berlinski voiced
not only his personal opinion but rendered the credos of the other
parties, which were eager for battle, and particularly of the youth
organizations. "Even if the fighting should take on a restricted
character (not with firearms)," he wrote, "there is no other way."
He was convinced that if the masses were informed of the true
facts, thousands of young men and women would be prepared to
join in the struggle, armed with knives and axes, sticks and rods,
salicylic acid and sulphur "to strike back at our mortal enemy."
What Berlinski sought was to "show the world that we did not go
as sheep to the slaughter. Let our desperate act be a sign of protest to the world which did nothing against the shameful acts of the
Hitlerite murderers, who are bringing about the destruction of
hundreds of thousands of Jews." "Neither Soviet Russia and certainly not the Allied powers can help us in any way in our great
distress. The underground Polish Government, which could ex-
tend real aid to us, will not do so," he went on to say.

Berlinski renders highly important information on the important social centre, which developed after the *akzia* in the
Ostdeutsche Bauwerk Tischlerei shop, one of whose managers
was Alexander Landau, patron of Hashomer Hazair, who placed
himself and his property at the disposal of the defence of Warsaw
Ghetto. Thereby all members of Hashomer Hazair, the leadership
of Hashomer Hazair, the leadership of the Left Poalei Zion,
the Polish Party and leaders of the Jewish Mutual Aid, including

Oneg Shabbat [members working on the Underground Archives—the Ringelblum Archives], obtained legalization as workers employed in the shop.

Berlinski expands on the conference held in the Hashomer Hazair hostel at Mila St. 61 at which the following decisions were made: (1) "to set up the Fighting Organization in order to organize the defence of the Warsaw Ghetto"; (2) "to teach the Jewish Police and the *Werkschutz* [the internal police of the 'shops'], the managers of the shops and the provocateurs a lesson."

The details given of the establishment of "defence authorities" are highly interesting. The representatives of the Hashomer Hazair and Hechalutz were in favor of the establishment of a Fighting Organization but the members of the Left Poalei Zion succeeded in persuading the participants of the need "to set up another authority which, on the basis of sober political assessment, would decide the right time to embark upon armed resistance."

In November a Coordinating Committee with the Bund was established and the Headquarters of the Jewish Fighting Organization was appointed. Twenty fighting squads, each comprising five members, were organized.

The arsenal of the Fighting Organization was incredibly meagre. It comprised no more than two revolvers. The fighting squads were armed "with sticks, knives, knuckle dusters, salicylic acid, sulphur, paraffin and petrol." This was all. "These are our (first) arms," wrote Berlinski. "With these arms our people embarked upon the development of the Fighting Organization. How much faith, devotion, courage and stamina must the members of the Organization have had to generate the necessary enthusiasm in themselves and their comrades in order to go out to battle."

Information on the battle against the *Werkschutz* and the managers of the shops goes far beyond the details we have from other sources.

Berlinski is the only source for information on the internal disputes regarding the distribution of the first consignment of arms, which the Organization received from the "Delegatura"—the underground representative body of the Polish Government-in-Exile in London—in December 1942. Similarly, it is only from Berlinski that we learn precise details of the demonstration which the Fighting Organization planned to stage in the Muranow Square under the slogan, "Honor to the fallen—half a year of destruction, 22.7.42–22.1.43." It was to be headed by Mordecai Anielewicz and his deputies, Berlinski and Marek Edelman, but the unexpected *akzia* in January prevented the holding of the demonstration that had been planned.

Berlinski's notes on the January Rising also possess a special significance. In this Rising, Anielewicz was successful in capturing a rifle and a Parabellum revolver. Berlinski gives us information about the battle that took place at the corner of Zamenhof and Niska Streets: ". . . While marching with a group of detainees (arrested by the Germans), he opened fire and commanded the battle that ensued. Some of the SS men were wounded or killed, while the rest fled, leaving behind their caps, and some of them even their arms. The Germans thereupon set fire to the building in which he and his men had taken up position. Mordecai (Anielewicz) succeeded in escaping. I greet his victory with a comradely handshake." Berlinski analyzed the January Rising and drew a number of conclusions. The Gordonia unit had not fought badly and had even captured some arms (it was accepted into the Fighting Organization after the January *akzia*). The fighting finished at the corner of Zamenhof and Niska Streets, where Mordecai and two other members fought the Germans courageously. Taking up position in a timber store, he kept the Germans at bay, capturing the arms of those who were wounded and using these weapons in the course of the battle. When the SS men set fire to the store he was forced to retreat. His two comrades were burnt to death. "When I complained to Mordecai about the non-distribution of the arms, which prevented the other units from taking part in the fighting, Mordecai replied: 'It makes no difference which of the movements was in action. The fighting was done by the Fighting Organization. The battle and its results are shared by all of us equally.' To my demand that there be a just distribution of arms I received the reply: 'We cannot deprive our comrades of the weapons with which they fought. In the course of our work we shall achieve equality and injustices will be put right.' "

It must be added here that Anielewicz kept his promise as soon as a new consignment of arms and ammunition was received from the Polish Underground (after the January *akzia*).

Ringelblum's biographical note, entitled "Mordecai Anielewicz —Commander of the Warsaw Fighting Organization," is of primary importance. Ringelblum, it transpires, first got to know Anielewicz at the beginning of the war. "Since then," Ringelblum wrote, "he used to come to me frequently to borrow books on Jewish history and economics, in which Mordecai took a deep interest. Who would ever have thought at that time that this quiet young fellow, so modest and so likeable, would, within three years, become the most important person in the ghetto, spoken of by everyone—with respect or with fear."

In the winter of 1941/42 Ringelblum witnessed Anielewicz's assumption of the post of commander of the Hashomer Hazair during a parade of the *Ken* (local organization) in Warsaw, when members of the movement were raised in rank. This ceremony required a formal avowal of loyalty to the movement. The occasion provided evidence of the love, respect and devotion which surrounded the personality of Mordecai. "He was surrounded by a similar aura later when he was commander of the Fighting Organization, but responsibility and authority did not go to his head. He remained as modest in his bearing as he had been always."

Young Mordecai, who matured with extraordinary rapidity, was one of the first to understand, after reports had been received of the massacres in Vilna, Slonim and other towns in the East, that all the Jews of Poland would be slaughtered. He deeply regretted that he and his comrades had wasted three years of the war in educational and cultural activities (in organizing advanced study circles and seminars). "We did not appreciate the significance of this new era of Hitler," Mordecai stated with sorrow. "We should have trained our youth in the use of firearms and other weapons. We should have educated them in a spirit of revenge against the greatest enemy of the Jews and of mankind."

Mordecai devoted himself entirely to the organization of defence. He was not only leader of the Jewish Fighting Organization (an appointment which he received from the Coordinating

Committee of Political Organizations), but one of the most devoted workers it had. He was not a commander of the type that sends his men into the firing line. He was endowed with a rare loyalty to his comrades, for whom he was ready to make every sacrifice, and his comrades reciprocated in kind. This was proven in the skirmish at the corner of Zamenhof and Niska Streets, during the January *akzia*.

A few days prior to the outbreak of the Rising, Dr. Ringelblum had an opportunity of visiting the arsenal of the ZZW (the Jewish Military Organization—the Revisionist body), which occupied a six-room apartment, on the first floor of an abandoned building at No. 7 Muranowska Street (this area was later known as "no-man's-land"). In the executive office, in which Ringelblum spent several hours, was an excellent radio set, capable of receiving transmissions from all parts of the world. Next to it was a typewriter. The leaders of the organization were well-armed. In the large halls were hung various types of weapons, including light machine guns, rifles, revolvers and pistols, hand grenades, bandoliers full of bullets, and German uniforms, of which full advantage was taken in the course of the fighting. The room was full of activity, just as in a proper army HQ. Orders were issued and transmitted to the various concentration points of the fighters, reports were received of many expropriation operations on behalf of the Arms Fund of ZZW. At the time of Ringelblum's visit, a transaction was concluded involving the payment of a quarter of a million zlotys to a former Polish army officer. Among other weapons, two machine guns were purchased at a price of 40,000 zlotys each, as well as a large quantity of grenades and bombs. The officer received an advance payment of 50,000 zlotys.

To his question as to why the arms-store was not properly concealed, Ringelblum was told that there was no fear of treachery among the members of the organization, and even if any undesirable guest such as a gendarme happened to drop in, he would not be left alive.

At that time, Dr. Ringelblum also visited the concentration point of the Fighting Organization, which was in a two-room apartment in 33 Swietojerska Street. Three floors below stood a German policeman guarding the shop. In the hall were ten armed fighters

IMPOSSIBLE

ready for action (friends and sympathizers of the Left Poalei Zion). They were forbidden to leave the hall, entrance to which was obtained via an attic of a neighboring building. Three girl fighters were preparing a meal, besides undertaking various dangerous missions for the organization. This group must be credited with a number of successful expropriation missions on behalf of the Arms Fund of the Fighting Organization.

It may be added that in view of the surprise tactics adopted by the Germans, all fighting units were generally ready to take action at a moment's notice.

Not only the Fighting Organization manufactured and used bottles containing explosive liquids. (Before the outbreak of the Rising, Halmann's "shop" at 53–55 Nowolipki Street, in which a large store of furniture had been prepared for the German Army, was destroyed with the aid of bottles of this kind.) Similar bottles were prepared in the individual positions, in addition to the collection of cold weapons, including axes, hammers, iron rods and the like.

Ringelblum gives us much information on the mood of the Fighting Organization and records remarks of the members regarding the inequality of the two sides, the combating of informers and Gestapo agents, the "shop" police and managers. Ringelblum prepared a list of those who had been shot "upon the orders of the Fighting Organization."

He proceeds to describe how the organization succeeded, "by propaganda and bullets," in imposing its authority upon the community.

From a talk between Ringelblum and Anielewicz we learn how soberly the latter assessed the situation. He was convinced that he and his comrades would fall in the hopeless battle ahead, that no man would know where and how they had fallen.

Ringelblum's assessment of the January (18.1.1943) *akzia* is highly instructive. In this *akzia* the Jews of Warsaw demonstrated obstinate opposition. To the credit of the Fighting Organization it must be said that the SS units were compelled to enter the ghetto in full battle order, supported by small tanks and light field artillery, grenades, light and heavy machine guns, etc. Ringelblum could not arrive at any assessment of the number of Germans that were killed and wounded, but he was convinced that they totalled dozens. Of the ten thousand Jews concentrated for despatch to Treblinka, one thousand were killed on the spot for disobeying orders. Notwithstanding the respect evoked among the Polish population by the heroic attitude of the Jews, the repeated appeals made to the Underground Government by various Jewish Underground leaders to supply arms to the ghetto remained unavailing. The quantity of arms that came from this source was, to use Ringelblum's term, "homeopathic."

Ringelblum wrote several accounts of the April Rising. His heart bled to see a mere handful of ill-armed fighters, the cream of Jewish youth, forced to wage battle with the German army, knowing that the outcome was a foregone conclusion. He himself observed the battle from the rooftops, from which fluttered the Polish and Jewish flags. He watched the battle in Muranowska Street from the fourth floor of the building at 32 Nalewki Street, on the afternoon of April 18. He also saw the fighters open fire on the SS units marching through (e.g. from 76 Leszno Street, from K. G. Schultz's shop).

Ringelblum also rendered an account of the battles waged outside the confines of the ghetto by Jewish units which had succeeded in breaking through the surrounding German positions. He expanded the accounts of the heroic exploits of Jewish fighters. The source of the story of a Jewish Joan of Arc dressed all in white, reported to have been seen from Swietojerska Street, firing accurately at the Germans with a machine gun and miraculously immune from all German shots at her, can be traced to the fact that women did indeed operate a machine gun from one of the roofs.

Ringelblum likened the brutality of Jürgen Stroop, in command of the operations against the ghetto, to that of Suworow, the Russian conqueror of the Praga quarter of Warsaw in Kosciuszko's rising. But in the eyes of an historian of Ringelblum's calibre the acts perpetrated by Suworow's soldiers were child's play compared to the horrors committed by Stroop and his minions.

The Germans made plans of their own. In January, Himmler visited Warsaw. There he got the information that about 40,000

Jews were still in the ghetto. (Actually, the number was about 70,000.) He decided that there were too many and ordered that 8000 be deported at once; from the remainder he wanted to save about 16,000 for forced labor camps. To Oberst Freter of the Armament Command in Warsaw he remarked that Keitel had agreed to this plan.

The January push came quite suddenly and caught the ghetto defenders by surprise. Sixty-five hundred Jews were snatched away. In the ensuing fracas one German police captain was severely wounded in the abdomen.

After this encounter Himmler ordered the total dissolution of the ghetto. The emptied Jewish quarter was to be torn down completely. No Poles were to be permitted to settle there, for Himmler did not want Warsaw to grow back to its former size.

The German SS and Police Leader in Warsaw, Oberführer von Sammern-Frankenegg, expected some difficulties in the operation and therefore concentrated his own forces and secured some assistance from the army's *Oberfeld-kommandantur* in Warsaw. He made his preparations thoroughly and, on the first day of the *akzia,* handed over his command to his successor, Brigade-führer Stroop.

Guerrilla Warfare

RAUL HILBERG *

This account is based on German sources.
However, Jewish scholars have insisted that the
German commanders grossly underestimated
their own losses in the final reports sent to
their superior officers. This was not to deny, of
course, the tremendous advantage of the Germans in the manpower and firepower available
for their use in the destruction of the ghetto.

Comparative Strength of Opposing Forces in Warsaw Ghetto*

JEWS	GERMANS
ZOB (*Zydowska Organizacja Bo-jowa*) Twenty-two platoon-size "battle groups" (men and women between 18 and 25)	*WAFFEN-SS* (with three or four weeks of basic training only) SS-Armored Grenadier Train-ing and Replacement Battal-ion No. 3, Warsaw SS-Cavalry Training and Re-placement Battalion, Warsaw
IZL (*Irgun Zwai Leumi*) Three battle groups	
A few Poles who were inside the ghetto and Polish partisans (Communists and national-ists) who carried out diver-sionary attacks outside the ghetto.	Order Police (including veterans of the eastern front) 1st and 2nd Battalions of the 22nd Police Regiment Technical police Polish police

* *Op. cit.*, pp. 322–327.

Comparative Strength of Opposing Forces
in Warsaw Ghetto * (*cont.*)

JEWS	GERMANS
	Polish fire brigade
	SECURITY POLICE (small detachments)
	ARMY 1 light anti-aircraft battery 1 howitzer crew 2 engineer platoons 1 medical unit
	COLLABORATORS (Ukrainians) 1 Battalion from Trawniki camp
Total armed strength: about 1500	Total armed strength: about 2000–3000
Equipment: 2 or 3 light machine guns 100 rifles and carbines (give or take a few dozen) A few hundred revolvers and pistols A few thousand hand grenades (Polish and homemade) Homemade Molotov cocktails A few pressure mines and other explosive contraptions Gas masks German steel helmets German uniforms	Equipment: 1 captured French tank 2 heavy armored cars 3 light anti-aircraft guns 1 medium howitzer Flame throwers, heavy and light machine guns, submachine guns, rifles, and pistols; grenades, smoke candles, and large amounts of explosive charges
Objective: To Hold Out as Long as Possible	Objective: To Clear the Ghetto in 3 Days

At three o'clock in the morning on April 19, 1943, the ghetto was surrounded, and three hours later the *Waffen-SS* entered the ghetto at Zamenhof Street. The invaders were met by concen-

* Chart adapted from Table 48 in *ibid.*

trated fire, and incendiary bottles put the tank out of action. The SS men withdrew with casualties. Later in the morning, raiding parties again entered the ghetto, and this time they proceeded systematically from house to house. By afternoon they encountered machine-gun fire. Since it became apparent that the ghetto could not be cleared in one sweep, the Germans withdrew again at night to resume operations in the morning.

On April 20 and 21 slow progress was made. The Jews held the factories, and it was decided, after some negotiations with the managers and the army, to destroy the buildings with artillery and explosives. By April 22 several sections of the ghetto were afire, and Jews jumped from the upper stories of the burning buildings after having thrown mattresses and upholstered articles into the street. The raiders attempted to drown Jews moving around in the sewers, but the Jews managed to block off the flooded passages.

After April 22, Jews were caught and killed in increasing numbers. Sewers and dugouts were blown up one by one. Captured Jews reported to the Germans that the inmates of the dugouts "became insane from the heat, the smoke, and the explosions." A few of the Jewish prisoners were forced to reveal hiding places and centers of resistance.

The Jews now tried to slip out of the ghetto through the sewer system; the army engineers countered this move by blowing up the manholes. Smoke candles were lowered into the underground passages, and Jews who mistook the candles for poison gas came up for air. In May the ghetto was a sea of flames. Only a few parties of Jews were still above ground in the burning buildings, and in their dugouts they were buried in debris and suffocated. Corpses were observed floating in the sewers. One desperate Jewish unit, emerging from a sewer, seized a truck and staged a successful getaway. The Jews were thinning out rapidly.

On May 8 the Jewish commander, Mordecai Anielewicz, was killed. The Germans now sent night patrols into the ghetto, and the remaining Jewish dugouts were systematically destroyed. By May 15 the shooting became sporadic. The Jews had been overwhelmed. At 8:15 P.M. on May 16 the German commander, Stroop, blew up the great Tlomackie Synagogue, in the "Aryan" section of the city, as a signal that the Warsaw Ghetto battle was over.

Several thousand Jews had been buried in the debris, and 56,065 had surrendered. Seven thousand of the captured Jews were shot; another 7000 were transported to the death camp at Treblinka; another 15,000 were shipped to the concentration camp and killing center at Lublin; the remainder were sent to labor camps. Nine rifles, fifty-nine pistols, several hundred grenades, explosives, and mines were captured. The rest of the Jewish equipment had been destroyed.

After the armed resistance of the Jews was broken, two tasks had to be completed. In accordance with Himmler's wish the entire ghetto was to be razed, and every dugout, cellar, and sewer was to be filled in. After the conclusion of this work the whole area was to be covered with earth and a large park was to be planted. The work was interrupted in July, 1944, before the park could be planted. For the incomplete job Himmler presented to Finance Minister von Krosigk a bill for 150,000,000 reichsmarks.

More difficult but a little less expensive than the rubble clearance work was the task of rounding up 5000–6000 Jews who had escaped from the ghetto before and during the battle and who were now hiding in various parts of the district. The Poles appeared to have aided the Germans in this roundup only "in a handful of cases" (*in einzelnen Fällen*). However, Polish gangs were roaming the city, seeking out Jewish hiding places and forcing the victims to pay high sums of money or face denunciation.

After the conclusion of the Warsaw Ghetto fighting, only a few major ghettos were still in existence, particularly Lwow in the Galician district, the Bialystok ghetto, and the Warthegau ghetto of Lodz. When Brigadeführer Katzmann, the Galician SS and Police Leader, moved into what was left of the Lwow ghetto in June, 1943, he discovered that the 20,000 Jews in the ghetto had begun to build dugouts and bunkers on the Warsaw pattern. "In order to avoid losses on our side," Katzmann reported, "we had to act brutally from the beginning." Blowing up and burning down houses, Katzmann dragged 3000 corpses out of the hiding places.

Last Days

ALEXANDER DONAT *

. . . my wife, Lena, and I thought constantly about saving our little boy. We went over and over the list of the "Aryans" we knew, trying to think which of them might be both willing and able to take him. I began to write letters to our Polish friends, telling them of our situation and begging them to save the life of an innocent child. Needless to say, these letters could not go through the mails: they had to be delivered by messenger. But even if one got hold of someone willing to deliver a letter outside the walls, the recipient was usually reluctant to accept a letter from the ghetto brought by a stranger: there was too much danger of blackmail. So I first had to alert my friends by phone, and tell them to expect a letter from me. To make these calls, I used the phone in the office of the T.O.Z. (one of the Jewish welfare agencies) at 56 Zamenhof Street, which I could get to through secret passages. The phone was in constant use: by people on errands like mine, or by smugglers contacting their confederates about conditions at the gates or arranging to receive parcels to be thrown over the wall. Each call took hours of waiting my turn. And then not everyone I wanted to reach had a phone. I would often call my former partner, Stanislaw Kapko, at his office and have him get a message to someone that he was to come to Kapko's office and await a call from me. Then I would have to call Kapko the next day to find out if the appointment had been made. When I finally spoke to the friend, I had then to

* "Our Last Days in the Warsaw Ghetto," *Commentary,* Vol. XXXV (May 1963), pp. 382–389.

persuade him to come and talk to me at the printing shop on Leszno Street. There was no danger for Gentiles in coming to the printing shop because it was located outside the ghetto, and they could always pretend to be out buying Jewish goods. Still, they were not easy to persuade. Some never came, some came and refused my request. Finally one possibility to save Wlodek began to take shape: the Maginskis.

Stefan Maginski had been a member of the group with whom I had fled Warsaw in September 1939 (whence I returned to be with my family). He was a brilliant journalist and a highly cultivated man. I loved him, and he treated me rather as if I were his younger brother. His wife, Maria, a former actress, was both a beauty and a great lady. They had no children.

Mrs. Maginski agreed to meet us in Leszno Street. She spoke of a friend in the country who, for a modest fee, would be willing to take the child. She vouched for the decency and honesty of her friend, and promised us that Wlodek would be well looked after. They themselves could not take him, because they were too old suddenly to appear with a five-year-old child, and they were, besides, working night and day with the Polish resistance. The fee was indeed modest, and happily we could afford it. Sometime earlier I had managed to increase my income by going into partnership with Izak Rubin to smuggle out some of the kerchiefs made from pillowcases in the ghetto. Thus I had the money to pay for Wlodek's care for several months in advance. By some child's instinct for self-preservation, Wlodek did everything in his power to win Mrs. Maginski, and she was much taken with him. She promised to make the necessary preparations. . . .

At the end of March, Mrs. Maginski came once more to Leszno Street—this time to tell us that all the arrangements for Wlodek had been made and we had two weeks in which to prepare him for leaving us.

Two weeks: in which we tried to memorize our five-year-old son to the look and to the touch, and in which I watched approvingly while my son's mother taught him to disavow his connection with us. "Remember, you have never lived in the ghetto. You are not a Jew. You are a Polish Catholic. Your father is a Polish army officer who was taken prisoner. Your mother is away in the country. Mrs. Maginski is your Auntie Maria."

The two weeks turned out to be only seven days. Mrs. Maginski unexpectedly returned to the printing shop one afternoon, terribly upset. The Polish Underground had received word that the liquidation of the ghetto was to take place any day now; the child must be smuggled out the next day. Next morning, Lena washed and fed her baby for the last time. At eight o'clock we joined the printers' marching column, and at eleven Mrs. Maginski came to the shop for him. Wlodek was quiet, smiling. But just as we were to say good-bye, he clutched his mother and said, "Is it true that I'll never see you again?" "What a silly boy you are!" she managed to say. "Just as soon as the war is over, I am coming to get you."

Mrs. Maginski took Wlodek's hand and walked briskly out of the building. Wlodek skipped beside her, and didn't look back once. They crossed Leszno and turned into Orla, out of sight. A Jewish policeman who was a friend of ours followed them for a little way on his bicycle. Everyone crowded around to congratulate us. We had been very lucky, they said. So, indeed, we had. . . .

On . . . Sunday (April 18) at 6 o'clock P.M., Polish police surrounded the ghetto. Within an hour the underground declared a state of emergency. The fighters were assigned to their posts. Weapons, ammunition, and food were distributed, along with supplies of potassium cyanide. By 2 A.M. the next morning (April 19) the Poles had been joined by Ukrainian, Latvian, and SS units, who ringed the ghetto walls with patrols stationed about thirty yards apart.

I had just come on guard duty at our apartment house when two boys from the Z.O.B. arrived to order us all to our shelters. They were about twenty years old, bare-headed, with rifles in their hands and grenades stuffed into their belts. It did not take long to alert everyone; by dawn the ghetto was a ghost town. I awakened Lena and the others in our flat; we put on the best clothing we could find, and took the linen bag we had filled with lump sugar and biscuits cut up into small squares. About thirty people gathered in our shelter.

We had only one weapon among us: Izak's revolver. Izak crouched at a peephole near the entrance to the shelter, from which he could see part of the courtyard. An ingenious network of tunnels connected us with the "outside" world. Through a tunnel extended to the front attic of our house, in turn connected with others, one could reach a spot just above the corner of Muranowska and Zamenhof Streets. The north side of the building, which fronted on Niska Street and the *Umschlagplatz*,[1] could be reached by a special passage that had been drilled through the carpenter's apartment. This same passage connected with No. 62 Zamenhof Street, where a resistance group was preparing to make its last-ditch stand. On the second floor a hole had been bored through to one of the lavatories in No. 42 Muranowska, from which we were put into connection with every building on the block.

Despite all our elaborate preparations, the German operation came upon us suddenly enough to upset all plans—those of the hundreds of people who had prepared to slip out to the "Aryan" side at the very last moment, and had documents and lodgings waiting for them, and, of course Kapko's grand scheme. That "very last moment" had come, and it was now too late for anything.

On Monday morning, the Germans marched into the ghetto through the gate at Gesia and Zamenhof Streets and took up positions in the little square opposite the *Judenrat* offices. Convinced that the resistance would not fire on Jews, they sent members of the Jewish police in their front ranks. Our fighters let the Jewish police go by, and barraged the Germans who followed with bullets, hand grenades, and home-made bombs. The intersection of Zamenhof and Mila Streets, where the resistance occupied the buildings on all four corners, became the scene of a real battle. Home-made incendiary bombs, flung from an attic window, hit first one tank and then another. The tanks burst into flames and

[1] This was the transfer point near the railway line which the mass deportations had made notorious.

their trapped crews were burned alive. The troops panicked and scattered in disorder.

I lay on the attic floor with Izak, watching all this going on below. Izak's orders were to cover the withdrawal of our unarmed people should it become necessary for them to leave the shelter; several times I saw him point his gun and then, reluctantly, withdraw it. Below us German officers were trying to urge on their panicked *"Judenhelden"* with pistols and riding crops: the men who had been so powerful and assured when dealing with women and children and old men were now running from the fire of the resistance. Scores of German bodies lay scattered on the pavement.

When Izak and I returned to the others in the shelter to report on what we had seen, people embraced and congratulated one another, laughing and crying. Some began to chant the Psalms, and an old man recited blessings aloud.

(Later we learned from some of the fighters that the first battle of the Warsaw Ghetto resistance had occurred at the corner of Nalewki and Gesia Streets, where a German unit marching into the ghetto had been caught totally off guard and where, after several hours, this first German unit withdrew, leaving behind their dead and wounded. But replacements came, and the fighting continued at this corner off and on all day. The resistance group's meager supply of grenades and bombs finally gave out, and they then had to retreat through the back of the house at 33 Nalewki Street. Before pulling back, they set fire to the warehouse at 31 Nalewki, where the SS stored their Jewish loot. The warehouse continued to smolder and burn until the very end.)

It was night before the gunfire, most of it coming from the direction of Muranow Square, seemed to have stopped. We waited till it got very dark, and then crept down into the courtyard to exchange information with our neighbors. Huge billows of smoke were rising from around Nalewki Street. There had been very little activity at the *Umschlagplatz,* we learned, and only a few Jews had been led out through Zamenhof Street. Two fighters came into the courtyard (giving us a bad moment—they were dressed in SS uniforms) and told us the day's happenings.

The shooting we had heard from Muranowska Street came

from a battle between a strong resistance group at 42 Nalewki Street and a German unit retreating from the fighting at Nalewki and Gesia Streets. This unit had backed into the doorway of the building and had been entirely wiped out from the rear. Later in the afternoon, a second German unit had appeared in the Square, this time armed with howitzers and flame-throwers. The resistance men there were under the command of Pawel Frenkel and Leon Rodal, and were the best armed and best trained in the ghetto. They occupied the houses along the eastern and southern sides of the Square, and using the passageways between the buildings, were able to keep changing the direction of their fire. The enemy retired from the ghetto after sunset.

The original battle, the one at Nalewki and Gesia Streets, had not gone so well for us. There had been heavy losses on both sides; but when our boys were forced to retreat from their position, the Germans took over Gesia Street and, with it, the ghetto hospital. The SS first worked its terrible vengeance on the sick, going through ward after ward with bayonets and guns; then they shelled the building and set fire to it. Those patients and staff members who had made it to the shelters died in the fire.

All day Tuesday we watched the glow in the sky that indicated shelling in the vicinity of the Brushmakers. The Brushmakers had its own independent fighting unit, headed by Marek Edelman; and when the Germans opened attack on the district—for only twenty-eight people out of 8,000 responded to the Germans' summons to report for deportation—they walked into a mined boobytrap at the entrance to 6 Walowa Street. Stroop then called for artillery fire on the entire Brushmakers' area. The resistance suffered very heavy losses, and house after house caught fire. Fighting was taken up again in Muranow Square. There the Germans had set up a concentration of tanks, heavy machine guns, and flame-throwers. The resistance, on the other hand, had an underground passage to the "Aryan" side, and throughout the battle was being supplied ammunition by the Polish resistance. Muranow Square was the only Jewish position that did not suffer from an extreme shortage of weapons. In the end, some of the Jewish fighters managed to escape through their passage to the "Aryan" side.

From our observation point, we could actually see flashes of the fighting going on in Zamenhof and Mila Streets. And from time to time there were columns of deportees moving up Zamenhof, under SS escort, to the *Umschlagplatz*. One of these columns was rescued by gunfire from 29 and 62 Zamenhof, which scattered the escort and allowed the deportees to get away.

The apartment house across the street caught fire, and the sparks carried by the wind constituted a real danger to us. In accordance with a plan previously agreed upon, I made my way to the building next door where—amazingly enough—there was still a telephone in working order. I calmly reported the fire to the fire department, and within a few minutes they appeared to put it out. It took some time before the fire department, undoubtedly under German orders, ceased responding to our calls.

Tuesday evening a blood-red glow hung over the southern end of the ghetto, and here and there throughout the rest of the ghetto a building was burning: in some instances, like that of the warehouse, from a fire set by the resistance, more often from the shelling and occasional air bombardment. That night the grapevine offered sensational news: the uprising had spread from the ghetto to the whole of Warsaw. Organizations like the AK (the Home Army) and the GL (the People's Guard) were joining their Jewish comrades; an unlimited supply of arms was making its way to the ghetto; more important, we heard, the Allies had promised to parachute troops and supplies to us. We would show the bastards yet!

For the first time in two days, we lit the stove and ate cooked potatoes and kasha from our reserve stock. We then went to sleep in our own beds, full of hope for tomorrow.

But Wednesday was no different from the day before. We could hear the same gunfire and explosions. The fires were spreading. This was the day that Stroop began to close in, using two thousand trained troops, and thirty officers, with tanks, machine guns, and air power. Ammunition was giving out. And our boys were retreating from one position to another. There was no question that we would be defeated—but everyone fought on.

For Stroop the major problem was the tens of thousands of

civilian Jews holed up in their shelters. Himmler's order had been categorical, but to pull the Jews individually out of their hiding places before destroying the ghetto might take months. The resistance understood this too, and after two days of street fighting, decided to save their ammunition for the defense of the bunkers. Stroop, then, was faced with the challenge of extricating Jews from the ghetto at the risk of a house-to-house skirmish for each and every one of them.

It was a challenge he was equal to. He called in the army engineers and ordered them to set fire to every building. The engineers moved methodically from house to house, drenching the ground floor with gasoline and setting off explosives in the cellars. The ghetto was to be razed to the ground. However much substance there might have been to Tuesday night's life-giving rumors, there would be nothing to save us now. And activity was stepping up at the *Umschlagplatz.*

The ghetto by day was filled with death: fire spreading unchecked, street fighting at an end, lines of contact from section to section broken; but by night, it became pure phantasmagoria: flames and clouds of smoke and the crackle of burning wood. The crash of collapsing buildings drowned out the sound of gunfire, but occasionally the wind would carry a nearby moan or a distant scream. In his report of April 22, 1943, Stroop wrote: "Whole families of Jews, enveloped in flames, leaped out of windows, or slid to the ground on bedsheets tied together. Measures were taken to liquidate these Jews at once."

Then came Easter Sunday. The day was bright, and the citizenry of Warsaw, dressed in their finest, crowded into the churches. I thought, perhaps Wlodek is among them. When the mass was over, the holiday crowds pushed through the streets to catch sight of Warsaw's newest spectacle (stopping for a moment, maybe, in Kraisinski Square, to see the new merry-go-round?). Batteries of artillery were set up in Nowiniarska Street, from which the Germans kept up a steady barrage against the ghetto. And everywhere the flame, and the stench of roasting human flesh. The sight was awesome—and exciting. From time to time a living torch would be seen crouched on a window sill and then leaping through the air. Occasionally one such figure caught on some obstruction and hung there. The spectators would shout to the German riflemen, "Hey, look over there . . . no, over there!" As each figure completed its gruesome trajectory, the crowds cheered.

Fighting of a sort was still going on inside the ghetto—scattered and disorganized, but determined. Those people who had been burned out of their shelters were roaming the streets, looking for hiding places. We allowed another ten people into our shelter.

It was now the ninth day of the uprising, Tuesday, April 27. Someone who had been sent out to reconnoiter brought us word that the Germans were coming into our street. We heard shots in the courtyard, and then the call: *"Alles 'runter! Alle Juden 'runter!"*

"They are setting fire to the staircases and the ground floor apartments," Izak whispered. We could hear nothing, but in half an hour the heat became unbearable and black smoke began to fill the shelter. Our turn had come.

Izak announced that we were to evacuate the shelter. Nearly half our companions refused to budge. They had chosen to use their potassium cyanide, and with a kind of gentle indifference they sat watching the rest of us scurrying around. Below us was an inferno: our only way out was by the roof. There were five of us now, Izak, Lena, I, and two other friends; I never saw what happened to the others. We crossed the roof to the neighboring house, not yet on fire. Then began a tortuous journey through attics, and passages and dugouts and cellars. Our plan was to get as far away from our burning house as possible, and, under cover of night, cross the pavement to the backs of the houses on Mila Street, then down Mila and across Nalewki to a certain house that still had a passageway out of the ghetto.

By late afternoon we were at the middle of the block. At dawn Izak went to scout: we had to cross the street, find a shelter, contact a fighting group. Before he returned, we heard the now-familiar sound of windows breaking and smelled the smoke. The staircases in this building were in worse condition than our own had been. We went to the roof again, and sat, dazed by the fresh air and sunshine, straddling the roof's peak. What were we to do now? The look of death had come over Lena's face and I discovered that in the scramble for the roof, the little bag she had been wearing around her neck had slipped loose and was gone. In that bag was our last refuge: cyanide. We had to decide, then, whether to remain on the roof and burn alive or to try to make our way down. One of our friends decided for us: "There is always time to die," he said. We scrambled down through the burning staircase and ran out of the doorway with our hands above our heads. We were led by a waiting German officer out into Muranowska Street. A large number of Jews from the surrounding apartment houses were already gathered there. Among them were a few of our neighbors.

One of the SS men kept staring at Lena and asked her her name. She gave him her married name, and he walked away without a word. They had been classmates together at the university.

We were lined up five across, and made our way toward the *Umschlagplatz*. As we passed Niska Street, Lena clutched my hand. A woman, holding a child by the hand, stood screaming at an upper-story window and then threw herself into the street. This was our last sight of the Warsaw Ghetto.

To Nowhere

KALMAN FRIEDMAN *

Life began to fade on Nowolipie Street. Reports, both confirmed and unconfirmed, made everyone's hair stand on end. The
people spent most of the hours of the day in the bunker and in the
evening disappeared completely inside it. The apartments and the
houses were abandoned. The street was abandoned and cut off
from the world.

In the bunker under the house in which I lived there were the
warehouse workers of Nowolipie Street. Despite the terrible reports and the echoes of shots that were heard from the outskirts
of the ghetto the night before, I decided to hold the first Seder of
Passover with my paralyzed neighbor Jacob Nussbaum. I thought
that if things became really dangerous, I would still manage to return to the bunker. Without any special preliminaries, we moved
the table close to the bed. We spread out a white tablecloth on it
and wrapped up three *matzot* in a towel. *"Ha Lachma Anya,"*
my neighbor began. I filled the glasses and then it was Yezhy's
turn to ask the Four Questions. Yezhy was Nussbaum's nephew.

The atmosphere was pregnant with meditation. Pictures and
memories filled our hearts. We remembered the holidays, particularly the last holiday that we had celebrated with our families.
We remembered the Seders of the past, celebrations filled with joy
and grandeur. Yezhy moved the chair next to the table, and sang
the Questions in Yiddish: *"Tatishe, ich well dich fregen fir
kashes"* (Father, I want to ask you four questions). *"Far vos iz*

* "In the Warsaw Ghetto in Its Dying Days," *Yad Vashem Bulletin* (October, 1963), pp. 24–30.

gevorn farendert die dozike nacht fon alle necht . . ." (Why is there a difference between this night and all other nights . . .) And he finished as usual: *"Tatishe, ich hob dich gefregt fir kashes, entfer mir a terutz"* (I have asked you four questions, please give me the answers).

My neighbor and I exchanged wordless glances. We felt that our breath was leaving us and our hearts were bleeding. Yezhy, apparently, did not understand the significance of his words. He had once learned to ask the Questions and now he asked them without thinking, and it is well that he did not understand.

That night nothing happened on the street; it was only that we passed it full of fear. In the morning I went down to the bunker in order to meet with my friends below. I did not bid farewell to my neighbor because I intended to see him again. As usual, I locked the door. Some distance from Nowolipie Street, in the streets of the ghetto, shots and explosions could be heard, and they gradually came closer. It was impossible to leave. We sat hunched together in the darkness, almost forgetting Passover and the Seder.

I did not for a moment forget Nussbaum. Several times I heard heavy footsteps in the yard and in the street, but not above. The night slowly passed. Finally we knew by our watches that it was already dawn.

Suddenly, group after group of soldiers came. Wild beasts filled the house and the yard. Savage cries and unceasing shots froze the blood of those sitting in the bunker. Every one of us feared that we would soon be discovered. Soon the door would be found, and then what? Perhaps we had been informed upon? But finally the danger passed and the bunker returned to life. Terrible anxiety filled our hearts; what had happened above to Nussbaum and to Yezhy? God only knows where they are. I very much wanted to go up and to see what had happened to them. I took off my shoes and slowly climbed up the stairs: it was just my luck that they creaked and frightened me unjustifiably, or perhaps justifiably.

The doors of the lower and upper floors had been broken open. The neighbor's door had also been broken open. I went into the flat and ran straight to his corner—and this is what I saw: the bed had been moved from its place; all the household goods were spread on the floor and Nussbaum was lying under the bed—dead. My body was covered with sweat and my heart stopped beating.

For a moment I forgot how dangerous the place was. I stood frozen to the spot and looked about. I remembered Yezhy, the loyal guardian. Where was he? I tried to call him in a whisper. I searched for him in the kitchen, opened the cabinet, but nothing was to be heard. I was frightened by the silence and by my own footsteps. What had happened to Yezhy? I returned to the bunker depressed and saddened. I did not understand why Nussbaum lay under the bed. Apparently the murderers had ordered him to rise, dragged him by force from the bed, and when they saw that he did not rise, murdered him. Poor Nussbaum! I had not managed to say good-bye. . . .

The murderers unceasingly searched for our bunker. The noise of men and dogs could be heard above us. Our life became a hell. Every outburst outside sounded like thunder below. Thus it was during the day and during the night. Finally two hand grenades overcame our stubbornness and the danger of a cave-in forced us to open the door of the bunker. We went out one after the other, shocked and wounded. The members of the Jewish Police took us together with others who had come out of bunkers toward the loading area (which was called the *Umschlagplatz*). This was Friday, the fourth day of Passover.

They put us into a building full of Jews—men, women and children—who sat on the ground paralyzed with fear, shadows of men who were awaiting their fate. We were guarded by booted and armed wild beasts in the form of men. We heard yells and cries together with the whistle of locomotives from outside. I sat absorbed in my pain and sensing that death was near. All hopes for salvation had gone. Suddenly someone surreptitiously pulled at me from behind. "Yezhy!" I wanted to shout, but the shout remained stuck in my throat. The child came closer, put his small head on me, snuggling up, and remained silent. I felt his quivering limbs, his burning cheeks, and I stroked his face that was wet with tears. I lifted his head in order to see him: his eyes had deepened and become black and his lips had none of the crimson of life. The two of us sat holding one another—brethren in sorrow. Both of us had been judged for the same "crime"; both of us faced the same sentence.

And Yezhy told me about the recent happenings. "They struggled with my uncle. They wanted him to rise and finally they threw him to the ground. All this time they fired at the bedding, the closet and even the stove. They took me out of the room and put me in the corridor, and I did not enter the house again. I do not know what they did with my uncle, but I understood that he had been shot. When they left the room and took me downstairs, no living voice was heard from above. Below there stood German soldiers laughing heartily. When they saw me, one of them came to me with a belt in his hands. His face was crimson and he ran toward me. I thought that he would whip me. But he lifted me up and smiled at me. He took out a biscuit and gave it to me—and then let me down. I didn't understand anything he said."

Yezhy completed his story and lay down on me. I felt the child's body. If I had been allowed to do so, I would have rested there forever; never to feel anything again! The time passed ever so slowly. We waited for twenty-four hours and finally our turn came to leave on the road from which there was no return. I went with Yezhy, holding his hand. They hit us, but I tried not to lose him. Blows, shots, a real hell! We stepped on people and on luggage until finally we saw the carriages. Two lines of soldiers stood ahead of us and each of us was forced to pass between these beasts. Blows, kicks, insults.

Yezhy and I were the last to enter. A black Ukrainian called loudly, "One hundred!" and locked the carriage. Finally we were inside. Each one tried to find his place. Each beaten and wounded man laid down his bones. People began to become nervous and, because of the crowding and the heat, began to quarrel. Sighs, shouts and curses could be heard. People fainted and asked for water. Those who sat in the middle of the carriage had no air. The heat was unmerciful. The sweat was burning. And the remaining air was filled with a conglomeration of curses and Psalms. Those who came in last crawled over the bodies to the cracks and breathed in the air from outside.

A soldier stood outside each carriage, stood quietly and comfortably. He did not know what it was to have life ebb away. The sun shone upon him. Air was free for him. Why did fire not come to consume us together with them? Why did not an earthquake come to bury the entire world?

PART SIX

Chimneys

The name Auschwitz has become the symbol for Germany's attempt to destroy European Jewry, but among Jews three words in particular have come to be used for conveying the total horror: *Shoa, Khurbn,* and "Holocaust." Each of the three has a history which began hundreds of years ago, and each has been used in many different contexts and with differing meanings.

Shoa, the Hebrew noun the Israelis use, appears in biblical literature, especially in the Psalms and some of the prophetic writings. Its meaning is secular: "wasteness," "desolation," "destruction," or "storm." The Yiddish *Khurbn* is also Hebrew in origin and secular in meaning; it is usually translated as "destruction" or "catastrophe." The English "holocaust" too may be defined in secular terms, but its origin and history involve it with the concept of purposeful sacrifice.

In the Greek translation of the Hebrew Bible, *ólokauston* was used for *olah* when it was clear from the text that the sacrifice was burnt and its smoke went up to God. In English, "holocaust" came to mean "an offering wholly consumed by fire," because the word entered the language by way of the English translations of the Bible. Until about the seventeenth century, the word "holocaust" does not appear to have carried any secular meaning at all; it applied only to religious sacrifices.

In subsequent centuries, "holocaust" began to be used in a nonreligious context. By World War I, English writers were employing it to describe disaster in general, and the Great War itself came to be known as a holocaust in some circles. The secular meaning, increasingly prominent in later years, was the one associated with the "Holocaust," the destruction of European Jewry.

There is something hauntingly disturbing about the term "holocaust," especially in view of the purely secular application of *shoa* and *khurbn.* The link between purposeful sacrifice and the destruction of European Jewry is awesome to contemplate, even for those entirely disinterested in the theological implications of the Holocaust. The most secular-minded of English-language readers may do well to remember that once upon a time the word "holocaust" was used like this:

> Ysaac was leid that auter on,
> So men sulden holocaust don.

Arrival at Birkenau— Auschwitz

ELIE WIESEL *

Few escaped the camps of annihilation alive. Among those who somehow lived long enough to see the day of liberation by the Allied armies, and who have written about life and death in that world of terror and horror, Elie Wiesel stands alone in his recreation of the experience of his first moments in Auschwitz and his later anguish in Buchenwald.

The cherished objects we had brought with us thus far were left behind in the train, and with them, at last, our illusions.

Every two yards or so an SS man held his tommy gun trained on us. Hand in hand we followed the crowd.

An SS noncommissioned officer came to meet us, a truncheon in his hand. He gave the order:

"Men to the left! Women to the right!"

Eight words spoken quietly, indifferently, without emotion. Eight short, simple words. Yet that was the moment when I parted from my mother. I had not had time to think, but already I felt the pressure of my father's hand: we were alone. For a part of a second I glimpsed my mother and my sisters moving away to the right. Tzipora held Mother's hand. I saw them disappear into the distance; my mother was stroking my sister's fair hair, as though to protect her, while I walked on with my father and the other men. And I did not know that in that place, at that moment, I was part-

* *Night* (New York: Hill and Wang, 1960), pp. 39–44.

ing from my mother and Tzipora forever. I went on walking. My father held onto my hand.

Behind me, an old man fell to the ground. Near him was an SS man, putting his revolver back in its holster.

My hand shifted on my father's arm. I had one thought—not to lose him. Not to be left alone.

The SS officers gave the order:

"Form fives!"

Commotion. At all costs we must keep together.

"Here, kid, how old are you?"

It was one of the prisoners who asked me this. I could not see his face, but his voice was tense and weary.

"I'm not quite fifteen yet."

"No. Eighteen."

"But I'm not," I said. "Fifteen."

"Fool. Listen to what *I* say."

Then he questioned my father, who replied:

"Fifty."

The other grew more furious than ever.

"No, not fifty. Forty. Do you understand? Eighteen and forty."

He disappeared into the night shadows. A second man came up, spitting oaths at us.

"What have you come here for, you sons of bitches? What are you doing here, eh?"

Someone dared to answer him.

"What do you think? Do you suppose we've come here for our own pleasure? Do you think we asked to come?"

A little more, and the man would have killed him.

"You shut your trap, you filthy swine, or I'll squash you right now! You'd have done better to have hanged yourselves where you were than to come here. Didn't you know what was in store for you at Auschwitz? Haven't you heard about it? In 1944?"

No, we had not heard. No one had told us. He could not believe his ears. His tone of voice became increasingly brutal.

"Do you see that chimney over there? See it? Do you see those flames? (Yes, we did see the flames.) Over there—that's where you're going to be taken. That's your grave, over there. Haven't you realized it yet? You dumb bastards, don't you understand anything? You're going to be burned. Frizzled away. Turned into ashes."

He was growing hysterical in his fury. We stayed motionless, petrified. Surely it was all a nightmare? An unimaginable nightmare?

I heard murmurs around me.

"We've got to do something. We can't let ourselves be killed. We can't go like beasts to the slaughter. We've got to revolt."

There were a few sturdy young fellows among us. They had knives on them, and they tried to incite the others to throw themselves on the armed guards.

One of the young men cried:

"Let the world learn of the existence of Auschwitz. Let everybody hear about it, while they can still escape. . . .

But the older ones begged their children not to do anything foolish:

"You must never lose faith, even when the sword hangs over your head. That's the teaching of our sages. . . ."

The wind of revolt died down. We continued our march toward the square. In the middle stood the notorious Dr. Mengele (a typical SS officer: a cruel face, but not devoid of intelligence, and wearing a monocle); a conductor's baton in his hand, he was standing among the other officers. The baton moved unremittingly, sometimes to the right, sometimes to the left.

I was already in front of him:

"How old are you?" he asked, in an attempt at a paternal tone of voice.

"Eighteen." My voice was shaking.

"Are you in good health?"

"Yes."

"What's your occupation?"

Should I say that I was a student?

"Farmer," I heard myself say.

This conversation cannot have lasted more than a few seconds. It had seemed like an eternity to me.

The baton moved to the left. I took half a step forward. I wanted to see first where they were sending my father. If he went to the right, I would go after him.

The baton once again pointed to the left for him too. A weight was lifted from my heart.

We did not yet know which was the better side, right or left; which road led to prison and which to the crematory. But for the moment I was happy; I was near my father. Our procession continued to move slowly forward.

Another prisoner came up to us:

"Satisfied?"

"Yes," someone replied.

"Poor devils, you're going to the crematory."

He seemed to be telling the truth. Not far from us, flames were leaping up from a ditch, gigantic flames. They were burning something. A lorry drew up at the pit and delivered its load—little children. Babies! Yes, I saw it—saw it with my own eyes . . . those children in the flames. (Is it surprising that I could not sleep after that? Sleep had fled from my eyes.)

So this was where we were going. A little farther on was another and larger ditch for adults.

I pinched my face. Was I still alive? Was I awake? I could not believe it. How could it be possible for them to burn people, children, and for the world to keep silent? No, none of this could be true. It was a nightmare. . . . Soon I should wake with a start, my heart pounding, and find myself back in the bedroom of my childhood, among my books. . . .

My father's voice drew me from my thoughts:

"It's a shame . . . a shame that you couldn't have gone with your mother. . . . I saw several boys of your age going with their mothers. . . ."

His voice was terribly sad. I realized that he did not want to see what they were going to do to me. He did not want to see the burning of his only son.

My forehead was bathed in cold sweat. But I told him that I did not believe that they could burn people in our age, that humanity would never tolerate it. . . .

"Humanity? Humanity is not concerned with us. Today anything is allowed. Anything is possible, even these crematories. . . ."

His voice was choking.

"Father," I said, "if that is so, I don't want to wait here. I'm going to run to the electric wire. That would be better than slow agony in the flames."

He did not answer. He was weeping. His body was shaken convulsively. Around us, everyone was weeping. Someone began to recite the Kaddish, the prayer for the dead. I do not know if it has ever happened before, in the long history of the Jews, that people have ever recited the prayer for the dead for themselves.

"Yitgadal veyitkadash shmé raba. . . . May His Name be blessed and magnified. . . ." whispered my father.

For the first time, I felt revolt rise up in me. Why should I bless His name? The Eternal, Lord of the Universe, the All-Powerful and Terrible, was silent. What had I to thank Him for?

We continued our march. We were gradually drawing closer to the ditch, from which an infernal heat was rising. Still twenty steps to go. If I wanted to bring about my own death, this was the moment. Our line had now only fifteen paces to cover. I bit my lips so that my father would not hear my teeth chattering. Ten steps still. Eight. Seven. We marched slowly on, as though following a hearse at our own funeral. Four steps more. Three steps. There it was now, right in front of us, the pit and its flames. I gathered all that was left of my strength, so that I could break from the ranks and throw myself upon the barbed wire. In the depths of my heart, I bade farewell to my father, to the whole universe; and, in spite of myself, the words formed themselves and issued in a whisper from my lips: *Yitgadal veyitkadash shmé raba. . . .* May His name be blessed and magnified. . . . My heart was bursting. The moment had come. I was face to face with the Angel of Death. . . .

No. Two steps from the pit we were ordered to turn to the left and made to go into a barracks.

Never shall I forget that night, the first night in camp, which has turned my life into one long night, seven times cursed and seven times sealed. Never shall I forget that smoke. Never shall I forget the little faces of the children, whose bodies I saw turned into wreaths of smoke beneath a silent blue sky.

Never shall I forget those flames which consumed my faith forever.

Never shall I forget that nocturnal silence which deprived me, for all eternity, of the desire to live. Never shall I forget those moments which murdered my God and my soul and turned my dreams to dust. Never shall I forget these things, even if I am condemned to live as long as God Himself. Never.

The barracks we had been made to go into was very long. In the roof were some blue-tinged skylights. The ante-chamber of Hell must look like this. So many crazed men, so many cries, so much bestial brutality!

There were dozens of prisoners to receive us, truncheons in their hands, striking out anywhere, at anyone, without reason. Orders:

"Strip! Fast! *Los!* Keep only your belts and shoes in your hands. . . ."

We had to throw our clothes at one end of the barracks. There was already a great heap there. New suits and old, torn coats, rags. For us, this was the true equality: nakedness. Shivering with the cold.

Some SS officers moved about in the room, looking for strong men. If they were so keen on strength, perhaps one should try and pass oneself off as sturdy? My father thought the reverse. It was better not to draw attention to oneself. Our fate would then be the same as the others. (Later, we were to learn that he was right. Those who were selected that day were enlisted in the *Sonder-Kommando,* the unit which worked in the crematories. Bela Katz— son of a big tradesman from our town—had arrived at Birkenau with the first transport, a week before us. When he heard of our arrival, he managed to get word to us that, having been chosen for his strength, he had himself put his father's body into the crematory oven.)

Blows continued to rain down.

"To the barber!"

Belt and shoes in hand, I let myself be dragged off to the barbers. They took our hair off with clippers, and shaved off all the hair on our bodies. The same thought buzzed all the time in my head—not to be separated from my father.

Agony at Buchenwald

ELIE WIESEL *

At the gate of the camp, SS officers were waiting for us. They counted us. Then we were directed to the assembly place. Orders were given us through loudspeakers:

"Form fives!" "Form groups of a hundred!" "Five paces forward!"

I held onto my father's hand—the old, familiar fear: not to lose him.

Right next to us the high chimney of the crematory oven rose up. It no longer made any impression on us. It scarcely attracted our attention.

An established inmate of Buchenwald told us that we should have a shower and then we could go into the blocks. The idea of having a hot bath fascinated me. My father was silent. He was breathing heavily beside me.

"Father," I said. "Only another moment more. Soon we can lie down—in a bed. You can rest. . . ."

He did not answer. I was so exhausted myself that his silence left me indifferent. My only wish was to take a bath as quickly as possible and lie down in a bed.

But it was not easy to reach the showers. Hundreds of prisoners were crowding there. The guards were unable to keep any order. They struck out right and left with no apparent result. Others, without the strength to push or even to stand up, had sat down in the snow. My father wanted to do the same. He groaned.

"I can't go on. . . . This is the end. . . . I'm going to die here. . . ."

* *Ibid.*, pp. 106–113.

He dragged me toward a hillock of snow from which emerged human shapes and ragged pieces of blanket.

"Leave me," he said to me. "I can't go on. . . . Have mercy on me. . . . I'll wait here until we can get into the baths. . . . You can come and find me."

I could have wept with rage. Having lived through so much, suffered so much, could I leave my father to die now? Now, when we could have a good hot bath and lie down?

"Father!" I screamed. "Father! Get up from here! Immediately! You're killing yourself. . . ."

I seized him by the arm. He continued to groan.

"Don't shout, son. . . . Take pity on your old father. . . . Leave me to rest here. . . . Just for a bit, I'm so tired . . . at the end of my strength. . . ."

He had become like a child, weak, timid, vulnerable.

"Father," I said. "You can't stay here."

I showed him the corpses all around him; they too had wanted to rest here.

"I can see them, son. I can see them all right. Let them sleep. It's so long since they closed their eyes. . . . They are exhausted . . . exhausted. . . ."

His voice was tender.

I yelled against the wind:

"They'll never wake again! Never! Don't you understand?"

For a long time this argument went on. I felt that I was not arguing with him, but with death itself, with the death that he had already chosen.

The sirens began to wail. An alert. The lights went out throughout the camp. The guards drove us toward the blocks. In a flash, there was no one left on the assembly place. We were only too glad not to have had to stay outside longer in the icy wind. We let ourselves sink down onto the planks. The beds were in several tiers. The cauldrons of soup at the entrance attracted no one. To sleep, that was all that mattered.

It was daytime when I awoke. And then I remembered that I had a father. Since the alert, I had followed the crowd without troubling about him. I had known that he was at the end, on the brink of death, and yet I had abandoned him.

I went to look for him.

But at the same moment this thought came into my mind: "Don't let me find him! If only I could get rid of this dead weight, so that I could use all my strength to struggle for my own survival, and only worry about myself." Immediately I felt ashamed of myself, ashamed forever.

I walked for hours without finding him. Then I came to the block where they were giving out black "coffee." The men were lining up and fighting.

"Eliezer . . . my son . . . bring me . . . a drop of coffee. . . ."

I ran to him.

"Father! I've been looking for you for so long. . . . Where were you? Did you sleep? . . . How do you feel?"

He was burning with fever. Like a wild beast, I cleared a way for myself to the coffee cauldron. And I managed to carry back a cupful. I had a sip. The rest was for him. I can't forget the light of thankfulness in his eyes while he gulped it down—an animal gratitude. With those few gulps of hot water, I probably brought him more satisfaction than I had done during my whole childhood.

He was lying on a plank, livid, his lips pale and dried up, shaken by tremors. I could not stay by him for long. Orders had been given to clear the place for cleaning. Only the sick could stay.

We stayed outside for five hours. Soup was given out. As soon as we were allowed to go back to the blocks, I ran to my father.

"Have you had anything to eat?"

"No."

"Why not?"

"They didn't give us anything . . . they said that if we were ill we should die soon anyway and it would be a pity to waste the food. I can't go on any more. . . ."

I gave him what was left of my soup. But it was with a heavy heart. I felt that I was giving it up to him against my will. . . .

He grew weaker day by day, his gaze veiled, his face the color of dead leaves. On the third day after our arrival at Buchenwald, everyone had to go to the showers. Even the sick, who had to go through last.

On the way back from the baths, we had to wait outside for a long time. They had not yet finished cleaning the blocks.

Seeing my father in the distance, I ran to meet him. He went by me like a ghost, passed me without stopping, without looking at me. I called to him. He did not come back. I ran after him:

"Father, where are you running to?"

He looked at me for a moment, and his gaze was distant, visionary; it was the face of someone else. A moment only and on he ran again.

Struck down with dysentery, my father lay in his bunk, five other invalids with him. I sat by his side, watching him, not daring to believe that he could escape death again. Nevertheless, I did all I could to give him hope.

Suddenly, he raised himself on his bunk and put his feverish lips to my ear:

"Eliezer . . . I must tell you where to find the gold and the money I buried . . . in the cellar. . . . You know. . . ."

He began to talk faster and faster, as though he were afraid he would not have time to tell me. I tried to explain to him that this was not the end, that we would go back to the house together, but he would not listen to me. He could no longer listen to me. He was exhausted. A trickle of saliva, mingled with blood, was running from between his lips. He had closed his eyes. His breath was coming in gasps.

For a ration of bread, I managed to change beds with a prisoner in my father's bunk. In the afternoon the doctor came. I went and told him that my father was very ill.

"Bring him here!"

I explained that he could not stand up. But the doctor refused to listen to anything. Somehow, I brought my father to him. He stared at him, then questioned him in a clipped voice:

"What do you want?"

"My father's ill," I answered for him. "Dysentery. . . ."

"Dysentery? That's not my business. I'm a surgeon. Go on! Make room for the others."

Protests did no good.

"I can't go on, son. . . . Take me back to my bunk. . . ."

"Try and sleep a bit, father. Try to go to sleep. . . ."

I took him back and helped him to lie down. He was shivering. His breathing was labored, thick. He kept his eyes shut. Yet I was convinced that he could see everything, that now he could see the truth in all things.

Another doctor came to the block. But my father would not get up. He knew that it was useless.

Besides, this doctor had only come to finish off the sick. I could hear him shouting at them that they were lazy and just wanted to stay in bed. I felt like leaping at his throat, strangling him. But I no longer had the courage or the strength. I was riveted to my father's deathbed. My hands hurt, I was clenching them so hard. Oh, to strangle the doctor and the others! To burn the whole world! My father's murderers! But the cry stayed in my throat.

When I came back from the bread distribution, I found my father weeping like a child:

"Son, they keep hitting me!"

"Who?"

I thought he was delirious.

"Him, the Frenchman . . . and the Pole . . . they were hitting me."

Another wound to the heart, another hate, another reason for living lost.

"Eliezer . . . Eliezer . . . tell them not to hit me. . . . I haven't done anything. . . . Why do they keep hitting me?"

I began to abuse his neighbors. They laughed at me. I promised them bread, soup. They laughed. Then they got angry; they could not stand my father any longer, they said, because he was now unable to drag himself outside to relieve himself.

The following day he complained that they had taken his ration of bread.

"While you were asleep?"

"No. I wasn't asleep. They jumped on top of me. They snatched my bread . . . and they hit me . . . again. . . . I can't stand any more, son . . . a drop of water. . . ."

I knew that he must not drink. But he pleaded with me for so long that I gave in. Water was the worst poison he could have, but what else could I do for him? With water, without water, it would all be over soon anyway. . . .

"You, at least, have some mercy on me. . . ."

Have mercy on him! I, his only son!

A week went by like this.

"This is your father, isn't it?" asked the head of the block.

"Yes."

"He's very ill."

"The doctor won't do anything for him."

"The doctor *can't* do anything for him, now. And neither can you."

He put his great hairy hand on my shoulder and added:

"Listen to me, boy. Don't forget that you're in a concentration camp. Here, every man has to fight for himself and not think of anyone else. Even of his father. Here, there are no fathers, no brothers, no friends. Everyone lives and dies for himself alone. I'll give you a sound piece of advice—don't give your ration of bread and soup to your old father. There's nothing you can do for him. And you're killing yourself. Instead, you ought to be having his ration."

I listened to him without interrupting. He was right, I thought in the most secret region of my heart, but I dared not admit it. It's too late to save your old father, I said to myself. You ought to be having two rations of bread, two rations of soup. . . .

Only a fraction of a second, but I felt guilty. I ran to find a little soup to give my father. But he did not want it. All he wanted was water.

"Don't drink water . . . have some soup. . . ."

"I'm burning . . . why are you being so unkind to me, my son? Some water. . . ."

I brought him some water. Then I left the block for roll call. But I turned around and came back again. I lay down on the top bunk. Invalids were allowed to stay in the block. So I would be an invalid myself. I would not leave my father.

There was silence all round now, broken only by groans. In front of the block, the SS were giving orders. An officer passed by the beds. My father begged me:

"My son, some water. . . . I'm burning. . . . My stomach. . . ."

"Quiet, over there!" yelled the officer.

"Eliezer," went on my father, "some water. . . ."

The officer came up to him and shouted at him to be quiet. But my father did not hear him. He went on calling me. The officer dealt him a violent blow on the head with his truncheon.

I did not move. I was afraid. My body was afraid of also receiving a blow.

Then my father made a rattling noise and it was my name: "Eliezer."

I could see that he was still breathing—spasmodically.

I did not move.

When I got down after roll call, I could see his lips trembling as he murmured something. Bending over him, I stayed gazing at him for over an hour, engraving into myself the picture of his bloodstained face, his shattered skull.

Then I had to go to bed. I climbed into my bunk, above my father, who was still alive. It was January 28, 1945.

I awoke on January 29 at dawn. In my father's place lay another invalid. They must have taken him away before dawn and carried him to the crematory. He may still have been breathing.

There were no prayers at his grave. No candles were lit to his memory. His last word was my name. A summons, to which I did not respond.

I did not weep, and it pained me that I could not weep. But I had no more tears. And, in the depths of my being, in the recesses of my weakened conscience, could I have searched it, I might perhaps have found something like—free at last!

SS Central Office of Economy and Administration

"Estimated Profit (from Exploitation of Inmates of Concentration Camps)" *

Average daily income from hiring out [an inmate]	RM 6.00
less food	RM .60
less amortization for clothes	RM .10
Net income	RM 5.30
Average life expectancy 9 months x RM 5.30 =	RM 1431
Income from an efficient utilization of corpses	
(1) gold from teeth (3) valuables	
(2) clothes (4) money	
less cost of burning [the corpses]	RM 2.00
Average net profit	RM 200
Total profit after 9 months	RM 1631
To which must be added income from utilization of the bones and ashes	

* Jacob Robinson, "Research on the Jewish Catastrophe," *The Jewish Journal of Sociology,* Vol. VII (December 1966), p. 198.

PART SEVEN

Liberation

Just as the power of the German armies created the territorial shelter for the killing of Jews, the might of the Allied armies destroyed that shelter and liberated the few Jews who had managed to stay alive. But what did that liberation mean? There were after all many liberations, and responses by various camp inmates and liberators differed greatly. The selections that follow—all eyewitness accounts—give some indication of the incredible range of experience in the moments of liberation and in the days immediately following the arrival of Allied troops, when men began to relate themselves to a future.

Westerbork: Two Survivors

Muted Enthusiasms

WALTER LENZ *

This excerpt is based on a memoir by Walter Lenz, who crossed into Holland from Germany just before World War II only to be interned by the Dutch government; he recalled his moments of liberation many years later.

My view of their departure was perfect. I was sitting in an office just on the outskirts of the camp. I had a full view of the commander's villa and the special building we had constructed for the SS.

The SS began leaving on the afternoon of the eleventh of April, 1945. The girl friend of the camp commander in her role as secretary carried his beautiful leather boots as they left.

My sense that liberation was near was confirmed when SS officers came to me, gave me their hand, and said *"Auf Wiedersehen,* Herr Lenz." In the past they had usually greeted me with just "Lenz." Actually, all of us in the camp knew that the Allies were near as we heard them fighting at the Orange Canal, a few miles to the east of us.

The evening and night of the eleventh became one of apprehension as the Germans were on the way out and the Allies on the way in. We had no way of knowing what each hour would bring or how the Germans would behave as they left the camp. We were reasonably sure that the camp commander and most of the aged

* The original transcript is on deposit with Cornell University's Oral History Program, Ithaca, New York.

partially disabled SS guards would not harm us. They had let it be known in many different ways that as far as they were concerned the war was over; in fact the camp commander appeared to have made that decision in the fall of 1944; he appeared simply to have decided to make Westerbork his last peaceful stand and thus precluded any effort on his part to go east and join in the fighting. Many of the guards agreed with him and acted accordingly.

On the other hand some, like one of the SS officers I encountered on the eleventh, were of a different predisposition. This young man knew that his older commander had ordered the raising of a Red Cross flag and had instructed the camp's guard not to fight within the camp. The young officer told me, "You know what I would have done if I would have been in the commander's place? I would leave you all dead here." Since we had no sure way of knowing how many guards shared his views, we allowed for the possibility that some shooting could break out before the Allies arrived. In any event we posted our own guards to at least sound the alarm if danger threatened. We could do little more as we had no guns.

By three o'clock in the morning they had left, and around eight, contrary to orders not to leave the camp, I and two others walked to the German command post and took a volume on art history from the library of the commander. I also went to the now unoccupied SS barracks to see if the soldiers had left anything of value: I found my own skis and poles, and took them back.

Then I and someone else went outside the camp to a bunker which we now used as an observation post. I had helped build that bunker for unusual reasons. Allied planes had dropped dynamite and other weapons to the Dutch Underground operating in Drenthe Province. Where that Underground was supposed to have been I did not know, but I did know that Drenthe had many Dutch Nazis and these collected the deadly manna and brought it to Westerbork. When this material came into the camp the commander ordered me to "build something which would not blow up if hit by a light bomb." So I and some others built it and camouflaged it with earth and trees so that it all looked like a small hill with trees on it. Now we went to sit among the trees to see the approaching Allies. But instead of approaching Allies I saw my only tank battle. Directed by spotters, Allied tanks were shooting at German tanks which were slowly retreating. Unfortunately, the Allied tanks did not advance in the direction of the camp. In fact, after some shooting they seemed to be retreating.

I returned to the camp and reported my news to Kurt Schlesinger, who for me was the Jew in command. In the afternoon A. van As, the leading Dutch commander, made all of us assemble in the camp's Great Hall, and while we were there other observers were sent out to bring more information about the position of the Allies. Suddenly someone thought of phoning to a farm between the camp and the canal. Now we learned the Allies had in fact crossed the canal and were on their way to the camp.

With a feeling of unbelievable excitement we ran from the hall in the direction of the Allies. And as we ran, my wife or my friend's wife called to my friend: "It's time, after all these [camp] years, that you and Walter say *Du* to each other." Suddenly, in this later afternoon of an unusually warm spring day, we saw the German soldiers we had seen moving up to the canal in the morning following Allied soldiers as prisoners! We raced toward the Allies, and wild jubilation broke out. That night the camp had a fantastic celebration, but I did not participate. I was completely exhausted, having hardly slept in the previous twenty-four hours and feeling the strain of tension I had been under. I went to sleep.

But the next day, for me, but not for many others, three events occurred which muted my enthusiasm. I do not now remember how important each of these was, but I do recall clearly that each saddened me. Let me explain. Roosevelt's death shook me. News of his passing came to us the day after our liberation, and I at least was quite troubled by this revelation. Secondly, on the day after our liberation, and completely contrary to any of my expectations, the Canadians took some twenty Jews into custody, and as it turned out, held them about two weeks for interrogation. These arrests came as a blow. The men were persons I knew and had worked with, but they had also been involved in the transports, an involvement I did not share. The Canadians had their names from lists Dutch Underground members present in Westerbork had provided the Allied soldiers. I and others had not known the

Underground was in Westerbork and now I at least was doubly furious. We had tried to contact the Underground to block some of the transports leaving Westerbork. Underground fighters probably could not have stopped most of the guarded transports, but the one that turned out to be the last one probably could have been stopped. And we had tried to get the Underground to stop that train, the one that carried the Frank family to Auschwitz. Well, as in the past in the camp, the Underground had done nothing. But now, as we were liberated, its members turned up with lists of names of people almost all of whom could truly not have been accused of malicious and vicious collaboration with the Germans. As events turned out I was completely vindicated because the Canadians released all but one of those whom they had taken into custody. But all that came later. At that moment, on the day after our liberation, their arrest deeply disturbed me.

The third element that muted my feeling of liberation was completely different from the other two, but in many respects far more profound. Shortly after the Canadians arrived it became clear that something was bothering them. They asked a number of questions that made little sense to us at the time. Why were we so well fed? Why were we not sickly, on the verge of death? In fact, as cruel as it may sound now, I had the feeling that our liberators were in a sense let down, for as we soon learned, they had steeled themselves for liberating another Bergen-Belsen.

While this reaction helped mute my enthusiasm, it also began to open wide the door to the horrors we had all escaped. Having worked with men who repaired radios I had heard in 1943 a BBC report that a British MP by the name of Golan had told Parliament the Germans were killing large numbers of Jews with poisonous gas. But I remembered my young days in Vienna during World War I when the British accused the Germans of using their bayonets for tossing Belgian babies into the air. Then I had refused to believe that Germans were capable of such atrocities, and as a much older man I heard that 1943 BBC report with that memory of World War I.

From time to time we had used different devious ways to learn where the transports were going. We assumed that they were headed for Auschwitz—except for a few, all in fact did go there—

but try as we would we could not find out what went on at Ausch-witz. One of the Green Police accompanying the transport in-formed one of our people that even if he wanted to he could not tell what went on there because some twenty kilometers from Auschwitz the SS took charge of the train and he and others of the Green Police headed back to Westerbork. And to my knowl-edge no one, including the Dutch Underground, ever informed anyone in the camp of the fate of those transports, about death camps, about *Einsatzgruppen*,[1] or about systematic starvation.

Speaking for myself, I assumed that the transports were destined to prison camps like Dachau, where I had been before coming to Westerbork. To me that meant camps where an able-bodied person had a certain chance to survive. It was clear to me that at such camps the Germans would not feed us very well, that the future there was black for our small children and old people. But being then in my early forties, having survived Dachau, I was reasonably confident I would also survive the kind of camp to which I thought the transports were going.

When liberation brought with it radio news from the American army, we slowly learned of the extermination centers and death camps for the first time. And horrible as it was I found myself listening primarily to the names being broadcasted from Theresien-stadt in late April, for I had reason to believe my mother was there. In fact, news from other camps became really secondary.

In retrospect one could hardly have blamed the Allied soldiers who were surprised at our excellent condition. Westerbork was simply different. The winter before our liberation, for example, the Germans scoured the surrounding countryside for food and pro-vided the camp inmates with more sustenance than many a Dutch-man had living in the area. Those of us who had somehow survived the transports were reasonably well fed and well clothed, and in the months before our liberation had little to fear except being caught in battle between Germans and Allies. In fact, a number of us immediately offered our services to help the Allies in their war against the Germans. But except for some of the doctors in our camp, whom they took with them, they rejected all of us. I was told, for example, the following: "Look, what are you?" "I'm

[1] Mobile teams of machine gunners whose job was to shoot Jews.

an Austrian Jew, eager to help the Allied cause." The Canadian
captain then said: "No, you are not. You are a German Jew, and
we don't want German Jews in any capacity, but as nurses and
doctors. If you are neither, I am sorry, I can't help you."

For many others in the camp, however, nothing muted their
sense of exhilaration. They were jubilant that the Germans were
finally gone, that they had survived, that freedom had returned.
As excited and pleased as everyone was to have outlived the Occupation, almost no one could leave the camp. To be sure, we
gained permission to walk just outside of the camp's perimeter.
But movement beyond that was impossible in the initial days of
liberation.

There were a number of different reasons why liberation did
not bring with it freedom of movement. Those who had or thought
they had a place to go to in Holland could not go because of military reasons. The Allies, on their northern front, drove eastward
toward Germany, and did not stop their main advance because
of Holland. Instead part of their units swung north into Holland to
cut off most of its inhabited parts. Thus, almost all of populated
Holland was still occupied by Germans and subject to military
activity. Essentially then, all movement had to wait until the
Allies secured Holland.

The process of release from the camp also affected our freedom
to move. After a few days the few Canadians who had governed
us left and turned the camp over to Dutch officials. These let the
Dutch leave the camp first, apparently following the principle of
last in, first out. After the Dutch the officials released those refugees who had places to go to in Holland. Then they turned to the
real refugees, who really had no place to go. It was not until early
July that the last refugees were let go. These were some 100 or
150 of the original refugees who had helped establish Westerbork.
In short, although liberation made it possible to go just outside
the camp and for some like myself to go some distance from the
camp, liberation did not bring with it the instant right of free movement.

Nor did liberation bring with it a quick change of routine. The
Dutch authorities maintained the routines of the camp. In fact,
I personally found myself under more rigorous discipline than in

the last months under German rule. Taking into account the fact that in the first few days after liberation there was no sure way of knowing that the Germans might not return and reoccupy Westerbork, liberation really brought with it the possibility of committing oneself again to the abstraction of freedom. And that in itself was a great event for those who had survived.

Tears of Joy

MAX O. KORMAN *

My liberation came April 12, 1945. There are no words to describe the feelings, the emotions that went through our souls and bodies that day. In all those years since 1933, they were suppressed and bottled up and now a sudden release. It was an explosion. The Nazis left the camp the previous day. We were still trembling. We were left to ourselves, only detachments of retreating troops kept moving throughout the day and all night. We were afraid of last minute executions, and if we were to survive that, we were afraid of vengeance in case of a comeback. Then complete stillness. Around 11:00 A.M. a few came running and shouting, "The Canadians." "The Canadians are coming." Everybody started running down the road. Through the mass of people I finally sighted something. It looked like a moving beehive, then another, then another. There were tanks packed with people who had encountered them first. We saw the Canadians between those people. It was like a breakthrough period, tears were running unashamed. We cried and laughed, kissed one another. Could someone describe this moment? No, no one could. You could only live it. As we later gathered in the Great Hall and sang the hymn, we sang it with all our heart. These words of *frijheid* and "free," they were not mere words. They were living pillars of our beings which were torn from us through all those years.

* From the unpublished *Korman Papers, loc. cit.* This was written in 1962.

Dachau

JOSEPH ROTHENBERG *

I was with a medical unit with the army advancing through Germany. We moved depending upon how the army moved. We didn't have a fixed destination; our movements were governed by strategic considerations. And we didn't know until we got into Augsburg that we were near Dachau.

After we set up our medical unit in the city of Augsburg a group of medical officers were detailed to Dachau, not so much to treat inmates as to observe what was going on. So, on the day after the camp's liberation my unit's medical group went to Dachau. There were two or three of us Jewish physicians, but the group was largely non-Jewish. I think we all had pretty much the same motive —maybe curiosity is the right word. We were anxious to see what had really happened.

We went by jeep to the concentration camp. On the road we passed many units of the 12th Armored Division traveling northward, their job apparently completed. I kept looking for my brother-in-law, David, who was with an armored unit, and I did find him a couple of days later. We had permits. We had to be fumigated going in and coming out because they were in the midst of a typhus epidemic in that particular area, in that particular camp. Some of their recent trainloads had brought in typhus from Eastern Europe, and their highest mortality at the time was from typhus deaths. On May 2, 1945, I wrote the following in my diary:

* Dr. Rothenberg kept a detailed diary of his days as an American soldier, and much of his account dates from entries made in 1945. The original transcript is on deposit with Cornell University's Oral History Program, Ithaca, New York; the diaries are in Dr. Rothenberg's possession.

"The prison is completely enclosed by a stone wall, surmounted by a barbed-wire fence. Outside the walls are the pretentious homes of the SS troops who presided over this hell. Outside also was the crematorium which is the place we first visited. On the railroad tracks leading into the enclosure were forty or fifty freight cars with the bodies of ten to twenty people lying on the floor of each. These were people who had been transferred to this camp from others as the Nazi retreated. Either they had died en route or they were clubbed to death by the Germans before they evacuated. Before the crematorium were piled the bodies of the dead. I would estimate 150 to 200. They lay in the awkward positions in which they had been tossed on the heap, legs intertwined, arms dangling, heads twisted in all directions. They all appeared to be males. The first glance was shocking, the second revolting—not revolting because of the bodies but because of the cruelty that produced such corpses. They were all wasted. Their numbers were tattooed on their arms, and Jews were indicated by a delta beneath the number. In the building another room was filled with the dead piled two or three deep. Adjoining this were the furnaces, which looked something like brick kilns. Behind the building were piles of discarded clothing removed from the dead. Still another room, marked 'shower bath,' was built very much like a gas chamber, and I strongly suspect that it was just that.

"Then we entered the compound proper. We asked the director, a prisoner, to act as our guide, which he consented to do. He was a Yugoslav anthropologist, apparently jailed because he couldn't foster the theories of a master race. The prison for political prisoners of all nationalities was built to accommodate ten to twelve thousand prisoners, but at the moment thirty-two thousand were interned there. I doubt that we'd put thirty-two thousand pigs in that compound. All nationalities were represented, as we soon learned by the numerous flags now flying in different places. My chief interest was in seeing the medical facilities. The operating room and dispensaries looked reasonably good, but for three thousand patients there were only four doctors and no nurses. In one room, the surgical ward, were 112 patients arranged in triple-decker beds in a ward in which we would ordinarily accommodate twelve or fifteen patients. Few medications and dressings, little nursing care. A pail in the center of the room served as a urinal, and on the rim of a second pail sat a man defecating. The tuberculosis ward was somewhat less crowded; they have eight hundred cases at present and several hundred additional ambulatory cases. I reviewed a few dozen admission X rays, all showing far-advanced disease with cavitation, and several with miliary tuberculosis. A number of thorax transectories were performed, but the technique was abandoned because of the 100-percent mortality—inadequate postoperative care. At present there is a typhus epidemic and I saw a group of such cases.

"The inmates all wear striped suits, gray and black, which look like awnings. By the degree of emaciation, one could guess the duration of their incarceration in concentration camps. The director showed us his daily mortality rates. At present, because of typhus, there is [a rate of] 100 to 120 a day. He explained that whenever prisoners arrived from other camps the rates would rise because the people usually arrived badly starved. The journey might require five to ten days, and they would have little or nothing to eat during this entire time. These people frequently died. At other times there would be epidemics of dysentery or typhoid fever. These sights are terrible—unholy, unspeakable. But for me, worse than all this is the knowledge that there are individuals who can so degrade themselves."

The inmates just sat there apathetically or were lying down. They were ill, too weak to move. They . . . they didn't do anything. They weren't even happy, I mean, or if they were, they certainly expressed no emotion.

They were quite different from the slave laborers I saw. These were for the most part Poles and Russians and I think French. They also wore uniforms and whatnot, but they didn't show the extreme emaciation. They were better fed because they were working. But the striking thing about that group after the liberation was the way they immediately were on their own. They always moved in bands, and the Germans were terrified of them because they took anything they wanted. If a German were riding along on a bicycle, they just threw him off the bike and took the bike.

And . . . nobody stopped them, because they had complete sympathy. They were independent, and they knew they were going home, and they . . . they took off and they left.

Those others in the concentration camp were too sick to move.

They had to have assistance. The place was strewn with them. You could walk . . . would walk through and there were people who had just died who were still lying there.

After the first impact in the first days in the first week, we just tried to put it out of our minds. I think it was like air raids, trying to forget about them afterward because it was . . . the air raid was too terrifying to think about and it was easy enough not to think about it. And I think after seeing all this and talking about it and writing home about it, then it was . . . then we didn't see it any more because then we had no contact. Then we were in the city of Augsburg and we were working and we saw [the] German population who were really well off compared . . . well, they *were* well off compared to what we had seen. So it was much easier to live in that atmosphere in a . . . in a good, clean city than to think about what we had seen.

But in Augsburg something unusual did happen. Listen to my diary:

"Went to synagogue today here in Augsburg. The first time in twelve years that this building has been used as a place of worship. The Germans had converted it into barracks for slave laborers. Although the chaplain had arranged for clearing of most of the building, scaffolding which had held the bunks still remained. All the synagogue ornaments and scrolls had disappeared. Three days later they were discovered safely hidden in Munich. They would be restored to the temple, and next Saturday, which is Shavuot, will be celebrated as Hanukkah instead. A single civilian was present. He told us that only a few Jews in the community had survived the ordeals of the past years. Some married to Christians had been treated a little less severely, but in February, when Nazi fortunes were at their lowest, all Jews were gathered for slave labor. A few managed to escape and lay hidden for a few months until the city was liberated. These very sad-looking boys, wearing the striped uniform of the slave laborers, were there too. Two were Polish, the third Czechoslovakian, about fifteen years of age; [they] had spent several years in various camps. They know that their parents are dead. Their faces remained very sad during our short talk. They were being cared for by these few remaining Jewish civilians. Relief agencies are entering the community."

Mauthausen

All Part of the American Occupation

TRENCH MARYE *

DEAR JACK:

I have been for two weeks in a concentration camp. But let's begin at the beginning:

After fourteen months in England I finally moved over to France, and from there was ordered on May 3 to set out on a special trip up near the front. Being alone, the only way I could travel was to hitchhike. The first thirty-five miles (to Paris) I drove in style in the staff car belonging to our unit, with a GI driver; from there on I was dumped into anything that was going my way. First was a "courier" carrying mail and supplies in a "recon car" (a glorified jeep), then . . . a truck convoy carrying newly trained Military Government officers forward into Germany. . . .

There is no wheel traffic on the roads in Germany except an almost endless succession of army trucks—because there are no other vehicles, there is no gasoline, the main roads are barred to civilian traffic, and besides nobody is allowed to leave the town where he now is without a special permit from Military Government. Nevertheless the road is dotted as far as the eye can reach with trudging people with packs on their backs or pushing baby carriages or carts full of possessions or sometimes (the lucky ones)

---

* The author was a soldier serving with the American Military Government. This letter, written to a former associate, was mimeographed and circulated by the Federal Security Agency, Office of the General Counsel, as Shop Letter No. 4.

riding bicycles—the D.P.'s (displaced persons), estimated to be as many as twenty million. For hundreds of miles it looked like the circus or a camp meeting breaking up. Every little while a truck convoy comes lumbering along filled with them, often with a French flag flying.

In Paris I had seen the temporary buildings erected inside the railroad stations all ready to receive the flood of repatriates when they arrive. The system for handling them is to post notices all over Germany indicating where the nearest "collection point" is located, and there in some former barracks or other group of buildings they are housed and deloused and fed and clothed and divided up by nationalities and finally loaded into trucks (and later into trains when these get going) and sent on to the next relay point and so on. Of course thousands of them simply "take off" across country on their own, and down where I am now you hear all sorts of stories of wholesale appropriation, or looting, and worse.

The villages and countryside are practically uninjured and the farm work is being carried on, though with oxen and often cows instead of any tractors they may have had—and workers are largely women, often gray-haired women. The fields are thoroughly planted, but the slave labor that did it is streaming away toward home, and the younger men are still with the army.

This, however, is the only work that *is* being done, for the economy of the country is back where it was two thousand years ago (with the exception of the fact that there is generally electric light). In a seven-hundred-mile stretch I have seen exactly two locomotives moving (scores of smashed ones), the bridges on the railroads are down (the engineers have patched up those on the main roads spendidly), the factories for metal products are all destroyed (and I mean all), the shops are either gutted or their shelves are empty and the door locked, since there is nothing to sell. Therefore there is no occupation for the people except to stand in line for groceries (I have seen long lines waiting at six in the morning for the stores to open, and every person carries a little handbag or market bag perpetually). The schools being closed, by Military Government order, the children are everywhere in evidence, frolicking in the sun along the roads, or playing in the streams, and if the car stops for a minute they spring up out of the ground and cluster around.

The cities are ghastly beyond description. We reached the first (Saarbrücken) within five minutes after crossing the border from France, and I shall never forget the terrific impression as of a city's skeleton gaping at us as we rolled through the empty streets— houses for forty thousand people empty shells and not a human soul visible. After that one became used to it and it was the occasional city area that was not ruined that attracted one's attention. In most cities the population was considerably in evidence, moving about the streets as if this were their normal way of living. The matter of removal of debris is in startling contrast to the treatment in England, where they have made it a point of morale to tidy up almost before the walls stopped falling. Here there has been apparently no effort whatever in that direction except to clear the roadway. The buildings stand there half collapsed, piles of plaster and bricks and wood lying where they fell and out on to the sidewalk. (I saw a crowd in Wiesbaden the other day standing fascinated by one of our bulldozers pushing the rubble into a vacant lot—the GI driver nonchalantly puffing a cigar as he shoved the remains of the city around!)

As regards the people's attitude, I would say that anyone could diagnose it any way he is inclined. We are forbidden to talk to them except on business (and couldn't anyway with any facility), and therefore one main road of finding out is closed. We carry our side arms at all times. On the street they look at you, then look away (and you do the same yourself), but if you ask a direction they are eager to tell you. They do not to me seem stricken or proud or defiant or resentful—they seem to be the same they always were, just people living their lives. At eight in the evening the streets suddenly become deserted as the curfew takes effect, and then the sound of the Yank is all that is heard through the empty thoroughfares—loud conversations that reverberate among the ruins, jeeps tearing about, radios blaring. The only sign that there is any other population is a face here and there at a window, watching.

We of course occupy the hotels, operating them with D.P. labor and an occasional German where he is essential. But there is little service—you are lucky if there is hot water or an elevator running —just a lot of rooms under one roof. When you arrive you walk into the room assigned you by the billeting office, unroll your bed·

ding roll on the first bed you see, and that is your home for the night. By bedtime you have several roommates whom you never saw before and will never see again. In smaller places you simply find a place in the camp of the local detachment, which is usually a German barracks, often pretty well battered by our air attacks.

V-Day we happened to end up at General Patton's headquarters, where we found a celebration dinner going on, with plenty of champagne (German), a GI orchestra and Russian waitresses to give the thing a touch of color. That day for the first time we had seen long strings of our trucks loaded with German prisoners. Next day, and ever since, the roads have been full of them moving under their own power—singly, in groups, in their own trucks, sometimes still in military organization, all headed for home or a demobilization point. They look like anything but the terrors of the universe, with their nondescript clothes and generally battered appearance. That night we spent in a village far up in the mountains that separate Bavaria from Czechoslovakia, where a corps headquarters is temporarily located. The contrast presented was terrific—a typical picturesque Bavarian pastoral mountain village, the streets filled with huge U.S. Army trucks and other paraphernalia, and the air full of good raw American language. (During the day we had passed through Nuremberg. Formerly it was a perfect set piece for a medieval pageant; now it is a twisted tangle of ruin—the old castle and the new Nazi area merely a part of the general desolation.) Next day we wound through beautiful mountain scenery and then down along the Danube where it breaks through the mountains, to our destination, the city of Linz in Upper Austria.

Our first job here was to report on the condition and needs of the concentration camp at Mauthausen, about fifteen miles below Linz. We set out and followed a dirt road along the riverbank, through tiny villages, showing little signs of war except for an occasional roadblock (heavy piles driven in on both sides, between which a barrier could be quickly put in place) or where there had been an air attack on a road convoy and the fields nearby were dotted with huge craters and up in the woods the tall pines around each crater were uprooted or stripped of their branches. Finally, at a turn of the road, up above us on the summit of the line of hills that edge the broad valley, we saw the place—a typical great granite-built penitentiary, with colonies of wooden barracks surrounding it. The location is superb, the valley below with the river winding through it, towns here and there, and over yonder some fifty miles away the long jagged line of the Alps, in some places snow-covered.

As we rolled in through the gate, there spread all over the enclosure was the raw material of this torture factory—human beings by the thousands, including women and a few children, in all forms and quantities of attire, and in all degrees of health, some in very good condition, but the vast majority mere walking skeletons. They were mostly sitting or lying in the bright spring sunlight, or simply milling about. The camp had been liberated just four days before by an advance unit of the army and up to then there was little they could give them except sunlight and thick soup. They couldn't be given freedom outside the camp yet until they had been fattened up and sorted and disinfected and orderly arrangements made for their reception and transportation after they left.

It is all just as we have read about these camps in the papers—machinery for continuous extermination, gas chambers, shooting rooms, ovens . . . Apparently, however, the most reliable continuous method was starvation, and the limit upon the rate of extermination was the limit of the means of disposition of the bodies. (Why they didn't dig pits and dump them in, as we have been doing with the twenty-five to fifty that are still dying in spite of our efforts to save them, I can't understand.) The scenes in the barracks that I saw the first day were horrible, even after four days of good treatment. In some barracks there are bunks (three-tiered), but there were two of these emaciated scarecrows in each bunk, and before we came there were six! If a man had to get up in the night he lost his place to one of those who had none at all. In the worst huts there are no beds—there lay these wretched creatures all over the floor, a couple of feet apart, just lying there or sitting up and gazing blankly at you as you stood at the door. The latrine was placed on a terrace up about ten steps, and many of them were too weak to make it formerly, so that the general stench all over the camp was nauseating. That has disappeared now, but we had to burn down one of the attached camps. There had never been any drinking water in the camp, and we had difficulty in getting a supply of even washing water up here, but fortunately the Vienna fire department had sent a lot of its engines up here for safety and our people just set them to work and supplied the cisterns through fire hoses. (The firemen were put to work as guards after the SS men left, and now they are having a hard time getting home, what with the prohibition of circulation and the fact that Vienna is in the hands of the Russians.)

When the guards left, the prisoners themselves took over, the Russians being largely in control, they and the Poles forming the largest contingent. (Even under the Germans they were all organized into national groups, and much of the administration was handled through these groups.) They had set up courts and had already condemned some of their own number to death for trafficking with the Germans. When our troops arrived and took over, it put an end to that regime and its edicts, of course, but the next night three of them were murdered right in the camp streets. So the commandant had to physically segregate them into separate barracks by nationalities, and even so there were frequent fights between Russians and Poles and between Mihailovicz-Yugoslavs and Tito-Yugoslavs.

At one of the subsidiary camps the prisoners simply all left. However, after wandering about for a few days they began coming back in great numbers, for food and shelter. There is of course a great amount of disease, including typhus, but one of our hospital units has moved in and set up a hospital in one of the barracks and has things in good shape. (With our inoculations and our knowledge of the effectiveness of DDT powder none of us have practically given a thought to contagion.)

As indicating further the shadings, there were other than pure black in the picture. I heard to my astonishment an orchestra playing out in the prison yard the first afternoon I was here. I was told that it was instituted for the purpose of drowning the cries of those that were being tortured, but at any rate it was an apparently well-practiced orchestra of prisoners. Shortly after my arrival there appeared a young Russian officer (their zone of occupation extends to within about twelve miles of here), who announced that there was a group of higher officers on their way here to take the Russian prisoners with them. The news spread around and presently here came a great crowd of Russians from their part of the camp surging down to the gate carrying a banner with a picture of Stalin. The visitors didn't take them away then, but the result was that they have now gone.

Some of the most gruesome pictures photographed here (showing for instance the five-hundred naked bodies that our men found here upon their first arrival, stacked like beef carcasses) are posted in the city of Linz and there is a crowd around the board all the time. Whether there is any feeling of responsibility or remorse on the part of the spectators would require more cross-examination and psychological analysis than I possess the power of. When I stopped to look, one man edged over to me and said in English: "We never dreamed that the Germans were doing such things." But I was an American, so you can draw almost any conclusion you like from that. Personally I am inclined to conclude that one of the officers was right when he said, after visiting Buchenwald, that the people in town knew probably just as much as and no more than we ordinarily know about what goes on in the asylum just outside town. It is pretty certain that at least 150,000 people came to their deaths here in the seven years that it has been in operation. . . .

Steps Beyond the Grave

SIMON WIESENTHAL *

It was ten o'clock on the morning of May 5, 1945, when I saw a big gray tank with a white star on its side and the American flag waving from the turret. I stood on the windswept square that had been, until an hour earlier, the courtyard of the Mauthausen concentration camp. The day was sunny, with a scent of spring in the air. Gone was the sweetish smell of burned flesh that had always hovered over the yard.

The night before, the last SS men had run away. The machinery of death had come to a stop. In my room a few dead people were lying on their bunks. They hadn't been taken away this morning. The crematorium no longer operated.

I do not remember how I'd got from my room into the courtyard. I was hardly able to walk. I was wearing my faded striped uniform with a yellow *J* in a yellow-red double triangle. Around me I saw other men in striped dungarees. Some were holding small flags, waving at the Americans. Where had they gotten the flags from? Did the Americans bring them? I shall never know.

The tank with the white star was about a hundred yards in front of me. I wanted to touch the star, but I was too weak. I had survived to see this day, but I couldn't make the last hundred yards. I remember taking a few steps, and then my knees gave way and I fell on my face.

Somebody lifted me up. I felt the rough texture of an olive-drab

* The Murderers Among Us: The Simon Wiesenthal Memoirs, edited by Joseph Wechsberg (New York: McGraw-Hill, 1967), pp. 45–56. This book records Wiesenthal's career as a hunter of German war criminals.

American uniform brush against my bare arms. I couldn't speak; I couldn't even open my mouth. I pointed toward the white star, I touched the cold, dusty armor with my hands, and then I fainted.

When I opened my eyes after what seemed a long time, I was back on my bunk. The room seemed changed. There was only one man on each bunk, no longer three or four, and the dead had been taken away. There was an unfamiliar smell in the air. It was DDT. They brought in big kettles with soup. This was *real* soup, and it tasted delicious. I took too much of it—my stomach wasn't used to such nourishing fare—and I got violently sick.

The next days went by in a pleasant apathy. Most of the time I dozed on my bunk. American doctors in white coats came to look at us. We were given pills and more food—soup, vegetables, meat. I still was so weak that a friend had to help me when I wanted to go out. I had survived, I didn't have to force myself to be strong any longer; I had seen the day I'd prayed for all these years, but now I was weaker than ever. "A natural reaction," said the doctors.

I made an effort to get up and walk out alone. As I shuffled through a dark corridor, a man jumped at me and knocked me down. I collapsed and lost consciousness. I came to on my bunk, and an American doctor gave me something. Two friends sat next to me. They had picked me up in the corridor and carried me to my bunk. They said that a Polish trusty had beaten me. Perhaps he was angry because I was still alive.

People in room A said I must report the trusty to the American authorities. We were free men now, no longer *Untermenschen.* The next day my friends accompanied me to an office in the building that had formerly been the camp headquarters. A handwritten sign WAR CRIMES was on the door. We were told to wait in a small anteroom. Somebody brought me a chair, and I sat down.

Through the open doors, I saw American officers behind desks who interrogated SS men who stood at attention in front of them. Several former prisoners worked as typists. An SS man was brought into the room. Instinctively I turned my head sideward so he wouldn't see me. He had been a brutal guard; when he walked through the corridor and a prisoner did not step aside quickly and snap to attention, the SS man would whip the prisoner's face with the riding crop he always carried. The sight of this man had always brought cold sweat to the back of my neck.

Now I stared; I coudn't believe it. The SS man was trembling, just as we had trembled before him. His shoulders were hunched, and I noticed that he wiped the palms of his hands. He was no longer a superman; he made me think of a trapped animal. He was escorted by a Jewish prisoner—a *former* prisoner.

I kept staring, fascinated. I didn't hear what was said as the SS man stood before the American interrogator. He could hardly stand at attention, and there was sweat on his forehead. The American officer motioned with his hand and an American soldier took the SS man away. My friends said that all SS men were being taken to a big concrete pillbox, where they were to be kept under guard until they were tried. I made my report on the Polish trusty. My friends testified that they had found me lying unconscious in the corridor. One of the American doctors also testified. Then we went back to our room. That night the trusty apologized to me in front of our comrades, and extended his hand. I accepted his apology but did not give him my hand.

The trusty wasn't important. He was already part of the past. I kept thinking of the scene at the office. Lying on my bunk with my eyes closed, I saw the trembling SS man—a contemptible, frightened coward in his black uniform. For years that uniform had been the symbol of terror. I had seen apprehensive German soldiers during the war (the soldiers, too, were afraid of the SS men), but never a frightened SS man. I had always thought of them as the strong men, the elite, of a perverted regime. It took me a long time to understand what I had seen: the supermen became cowards the moment they were no longer protected by their guns. They were through.

I got up from my bunk and walked out of the room. Behind the crematorium, SS men were digging graves for our 3000 comrades who had died of starvation and exhaustion after the arrival of the Americans. I sat down, looking at the SS men. Two weeks ago they would have beaten me half-dead if I had dared look at them. Now they seemed to be afraid to walk past me. An SS man begged an American soldier for a cigarette. The soldier thew away the cigarette that he'd been smoking. The SS man bent down, but another SS man was faster and got hold of the butt, and the two SS men began to scuffle until the soldier told them to get away.

Only two weeks had gone by, and the elite of the Thousand Year Reich were fighting for a cigarette butt. How many years had it been since we had been given a cigarette? I walked back to my room and looked around. Most of my comrades were lying apathetically on their bunks. After the moment of exhilaration many of them suffered attacks of depression. Now that they knew they were going to live, they were aware of the senselessness of their lives. They had been spared—but they had no one to live for, no place they could go back to, no pieces they could pick up. . . .

[Days later]. They would ask each other: "Who else is alive?" One couldn't understand that one had survived, and it was beyond comprehension that others should still be alive. They would sit on the steps to the office [of the Jewish Central Committee in Linz] and talk to one another. "Can it be that my wife, my mother, my child is alive? Some of my friends, some of the people in the town where we lived?"

There was no mail service. The few available telephone lines were restricted to military use. The only way to find out whether someone was alive was to go and look. Across Europe a wild tide of frantic survivors was flowing. People were hitchhiking, getting short jeep rides, or hanging onto dilapidated railway coaches without windows or doors. They sat in huddled groups on haycarts, and some just walked. They would use any means to get a few miles closer to their destination. To get from Linz to Munich, normally a three-hour railroad trip, might take five days. Many of them didn't really know where to go. To the place where one had been with his family before the war? To the concentration camp where the family had last been heard of? Families had been torn apart too suddenly to make arrangements for the day when it would be all over.

. . . And yet the survivors continued their pilgrimage of despair, sleeping on highways or in railroad stations, waiting for another train, another horse-drawn cart to come along, always driven by hope. "Perhaps someone is still alive. . . ." Someone might tell where to find a wife, a mother, children, a brother—or whether they were dead. Better to know the truth than to know nothing. The desire to find one's people was stronger than hunger, thirst, fatigue. Stronger even than the fear of border patrols, of the CIC and NKVD, of men saying "Let's see your papers."

The first thing we did at the Committee in Linz was to make up lists of known survivors. People who came in to ask for someone were asked where *they* were from. They were nomads, vagabonds, beggars. But once upon a time they had had a home, a job, savings. Their names were put on the list of some town or village. Slowly the lists grew. People from Poland, Czechoslovakia, or Germany brought us lists. We gave them copies of our lists. We worked long into the night to copy these lists. Early in the morning, the first people would arrive to look up names. Some waited all night to get in. Behind a man another waited for a glance that might mean hope or despair. Some people were impatient and there were brawls. Once two men began to scuffle because each wanted the same list. In the end they tore up the precious piece of paper. Another time two men started to argue, their eyes glued to the list in the hands of a third man. Each wanted it next. Suddenly they looked at each other and gasped, and the next moment they were in each others' arms. They were brothers and each had been trying to find the other for weeks.

And there were moments of silent despair when someone discovered that the person he was looking for had been there only a few days before, looking for him. They had missed each other. Where should one look now? Other people scanned the lists of survivors, hoping against hope to find the names of people they had seen killed before their very eyes. Everybody had heard of some miracle.

I hardly ever looked at the lists. I didn't believe in miracles. I knew that all my people were dead. After the Pole from Warsaw had told me what happened in Topiel Street, I had no hope that my wife was alive. When I thought of her, I thought of her body lying under a heap of rubble, and I wondered whether they had found the bodies and buried her. In a moment of illogical hope I wrote to the International Committee of the Red Cross in Geneva. They promptly answered that my wife was dead. I knew that my mother did not have a grave; she had died in the death camp of Belzec. I hoped that at least my wife might have a grave.

One night, when I had nothing else to do, I looked at a list of survivors from the Polish city of Cracow and found the name of an old friend from Buczacz, Dr. Biener. I wrote him a letter. I told him that my wife's body might still be lying under the ruins of the house in Topiel Street. I asked him to go to Warsaw and look at what was left of the house. There was no mail service to Poland, so I gave the letter to a man who specialized in getting things through Czechoslovakia to Poland.

I didn't know that a miracle had indeed happened. My wife told me all about it later. When the German flame-thrower squads had closed in on Topiel Street, in the darkness and confusion my wife and a few other people had managed to get away. For a while they hid. After the battle of Warsaw, the few survivors were driven together by the Germans and assigned to forced-labor transports for Germany. My wife was sent to a factory in Heiligenhaus, near Gelsenkirchen in the Rhineland, where they made machine guns for the Wehrmacht. The Polish laborers were decently housed and fed, and the Gestapo left them alone. The Germans knew that the war was lost.

My wife was liberated by the British, who marched into Gelsenkirchen on April 11, 1945. (That day I was lying on my bunk in the death block of Mauthausen.) My wife went to the British authorities and reported that she was Cyla Wiesenthal, a Jewish woman from Poland. Six women in her group turned out to be Jewish, but they had not known of each other. One of them told my wife that she was going home.

"Home?" asked my wife. "Where is home?"

"To Poland, of course. Why don't you come with me?"

"What for? My husband was killed by the Gestapo in Lwow last year. Poland has become a large cemetery to me."

"Have you proof that he's dead?"

"No," said my wife, "but . . ."

"Don't believe it. Now, suppose he were alive: where is he likely to be?"

Cyla thought it over. "In Lwow, I would think. We spent the years before the war there."

"Lwow is now in the Soviet Union," said her friend. "Let's go there."

The two women left Gelsenkirchen in June 1945. (At one point on her journey, we later discovered, my wife had been less than thirty miles from Linz.) After an arduous trip, they reached the Czechoslovak-Polish border at Bohumin. They were told that a train left that night for Lwow. They got on the overcrowded cars and arrived in Cracow, Poland, in the morning. It was announced that there would be a four-hour stop.

At the Cracow railroad station somebody stole my wife's suitcase with everything she owned. That was her homecoming. To cheer her up, her friend suggested that they walk into town. Perhaps they would meet someone they had once known. The beautiful old city of the Polish kings looked deserted and ghostlike that morning. Suddenly my wife heard her name called out, and recognized a man named Landek, who had been a dentist in Lwow. (Landek now lives in America.) For a while they exchanged hectic questions and unfinished sentences, as always happened when survivors met. Landek had heard that Simon Wiesenthal was dead. He told my wife to talk to Dr. Biener. He might know more.

"Dr. Biener from Buczacz?" asked my wife. "Is he in Cracow?"

"He lives five minutes from here." Landek gave her the address and hurried away.

When they came to Dr. Biener's house, my wife asked her friend to wait downstairs. She walked up the stairway with a heavy heart. On the third floor she saw a sign reading Biener and rang the bell. The door was opened. For a moment she saw Dr. Biener's face and heard a muffled cry. Then the door was quickly shut again.

"Dr. Biener!" my wife shouted, banging her fists against the door. "Open up! It's Cyla. Cyla Wiesenthal from Buczacz!"

The door was opened. Dr. Biener was pale, as if he were seeing a ghost.

"But—you are dead," he said, "I just got a letter. . . ."

"I'm very much alive," my wife said angrily. "Of course I *look* half-dead, after spending the night on the train."

"Come in," Dr. Biener said hastily, and closed the door. "You don't understand. Yesterday I had a letter from your husband. Simon writes that you died under the ruins of a house in Warsaw."

Now my wife got pale. "Simon? But he's dead. He's been dead for over a year."

Dr. Biener shook his head. "No, no, Cyla. Simon is alive, in Linz, Austria. Here, read the letter."

They called my wife's friend from downstairs. She was not at all surprised. Hadn't she told Cyla that her husband might be alive? They sat down and talked, and when they remembered the train it was much too late. If my letter hadn't reached Dr. Biener the day before, if my wife hadn't met Landek, if Dr. Biener hadn't been at home, the two women would have gone back to the station and continued their journey to the Soviet Union. My wife might have been sent into the interior of the USSR, and it would have taken years to find her again.

My wife stayed in Cracow, and tried to get in touch with me. Dr. Biener knew several illegal couriers who would carry letters for a fee, with no guarantee of delivery. She wrote three letters and gave them to three men working different routes. I received one of them, from a man who had come to Linz by way of Budapest— which is quite a detour.

I'll never forget the moment when I saw Cyla's handwriting on the envelope. I read the letter so many times that I knew it by heart. I went to see the OSS captain for whom I was then working and asked him to give me travel orders to Cracow. He didn't like the idea of my going to Poland. He said I might never be able to come back. He suggested we think it over until next morning.

I didn't go to the Jewish Committee that afternoon. I was happy and perhaps feeling a little guilty at being a happy man among so many unhappy people. I wanted to be alone. I knew a peasant not far from where I lived who had a few horses. I thought of my summer vacations in Dolina, where I loved to ride horses. I asked the peasant to let me have a horse for an hour. I forgot that I was a little older and not yet in good physical condition. I mounted the horse. Something went wrong. I suppose the horse sensed at once that I was still weak. I was thrown and landed in a potato field with a broken ankle.

I had to stay in bed. That settled the matter of my projected journey to Poland. I asked a Jewish friend, Dr. Felix Weisberg, to go to Cracow and gave him a letter for my wife. He promised to bring her back to Linz. My OSS friends made out the necessary travel documents for her, so she would have no difficulty in getting into the U.S. Zone of Austria.

They were fine travel documents, but unfortunately my wife never received them. Crossing Czechoslovakia on his way to Poland, Dr. Weisberg was warned that there was an NKVD roadblock ahead, with "very strict controls." He got nervous; if the Soviet secret police found any American *dokumenty* on him, they might arrest him as a spy. He destroyed the documents. Too late he realized that he had also destroyed my wife's address in Cracow. As it turned out, NKVD didn't even search him. In Cracow, he went to the local Jewish Committee and put a notice on the bulletin board. Mrs. Cyla Wiesenthal, the wife of Simon Wiesenthal, was asked to get in touch with Dr. Felix Weisberg, who would take her to her husband in Linz.

My wife saw the notice the next morning and went to see Dr. Weisberg. She was not the first visitor. Two other women were already there, each claiming to be the one and only Cyla Wiesenthal. A lot of people in Poland were trying to get to Austria, hoping they might later try to get to America. Poor Felix Weisberg had a trickier problem than the mythological Paris. Weisberg didn't know my wife. In all the excitement preceding his sudden departure, I had foolishly forgotten to give him her exact description. He faced the unpleasant possibility of bringing back the wrong Mrs. Wiesenthal. Weisberg told me later that he'd asked each of the three women to describe how I looked. Two seemed rather vague, but one knew a lot of details, naturally. Also, Weisberg admitted to me, he'd liked her best. He decided to take a chance and bought false travel papers for her in the black market.

One evening, late in 1945, I was early in bed as usual. My broken ankle still gave me a lot of trouble. There was a knock at the door. Felix Weisberg came in, confused and embarrassed. It took him quite a while to explain how he'd foolishly thrown away the American documents, and his dilemma over three women each claiming to be Mrs. Cyla Wiesenthal.

"I brought one of them with me. She's waiting downstairs. Now, don't get excited, Simon. If she isn't your wife, I'm going to marry her myself."

"You?"

"Yes, my word of honor. You're under no obligation whatsoever. To tell the truth, I thought it safest to bring the one I liked best. That way, I knew even if she was not your wife I would ——"

But then she came into the room, and Felix Weisberg, God bless him, knew that he could not marry her.

Salzwedel: Death to the Jews

JOHN TOLAND *

*Toland, who wrote his history of the ending
of the European war with the aid of interviews with survivors, describes events in the
town of Salzwedel, Germany, where liberated
slave laborers went berserk, unleashing terror
and revealing how their hatred of Jews also
survived concentration camps.*

On the day of Hitler's breakdown a motorized column of the
American 84th Division rolled into the town of Salzwedel, 100 air
miles west of the bunker. Huddled in the houses, almost as frightened as the local citizens, were about 4000 concentration camp
inmates and slave laborers abandoned by their guards.

Tadeusz Nowakowski was one of the first to venture into the
street. In 1937, at the age of seventeen, he had won the Polish
Academy of Literature's prize for young writers. Two years later
he and his father, who had worked together with Paderewski at
the time of the Versailles Treaty, were arrested for publishing the
underground paper, *Poland Still Alive.* The elder Nowakowski
never lived to see his concentration camp, Dachau, liberated; he
was beaten to death with a shovel by an enraged guard. But his
son endured a succession of Gestapo prisons and camps. He escaped in early February and fled west to Salzwedel, where he found
refuge with Polish slave laborers at a sugar factory.

The streets of Salzwedel were jammed with U.S. motorcycles,

* *The Last 100 Days* (New York: Random House, 1965, 1966), pp. 443–
446.

jeeps, trucks and armored cars churning up clouds of smoke and dust. Nowakowski could hear the roar of planes. It was the scene of liberation he had dreamed of for so many years.

A jeep stopped and a huge Negro stopped out to wild applause and a deluge of flowers. He pushed the crowd aside and nailed a SLOW sign on a telephone pole. He fanned himself with his helmet, shoved his way back to the jeep and drove off with a blast of his horn.

The other Americans were just as bored and looked at the prisoners with indifference, even as they flipped out packs of Chesterfields. They were far from arrogant, yet their behavior suggested a barely concealed contempt at the sight of the miserable and helpless. Or perhaps, Nowakowski thought, they were just tired of it all.

Only a crew of cameramen showed special interest. They persuaded the emaciated prisoners to return to the nearby concentration camp so that they could be filmed behind barbed wire. Some of the children cried when asked to go back through the gate.

In town, mobs of slave laborers roamed the streets, looking for ways of revenge. Barefooted Rumanians emptied buckets of marmalade onto the sidewalk, enraged women smashed store windows with their hands, and a Russian tossed fistfuls of herrings into the air.

A wounded SS man was dragged out of a garage and trampled to death. Prisoners, whose bodies were bloated from hunger, moved painfully up to the corpse. They kicked at it feebly, then flung themselves down and began tearing the hated flesh with hands and teeth. Nowakowski wanted to join them, to shout, "Tear his eyes out! For my tortured father, for my companions, for my bombed city!" But the words stuck in his throat. He laughed hysterically, tears streaming down his cheeks. He thought, I am alive, you sons of bitches!

An American patrol in a jeep fired a burst just over the heads of the clawing mass, tooted a horn reprovingly and passed on. It was a surrealistic nightmare. In front of a department store Nowakowski saw two drunken Frenchmen, entangled in a shredded bridal gown, kissing each other on the mouth and stoking each other's hair. An old Polish woman was vomiting blood as gypsy children emptied a bag of flour on her.

Across the canal he saw prisoners clamber onto a railroad tank car full of alcohol. When no one could open the valve someone found an ax, and soon the liquid spurted out in a great jet. The shrieking mob held out mess tins, hats and shoes. A Czech boy shouted, "It's methyl alcohol! It's poison!" but no one would listen.

A group of Russians tied the Bürgermeister to a tombstone and stripped his wife and daughter of their clothes. The Bürgermeister reared up and screeched like a cock crowing. A red-faced Russian shouted that his own wife had suffered the same fate in Kharkov, and roughly pushed several young countrymen up to the daughter. The mother threw herself on the ground and in supplication tried to kiss their feet.

There was a moment's hesitation. Then a squat Kalmuck grabbed the girl and forced her down. Her father made a mighty wrench. He tore the tombstone out of the earth—and dropped dead. Nowakowski watched the prisoner who had started it all walk away, with hands in pockets; he sat down on the bank of the canal and buried his face in his hands.

The riot reached such proportions that the Americans were forced to pen up the prisoners again. With hundreds of others, Nowakowski was locked in the gymnasium of a former army camp. But the nightmare continued. A group of young girls sang the Polish song "All Our Daily Concerns," while a few yards away men poisoned by the alcohol writhed in agony and vomited violet liquid. Those suffering from diarrhea had to relieve themselves on the spot and were shoved away by angry neighbors.

A group of boys found the gymnastic equipment and began clambering up ropes and swinging on trapezes like monkeys. They did not even stop their yelling and laughing when one of them dropped onto a pile of scrap iron, screamed a few minutes, then died.

By midnight the situation had become intolerable. A mob of men broke into the huddles of sleeping Polish and Ukrainian women. Nowakowski heard scuffles, short cries, curses, laughing, crying and whimpering. One man lamented over and over, *"A ja ne mohu, ne mohu!"* ("But I can't, I can't!")

An Italian poisoned by alcohol had a fit. Like an animal he crawled frenziedly over sleepers, meowing and barking. When he reached the wall he kept smashing his head against it until he slumped under a radiator, finally at peace.

It wasn't until dawn that the Americans unlocked the gymnasium and told the French, Dutch, Belgian, Luxembourgian and Czech prisoners to come out; they were to be transferred to the officers' quarters. This brought screams of outrage from those left, who began cursing the Americans and the day of liberation. "We're allies too!" an indignant Italian shouted.

A wave of hysteria swept the big room. A Ukrainian woman who thought a Polish woman had stolen her comb ripped off the offender's necklace. She screamed for help from fellow Poles and a cry went up: "Kill the Ukrainians!"

Suddenly a loudspeaker boomed "Hello, hello," and in five languages announced that the hall was going to be inspected. At eight o'clock several American officers peered in and, appalled, quickly withdrew. They ordered all children brought outside at once. A rumor started that Jewish women were being quartered in villas and given white bread, eggs and chocolate. Shouts of rage went up: "They take hot baths and walk around in kimonos!" "They sleep with Americans."

"You see how these sons of bitches look after their own people!" someone called out. "A Jew will always help a Jew, but the Christians are left to die like dogs!"

"Like dogs!" a hundred others repeated.

"That's because we're not dirty Jews like them!" screamed an old woman wearing a man's cap.

A girl angrily shouted back, "That's because they burned us in the crematorium ovens while you were screwing German farmers in barns!"

The room went quiet. Everyone stared at the girl. She was small and ugly, with a big head that looked like a pumpkin on top of a pole. Her red ears stuck out. "Go ahead, hit me!" she cried hoarsely.

"*Jüdin!*" someone screamed, and the mob rushed at the girl. An elderly bespectacled man who looked like a professor circled the girl with a protecting arm. "Don't touch her!"

The frenzied attackers threw them both to the floor and smothered them with sacks. The "professor" was overwhelmed; the women tore out the girl's hair in chunks and jabbed fingers in her eyes. "That's for the milk!" one shouted. "That's for the chocolate! That's for the farmers in the barn, you dirty Jew!"

Her defender stopped struggling, his body went limp.

"Oh, Jesus!" a woman cried. "They're dead!"

The women scattered, but two Russians wiped the blood off the victims' faces, dragged them to a corner and dumped them on top of several other corpses.

Death Against Life

ELIE WIESEL *

I had to stay at Buchenwald until April eleventh. I have nothing to say of my life during this period. It no longer mattered. After my father's death, nothing could touch me any more.

I was transferred to the children's block, where there were six hundred of us.

The front was drawing nearer.

I spent my days in a state of total idleness. And I had but one desire—to eat. I no longer thought of my father or of my mother.

From time to time I would dream of a drop of soup, of an extra ration of soup.

On April fifth, the wheel of history turned.

It was late in the afternoon. We were standing in the block, waiting for an SS man to come and count us. He was late in coming. Such a delay was unknown till then in the history of Buchenwald. Something must have happened.

Two hours later the loudspeakers sent out an order from the head of the camp: all Jews must come to the assembly place.

This was the end! Hitler was going to keep his promise.

The children in our block went toward the place. There was nothing else we could do. Gustav, the head of the block, made this clear to us with his truncheon. But on the way we met some prisoners who whispered to us:

"Go back to your block. The Germans are going to shoot you. Go back to your block, and don't move."

We went back to our block. We learned on the way that the

* Op. cit., pp. 114–116.

camp resistance organization had decided not to abandon the Jews and was going to prevent their being liquidated.

As it was late and there was great upheaval—innumerable Jews had passed themselves off as non-Jews—the head of the camp decided that a general roll call would take place the following day. Everybody would have to be present.

The roll call took place. The head of the camp announced that Buchenwald was to be liquidated. Ten blocks of deportees would be evacuated each day. From this moment, there would be no further distribution of bread and soup. And the evacuation began. Every day, several thousand prisoners went through the camp gate and never came back.

On April tenth, there were still about twenty thousand of us in the camp, including several hundred children. They decided to evacuate us all at once, right on until the evening. Afterward, they were going to blow up the camp.

So we were massed in the huge assembly square, in rows of five, waiting to see the gate open. Suddenly, the sirens began to wail. An alert! We went back to the blocks. It was too late to evacuate us that evening. The evacuation was postponed again to the following day.

We were tormented with hunger. We had eaten nothing for six days, except a bit of grass or some potato peelings found near the kitchens.

At ten o'clock in the morning the SS scattered through the camp, moving the last victims toward the assembly place.

Then the resistance movement decided to act. Armed men suddenly rose up everywhere. Bursts of firing. Grenades exploding. We children stayed flat on the ground in the block.

The battle did not last long. Toward noon everything was quiet again. The SS had fled and the resistance had taken charge of the running of the camp.

At about six o'clock in the evening, the first American tank stood at the gates of Buchenwald.

Our first act as free men was to throw ourselves onto the provisions. We thought only of that. Not of revenge, not of our families. Nothing but bread.

And even when we were no longer hungry, there was still no one who thought of revenge. On the following day, some of the young men went to Weimar to get some potatoes and clothes—and to sleep with girls. But of revenge, not a sign.

Three days after the liberation of Buchenwald I became very ill with food poisoning. I was transferred to the hospital and spent two weeks between life and death.

One day I was able to get up, after gathering all my strength. I wanted to see myself in the mirror hanging on the opposite wall. I had not seen myself since the ghetto.

From the depths of the mirror, a corpse gazed back at me.

The look in his eyes, as they stared into mine, has never left me.

Epilogue:
A Personal Note

There was a time when I lived with the Holocaust. A day did not pass when I did not in some way think about its horror. Then there came one Ninth of Av, the fast day commemorating the destruction of the Temple in Jerusalem, when I spoke with a rabbinic friend about the many destructions in Jewish history. And I remember saying to him: "I really don't need Tishah B'av for remembering destructions. After the Holocaust, every day is Tishah B'av." My friend pleaded with me to change my attitude. The living, he said, must remember regularly, but only on occasion. To convert every day into Tishah B'av would destroy the very life the survivors had struggled to maintain.

Slowly, days began occurring when I did not think about the Holocaust. But when, in 1967, Israel lay under heavy threat, the destruction of European Jewry assumed new vividness. Then, after a while, days without thought of the Holocaust began to reappear, and soon I even came to think I could relegate its memory to Tishah B'av or Yom ha-Shoa, the new day set aside for remembering the six million.

During the summer of 1968 my family and I traveled through Europe, stopping here and there to seek out remnants of Jewish life. While in Holland, we drove from Amsterdam to Westerbork, where my father had spent many months. When we reached the vicinity and started to ask where the camp had been, no one seemed to know. Finally I learned from a restaurant owner the magic words "the old *Jodenkamp*." In late afternoon we were inside the camp area, where we met four Dutch travelers who paid regular visits to the *Jodenkamp* site. They took us off the road

305

among trees planted after the war, and showed us the base of the water tower and the railhead from which the transports had begun their terrible journeys.

As I stood there wondering about my father and others who had survived, Ezra, my youngest son, tears streaming down his face, came running to tell me we were locked out of our car. For the next few seconds I felt trapped with my family at the very spot where my father had been imprisoned. The feeling was momentary: the Dutch travelers helped us open the car door and soon we were on our way back to Amsterdam.

A few days later, in Zurich, in a kosher butcher's shop, we struck up an acquaintance with an elderly gentleman who offered to escort us to a Jewish bakery. While in our car he told us that he had come from Amsterdam and had been in Westerbork. No, he did not know my father, he said as we parted.

Two days later, while crossing the main railway station, my sons and I suddenly found a stamped letter on the floor. I picked it up and started to walk to a mailbox, when I heard the voice of the same elderly man saying: "Oh, thank you for finding my letter. Perhaps you have my pen also." In fact, I did have his pen, which he had lent me while we were in the bakery and which he had forgotten to reclaim. "Well, good-bye, and give my regards to your father. I remember him well." I winced: I had told him on our first encounter that my father had died some years before.

The following summer, in Europe once again, when our itinerary made it necessary to drive across Germany, we decided to consider ourselves as just passing through. I was apprehensive because I could not predict my reactions on returning to the land and people that had unleashed such horrors a generation earlier. Still, I told myself, what could happen on the Autobahn, the superhighway, which we would be taking from Basel to our destination, the ferry-crossing in Denmark?

From the moment we crossed the German border, however, I found myself looking at the inhabitants with a special eye. I silently judged and accused everyone over forty whom I happened to encounter. They said nothing. I said nothing. But my special eye fused each one with weird images of the Holocaust. As we drove past the turnoff to Hanover, I remembered "my" sealed transport train pulling out of the railway station , and the platform guard contemptuously scattering the shreds of the postcard my mother had asked him to mail to her parents.

As we approached Hamburg, my children asked me to stop. For a moment I hesitated, looking desperately toward my wife, who understood all too well what such a decision implied. I drove into Hamburg.

Within minutes I found my way to the neighborhoods I had known, but suddenly, having gone too far, I stopped the car. Out of nowhere another car appeared; its young, blond, blue-eyed driver asked, in accented English, how he could help, and I told him, inexplicably, in German, and without any of the malaise I had been enduring since Basel. He showed me where to go, and for a moment, I was an ordinary tourist.

Upon driving toward the place where "my" great synagogue had once stood, the evil images reappeared. I sensed the approach of the crisis I was creating as soon as I saw, off to my right, the street name Bornstrasse. I glanced left for the street sign of the famous Bornplatz, whose name a synagogue had also carried. . . . No Bornplatz!!! . . . This was now the home of Hamburg's university. . . . Surely someone would remember. . . . I asked a woman passing by . . . looked at her . . . and understood everything when she responded with a curt "Yes" to my question, "Is that where the Bornplatz used to be?" I drove across the street, and stopping in a little square, saw a strange, unfamiliar street name above me. There was no more Bornplatz.

I lost control. "I will not get out of this car," I decided. "We will not get out of this car. The wheels have to touch this soil, but we do not." I threw the car into gear and fled. We remained in flight until we reached the ferry.

When they remember these events, I hope my children will understand why the Holocaust of the past remains for me an eternal, painful present.

Further Reading

Hans Buchheim, *et al. Anatomy of the SS State* (London: Weidenfeld and Nicholson, 1969).

Arthur Bulloch, *Hitler: A Study in Tyranny* (New York: Harper & Row, 1964).

Lucy S. Dawidowicz, ed., *The Golden Tradition: Jewish Life and Thought in Eastern Europe* (New York: Holt, Rinehart and Winston, 1967).

Philip Friedman, Jacob Robinson, *et al., Guide to Jewish History Under Nazi Impact,* 9 vols. (New York and Jerusalem: Yad Vashem-YIVO, 1960–1966).

Oscar Handlin, "Jewish Resistance to the Nazis," *Commentary,* Vol. XXXIV (November 1962), pp. 398–405.

Raul Hilberg, *The Destruction of the European Jews* (Chicago: Quadrangle, 1961).

Robert Koehl, *RKVD* (Cambridge: Harvard University Press, 1957).

Guenther Lewy, *The Catholic Church anl Nazi Germany* (New York: McGraw-Hill, 1964).

George L. Mosse, *The Crisis of German Ideology: Intellectual Origins of the Third Reich* (New York: Grosset & Dunlap, 1964).

Elizabeth Wiskeman, *Europe of the Dictators, 1919–1945* (New York: Harper & Row, 1966).

Contributors

Max O. Korman, a salesman from Hamburg who became a refugee in 1938 when he was deported to Zbaszyn, Poland. He was a passenger on the ship *St. Louis* and survived the Westerbork concentration camp.

Nathan C. Belth, a research analyst (in 1939) for the American Jewish Committee.

Clarence E. Pickett, for many years executive secretary of the American Friends Service Committee.

Quentin Reynolds, in the 1930's a reporter and an associate editor of *Collier's* who was sent to Germany in 1938.

Chaim A. Kaplan, a Hebraist and schoolteacher who kept a diary in Warsaw between 1939 and 1942.

Shmaryahu Ellenberg, an activist among the Jews of Poland. He later became an educator in Israel.

A. H. Hartglass, a leader among the Jews of Poland, a journalist, and a member of the Polish parliament. He died in Israel in 1953.

Zvi Yavetz, a teen-ager in Czernowitz when World War II began. He became an academician in Israel.

Hans Goldberger, a textile merchant from Bratislava who became a refugee. He was a passenger on the ship *Pentcho*.

Jacob Kahn, a jeweler from Mannheim who became a refugee in 1940.

Alexander Grin, a resident of Belgrade who became a refugee in 1941.

Samuel Silverman, a furrier from Brussels who became a refugee in 1940.

Raul Hilberg, an American scholar who has written one of the important studies of the destruction of European Jewry.

J. Kermish, presently a director of the Yad Vashem Archives in Jerusalem.

Alexander Donat, a journalist from Warsaw who survived the Warsaw Ghetto. He is now a writer in the United States.

Kalman Friedman, a survivor of the Warsaw Ghetto who became a public-relations director in Jerusalem.

Elie Wiesel, who as a teen-ager survived Auschwitz and Buchenwald. He became an influential writer and teacher, with the Holocaust as his subject.

Walter Lenz, a Viennese student of art history before he became a refugee in 1938. He survived the Westerbork concentration camp.

Joseph Rothenberg, a physician from New York City, who as a soldier in the American Army helped to liberate the concentration camp Dachau.

Trench Marye, a major in the American Army who visited the concentration camp at Mauthausen just after its liberation.

Simon Wiesenthal, a survivor of the concentration camp at Mauthausen who became a famous hunter of Nazi war criminals.

John Toland, an important American writer of historical accounts about World War II.

ACKNOWLEDGMENTS

(Continued from copyright page)

American Jewish Year Book: From *The Refugee Problem* by Nathan C. Belth.

Commentary and Alexander Donat: From *Our Last Days in the Warsaw Ghetto* by Alexander Donat. Reprinted from *Commentary,* by permission; Copyright © 1963 by the American Jewish Committee.

Hill and Wang and Georges Borchardt, Inc.: From *Night* by Elie Wiesel. English translation © MacGibbon & Kee, 1960. Reprinted by permission.

The Macmillan Company and Hamish Hamilton Ltd.: From *Scroll of Agony: Chaim A. Kaplan's Journal of the Warsaw Ghetto,* translated and edited by Abraham Katsh. Copyright © Abraham Katsh, 1965.

McGraw-Hill Book Company: From *The Murderers among Us: The Wiesenthal Memoirs* edited by Joseph Wechsberg. Copyright © 1967 by Opera Mundi, Paris. Used with permission of McGraw-Hill Book Company.

Quadrangle Books, Inc.: From *The Destruction of the European Jews* by Raul Hilberg, Copyright © 1961, 1967 by Quadrangle Books, Inc. Random House, Inc., and Arthur Barker Ltd.: From *The Last 100 Days* by John Toland. Copyright © 1965, 1966 by John Toland. Reprinted by permission.

Yad Vashem: From *My Meeting with Adam Cherniakow* by Shmaryahu Ellenberg, *A Second View of Cherniakow* by A. H. Hartglass, *In the Warsaw Ghetto in Its Dying Days* by Kalman Friedman, *First Stirrings* by J. Kermish.

313

Index

Himmler, Heinrich, 219, 229–30, 234, 242
Histadrut, 137
Hitler, Adolf, 87, 89, 100, 101, 105, 107, 121, 139, 149, 226, 301
Hitler Youth Organization, 91
Hoare, Sir Samuel, 61
Holland, 43, 55, 61, 69, 267, 299, 307; Jews and, 42, 46, 65, 79, 177–78, 272; Underground in, 268, 269–71
Holy Land, see Palestine
Hoover, Herbert, 26
Horedenke Rebbe, the, 143
Housing confiscated, 109–10
Hungary, 59, 64, 74, 164

Intergovernmental Refugee Committee, 56–58, 60, 62
Israel, State of, 21, 22, 129, 136, 137, 307
Italy, 43, 173–75; and Jews, 64, 152, 154, 165, 166, 182

Jabotinsky, Vladimir, 118, 136, 137–38
Jewish Colonization Association, 67
Jewish Committee (Nice), 183
Jewish Journal of Sociology, 264n
Jewish Journalists and Authors Association, 100
Jewish Merchants and Artisans Organizations, 125
Jews: attitude toward Bolsheviks, 115; bounty on, 181; census of, 117–18, 179; children, 73–74, 77–78, evacuation of, 66, placed with Gentiles, 236–37, see also Refugees; deportation of, 143, 156, 164, 174, 175, 179, 181, 190, 192–93, 248; detained after liberation, 283; family life, 74, 78; forced labor of, 114, 119–20, 142, 143, 149, 191, 213, 230, 234, 277, 278, 291; humor, 120, 139; morality, 113; population, in Europe, 18–19, 22, 24, 32, 35, 37, 40–44, 46; systematic starvation of, 187–88, 194–95, 287, 301–303; *see also* entries under specific countries
Joint Distribution Committee, 50n, 51, 54, 59, 66–70, 117–19, 131
Judische Ordnungs-Dienst (Jewish Order Service), 211

Kalmanowich (German agent), 214, 215

Kamiel, Joseph, 94n
Kahn, Jacob, 156
Kanal, Israel, 211
Kapko, Stanislaw, 235–36, 238
Kaplan, Chaim A., 96–97, 99, 124, 189ff.
Katsh, Abraham I., 41n
Katz, Bela, 256
Katzmann, Brigadeführer, 234
Keren Kayemet (Jewish National Fund), 140
Kermish, J., 209
Kerner, Moshe, 125
King Alexander, S.S., 173
Kishinev pogrom, 27, 137
Komsomol, 139
Kora, S.S., 173
Korman, Ezra, 308
Korman, Max O., 47
Kosowsky (Jewish policeman), 216
Kristallnacht, 33. See also November 10 (1938)
Krosigk, Minister von, 234
Kumanovo, S.S., 173

Labor Zionist Movement, 137n
Landau, Alexander, 223
Landau, Margalit, 213
Last 100 Days, The, 296
Latin America and Jewish refugees, 66–68
Latvia, 121, 237
League of Nations, 58, 61–63; High Commission for Refugees, 69
Lehman, Herbert, 33, 34
Lehman, Irving, 33, 34
Lemwright, Martin, 89
Lenz, Walter, 267
Lessing, Gotthold, 29
Levin, Yitzhak Meir, 133
Leykin, Yaacov, 213–14
Lilienthal, David, 33
Lodz, 39, 40, 59, 95, 124, 129, 200, 234
London, 69, 86, 127n
Lontzki, Captain, 216, 219
Lubiana, 166, 167, 168, 169
Lublin, 28, 94, 95, 104, 121, 210, 234
Luboszycki, Aron, 200
Luther, Martin, 20–21, 87, 89
Lutherans, Nazi persecution of, 87, 89
Lwow, 28, 40, 59, 95, 140, 143, 234, 291, 292

McAdoo, William G., 26n